Tales of the
Chi-Town 'Burbs™

Palladium Books® Inc.

First Printing – August 2008

To my dear friend, *Erick Wujcik,* my mother, *Florence,* both passed, and father, *Henry,* who encouraged me to unleash my imagination and made me believe I could do anything.

To everyone listed in this book, and to Palladium's many talented writers, artists and creative geniuses, who inspire me to continue to write, create and reach for the stars.

And to the human spirit that keeps those imaginations burning bright.

– Kevin Siembieda
Writer & Publisher, 2008

Editors:
Alex Marciniszyn
Kevin Siembieda
Wayne Smith

Story Construction: **Kevin Siembieda**

Proofreader: **Julius Rosenstein**

Cover Art: **Slawek Wojtowicz**

Layout and Typesetting: **Wayne Smith**

Art Direction: **Kevin Siembieda**

Story Consultation: **Kathy Simmons**

Authors:
Braden Campbell
Carl Gleba
Jeffry Scott Hansen
Josh Hilden
Jason Marker
Mark Oberle
John Philpott
Jason Richards
Kevin Siembieda
Josh Sinsapaugh
Taylor White

Based on the Rifts® RPG world, setting, characters and concepts
created by *Kevin Siembieda*.

Website: **www.palladiumbooks.com**

Contents

Perspective

By Kevin Siembieda

"Hah! I'm telling you, we are so close to Chi-Town we have'ta stop at the 'Burbs. It'd be crazy not to. The boys can get a little R&R, we can resupply, and you and yer families can git a bath and a hot meal."

"And I'm telling you, Jocko, it's much too dangerous, especially with the children."

"Rubbish," laughed the rowdy merc leader. "Whatcha think is gonna happen? A mob of thieves is gonna leap outta the shadows and converge on ya all to rob you down to yer underpanties? It ain't gonna happen. Just gotta make sure the little ones and other ladies don't wander off, is all. These thugs yer so worried about ain't gonna mess with a group of people. Especially – and I mean no offense – folks as ordinary and unassuming as yerselves. They're more like jackals than lions. They pick off them who wanders off from the group. 'Sides, the 'Burbs ain't as bad as people think."

"How can you say that?"

"You ever bin there?"

"No, but . . ."

"But you've heard all the stories. Yeah, yeah, yeah. And mosta them stories is exaggerations and pure hogwash. Gotta be smart and careful, is all. It's the big city and you can't go around thinkin' everyone is the friendly farmer down the road. There's cutthroats to be sure, but ya gotta go lookin' fer trouble most of the time for it ta find ya. There are plenty of places women and children don't belong, and ya avoid 'em, is all. There are many more places perfectly safe fer families and visitors such as yerselves."

"Right. Perfectly safe my eye."

"No, really. Them Old Town 'Burbs are more safe and civilized than Kingsdale or MercTown let me tell ya, and you've been ta both! And even the Shanty Towns and New Towns are made up of families just like yer own. It's the vermin that's out to prey on them ya gotta watch out fer, and they ain't likely ta mess with a group of us, and me and the boy will cover yer backs iffen they do."

"Even if that were true, Jocko. What could possibly make you want to go there? It's a filthy, horrible place."

"Horrible from the lass who ain't never bin there. Let me tell ya lady, as far as I'm concerned it be *paradise* on earth! I mean that."

That comment only rattled the cages of most everyone and got a number of the men and women arguing with Jocko and the mercenary band that had been escorting them from Kingsdale.

"Simmer down, all of ya," said Jocko with a laugh. The grizzled old Glitter Boy pilot stood up to continue his presentation on the wonders of the *Chi-Town 'Burbs, Heaven on Earth*.

"This is what you need ta understand about the Chi-Town 'Burbs. It be the new cradle of humanity. Forgit about life inside the fortress city. That's where all the cowards and soft people with their heads buried up their . . ."

"Jocko!!" shouted the protective mother of four.

"Oh, yeah . . . heads buried in the sand," he said with a wink and a hefty laugh, accompanied by the laughter of his merc squad.

"The 'Burbs is where the living is done. This is where people from all walks of life come ta build a new, better life. They come with their little ones in tow from all around, because it's safer in the 'Burbs than where we are sitting right now. There ain't hardly no demons or monsters or crazy Necromancers afoot, like there might be back in them woods. Why? Because like 'em or not, the Coalition sees to it there ain't any. 'Cepting for some slimy creature that snuck in or was summoned up by a dang Shifter or some such, there ain't no vampires, or werebeasts. No Brodkil or Witchlings or Splugorth, or any number of a hundred monsters found out here. Thet's why they call the wilderness the 'Wildlands' and we're all branded 'Wildlanders.' Because the 'Burbs is civilization.

"Sweet civilization. Half of the 'Burbs have indoor plumbing and electricity, a third have television pirated from Chi-Town herself. The Old Town 'Burbs have lit, paved streets, fancy buidlings, and even skyscrapers. And the shopping, ladies, ya name it, it's there to be had. Fabric fer making dresses and clothing, tailored clothing, shoes, perfume, spices, breads, pies, meats, coffee, medical supplies, tools, bionics, bikes, cars, power armor, and all the rest. Ya just need ta know where ta look. Hell, um excuse my language, ya can practically find anything iffen you know where to look.

"Oh, and fer those of ya missing the creature comforts, there's the warm beds and hot bath of a hotel, dance halls, nightclubs, and taverns, and gambling, and girls, oh sweet god, them girls are . . ."

"Jocko!"

"Well, you git the idea. Civilization in all its colors and glory is what Chi-Town be."

As Jocko and his boys laughed it up, grunted and patted each other's backs in agreement, the family members launched a counteroffensive.

* * *

"I must respectfully disagree," began Samuel, the husband of the woman Jocko had been addressing. Many of the other parents and young adults gathered around to lend their support.

"Chi-Town is the home to oppression and imperialism. The 'Burbs that lay in its dark shadow are squalid dens of iniquity where the desperate and homeless try to eke out a wretched and shameful existence. Yes, there may be some vestige of civilization, but at what cost? Every vice is known to exist there. Aren't the 'Burbs home of the Black Market and other gangs of criminals?"

"Yeah, the same Black Market we bought half your gear and vehicles for this trek of yers," interrupted one of Jocko's men.

"If I may continue," grumbled Samuel. "Yes, there may be families and children living in the 'Burbs, but we've all heard about the press of humanity at the 'Burbs. The overcrowding. The squalid conditions. The open sewers. The children running wild in the streets and calling themselves *City Rats*. There are gangs who would as soon shoot a person dead and take their belongings as look at you. There are villains who attack and overpower Headhunters and urban cyborgs who are dismembered like cattle for their bionic parts, and you talk about the safe streets?

"And while there may be mages and D-Bees present, they are the minority and must come out mainly at night and hide in the shadows. Others are slaves or indentured servants or the impoverished struggling to feed their families and praying for salvation.

"And let's not forget about the Coalition States. The Chi-Town 'Burbs is not civilization, it is a lawless no-man's zone of human depravity, despair and violence at the mercy of the Coalition States. A place where the Coalition Army may ride in and destroy entire neighborhoods in the name of justice, security or the preservation of human life. How can you call that civilized?"

"Beggin' yer pardon Sammy, but yer overstating the case. It ain't exactly like that. Purges' ain't all that common and the rest, well you've presented it all in the darkest possible way. Taking a page from Emperor Prosek's chapter on fearmongering are ya?"

"Now see here!"

"The little kiddies weren't shakin' in their boots when I was talkin', mister."

Arguing ensued until a young woman stood up and spoke.

"Mr. Jocko, even the esteemed Erin Tarn described the Chi-Town 'Burbs in her book, *Traversing Our Modern World,* as, and I quote," the young scholar proudly recited the following passage from memory:

"'The 'Burbs are crime ridden, especially the shanty-town areas, Body-Chop-Shops are common, as are gambling houses, and all manner of places of ill repute. Roaming street gangs, bandits, slavers, crazed mystics, vicious psychics, malicious D-Bees, and supernatural predators all prowl the 'Burbs in search for victims and easy prey. Dog Packs and Psi-Stalkers are an ever present force on the streets, just as the SAMAS and Sky Cycles are in the air. However, these police/soldiers are not so much concerned with protecting the people in the 'Burbs as they are with containing the criminals to the 'Burbs. Yes, this is Chi-Town's first line of defense against non-humans and malevolent forces.'"

With that, everyone turned to a silver haired woman in a hooded cloak. Both sides clearly expected her to set the other side straight. That happens a lot when you are considered the greatest historian of your day, and a voice of truth and reason.

"Well, Miss Tarn, who's right?" Asked the young woman, confident that the famed historian would side with the families.

"I think you've both made compelling arguments, but I think you both overstate your case."

"But if you had to pick one side . . ."

Erin smiled warmly at the woman with the pleading face. "But I don't have to pick one side, do I? Shouldn't the debate continue with cooler tempers?"

"But Miss Tarn," protested the young woman. "You also wrote in *Traversing Our Modern World* that the people in the 'Burbs who survive the squalid conditions, famine and disease, will fall victim to demons and D-Bees. And the survivors must fight a daily battle against dark forces. Still, there are other hopefuls to take their place. Didn't you?"

Erin Tarn hated it when her own words were tossed back at her. It always felt like, 'But Mom, you said . . .'

Erin took a deep breath, sighed, and confessed, "I'm afraid I'm as guilty of painting the 'Burbs as only a terrible, dangerous place as you and so many others, but like many places, that is not the whole story. It's one piece of a much bigger story. Mr. Jocko is correct in that much."

"Hah, told ya," chortled Jocko and crew.

"How can that be?!" exclaimed one of the parents.

"I don't understand," sighed the young woman.

Erin repositioned herself near the bonfire to sit in a more comfortable position. She pulled down her hood so everyone could see her face and settled in for what she imagined would be a long chat. Mercs, parents, young adults and children all gathered around closer. The children squeezing to the front where they could be close to the soft-spoken, motherly figure. Erin surveyed her audience and gave them a disarming smile.

"Well, my darlings," said the matron of truth in a warm tone. "The Chi-Town 'Burbs are certainly not heaven on Earth as our esteemed guide would have you believe."

A glance in Jocko's direction showed him smirk, bow his head and raise his glass to her in deference.

"Just as you and the other educated parents and families overstate the evils and horrors of the 'Burbs." A few people began to open their mouths to offer words in defense of their position, but Erin Tarn silenced them by continuing to talk, herself.

"I take some responsibility for that, as my book, *Traversing Our Modern World* – published without my consent or final rewrite, I might add – has helped to form many people's opinions on Chi-Town and many other places. But we – *all of us* – must never get so smug or believe we are so educated and smart that we never reassess what we know or question what we hold as truth. The road to perdition is paved with good intentions and strongly held beliefs, my dears. Never forget that or you'll be no better than the government of the Coalition States."

That statment prompted a number of people to looked at each other and whisper. Erin liked getting people to put down their own bias and think for a minute. She paused, took a drink from her canteen, and continued.

"So here is what I can tell you about the Chi-Town 'Burbs, with as much knowledge, truth and objectivity as I can offer. I have been to the 'Burbs many times. I can say with complete confidence that like all 'Burbs, it is very different from the towns and homes you know. That in and of itself makes them dangerous places, because you are out of your element. You don't understand the culture or the local customs, so you don't know what to expect and may not recognize or understand warning signs that might otherwise save your life.

"The Chi-Town 'Burbs is, indeed, located in a no-man's land over which the Coalition Army has complete jurisdiction, but little concern for the people who live there. The Coalition seeks to contain and control the 'Burbs as best they can, and if they could eliminate it without looking like monsters themselves, they most certainly would.

"It's also true that the 'Burbs can be lawless and violent. The Black Market flourishes there like weeds. Larceny, cruelty, and all of humanity's vices are on display like the open sewers of the Shanty Towns. All manner of rough people, human and D-Bee, warriors and mages, adventurers and thieves, come to the Chi-Town 'Burbs as if they were moths to a beacon of light. Why? Because there is opportunity there.

"Some who seek opportunity come to make an honest living. Others come to prey on the foolish, the innocent and the unsuspecting. Some trade in tangible goods, some in secrets, others traffic in vice and dark desires best not discussed here with so many children present. Others come to find entertainment and reward by gambling, drinking, rough-housing, and taking part in other pleasures, wholesome and otherwise.

"For some, the 'Burbs are a resource. A place to trade the crops they grow, or where they can trade ancient artifacts dug up from the earth, or where they can trade animal skins, crafts and other goods or services for the supplies, food, medicine or tools they need back home. For them, the 'Burbs may be the only place to resupply before going back into the Wildlands, or the only place to find work to support their families.

"For still others, the 'Burbs is a place to feel *alive* by spending their hard earned money on pleasure, be it a warm bath, hot food, rare spices, fruit, vegetables, drink, or the company of others, even if that company is bought and paid for. Warriors and adventurers lead hard, often short, violent lives, so for them, the 'Burbs, with all it has to offer, may, indeed, seem like paradise.

"To those of you who have simpler tastes and different values, the 'Burbs may seem like a harsh, heartless environment filled with selfishness, greed, crime and cruelty. To you I say, look deeper, for there is more, much more, beneath the surface.

"Human nature being what it is, some drink too much and party too hard. That can lead to foolishness and loss of control, and all of you know what happens when you don't control yourself."

"You make too much noise or break things by accident," piped in one youngster eager to contribute to the discussion.

Erin and the adults all smiled and chuckled.

"Why yes, dear, you are correct. When you get carried away and lose control you may do foolish, foolish things, break something or hurt the people around you by accident. Many of the soldiers and adventurers live such dangerous lives in the Wildlands that when they unwind they get careless and start fights or get into drunken brawls. Packed too tight, some get on the others' nerves and can cause misunderstandings and fights that might lead to duels and bloodshed.

"With so many people coming to the 'Burbs to resupply, spend money and find entertainment, it attracts all kinds of businesses and other people. Let's ask the children a question. What happens when you throw bread out in a field?"

A dozen hands from the youngsters sprang into the air and waved above their heads with a chorus of, "I know. I know."

"Yes, dear," said Erin, pointing to a particular young girl.

"Birds come to eat it all up!" she exclaimed.

"Just one kind of bird?" asked Erin.

"No! All kinds of birds," piped up several others.

"Not robins. Robbins eat worms," added a boy.

"That's true, not robins."

"Squirrels, too," offered another one of the boys.

"Noooo, not squirrels!" snorted back some of the girls.

"Uh huh. Ain't that right, Miss Tarn? Squirrels might come to eat the bread."

Erin smiled and motioned up and down with her hands to quiet the children.

"The point is, where there's bread, many birds, and maybe a hungry squirrel or two, come to eat it. Chi-Town economics works in a similar way. With so many people coming there and setting up homes, it attracts businesses. Businesses attract more people. Sadly, all this activity also attracts bad people and criminals who prey upon the good people."

"Like a cat might stalk the birds," offered one of the girls.

"Exactly," smiled Erin Tarn. "So bandits and thieves, Cyber-Snatchers, the Black Market, Body-Chop-Shops, criminals and thugs of all flavors come to Chi-Town and set up their own businesses, robbing and hurting people, selling drugs and doing other things that are wicked or hurtful."

"Monsters and demons too, right?" asked one frightened looking blonde girl.

"Sometimes, yes, but like Mr. Jocko said, the Coalition soldiers try to chase away monsters whenever they find one, even near the 'Burbs."

"But if heroes and adventurers go there," asked one of the boys, "why don't they kill the monsters and the bad people? Shouldn't they protect the families? Don't they like little kids and mommies?"

"Well," said Erin firmly, "they do exactly that whenever they can, but because there are no official laws in the 'Burbs, it is much harder to find and stop the bad men. And that's one of the things that make the 'Burbs so dangerous, there are no formal laws or police force to protect all the people. Each community in the 'Burbs has its own laws, and some are safe while others are very dangerous."

"So if we go to Chi-Town we stay away from the bad places," announced one of the boys like he just found the answer to all their problems.

"Oh yes, that's very smart," confirmed Erin. "But I'm afraid the 'Burbs aren't clearly marked with signs like most true cities, so it's easy to walk from a safe community into a dangerous one without ever realizing it. Furthermore, so many people, good and bad, come and go so quickly at the 'Burbs, it's hard to keep order or find and punish a bad guy who just came for a visit and leaves after he's caused mischief."

"So how can you side with Jocko?" asked the young woman who started the conversation by quoting the esteemed Miss Tarn.

"Because the 'Burbs are also a place of hopes and dreams, my dear. We see and hear about all the crime, villainy, bloodshed and monsters, but we forget the 'Burbs are filled with people just like you and me.

"Remember when I said look deeper? This is what I meant. Look beyond the ugly, scary, noisy parts and you know what you find? Mothers and fathers, sisters and brothers, families who are not villains or monsters, but ordinary people trying to build a better life."

"But why would good people go there if the 'Burbs are so scary and full of bad people?" asked the littlest child, listening intently.

"Oh sweetheart, because the 'Burbs aren't all scary and full of bad people. Because the hard working families build homes and churches and places where good people can live safely and raise a family. They open stores and businesses that treat people fairly and treat others with respect."

"Even D-Bees?" asked a D'norr Devilman child.

"Yes, even D-Bees, at least in certain parts of the 'Burbs, but D-Bees and practitioners of magic must be especially careful because a lot of the people still don't accept them and will try to drive them away, or hurt them."

"Just because they aren't human," stated one of the older girls.

"Yes, Talia, I'm afraid so."

"That's stupid," growled one of the boys.

"Yes, it's ignorant and foolish. That's why we try to teach tolerance and acceptance of all people regardless of their nature and appearance. We must all learn to live together in peace or else we can never be free of hatred and violence. And if we're not careful, we'll all destroy ourselves."

"But the Coalition hates and fears us all," whimpered the D'norr girl.

"No, darling, not all the people in the Coalition, and certainly not all the people in the Chi-Town 'Burbs. Even in the shadow of the great fortress city of Chi-Town, there are communities in the 'Burbs where D-Bees are welcomed as equals. There are people throughout the 'Burbs who are kind to D-Bees and help them hide from and escape Coalition soldiers.

"That's why you must never let yourselves embrace hate like the citizens inside the fortress cities do. Those poor souls live in fear and ignorance. They don't know better, because they allowed their leaders to spin a web of lies. And because they don't question what they think they know like we do – like we're doing right now – and talk about their fears, they don't try to understand or accept people who are different. Instead they see them as monsters and they live in constant fear. And being afraid is a terrible, terrible way to live.

"That's why, in some ways, the Chi-Town 'Burbs is very special. It may represent hope for all of us. It is filled with hundreds of thousands of people, humans and D-Bees forced to live together and learn about each other, and come to care about each other. These people learn that D-Bees aren't monsters at all, but people just like them, just in a different shell. Together, these human beings and D-Bees battle the demons and monsters of poverty, corruption, injustice, fear and hatred. They are people who, I hope, one day will learn the lesson that we must all accept each other and learn to live together as equals. Am I crazy to believe this is possible?"

Erin smiled as all the children said "noooooo" in hushed voices.

"I think not, because as big and powerful and scary as the Coalition may be, they cannot crush the hopes and dreams of all people. The 'Burbs exist because no matter how many times the CS waged purges in the communities and tried to drive everyone away, people always came back. And not just the people they drove away in the first place, but thousands and thousands more. And every single day, more people come to the Chi-Town 'Burbs in search of their dreams. Dreams of a better, safer life. Dreams that expose them to all races, all beliefs and all people. People who, despite their appearance or the practice of magic, all share similar hopes and dreams. People who are not so different after all. And that makes Chi-Town a true place of hope for us all."

After a moment of thoughtful silence (one could almost hear the unspoken 'wow') a bunch of hands and voices raised up again. Erin Tarn knew she'd be answering questions and weaving stories for hours to come. And she loved every minute of it.

A While Longer

By Braden Campbell
& Kevin Siembieda

Today marked a pair of anniversaries for me. Conventional wisdom says the average human applying for citizenship to the Coalition States has a waiting period of six years. At least, that's what people will tell you. Even Erin Tarn said so in *Traversing Our Modern World*, which, if the local constabulary asks, I most definitely have *not* read.

They don't tell you that when you register for citizenship, of course. About the six-year-if-you-are-lucky-wait, I mean. They just ask you some questions while a nice young lady in a white smock takes a sample of your blood.

Are you fully Human?

Has there ever been, to the best of your knowledge, a history of mutation in the family?

Have you ever dated a D-Bee?

Has anyone in your family gotten involved with a D-Bee?

Do you practice, or have you ever practiced, magic?

Do you know anyone who practices magic?

If so, what are their names?

Do you have any psychic powers of which we should be aware?

Has anyone in your family exhibited psychic abilities? Premonitions or Deja vu?

Could you look directly into the camera lens and try not to blink?

And a whole lot more.

Then you sign your name at the bottom of the form, or make an X if you can't read or write (and it's best if that is the case), and you are dismissed. Send in the next applicant on your way out. That's the drill.

My God, I can't believe that was so long ago. Could it really be that long since I first arrived here, since I first saw the fortress city of Chi-Town?

I so clearly remember the day our caravan crested that hill, and stopped to take a long look at the *Promised Land.* The seat of power for the new America. The home of humanity. We could see the Mackinaw River twisting though the countryside, flowing steadily by just as it had long before the Coming of the Rifts. In the distance behind it, the great fortress city, Chi-Town, loomed like a man-made volcano, as grey and artificial as any single thing could be. Yet at the same time it seemed majestic and powerful. Beautiful and comforting. Just looking at it, you knew it was a safe place to live.

All around the great fortress were the 'Burbs, teeming with people. Tens of thousands of them. Maybe hundreds of thousands. All waiting to be let in, to finally feel safe behind those massive walls and to become a noble Coalition citizen.

We stumbled down the hill giggling and chattering like children. Some of us had been on the road for weeks, steadily walking, and our strength was all but used up. My brother, Daniel, who was three years older than me, had lost fifteen pounds and his pants were now being held up by a fraying piece of rope.

We came down the hill and snaked our way through the twisting, narrow pathways of the Shanty Town 'Burbs, then through the dirty streets of Newtown 'Burbs, and then the paved streets of an Old Town 'Burb. The closer we came to the fortified city, the cleaner, more civilized and modern the streets became, as if just being closer to the city made life better.

Chi-Town was our goal. No one walks from Arkansas to live in the 'Burbs. It's Chi-Town that everyone wants. Everyone human that is. And there would be plenty of D-Bees too if they were allowed inside.

When we finally got to the gates it was like the end of a pilgrimage. Like taking a six hundred mile-long road through a wilderness Hell to the Pearly Gates of Heaven. Only, it wasn't an angel that met us there, but a group of armed *Dead Boys* in shimmering black armor.

That was the first time I'd ever seen a real soldier of the Coalition States and their famous black combat armor. I'd heard of them, of course. Everyone had. But seeing them was so exciting. Helmets molded to look like ebony skulls with glowing red eye lenses, uniform and faceless. There were six of them, all carrying energy rifles, standing around the *Registration Center*, keeping things under control. And when a quartet of SAMAS flew by, no more than a hundred feet above us, all of us newbies pointed and cheered.

It was a slow day when Daniel and I arrived, only a few hundred people in line ahead of us. We glanced timidly towards the skull-faced gunmen, not wanting to offend or show that we had never seen one before, and wanting, oh so badly, for them to be our friends. And so we waited patiently. We answered the questions. Then, when it was all over, we waited some more.

My brother and I were lucky in that our dear mother had managed to save seven gold coins, which she bequeathed to us, her only sons, just a couple hours before coughing her last breath. She died of tuberculosis that winter, but not before making us each swear on our honor to go to Chi-Town and make a better life for ourselves. The gold coins weren't much, certainly not enough to buy a hovercycle, but used sparingly, it would give us food and shelter for a while. Until we could make it to Chi-Town and find temporary work in the 'Burbs till we became citizens.

So that first night in the Chi-Town 'Burbs, while many of the others we had come to town with slept in the streets, Daniel and I rented a room. Room number three, to be exact. The one right above the back kitchen of an all-night tavern, where the sound from the jukebox pounded through the floorboards and the smells from the kitchen traveled up through the vents in the floor. I don't know why we spent the money on a room. We were so wound up that we couldn't sleep half the night it seemed so wonderful. Like something out of a dream. Of course, reality would hit us square in the face within a few weeks, but that night, that night was magical.

I remember it like it was yesterday. Mrs. Lowery was the owner. A wrinkled wisp of a women, with white, curly hair. She smoked constantly, and her teeth were yellow from a lifetime of filterless cigarettes. She seemed stern and talked fast and matter of fact.

"Only got one room what's got two beds," she had said, "and it's seventy-five credits a night. Meals are extra." Dan rubbed his eyes wearily, and gave her one of our remaining three gold coins, which was enough for two weeks' worth of shelter from the streets. It was one-third of our entire, remaining, personal fortune, such as it was, but the sight of gold brought a twinkle to the old lady's eye. "Bless yer hearts," she said with a smile, and led us through the bar to the back staircase, then up to the second floor. I guess she took pity on a couple of young Wildlanders bearing gold.

Our room was at the end of the hall. Widow Lowery unlocked it with a heavy key and swung the door open. It wasn't much, but in the weeks to come we'd learn it was a real bargain and real nice. There was a window that looked out onto a gravel street, and you could hear music, laughter and the clink of bottles and glasses through the floor. The room had two single beds, a couch and a desk, on top of which was a small tube-set radio. The carpet was drab and worn, and the quilts on the beds had several gaudy patches on them. Through the window, I could see that it had started to rain. People ran under awnings or pulled hoods over their heads and hats over their eyes. I was glad to be out of the rain and have any kind of room at all.

Being young and stupid, I thought that our applications as CS citizens would be processed in a day or two. Maybe a week. Hey, I was a 19 year old kid from the Wildlands, what did I know? The very next morning, while Dan was still asleep, I got up, quietly pulled on my boots, and crept out into the hall. One of Widow Lowery's infinite number of cats was stretched out at the top of the staircase. It looked up at me as I stepped over its fluffy black and white body, and meowed forlornly. I made my way through the darkened bar, and out into the street.

The rain had turned into a light drizzle. The clouds were low and the general feeling of the morning was one of dampness and chill. I walked two or three blocks down the street to a little place that sold baked goods and hot grass tea. Yeah, that's right. Tea made from grass and weeds. I liked it. People talk about coffee that comes from South America like it's God's gift. Me, I don't much care for it, and I'm not going to pay what they want for one lousy cup. I don't care what kind of perils the importer must face to get it here. Funny, that's one of the things people talk about when they apply for Coalition States citizenship: the CS has coffee thanks to a trade deal with the Colombians. If you live in Chi-Town, you can drink all the coffee you want. Hot, iced, black, cream and sugar. You can have it all. Cheap too, compared to what they charge in the 'Burbs. You just gotta wait long enough to get citizenship.

For breakfast that morning I had a delicious honey-dipped bun and drank my tea. When I was done, I picked the dandelion seeds out of my teeth, and walked to the Registration Center. Another line up. More people waiting. When I finally got to the window where a little man in a grey uniform was sitting, I told him my name and asked if my application had been put through yet. He just looked at me with a pained expression. Like he'd heard the question a million times before. Shook his head no, and called the next person forward as if I wasn't there. I told him I'd come back the next day, but he ignored me.

Things went on like that for two weeks. Every morning, I'd get up before Dan and head over to the Registration Office. I would wait in line with rest of the teeming masses, and when I got to the window, I would tell the uniformed clerk my name. Some days it was the little man. Some days it was a lovely woman with dark skin and blue eyes. But always the same shake of the head. Finally, I came out and asked the lady point-blank just how long it would take. The dark-skinned woman sighed heavily. "Mister Sussex," she said, "do you see these?" She pointed over her shoulder, where cardboard boxes were stacked to the ceiling. There might have been thirty of them or more. "Each one of them holds 250 applications, just like yours. And that's just from this month. We operate on a first come, first served basis here. It's the only fair way to go about it. When we get to your file, we will contact you, but until then, you need to stop wasting our time and yours. They'll find you when your time comes. Understand?"

I was nineteen and thought I owned the world. "I understand. It's already been two weeks! We lookin' at another couple of weeks? A month? What?"

I didn't understand, then, that this was just one of three Registration Offices or that there were years' worth of boxes of application forms ahead of us, not just the people in those thirty boxes. Most folks who come to Chi-Town to apply for citizenship don't know that when they come to the big city carrying their dreams in a sack, so it wasn't just the ignorance of my youth. I was so busy asking questions, like how would they find us when our papers came if they didn't know where we currently lived, to even see two of the Dead Boys shoulder their rifles and walk up behind me. I just kept on speaking to the lady with the ice blue eyes, my voice getting embarrassingly loud as I fired off my questions.

Suddenly, a hard, heavy hand clamped down on each of my shoulders. I jerked around to see the two soldiers, and took note of my startled reflection in the red glow of their eye lenses. They began to escort me out of the building.

"You're going to have to wait a while longer," the woman called after me.

"You need to wait your turn like everyone else, son," said a voice from the black armor. "Don't make us have to walk you out again. Understand? It'll go on your chart and you don't want that kinda trouble."

That was as close to a time frame as I was ever able to get out of the Coalition, 'a while longer.'

The next day, Daniel was murdered by a group of toughs while on his way back from the market. They took his money, his boots, the food, and his cybernetic left eye, and left him like a butchered animal carcass laying in the street. I wasn't with him at the time, but at least fifty people must have seen it happen. Stood there and watched, doing nothing. There's never a hero around when you need one. I only found out about it because by the time the Dead Boys finally showed up to investigate, I had become worried about Dan and had gone looking for him. I saw him from behind the yellow line of tape, lying in a puddle, slack jawed, barefoot. He was staring at the sky with one eye and one empty socket. I screamed like a madman.

My big brother, the guy who had taught me how to drive a car and how to undo a bra with one hand, was gone. So was our money. Our room above the bar was paid up for one more night. After that, I would be out on the streets like so many others living hand to mouth in the 'Burbs. I looked down at my brother's corpse again, and wondered how I was going to survive without him. He was the last of my family.

A Dead Boy walked up and handed me a claim ticket for the body, should I want to claim it. Then they took Daniel away, zipped up in a black plastic bag. I didn't have money to bury him, so that was the last time I'd see my brother. A claim ticket my only record of his death.

When I got back to the bar, Widow Lowery was waiting near the door.

"I heard about Dan," she said through a haze of cigarette smoke. "A shame. You're both nice boys. What're gonna do now, Dear? Got a place to go? Sit down here and talk to me."

So I spoke at length with the Widow Lowery, and arranged to work at the bar for my lodgings. Just in the short-term, I told her. Just until my papers for citizenship came through in a few months. She didn't shake her head like the clerks at the Registration Office. She smiled, showing me her yellow Cheshire cat teeth, patted my hand, and said, "Ok Dear, just until your papers arrive."

I started out working in the back kitchen, washing glasses and plates. Slept most of the day and worked mostly at night. The 'Burbs come to life at night. We'd see only a handful of patrons during the day, but the place would be near filled to capacity by sundown and not start to thin out till midnight. Even then, we'd have a couple dozen patrons who wouldn't empty out till four in the morning. Then there'd be the breakfast crowd from five to seven, coming for a quick bite to eat before work, and then, except for a few customers throughout the day, the bar would remain pretty much empty till late afternoon. By early evening, you had people stop in for a drink on their way home from work. Others came to party or get drunk, and others came to socialize, eat and hang out with neighbors after the sun went down. As dangerous as the streets of the 'Burbs could be during the day, they were far worse at night. The Dead Boys tried to take action against any mages, D-Bees and monsters that made a flashy appearance or started trouble, but they couldn't be everywhere or catch all of them, you know. Someone always got eaten by some slimy thing from another world or some such. And the people of the 'Burbs were expected to take care of their own and keep the peace as best they could. Big commotions, gunplay, and magic would always get a fast CS response, but most anything else could take hours if the authorities showed up at all. That meant a fair amount of lawlessness and chaos, especially in the Shanty Towns and New Town 'Burbs. So I was glad to have a night job where I felt reasonably safe.

Three months later, though surrounded by music and the sound of people having a good time, I was still thinking about Dan, and trying to fully grasp that he was gone and that I was now alone in the world. The deaths of my parents and my brother were all too fresh and overwhelming.

As a busboy, there was no way that I could earn seventy-five credits a day, so I had to move out of the room above the kitchen. Widow Lowery was kind enough to let me set up a cot in a corner of the basement, next to the old oil furnace. I threw myself into work to make me forget. I washed dishes. I reorganized, washed and painted the basement. I fixed the leak in the roof over the office. I installed new carpet in the other rooms. I spent three weeks stripping and staining the back stairs after I accidentally broke part of the railing and discovered that they were made of solid oak. I fixed broken bar stools, patched holes in the drywall and spent my nights bussing tables and washing dishes. I liked working hard, because it meant I was too exhausted to dream. I liked dreamless nights. I didn't want to dream about Dan or my old life in Arkansas. And I didn't want to dream about the future, as I didn't feel like I had one. I was doing what it took to survive on a day to day basis.

Widow Lowery kept saying 'time heals.' Darn if she wasn't right. I hadn't realized I started living again until the day the Widow blew a cloud of smoke my direction, flashed me her golden smile and said, "It's good to hear you laugh again, Allen."

You can only mourn so long before you either let the world swallow and devour you, or you start living in it again. That's one of Mrs. Lowery's sayings too. For me, it took about a year. A year of burying my head in work. By then, I knew every aspect of the bar's operation and had moved up from busboy and dishwasher to bartender. I got to know all the regulars, and most of them liked me. That meant I got to hear about lives, families, hardships and dreams along with the latest rumors and gossip. Widow Lowery loved gossip and during the quiet periods when I wasn't sleeping or learning my way around the 'Burbs, we compared notes and exchanged stories. I was lucky to have fallen in with Widow Lowery. All things considered, I liked working at the *Blue Lady Lounge*, and my life in the 'Burbs was pretty good.

That fall, Widow Lowery shocked me with news that she was leaving town. Permanently. She explained how the long hours and damp, Illinois/Wisconsin climate were getting to be too much for her arthritis and aching joints. She had a nice nest egg saved up and was going to try building a new life in the *State of Lone Star* – what the Golden Agers had once called Texas. The Coalition was desperately trying to populate that bleak and empty place, and was offering people farmland and housing for next to nothing. It sounded good to her, and she, her boyfriend, Thomas, and his kin were going to give it a go.

First, my mind swirled with thoughts of missing the Widow. She'd become like family to me and I would miss her and rest of the crew. Then my thoughts swirled back around to *me*. What was she going to do with the bar? Sell it? Close it? What would happen to me? My concern must have shown on my face because the Widow took my hand, sat me down and lit a new cigarette with the butt of an old one.

"You're honest and a good, hard worker, Dear. You ain't never done me wrong, and you done more than your fair share of work without asking me for anything more in return. Seeing as how I don't know how things are gonna work out in Lone Star, I thought I'd find me a body to manage the place for me. You know, an honest, hard working fella who wouldn't cheat me outta my percentage and who'd treat the *Blue Lady Lounge* like it was his own. I'm hopin' that fella would be you, Allen. What do you say? Interested in running my place? Actually Dear, that would be *your* place. I'd just be your silent partner."

I just sat there with my mouth open sucking in cigarette smoke.

"That's alright," the Widow Lowery said, patting my hand. "Give it some thought and let me know. Ain't no rush, Dear."

Like I said before, Chi-Town is where everyone wants to live. Not the 'Burbs. I still clung to that dream. Chi-Town houses more than two million of my fellow human beings, making it one of the largest, single concentrations of our people in all the known world. A haven for humanity. A place to raise a family and live in peace. However, managing the Blue Lady would give me a better life while I waited. Sure, I was still stuck in the 'Burbs, where trouble lurked on every street corner, but I'd have my *own* place, and I could save some money for when the CS Citizen's Agent came for me with my papers.

"Sure, Mrs. Lowery!" I told her with genuine appreciation. "I'd be happy to take care of the place for you."

It must have been the answer she was looking for, because the Widow positively beamed, asked if I was sure I didn't want to take more time to think about it before accepting. I told her, heck no, and we sat down to work out the details. I'd effectively own the bar and I'd put one quarter of the profits in Widow Lowery's bank account. When I sold the place after becoming a Chi-Town Citizen, we'd split the proceeds fifty-fifty. It was a great deal. After only a year and a half living in the 'Burbs I owned my own business. Not bad.

Now, some of you might think that operating a bar is one long party. It's not. It is a lot of hard work and garbage runs uphill to the boss, which was me now. But you know, owning your own business is also fun and challenging. Every day is the same in some ways, but different in others. Running a bar is especially interesting. You get new people coming in everyday, and they have different stories to tell than the regulars. You get to see all kinds of folks, human and nonhuman, though I try to discourage those types, if you know what I mean. Being in the Chi-Town 'Burbs, all kinds of people come and go. That means Chi-Town 'Burbies hear more about the outside world than most anyone else in the entire country. A lot of it will scare the living bejeezus out of you. All of it is interesting, though sometimes I hear stuff I'd rather not know.

A tavern by its very nature is a social environment, and a neighborhood bar is a social lynchpin. That means I inherited not only the building and hooch, but the neighborhood, the people in it, and all the regulars who considered the Blue Lady Lounge their home away from home. I'd already knew just about all of them on a first-name basis before I took over. Let me tell you, there were some real characters. There was *Kenny Philbrick*, a giant, bearded man whose wide and welcoming grin was tarnished only by his profound lack of teeth. There was *Bill Catlay*, our resident trivia expert. He was an Operator specializing in small engine repair, was smart as a whip, had an uncanny memory, could be annoying as hell, and was a full-blown alcoholic. His girlfriend, *Tandra Faulkner,* was typical of many young women in the 'Burbs: too much makeup on a starved-looking thing with peroxide blonde hair piled haphazardly around her head. *Zach Halloway* was the resident grouch who complained about everything from the weather to the drinks, to noise, to Emperor Prosek. *Angela "Angie" Vega* was an attractive middle-aged woman who looked worn out and seemed be the victim of a perpetual black cloud over her head; if something in her life could go wrong, it did go wrong. She had the worst luck I'd ever seen. *Roger Pittman* was a nice fellow, even if his long, white chin whiskers made him look like a billy goat. *Ian Polovich* was another nice fellow – a grizzled ex-Headhunter who, if his fantastic stories could be believed, must have been the veteran of a dozen major wars and several dozen skirmishes over the last half-century. In fact, we had a bunch of regulars who were once mercs and adventurers come in several nights a week to drink, play cards, throw darts, and share the stories of their youth with anyone willing to listen. Believe me, I've heard enough to write a book. Maybe several books. That's all part of the job.

My staff consisted of myself, Mario, my second-man bartender, Lenny, the scrawny busboy and dishwasher who fancied himself a ladies' man, Carlos and Benito, the hard working cooks in the kitchen, and my wait staff, Lisa, who was young, pretty and a mother of two, Samantha, a matronly flirt who the older men just adored, and Julie, a petite brunette who fancied herself a scholar just because she could recite the alphabet.

My very first weekend as the new proprietor of the Blue Lady Lounge was almost my last.

I had wanted to make it a big event, such as I could, to celebrate my taking over the Blue Lady Lounge. So, I had hired a live band and set them up in the pool room. That should have been enough of a draw, but I didn't stop there. I also paid *Bill Catlay* fifty credits to climb up on to the roof, and jury-rig the ancient cable box up there back to life. Now, not only would the Blue Lady have live music that night, but we could also watch the boxing match broadcast from the Metrobowl in Chi-Town. Television was rare in this part of the 'Burbs, and boxing was popular, so we packed people in like crazy.

Once Bill was done up on the roof, he took his usual seat at the bar and ordered a double vodka and soda with a wedge of lemon on the side. I felt I owed him for fixing the cable so I gave him his first six drinks on the house, even though the lemons had cost me an arm and a leg. Yeah, we have lemons in the 'Burbs.

By 10 o'clock, about the time the match was beginning on television, I took a quick look around. The place was packed and my three girls were busy serving both food and drinks, and the band was finishing their third set. I smiled to myself. It was really something. Widow Lowery would be proud. There were a lot of regulars and just as many new faces. One old face was Bill Catlay half asleep, as well he should have been. He'd been drinking since five that afternoon. His glass was full of mashed up lemon slices, because for some reason known only to him, whenever he finished one vodka and soda, he demanded that you serve the next one in the same glass and keep the old lemon rind in there too. By 9:30 I figured he was drunk enough, and so I cut him off. I asked his girlfriend, Tandra, to take him home, but Bill begged me to let him stay to see the boxing match. It was a good day, so I relented.

For the next few hours, I was in constant motion behind the bar, pouring, opening, shaking, stirring, cutting, garnishing. I only caught glimpses of the boxing match, but could tell when something important happened by the cheers and jeers. At three o'clock I rang the big brass bell that hung over the bar and announced last call. The band had left at two, most everyone had already gone home, and we started to tear down. The boxing match was a great success and I was thrilled no fights broke out at the bar. When it ended, half of the patrons went home. That was just fine with me and my staff. By that point, my apron was soaked through from ice water, booze and lemon juice, my feet were aching and I was exhausted. The girls were wiped out, too.

We had done well that night. In fact, we had so much hard cash in the till that I decided to pop it out of the register and quickly take it up to the safe in the office. Consequently, I only caught a glimpse of the group of newcomers who wandered in and seated themselves at one of the big round tables in the corner. When I came back downstairs, Samantha had served them a pitcher of foamy beer. I took off my apron, and watched for a second as Kenny and Roger rolled bottle caps down the length of the bar. Then I went out the side door, into the alley to cool off in the morning breeze.

It couldn't have been more than a minute when Roger appeared in the doorway, beckoning me to, "Come quick. A fight's goin' on in there."

I ran in to find Big Kenny wrestling with one of young guys who had been sitting at the round table. He had the kid in a headlock, and despite his best efforts, there was no way that this scrawny twenty-year-old was going to be able to get out of it. Kenny worked as a lumberjack for nine months out of the year, clear-cutting forests north of Cedar Rapids. He didn't use power armor or laser cutters either. He and the rest of his crew worked the old fashioned way: with axes and saws. Needless to say, even though he couldn't eat an apple with those last few bad teeth, Kenny could crush one with his bare hands. However, all the time I had known him, I had never heard him speak an ill word of anyone, let alone get physical.

"Kenny, what the hell are you doing?" I yelled. There was a glare and a fire in his eyes that quite frankly scared me.

"He was makin' trouble, Allen," Kenny groaned in explanation.

I thought I could defuse this situation, whatever the hell it was, all by myself. After all, I was the manager now, right? I didn't notice that Bill had managed to resurrect himself from on top of his bar stool, and was now standing slightly behind me with a bottle clenched in his fist.

"If Kenny lets you go," I said to the kid in the headlock, "will you promise to calm down?"

There was a muffled sound and a slight nod which I took to be a yes. My next question was going to be a repeat of the first, but I never got the chance. From out of nowhere, another of the round table kids, beefy, with a red face and short, dark hair, slammed into Bill with the force of a freight train. His flying tackle took the two of them right through the front window and out onto the sidewalk boards in a flurry of glass and blood. I heard a woman scream, and thought it might be Tandra.

I had fallen to the floor when Bill and his assailant went flying through the window. This spectacular sight and sound was enough to distract Kenny, and the headlock kid slipped out of his grasp, and ran to help his friend. He kicked me in the head on his way. Maybe by accident, maybe not. Anyway, it hurt like hell. Lisa appeared by my side and together, she and Kenny helped me to my feet. A crowd had gathered out front to watch the action. Twenty, maybe thirty people, some of them my patrons. All were standing in a rough semi-circle, watching with varied emotions as the two young guys proceeded to beat the crap out of Bill Catlay. The red faced kid was doing most of the damage, and reflecting on it later, I suspect that he was high on Crash, or Adrenathol, or some other street drug.

Yes, it was Tandra screaming. I saw her now, standing over by the big round table in the corner. Had she left Bill, half asleep and alone with his lemon slices, to flirt with the boys? Is that what started all this? I stood there stunned. Maybe my brother Dan would have done something more heroic. Hell, maybe if Dan had been here, the fight never would have happened in the first place.

"Jesus," Lisa whispered next to me, "they're going to kill him, Allen. Do something."

Kenny let go of my arm and started to move toward them, but suddenly, I saw the kid with the brown hair jerk like he'd been kicked in the guts. He rolled off of Bill and staggered to his feet. The crowd, moving as a single being, backed away to give him room. Through the shattered remains of my front window I could see wide eyes and slack faces. Bill's attacker had his hands clasped tightly across his stomach, and a torrent of blood was pouring from between his fingers like water through a cracking dam. I saw Bill get up. His face was a bloody mess. In his right hand he gripped a Vibro-Knife.

"I wanna go home," he was yelling now. "I just wanna go home."

And that's when the shot rang out. Bill's back arched in a terrifying way, and a huge red blotch appeared on his chest. Then he toppled forwards, landing on my pool room floor, his feet dangling lifelessly on the sidewalk. The tough kid, high on something, was cursing and spitting on Bill's corpse, waving the gun around to hold anyone else at bay. Then half his upper body exploded into a pink mist and the rest fell, landing face down in the dirty street. One precision energy blast from a Coalition Peacekeeper to take down the threat. Everyone else scattered like rats. I guess they saw the Dead Boys coming, and ran. Typical in the 'Burbs.

The next thing I remember was meeting *Lieutenant Richard Milne*. I was sitting at one of the bar stools. Lisa had poured cold water over a cloth, and I was now holding it up against my jaw to dull the swelling.

The Lieutenant made an impression right away. For starters, he walked into the bar through the broken window, ducking under the bands of yellow plastic tape that the other Dead Boys had erected. Glass crunched underneath his heavy, spiked boots. He wasn't dressed in a full suit of combat armor. Instead, he wore a shining black chest plate over the top of his grey Coalition uniform, and a heavy-looking overcoat with medals and ribbons on the lapels. As he entered the pool room and looked down at the white sheet covering Bill's corpse, he removed his hat.

Lieutenant Milne could have just stepped out of a CS recruiting poster: a square-jawed vision of Coalition spit and polish. His hair was neat and cut short. He was clean-shaven. His black skin was smooth and blemish free, and his teeth were white and straight, all of which he owed to the superior medical services available to Chi-Town citizens. His jaw line was tight and strong, he eyes piercing, his voice deep and a little intimidating, and even under his coat and armor he left you with the impression he was strong and muscular. As a military man, I imagined that he must begin each morning with an exercise regimen that would leave me in convulsions.

By contrast, I was short, white, fit but hardly a muscleman, my hair was thinning a bit and my belly was soft. I wore a full beard, not because just because it made me look older, but because it hid my weak chin. After a long hard day and harrowing fight, my hair was unkempt, my clothes were stained, and my mind unfocused. In short, Lt. Milne was my polar opposite, all the things that I was waiting to be. I was surprised at just how much he frightened me. It must have been his demeanor: cold and businesslike.

"You the owner?" he asked.

"Yeah. I'm Allen Sussex. I just took over the place."

He tucked his hat under his arm, and pulled some kind of electronic device from his coat pocket, pressed a button and addressed it.

"For the record: My name is Richard Milne, Lieutenant, currently acting on behalf of the ISS. This is investigation number zero-zero-three, September twenty-fifth, 103 P.A. Business proprietor is Sussex, Allen, Caucasian male, approximately 20-21 years of age."

Then he turned his gaze on me and began to ask questions.

"Mr. Sussex, this conversation will be recorded as part of my investigation. As an unallied non-Citizen of the Coalition States squatting on CS land people like you call *the 'Burbs*, you have no say in the matter, possess no right of due process, and, in fact, possess no legal rights at all. Do you understand?"

I didn't, but I nodded my head anyway. His accent was clean, formal, without a lot of slang and contractions. He sat down next to me, set the recording device between us, and asked me to clearly and succinctly tell him what had happened. I told him everything I knew, leaving out only the part where I asked Bill to hot wire the cable box so that we could leach video signals from the Chi-Town broadcast network. I wasn't sure if it was illegal or not, but I wasn't going to take any chances with this guy. He had the air of someone who was fresh out of officer's training, the kind of man who does everything by the book and to the letter, because any kind of human warmth he might have once possessed had been beaten out of him.

When I had finished telling my story, he set his hat down next to the recorder and looked around the room.

"No weapon detectors," he muttered to himself. Then he turned back to me. "Do you own a gun?"

I felt the blood rush out of my face. This was a trick question, surely. If I said yes, then I would be hauled away for having an illegal weapon. If I said no, then he likely wouldn't believe me, since just about everyone you meet out there in the world is packing something.

I stammered for a second, and he raised an eyebrow. "No," I finally spat out. "I can't afford one."

"Well, you might want to invest in something," he said. "To protect yourself and your property."

"Um, really?" I didn't confess guns make me uncomfortable and didn't really want to resort to owning one.

"Yes, of course. It's dangerous here and this is a nicer place than most I've seen."

"Uh, thanks. But, um, I . . . I don't plan on being here much longer."

"You're thinking of leaving town?" he asked pointedly.

"No. It's just . . . I just meant that I'm only doing this until my Citizenship papers come through, that's all."

"I understand. Thank you, Mr. Sussex. I'll contact you if I have any further questions," the Lieutenant said as he switched off his recorder and placed it back into the folds of his coat.

"I'm only here for an interim period as well. I expect to be promoted to a position better suited to my abilities. However, until I get that promotion and you become a Citizen, you and I need to come to an understanding."

I stared at him blankly.

"I'm in charge of policing your, um, neighborhood," he sighed. "This bar is going to attract a lot of attention, especially now. You help me keep things safe, quiet and orderly, and we won't have any trouble. You understand me? No trouble. I like order. I hate being bothered with incidents like this. Understand? No trouble, no problems from me. Become a magnet for trouble and my men and I will be camped on your doorstep. Understand?"

This was a warning, as he didn't even wait for my response before he stood up, put his hat back on, touched the brim, and nodded to Lisa.

"You try and have a good day now," he said, and again, instead of using the door, he walked out through the broken window.

I had the distinct impression that he felt he was above any kind of rules or courtesy that we *non-Citizens* might be living by.

He stopped, the glass crunching under his weight, and without turning around, said in a loud voice from outside, "One more thing, Mr. Sussex, the name of this bar, the *Blue Lady*. Do you play blues music here?"

"Uh, no. No I don't."

"Good. Change the name. The blues has certain unsavory connotations, and has been proven to promote independence, creativity, freethinking and rebellion. And we don't want this place to attract those kind of rabble-rousers, now do we? So I'd recommend you change the name as soon as possible."

As the ISS Officer walked way, his last remark burned. It snapped me out of my shock. Who the hell was this guy to tell me what I should and shouldn't do? The name of my bar was offensive to him? Promoted what kind of thinking?! No way was I going to change the name. No way.

The next morning I was still stewing over it all. I felt numb as I surveyed the carnage in my bar, and ran over the events of the night. Numb from lack of sleep and numb from anger. My head was spinning. I still couldn't believe Bill was dead. Replacing the window and making repairs would take two-thirds of the profits. The CS was likely to keep a closer eye on the place now. And the name . . .

At first I was determined to keep the name no matter what, but after a lot of thought I had an idea. I borrowed a ladder and bought a sign plank and a bucket of white paint from Mr. Lenn's hardware store across the street. I made a new sign and after I hung it, I crossed the street to return the ladder, and then Mr. Lenn and some other neighbors came over as I stood in front of the store to survey my handiwork.

"Sorry about Bill," said one.

"Too bad about the trouble, Kid," said another.

"Wish I didn't turn in early, maybe coulda stopped it before it went that far," added war vet Ian, who heard what happened and was coming by to see if he could lend a helping hand.

"Give it a few weeks," said someone else. "This will all blow over and be forgotten like it never happened."

"*A While Longer?*" said Mr. Lenn. "That's an odd name. I don't get it."

"I do," I replied, "and so will the powers that be."

* * *

With Ian's help, I spent the rest of the day replacing the window, which I am proud to say, has remained unbroken for the past six years now.

Six years. Man, time flies.

I look back now and laugh at how we thought things were going to turn out. I was going to get my papers any day and Richard, or should I say Lieutenant Milne, was going to get promoted the hell on out of here. Well, I saw the Lieutenant just the other day. He's a regular in my place, as a matter of fact. He comes in twice a week, Tuesdays and Thursdays, like clockwork. You see, he's been waiting too, putting in time, just like the rest of us. And he knows it now. You can tell by how much he's mellowed over the years, by how much he's stopped caring about protocol and stupid rules, and come to think of us 'non-Citizens' as people. He's one of the good guys. Not all Coalition soldiers and Peacekeepers are the scum of the earth the anti-Coalition factions would have people believe. Sure, some of the CS Peacekeepers abuse their power. Some are corrupt, do as they please, shake people down and are as rotten as Cyber-Snatchers. But not all of them. Some believe in justice and come to care about the 'Burbies. Richard is one of those. He tries to help people whenever he can, turns a blind eye to chicken-shit offenses, and hates the corrupt lawmen as much as we do.

I poured him a shot of rye and did likewise for myself. No charge, as usual. We didn't say anything of it, but we both knew this was the anniversary of our first meeting.

"Did you get anything in the mail today, Allen?" he asked. He was referring to my Citizenship papers.

"Nope. Did you?" I asked, referring to his promotion.

"Hell, no," he said with a chuckle.

He raised his shot glass, and I matched him.

"To one more year, and whatever it may bring," he said with a touch of bitterness.

I nodded and dumped the rye straight down my throat. There was a time the rough booze would have made me shudder, but I'm so used to it that now it doesn't even give me pause. I echoed his heartfelt sentiment.

"Just a while longer," I said.

Be Careful What You Wish For . . .

By Jason Marker

Awake. Swimming up from the anesthetic like a diver from his well. Sound crept into his brain. The clatter of steel instruments, the splash of running water, someone shuffling about in paper slippers. He tried to move and found that he was strapped down. Panic. He started to struggle against his bonds, then memory came flooding back.

He remembered the clinic, secreted away in an anonymous commercial center in a part of the 'Burbs where one in three streetlights still worked.

Other memories. The flickering fluorescents and cracked plastic tubing of the furniture in the waiting room. The doctor, broad, black, and bald, telling him to stare at a mural on the ceiling as the anesthetic took effect.

His tongue was swollen and dry, and there was a taste in his mouth like iron. He shifted again in the chair and said,

"Gah."

"How's my patient, awake finally?" the doctor's voice rumbled from somewhere in the room. He tried to open his eyes and for the first time noticed the gauze wrapped around his head, covering them.

"Don't worry about the bandages," the Cyber-Doc continued. "You bled a little more than usual so I wrapped you up."

"The eyes?" he whispered in a hoarse voice.

"Fine, just fine." He felt the Cyber-Doc suddenly beside him and the straps holding his arms loosened.

"The operation went well," continued the doctor as he proceeded to free the patient from the operating chair. "They went right in like they belonged there. No immediate signs of rejection. All signs positive. Can you stand?"

The doctor took the patient's arm and helped him to his feet. He swayed a bit and put his hands out, feeling for something to steady himself. The doctor steadied him, then helped him walk shakily to a chair. He sat heavily and his hands immediately went to the bandages, his fingers gingerly probing the new eyes through the gauze.

"Don't fiddle with them!" the Cyber-Doc chastised.

"When can I take the bandages off?" There was a noise like a child's rattle and the rustling of paper, then the doctor was beside him again, pressing a paper bag into his hands.

"Leave them on until tomorrow morning. There's enough painkillers and antibiotics there to last you a couple of weeks. Take the antibiotics twice a day on a full stomach, and try to use the painkillers only when you really need them."

"Tomorrow morning? I . . . I can't see. How am I going to get home?"

"I'll call you a cab."

Thirty minutes later found him in the back of a cab on his way back to his apartment. Since he couldn't see, his other senses had scrambled to take up the slack. The old cab shuddered as it pitched over bumps and splashed through potholes in the shattered asphalt. He could smell the cab smell; a mix of stale sweat, cigarette smoke and vomit. Sleet and rain pelted the roof, and through the thick safety divider he could just hear the whine of the turbine and the steady thump of the windshield wipers. He could feel the new eyes in their sockets, heavier and more real than his old meat eyes. He rolled them around and dull pain throbbed from behind them, proof that they were there.

The cab's engine dropped in pitch as it swung around a corner and came to a stop. The cabbie muttered something incoherent through the cracked speaker and he fumbled his credit chip into the slot. There was a clunk as the locks released and the door swung open and he slowly climbed out into a cold, stinging rain. The door of the cab swung shut again, narrowly missing him, and the cab sped away, leaving him standing there on the cracked sidewalk.

"Thanks a lot, asshole," he muttered as he tried to get his bearings. He figured the last turn had been onto South Street, and since he had gotten out of the passenger side of the cab, that he should be facing his building. He made his way carefully in the direction he hoped was the front of his building. Hands held out in front of him, he eventually found what felt like glass doors. He felt along them to the jamb, then along the jamb to where the card reader should be. There. He pulled his wallet out of his coat and held it up to the card reader. There was a beep and the sound of a bolt being thrown and he scrambled to catch the door before it locked again. The door swung shut behind him with a click and he was safe, at least as safe as he could be, in the lobby of his apartment building. He relaxed now and began to make his way slowly across the lobby to the stairwell. He'd walked this path a million times in the dark. The power was shut off to this part of town every night, and besides, he'd never seen more than one or two lights work in the lobby anyway.

He climbed the nine flights to his floor, and came out into his darkened hallway. He could hear what neighbors he had going about their evening's business. There was the low hum of the portable generators everyone used, a man's voice shouting and the sound of smashing crockery, a woman moaning and calling someone's name over and over. He walked along the corridor and trailed his fingers along the wall, counting the doors. He finally arrived at his apartment and fished his keys from his pocket. After a few false starts he found the right key and fit it into the lock. He rattled the key around in the stubborn lock and with a minimum of cursing and force he finally got it open.

He opened the door and saw a dark shape slide in front of him, and saw orange light flash from the knife blade as the figure lunged at him. He shrieked and threw his hands over his face. His feet got tangled in one another and he fell hard on his behind and scooted back until he hit the wall on the opposite side of the corridor. He waited there on the floor for the attack to come, but nothing happened. He lowered his arms and stared into the black inside of his bandages. With a hand on the wall he got shakily to his feet.

He was blind, bandages wrapped tightly over his eyes. How could he have seen anything? He remembered the vision vividly, though. The way the light flashed from the blade, but that didn't make any sense either. There wasn't any power on this side of town, and there wasn't a working streetlight on his block to begin with. He took a ragged breath and shook his head. He laughed it off as a combination of the anesthetic and the acute paranoia everyone possessed in the 'Burbs. He could hear doors opening down the hall, his neighbors peeking out to see what the trouble was. A muffled voice from somewhere shouted, "Keep it down out there!" He hurriedly entered his apartment and locked the door against the night.

* * *

The next morning he awoke to the insistent beeping of his alarm. He stumbled over a pile of unwashed clothes and made it into the kitchenette. He opened a drawer and began to rummage through it for something sharp. His hands closed around a pair of kitchen shears. He snatched them from the drawer and fumbled his way into the bathroom. Facing the mirror he slid one blade of the shears under his bandages and with his eyes still closed he cut through the heavy gauze. The bandages fell into the sink with a sound like leaves and he slowly parted his eyelids. At first he saw only a bright blur as the eyes compensated for the sudden light. Then everything snapped into place; he saw the dark commas of bruising under his eye sockets and stared into someone else's eyes in his face.

No, they were his now. The finest china blue he had ever seen, with a nearly invisible band of gold separating the iris from the pupil. He began to lean forward for a closer look then stopped. While waiting for the cab at the clinic, the doctor had given him instructions on how to control the features built into the eyes. He concentrated for a moment and the eyes zoomed in tight, giving him a sense of vertigo, and he seemed to be inches from the mirror. He drank in their perfection, the glow they seemed to have. He focused tighter and he could read the Triax logo curving around the outer edge of the irises in small gold capitals. With a thought his vision corrected to normal and he returned to the kitchenette.

He went to the window and looked out over the filthy sprawl of the surrounding neighborhood. His building was the tallest structure in six blocks, so he had a relatively unobstructed view. He let his gaze wander up the crazed surface of South Street, past ramshackle tenements and abandoned commercial plazas. Past weedy, empty lots and overgrown playgrounds where packs of feral dogs and semi-feral children roamed and broken glass and shell casings glittered among the ragweed like stars. Figures darted in and out of doorways, always looking over their shoulders, and a matte black ISS prowl car cruised slowly along a distant side street, shaking down citizens and keeping the peace. He looked past all of this, his eyes constantly adjusting for light and distance, filtering out the haze and smoke that hung over the 'Burb like a blanket. His gaze traveled further, past the blasted remains of his neighborhood to better ones. Past busier streets and more fashionable addresses, places where the police actually *policed* and life was worth more than whatever you had in your wallet. Finally, at the edge of the eyes' usable range, the bulk of Chi-Town rose above the smoke and morning fog, its marker lights flashing and a million windows throwing back the wan winter sunrise. Aircraft and hovercars orbited its landing pads like tiny moons.

He snapped his vision back and smiled at his reflection in the window. This, this right here, is why he had scrimped and saved and gone without for so long. He leaned his forehead on the cool window and closed his eyes. He rolled them around behind his eyelids and reveled again in the pain, the weight of them. Now he'd be noticed, now he'd be somebody. He'd been turned away from so many clinics so many times. Not enough money, not enough need. Finally, he'd met a man who knew a man, a man that could get him the eyes he'd wanted so badly. The price had been surprisingly less than he'd expected, even with the surgery, and he'd jumped at the chance. Things would change now. Things would be different, he could feel it. He opened his eyes again and smiled out at the ruined street. He wouldn't have to live here much longer, he just knew it. He slapped his palm on the wall and laughed, then started in to getting ready for the day.

* * *

He returned to the apartment after work and cranked up his electric generator. Power down was in an hour and he wanted a good charge so he could watch the news. Retrieving a beer from the fridge he settled into his chair and let it conform around him. He switched on the console and flipped over to a PostChannel to get his mail. After fifteen minutes of bills and solicitations, he switched to a random channel and got up for another beer. As he turned the corner to the kitchen he caught movement to his right. He spun around but there was nothing there. He remembered the vision from last night. He laughed nervously and continued into the kitchen.

The news that night was typical. Death, war and lies were all the rage on the Coalition's State News Agency channel. Nothing special in sports, all the good shows were repeats, so he switched off in the middle of a story about another cyberjacking victim found in the Point, her eyes and neural plug cut from her corpse. He spent a few hours playing video games, then turned in for the night.

He woke up screaming. He sat up on the futon, sweat soaked sheets pooling at his waist. He sat there shivering in the dark with his hands pressed to his abdomen. He had seen the man in the goggles. He had been grabbed by someone, and had seen the goggled man swing the blade up toward his stomach. Nightmares. He hadn't had nightmares since childhood. He lay back down and tried to get back to sleep, but all he managed was a fitful doze until his alarm.

He woke up tired and dragged himself into work right before the bell sounded. All day he had this odd feeling he couldn't shake, like fear or dread. He kept thinking about the nightmare. He turned it this way and that in his head, trying to make sense out of it. He thought maybe it was just a side effect of living in a bad neighborhood. He'd lived there for years, though. Sure his neighborhood was dangerous. He'd been mugged before, even caught in a firefight, but things had been quiet lately. He'd never had nightmares like this before. Feeling worried and afraid frustrated him. Why all of a sudden, when his luck had finally turned, should he feel like this? He should be feeling great! He finally had his new eyes, already he could see people looking at him differently. In the break room he'd made a point to mention the new eyes, even though he'd hardly spoken to anyone in the years he'd worked at the warehouse, and his coworkers were suitably impressed.

He'd have to be careful not to lord it over them, he thought. No one else he knew had such nice implants, or any implants at all. He pitied them in a way, these little people he was forced to work with. They'd never get to know how good it felt being just a little better than everyone else. He'd even mentioned it to his foreman, to make it known that he was a man to watch, a man who was going places. The foreman played like he was unimpressed, but he knew different. He knew the foreman just didn't want to make a scene. The rest of the day passed quickly, and by the time his shift was over he had nearly forgotten about his nightmare.

After work he returned to his apartment and changed into the best clothes he had. He took a cab uptown and ended up at a crowded bar where a largely untalented but enthusiastic band belted out simple and frenetic music from behind a wall of chicken-wire. He found a place at the corner of bar where the weary looking bartender hurried to keep up with his customers. He sat and waved down the bartender, who pulled him a draft and slapped it down in front of him with little fanfare. He spent an hour trying to strike up conversations with the other patrons, but the noise from the stage made it nearly impossible. At one point he bought a drink for a young woman at the other end of the bar, and when the bartender delivered it she looked over at him, smiled a tight, brittle smile and sent the drink back.

Less than two hours after he got there, he left the bar to hail another cab. Stinging with rejection and loneliness, he spent the ride deep in his own head. By the time he got back to his apartment he had worked himself into a bitter funk. He had just enough power stored in the generator to watch a little video, so with a beer sweating on the floor beside him, he fell asleep in his chair while the eye of his monitor flickered in the dark apartment.

The nightmare came again that night. He woke screaming again and stood up so quickly that he knocked his chair over backwards. He stood there in the dark, gulping air and trying to get his bearings. He had felt it this time, he had felt the knife slide into him, right below his breastbone. Shakily, he righted his chair and sank back into it. There he sat, staring out of the window until the sun came up.

* * *

He felt terrible the next day. He got to work twenty minutes late, unshowered and wearing yesterday's clothes. Twice he fell asleep in his crane, and he spent his lunch curled up on some pallets in a restless nap. The rest of the day dragged on. All he wanted was to get home and try to get some sleep. At one point a truck pulled into the warehouse and just for a moment the orange overheads flashed from its windscreen. He spooked and dropped a two ton shipping crate from fifteen feet up. It shattered on the warehouse floor, spraying shards of polycarb and machine parts and nearly crushing one of his coworkers. The foreman came out of his office raging. He plead an oncoming cold, was docked half a day's pay, and was sent home. On his way back to his apartment a shadow moved behind a pillar in the transit station and he jumped away with a shout, only to be gawked at by a mumbling squatter.

He tossed and turned all night, muttering and screaming. The lurid orange glow of the cloudy sky. Light flashing from the serrated blade of a combat knife. His limbs full of lead, barely moving, not quick enough to fend off the anonymous assailant. The bottle-green lenses of the nightvision goggles, and the harsh rasp of breath from the respirator. Falling, slowly, the killer's arm supporting him and laying him gently on the ground. Flash of the knife again as it dips toward his eyes.

The morning dawned fitful and gray. A few soot colored snowflakes ventured down out of the dirty iron sky. He sat in the chair staring blankly at the eye of his monitor. Happy faces, the product of this season's cosmetic fashion, babbled at him from behind a desk over in Chi-Town. After the nightmare, he hadn't even tried to get back to sleep. He reached out and dialed the number at work, turning the video off. He informed his foreman that he wouldn't be in because the cold had set in. The foreman grunted and told him to hurry up and get better. He called a cab next, dressed, shrugged into his old duffel coat, and left to get some answers from the clinic.

He returned well after dark, exhausted, terrified, and with no answers. First he had gone to the anonymous address in the vain hope that the clinic was still there. It was not. The door was chained shut and there were fresh boards over the windows. He spent the next few hours chasing leads and rumors in bars and on street corners, exhausting both his money and patience. By four in the afternoon he gave up, and with no money left on his credchip he began the long walk back to his building.

The onset of the early winter dusk lengthened shadows as the sun set, unseen, behind the clouds. He hunched his shoulders deep in his coat as the wind began to sing around him and snowflakes began to billow down from the sky. As it got darker and the streetlights began to wink on, he began trembling. Terror gripped him, his palms began to sweat, his mouth dried, and down every alley and around every corner he saw flashing steel and lenses of green glass. Finally, he made it to the relative safety of his apartment. He didn't bother with the generator. He just stumbled into his bedroom, collapsed onto his futon and began to sob, eventually drifting into a restless sleep. Light and shadow, flashing steel and livid green, arms like lead and the quicksand reflexes of nightmare. He thrashed and fought in his sleep, whimpering and screaming. He finally awoke in the cold pre-dawn, a shout dying on his lips, someone's name. He felt calm and he knew suddenly, and with absolute clarity, how to end the nightmares.

A week after he had called in sick, ISS cops responded to a panicky call from the building's manager. They entered the darkened apartment and the smell of death hit them like a fist. They found him there, curled fetus-like on the futon. His eye sockets were ragged holes, there were deep lines gouged in his cheeks and his face was caked with black, dried blood. His arms were crossed over his chest and his hands were clenched into fists. Blood had seeped between his fingers and dried there. One cop pulled on a pair of disposable gloves and pried his right hand open. A blood-streaked sphere trailing nervejacks and fiber optics clattered to the floor and rolled into the officer's boot, a perfect china blue iris staring up at him.

Love and Remembrance

By Kevin Siembieda & Josh Hilden

Ian Polovich walked down a street he had walked down a million times before. Only today it seemed different. The air seemed a little less acrid and he noticed things he hadn't noticed before, like the new drapes in Mrs. Carson's front window or that Katie, the Johnson family's dog, had given birth to seven pups. He couldn't help thinking how fresh and new and sharp everything seemed to be when you knew your time was coming to an end. *Funny how that works,* he thought to himself.

Ian had faced death many times on the battlefield. First, as a soldier in the Chi-Town Defense League before it became the cornerstone for the Coalition Army. Then in the CS Military, and later as an independent adventurer and mercenary for hire. Facing death in a pitched battle, you don't have time to think about anything but kill or be killed. This was different. He'd had the last 13 hours to think about who or what might be coming for him. 13 hours. Bad luck, that number.

Ian didn't know when it was going to happen, but he knew it would be sometime soon. Almost certainly today. It was just a matter of when and where. He didn't really care about who or how, and he already knew why: *For taking a stand when evil showed its ugly face.*

Ian Polovich had spent most of his life fighting someone else's battles. That all came to an end 19 years ago – or was it 20 – when he moved to the Chi-Town 'Burbs. He'd been drifting ever since. Drifting? *Hell,* he mumbled to himself. *Been more like sleep-walking. Just existing until last night.*

As he thought about it, he realized somewhere along the line he had given up on life. He couldn't remember when or why, heck, truth be told, he didn't even notice he had given up. It just happened. For God only knows exactly how long, he had gotten up every morning and went through the routine he had come to expect. Went through the paces, walked among the living, but wasn't actually living himself. Not really. *How does something like that happen and you don't even notice?* he pondered.

Ian took a deep breath and enjoyed the cool, moist crispness of the morning air as if it was his last sweet breath of life.

"Guess I just didn't care no more," he said aloud.

A crowd of City Rats pushed past Ian, three of them brushing against his metallic arm and armored chest.

"Watch where I'm going, old man," grumbled the oldest, a 19 year old who liked to call himself Street Shark.

The rest of the gang barely took notice of him. They were heading home or to their daytime flops. Most of these older City Rats ran the streets from dusk till dawn, calling it a night and turning in around six-thirty or seven in the morning. They wouldn't be crawling back out of their hidey-holes again till well past three or four in the afternoon. The youngins, the 8-14 year old City Rats, they'd be popping up and hitting the gravel any time now. It was almost like shift change at a factory, as one batch turned in, the others went to work. Kids grew up fast in 'Burbs, especially in New Towns and Shanty Towns like this one. Kids. That made Ian think of his nieces and nephews, and how he never had any kids of his own. He didn't mind really, but he wished he had spent more time with his own kin.

The morning wind danced across his face and shoulders like a Sprite. Even though it was Spring, the chilly wind had an autumn bite to it. Temperatures had plummeted during the night, and frost covered most everything: aluminum, steel, and painted wood that made up most of the huts, the glass and plastic windows, and the tarps and Mega-Damage materials that composed most of the doors to the huts and shacks of Clearview. What a name, Ian mused to himself, because there wasn't much of a view for ten miles around, unless you include the towering walls of the fortress city that loomed above everything. But it was off in the distance like a manmade mountain of technology and concrete. And even the view of it wasn't very good or clear. Half the time it was obscured by the haze of smoke and factories in the Old Town. He had to admit though, like it or not, the fortress city of Chi-Town was something to behold.

Clearview was one of the less impressive 'Burb slums built around the walls of Chi-Town. A collection of dreams, humanity and wreckage contained in a hodgepodge of buildings held together with bailing wire, rusty nails and hope for a better future. The streets were hard-packed earth or gravel, sometimes barely wider than two men's shoulders. There were only a half dozen thoroughfares wide enough for large trucks or giant robots. That made most Shanty Towns, and even the older 'Burbs, *mazes* that only long time residents like him, City Rats and the resident criminal element knew well. Oh, there were nicer parts of the Chi-Town 'Burbs, but Clearview wasn't one of them.

The neighborhood was much more settled and organized than it had been when Ian first decided to plant stakes here. Twenty years ago it was brand new – all tents, trucks and mud. Back then, this area was part of the outer ring of the Chi-Town 'Burbs. A wild and lawless slum and filth. Nothing like the venerable neighborhoods like *City Side* and *Hillcrest* in the Old Town 'Burbs. Heck, nothing like it is today. Even now, Ian didn't know if Clearview would become a permanent part of the 'Burb sprawl or not, but it had its share of permanent buildings made of wood and concrete, with more popping up every month. It still had a way to go, however, and nothing was truly 'permanent' in the 'Burbs. Not any of them. Even the Old Towns could be razed to the ground if the CS decided to do so.

It was crazy, but the 'Burbs were a weird, inhabited no-man's zone left to exist at the whim of the CS powers that be. In fact, there was a time when Coalition troops would chase away squatters and destroy their tents and shanties on a regular basis. Ian knew, he was part of those operations. Yet, no matter how many times they were destroyed or how many people died in the *cleansings*, they'd always come back. Always. *Like roaches,* they used to say, *an infestation of human roaches.* Destroying, chasing away, and even killing people by the dozens, became an exercise in futility, because the hopeful, the frightened and the desperate would always come back. Before you knew it, another Shanty Town was thriving. Then another and another, *like weeds in the garden,* as one of his commanding officers was prone to saying.

In fairness to the Coalition States, the throngs of people who came were more than the government and the city could handle without causing its economy to collapse. It was a hard choice, but even Ian had to admit it was the right one: *Save what people you could and leave the rest to fend for themselves.*

Sure the CS would help in small ways, extra food, sending medical supplies when outbreaks of disease occurred, and military patrols to root out the worst criminals and destroy dangerous monsters, but that was about it.

Of course, the CS could have done more. A lot more, mumbled Ian to himself. *Excepting that things were a might more complicated.*

The vast majority of the people pouring in from the Wildlands were uneducated and unskilled. A third were just dirt farmers. A third wilderness folk who lived off the land hunting, fishing, trapping and eating stuff no man should ever put in his mouth or his belly. The rest were pretty much vagabonds, nomads and drifters. Even so, the CS probably would have let the squatters and their Shanty Towns grow into something resembling a real city except for *the undesirables* that came with the people. Swindlers, druggies, thieves, bandits, con artists, punks and thugs, like rats and other vermin and parasites, all come, part and parcel, with human civilization.

Young toughs and even mercs tired of putting their necks on the line in somebody else's wars took up residence, organized street gangs and began to claim neighborhoods as their domains. Some of the gangs were more like citizen groups and militias with good intentions of keeping their communities safe, but most were criminals and thugs looking to capture themselves respect, power and money the old fashioned way: with threats and muscle. Intimidation and fear can be half the battle. That's why the Coalition used it, so why not the bottom feeders?

Then the criminals got smart and got organized. Most people don't know it, and the CS would never admit it, but the birthplace of the *Black Market* was right here in the Chi-Town 'Burbs. Took control of the gambling, saloons and prostitution first. Followed that up with drug dealing and all the rest. Body-Chop-Shops are a new invention of the last 30 or 40 years, but they were another gem in the Black Market's tarnished crown. Body-Chop-Shops, what an abomination, thought Ian. Half of them were human butcher shops and back alley clinics that killed as many people as they helped. And their existence bred scum like Cyber-Snatchers.

Lowlifes, con-artists, thieving murderers and organized crime were the least of the problems for the Coalition. Most outsiders wouldn't believe the number of D-Bees living in the 'Burbs. At least 20% of the inhabitants, mused Ian. Twenty percent! That was a considerable number. And the CS, even in the early days, had a problem with *the alien invaders.* That's what they called D-Bees back then, *inhuman aliens come to take what belonged to humankind.*

Then there were the practitioners of magic. That was a sad story. There was a time when magic was accepted by the leaders and people of Chi-Town, but the Federation of Magic changed all that. If D-Bees were the inhuman *boogie man*, practitioners of magic became *Enemy Number One.* People who called upon a force beyond human understanding. A power to be feared, loathed and shunned by all God fearing, peace-loving folk. Ian stopped to spit at that thought. It was crazy what people scared themselves with. What they convinced themselves to be true.

If things had gone differently, if the Federation of Magic hadn't laid siege to Chi-Town way back when, there would be a magic division within the Coalition Army right now. Funny how one event or one person can change everything. How fear can take hold and change people. Change a nation.

And that was the big problem with the 'Burbs: It was too much to control or even monitor. There were too many people. All kinds of people, and they brought all kinds of ideas and experiences that ran counter to the Coalition's own. That's what scared the Coalition government most: ideas and beliefs.

If they could, the CS would send them all packing, or better yet, just to be safe, wipe them all out. Problem was, destroying them was bad PR and terrible for their army's morale. It was one thing to kill nonhuman D-Bees, mages and lowlifes, but innocent human beings? No. There wasn't a Coalition soldier with the smallest shred of decency willing to go that far. After all, these were mostly humans coming to the 'Burbs. *Fellow human beings* coming to Chi-Town because they bought Prosek's story that the Coalition States was the last *bastion of humanity*. They believed the CS was humankind's great champion and only true hope. Ian chuckled to himself. Heck, he had lived and fought for that dream himself, for nearly 40 years. So yeah, thousands upon thousands of human beings came to Chi-Town longing to become citizens of the Coalition States and to live safe and free in the bossom of the fortified city. And when the authorities said, sorry there's no room for you right now, the people said, 'Okay, we understand. We'll just wait, right here, on your doorstep where you can find us.' And the 'Burbs were born. Not even Emperor Prosek's nastiest goons could endorse killing thousands of human beings who had come to them for the salvation they themselves enjoyed, believed in and promised to the world.

Of course, what the Coalition-haters don't understand is the CS aren't heartless goons who like to terrorize and kill. Almost every last one of them are patriots who believe in the dream. They see themselves as the 'heroes of humanity' and 'defenders of humankind.' They put their lives on the line every day to keep humanity safe. If that's a bad thing, it's because somehow that noble intention has been corrupted to represent only the humans who the Emperor and his government cronies deem worthy.

So the 'Burbs are allowed to exist. And because the dream continues they grow with the hopeful. The Coalition manages to maintain the illusion of benevolence and hopes by letting a few thousand cherry-picked 'Burbies earn their way into becoming true citizens and being given a life inside one of the fortified cities, tens of thousands more hopefuls are recruited into the army with the promise that their loyal service to the Coalition States will earn a gold star next to their name and win their family citizenship. Meanwhile, a million or more placed on lists wait. Wait and pray that they might be chosen. The Old Town 'Burbs are filled with families who have been waiting for a generation or more.

Ian spat on the ground and thought, *Yeah, that's the dream the Chi-Town 'Burbs, all 'Burbs, represented: Hope for a better life. If not for yourself, for your kids or your grandkids.*

Others, like himself, just chose to live in the 'Burbs for whatever reason. Even with all the corruption, lawlessness and influence of the Black Market, the 'Burbs were still safer than most of the alternatives.

"Dang," Ian mumbled to himself. "When did I git so, what's the word? Introspective. If I don't watch out I'll turn into a dang philosopher or something."

And that's why he was heading home. Since he realized he was going to die today, all kinds of memories and thoughts were filling his head. With them, Ian realized he had seen a great deal and knew a lot of things. No, not things. Truths. Truths he now wished he had imparted with others. Things he actually wanted to write down on paper. Things he wanted to get out of his system before . . . before it was too late.

"Good morning, Ian."

The cheerful voice and soft, cherub-like face of Alice Lancaster interrupted his thoughts. She was standing in the doorway to her bakery, smiling with all the warmth and brightness of a sunrise. She was a matronly woman around sixty-five years old, but she looked more like an attractive forty.

"Why do you look so surprised, Hon? Didn't you come to see me?"

Ian *was* surprised. He had been so lost in his thoughts that he hadn't realized his feet had carried him to the bakery like they did every morning.

"Um, morning, Sunshine. I . . . uh . . . guess I . . ." Ian fumbled.

"Kinda early in the morning to be daydreaming, isn't it?" Alice teased back, her glorious smile making him feel all fuzzy and lightheaded.

"Yeah, I reckon it is," Ian chuckled.

During her springtime years, Alice was a breathtaking beauty, and as far as Ian was concerned, she still was.

"It nice to see ya, Alice."

"It's good to see you, too. Coming inside?"

"Uh, 'fraid I can't today, Alice."

The woman looked surprised and her smile disappeared for a second.

"Why not? You know how much I love your morning visits."

"Wish I could," said Ian, smiling back at his sunshine. "But there are some things I hafta take care of before . . . before noon."

Truth was, he didn't want Alice or her shop to get caught in a crossfire in case they came for him while he was there. He was, admittedly, a creature of habit, and everybody knew he came to the bakery every morning like clockwork.

"Oh, alright," said Alice, her smile returning. "I'll put some rolls and blueberry muffins in a bag for you to take with you."

"That ain't necessary, Sunshine."

"Nonsense," she said with authority. "They're your favorites and it won't take but a minute."

Ian breathed in the delicious aroma of fresh baked breads and pastries that hung over the storefront. He loved Alice's baked goods almost as much as he loved her. In fact, he'd been in love with Alice years before her husband, Jefferson Lancaster, died from the *Black Frog Fever* seven winters ago. Of course, he had never told her. It wasn't right. Jefferson was his best friend, and buddies didn't take another friend's wife. Even though Jefferson was dead and Alice was clearly sweet on him, Ian's desire for the woman made him feel shameful. Jefferson was his best friend ever. Damn near a brother. Taking up with sweet, beautiful Alice felt like a betrayal of the man who had saved his life on more than one occasion. But would Jefferson begrudge seeing his wife and his best friend happy together? That question had been haunting Ian for some years now, and today, he knew the answer. Only it was too late.

Alice appeared in the doorway and pushed a paper bag of fresh rolls and three blueberry muffins into Ian's hands. A soft smile spread across her face and she said with a wink. "Honey, if you keep meeting me on the street like this every morning, people are going to think that you are sweet on me."

"You're too good to me, Alice," said Ian as he surveyed his prizes inside the bag: Blueberry muffins the size of softballs, a stick of butter, and a half dozen pumpernickel rolls.

"Yep, all my favorites," said Ian with a grin. "Still warm and steaming in the morning air."

"My, aren't you poetic this morning.

Ian grinned wider. "And let the neighbors talk, eh? I don't care if you don't."

Alice leaned into the human half of Ian's body and put her arm around his waist.

"Why Mr. Polovich, aren't you brash this morning?"

All Ian could do was smile. If his heart wasn't bionic, it would have skipped a beat. He wanted to take hold of Alice, lift her into his arms and profess his love. The love he should have given voice to years ago. Instead, he bit his tongue, looked at her in silence and drank in the moment. She was beautiful. And sweet. And kind. One of those special people who made life seem brighter, better, worth living. Strong willed, too. Kept the shop running despite her grief and loss when she lost Jefferson. An independent spirit who everyone admired, especially Ian.

"What?" asked Alice. "Is there something on my face?"

Of course, none of it mattered now, with him soon being a dead man, himself. His regret must have scrambled across his face, because the playfulness disappeared from Alice as she spoke again.

"Are you alright, Ian? Why don't you come in and sit for a while. I have some tea brewing."

"Nah, I'm . . . I'm okay. Just got a bit of business on my mind this morning.

"You sure?"

"Yep, that's all."

Her concern only stirred the emotions Ian was trying so hard to deny.

"Are you going to be able to drop in tonight? I'm having a big dinner for the orphans again, and the kids so adore you. They can never get enough of your stories. I love them too, you know."

"Um, yeah, about tonight . . . um."

"Please, Ian."

"Tell you what. If I can make it tonight, I will most definitely be there. But . . . uh . . ."

"But what, Honey?"

"Um, just don't be counting on it. This business, ya know."

"I understand, but try to make it, okay?"

"I'll do everything I can to be there, Sunshine. That's a promise."

Alice rose up on her tiptoes and kissed one cheek while she caressed the other. It was a firm, loving kiss born from concern.

"Are you sure you're okay?"

"Gotta go, Sunshine. See ya tonight . . . um, you know, if I can." Ian managed to muster a thin smile, rolled up the end of his bag of baked goods – as much out of nervousness as to keep the freshness – quickly turned and headed down the street.

Alice watched him until Ian turned and waved back at her as he rounded the corner. When he was out of sight, her shoulders slumped. She worried about Ian, and wondered if he cared about her as much as she cared for him. Before she got back to work she resolved to tell him she loved him tonight after the children went home. She didn't want to seem brash, but she couldn't wait for him to speak up any longer. Life was too short.

* * *

Around the corner, Ian paused and leaned against the side of a brick building. Everything in him wanted to turn around and go back. To finally tell Alice he loved her. Had for years. Even before Jefferson had passed away. How he used to envy his friend and his marriage. How he had secretly longed to make Alice his wife after Jefferson died, but he didn't. Too late now. Ian knew this was neither the time nor the place for that conversation. It was going to be bad enough when she'd get the news her old friend, Ian Polovich, was scheduled for execution. Telling her he loved her now would be nothing short of cruel and pointless. He had squandered his opportunity with Alice. He knew that now.

Ian felt his age as he moved across the hard dirt path. All around him were the sounds of the 'Burbs waking up, yet with each step he took, he could hear the whirr, clicks and whine of his bionic bits and pieces. He could have his old cybernetic relics replaced again with upgraded hardware, he had earned it, but Ian hadn't entered the city in more than twenty years. Foolish pride and resentment had kept him away, despite being eligible for free medical care and bionic restoration for the rest of his life. He was, after all, a decorated hero of the Coalition Army. Until today, however, the price of redeeming those benefits had seemed too damn high.

* * *

Ian sat at the tiny table in the kitchen area of his shabby little hut, a pad of paper in front of him and pen in hand. He took a deep breath, thought of Alice, thought of Emily and of his misspent life, and began to write.

I guess I'm writing this as a sort of memoir. Don't have time to write no book. So I'm writing what's been on my mind most as of late. Don't know if anyone but Alice and a parcel of orphans will miss me when I'm gone, but that's my own damn fault.

I'm near 137 years old. Always thought that was funny. From the books I've seen and things I've heard about the centuries before the Great Cataclysm, most folks died long before they hit one hundred years. That changed during the Golden Age of Man, when most diseases and stuff was taken care of, and bionics and medicine made it so a hundred year old man looked to be about thirty or forty. Lots of that tech has been rediscovered in Chi-Town, so the average citizen lives to a ripe old age and looks dang good until he passes a hundred and thirty. Hell, even in the 'Burbs folks regularly live to be one hundred plus unless their death is unnatural. It's away from the cities, out in the wilderness, where life is hard and short.

Me, I'm pushing one-forty. With my bionics and the medical treatment I can get as a CS veteran, I could probably go on till one-sixty or one-eighty easy. I'm a little bit worse for the wear you might say, but I could live some good years if I wasn't stupid last night. I'll get to that in a bit. First, I need to establish some background on myself.

I seen and done quite a bit in all my years on this charming little world. Done things I'm quite proud of and some I ain't so proud of.

I was born and raised in Chi-Town before it became the symbol of humanity and imperial power for the Coalition States. That's how I can read and write a fair amount. Don't get me wrong, I'm a soldier, not a scholar, but back before the Coalition come into existence, most kids went to school and at least half the folks in Chi-Town could read and write. It was a place of learning kind of like Lazlo or New Lazlo, only without all the magic. Chi-Town, the old Chi-Town I grew up in, focused on rediscovering the past and refiguring out lost technology. Makes sense when you consider this was home to the legendary Chi-Town Library. Visited the place many, many times, before it was destroyed. Me and my folks lived just a short piece away.

I have loved deeply, suffered heartbreaking loss, and I have allowed my pride and emptiness to make me a silent ghost while I was still alive. For too long, I have been existing without being a part of anything around me. For reasons I can't explain, I stopped being a ghost last night. I have to laugh at that, because it will probably hasten my death. So here I start living only when I'm going to die. You got to love the irony of that.

But you know what? It feels good to be alive and walk among the living again, even if it is only for one last day. I actually said a prayer this morning and thanked God that He let me live again before I died. Whether it be for a few hours or a few days, I'm grateful.

Not certain why I'm writing this. Now that my spirit has been rekindled and I feel alive again, my mind won't stop thinking. I keep pondering on the past and why things are the way they are. I want to tell other people not to be like I was. Not to give up on living or give up on people. And especially to not give up on yourself. We can make a difference. Maybe it's a little difference that the world and the God almighty don't barely notice, but we can make a difference to the people around us and the people we love. That's considerable when you stop and really think about it, and like I wrote, I've been thinking a great deal as of recent.

I feel like I have a pressing urgency to say what I'm thinking. I don't know if my writing this will make any difference to anyone. I don't know if anyone will ever read this or care one lick if they do. I guess I just need to get it out, so here goes.

I'm afraid most of my accomplishments have come from the barrel of a gun. I've lived a soldier's life. That's how I lost half my body, and for a while, a part of my soul.

My left leg and left arm got separated from my body more than a hundred years ago. The price I paid for going hand to hand with some kind of demonic cat during my tour of duty in the Ohio River Valley. They call it the Magic Zone for a reason, you know. In the end, I fed half of my limbs to that creature, and for what? That kid. What was his name? John, I think. John Sanchez, maybe?

I thought if I could distract the demon-cat, the kid could get away. Didn't work out that way. Damn fool just stood there transfixed in horror. I'd seen that before. Nothing you can do about it. I screamed and screamed for him to run even as the creature tore the limbs from the left side of my body, but the little bastard just stood there. Once the monster was finished with me for an appetizer, she went for the main course. The kid never even drew his weapon. Just stood there and died. Sad.

Don't know what happened next, other than waking up in a field hospital near the front lines, surprised I was still breathing. You could actually see the towers of the St. Louis ruins looming above the tree line from my cot. Could also see the blue glow of the Devil's Gate, too. A Rift that crackled to life on a regular basis to spew out more monsters at random intervals. The CS would eventually establish a military base to blast everything that emerges from the Devil's Gate, but back then there was nothing to stop the creatures born from its blue belly.

The hospital wasn't that bad, a dry bed and three hot meals a day, add to that a nightly shower with honest to God soap and clean hot water, and it was almost a vacation. If it weren't for losing my arm and leg, that is. That was soon to change, too. Seems all my screaming and effort to save the Sanchez kid impressed the lieutenant, and he put me in for cybernetic augmentation. A reward, they said, for extreme bravery under duress. In retrospect, it seemed more stupid than brave, but I wasn't gonna argue the point or turn down the chance to get a new arm and leg, even if they were made of tin. The operations went fine, my bionics, highly experimental back in 11 P.A. adapted to my body well. Still, I had to undergo an eight week recuperation and rehabilitation training program.

For a long time, the love of my life was a girl named Emily

That's where I met Emily. Captain Emily Carson, the most beautiful woman in the Coalition Army. She was in my rehab group, so I could see her damn near any time I wanted. Something about recovering from some kind of magic attack that shorted out her nervous system, forcing her to learn how to walk again. She was there before me and was making incredible progress by the time I arrived.

From the beginning there was that special something . . . that spark between us. A spark that ignited with our first kiss. It was wonderful.

These days if an officer and enlisted person are discovered to be romantically involved, they're separated by distance. One might get transferred to the *Iron Heart frontier* and the other to the *Lone Star Complex* or *Fort El Dorado* . . . I guess that's the *State of El Dorado* nowadays. Back then, things were a little more relaxed than that. You see, I've lived a long life and go back quite a ways. Back to a time when Chi-Town was just 'Chi-Town' and there weren't no Coalition States or an Emperor Prosek. Me, I fought alongside Joseph Prosek, the original, not the Emperor's offspring.

Anyway, my Emily, was amazing. She was full of fire. I don't know what she saw in me. Half man, half toaster, but we fell in love. It was so easy, too. So natural. So effortless. She was nearly eighteen years younger than me, and a commissioned officer, not an NCO like me. Didn't matter. Just like it didn't matter to me that she was a Military Specialist in an area that spooked some people even back then, *magic*.

Emily was a mage. I know that might sound crazy to you, but back then, the government recruited mages as part of their Special Forces. The current CS government whitewashes that part of our history, and most nobody today knows much about it, but back then, Chi-Town had a division of soldiers who were all mages loyal to humanity. This is just before the *Bloody Campaign* happened, and before magic became a buzz word for hate. People were leery about the use of magic, but I remember officers talking about *fighting magic with magic*.

Emily was one of those firebrand mages in the Coalition Army. Of course, there really wasn't a Coalition States back then. It was the City State of Chi-Town and we were part of the **Chi-Town Military Defense League**. A bunch of yahoos full of piss and vinegar.

Chi-Town was growing fast and that made it a target for raiders, would-be conquerors, demon hordes, Necromancers, monsters, and all kinds of human and inhuman trash, including the **Federation of Magic**. As for us soldiers, we saw ourselves as the defenders of humanity and dreamed of making Chi-Town the new pinnacle of human achievement. To make it the shining example that everyone else should strive to imitate. Guess we kinda done that, though Chi-Town has its share of tarnish these days.

Despite what you might hear, those were good times. Really good days, and we were feeling our oats. We had finally gotten the upper hand with the demonic hordes that had been laying siege to the humans in the area. Magic and psionics were used as tools to help keep the human race safe, and mages were accepted as productive citizens. For that matter, almost eight percent of the population of Chi-Town was D-Bees, back then. Before the Great War with the Federation of Magic, we were an open society. We felt it was our destiny to take the planet back from the monsters and make it safe for humanity again. For all peace-loving beings, really.

Anyway, one night, about a week before Emily was to be sent from Fort Sheldon on a liaison mission with friendly elements in the Kingdom of Tolkeen, I told her how I felt. I was terrified. I went to her quarters, reeking of too much cologne and alcohol-fueled courage, and knocked on the door. When she opened it I almost dropped the wildflowers I had picked and fled. But her smile stopped me in my tracks. It was so radiant. Made me feel like nothing else in the world mattered except for the two of us.

I confessed my love in one long running sentence without even stopping to breathe. My stomach was tied in knots. I felt that gravity was reversing itself and I was going to be thrown sky high and dropped to the ground. She listened to me patiently with this amused expression on her face. I remember it, because I kept thinking, oh, God, oh God, she thinks you are such an idiot!

When I was done blithering, she leaned forward to kiss me. Just a soft little kiss on my lips. Then she reached out with her small, soft hand, took my human hand and pulled me inside. The memory of that night has sustained me many a night since. The entire week together was, I have to say it, pure magic.

A week later, Emily was shipped out to Tolkeen to escort a diplomatic team from Chi-Town. Later I learned that the talks with the leadership at Tolkeen helped to keep them from joining the Federation of Magic and assailing our city from the north. A treaty was signed that kept a peace between the two powers for more than fifty years. When the recent war between the Coalition States and the Kingdom of Tolkeen was announced, I wept.

Emily and me corresponded daily, sometimes it would take several weeks for the mail to reach me, and I would get a dozen letters at once . . . those days were a treasure. It was even better when a Magic Pigeon would arrive, because when it spoke it had her sweet voice. She told me how things were in the north, and I told her about my duties here at Chi-Town.

The Battle for Chi-Town

Forty-six days after the nonaggression treaty was signed with Tolkeen, the *Federation of Magic* attacked Chi-Town. This was 12 P.A.

Them bastards only seemed to have one goal in mind: the utter destruction of our city and every person in it. It was one of the scariest times of my life. Dark mages and their demonic minions boiled forth from the ruins of Old Chicago, and more were summoned from the sheltered enclaves of the Ohio and central Mississippi River valleys. If you view the films that are the official CS history, or read the books provided to the CS educated elite, you hear how our victory was never in doubt, but that was not the case. Victory was never a certainty. The fighting was ugly and relentless. By the end of the third day, our lines of defense were broken and our forces scattered. We fought in the streets and we prayed for salvation.

The city's walls were actually breached six times during the course of the siege. I think them forty-seven days of battle aged me forty-seven years. We all fought with hardly any sleep. Used whatever weapon we could lay our hands on and did whatever had to be done to force them devils back.

Though they don't get no credit in the history books, our greatest heroes came from the Magic and Psionic Squads. I don't know if we would have won the battle if it weren't for them brave boys and gals. I'm serious. Without our own mages, I'm certain Chi-Town would have fallen. You have to remember, we did not have the invincible Coalition War Machine that we have today. We had the primitive forerunners of modern CS gear, and some pre-Cataclysm war machines that had been repaired and held in reserve for more than century. Most of the fighting was individual soldiers versus the magical and demonic horrors that had been unleashed against us. We needed every edge we could get and those relics, new-fangled bionics like I had, and the *magic* of our comrades helped win the day. Along with raw courage and pure desperation. We knew if we failed, we were all dead and Chi-Town would be no more.

The Federation forces seemed to take a special pleasure in killing our own magic forces. They called them traitors and fools, and seemed to focus their greatest wrath upon Chi-Town's magic defenders. That's why they suffered the greatest casualties, in excess of 50%, but our mages never wavered. None of us did.

The siege itself was long and terrible. When it was over, half of the city was in ruins. Our attackers had retreated back into the holes they had crawled out of in the Magic Zone, but we knew they remained strong and organized. That meant they'd be back. That we'd never be safe. That's when the great *General Joseph Prosek* stepped forward to lead the Defense League on the offensive. Our onslaught would become known as the **Bloody Campaign**, but it felt like justice to us. Hell, I don't care what folks call it, we done the right thing. If we hadn't, Chi-Town would have fallen under the next siege and there would never have been the Coalition States. We could never have survived another on-slaught like that. You can take my word on it.

The first place to fall to us in the Bloody Campaign was the mage infested ruins of **Old Chicago**. There was a large community of practitioners of magic who regarded the ruins of Chicago as a sacred place of power. The Federation of Magic used its lines of magic against us in their attack on the city, so we knew the ruins had to be cleaned out once and for all. When we took the ruins we'd hold on to them from that day forward – a no-man's zone where anyone found there had to be considered an enemy and destroyed.

I could tell you about the strange and contradictory things I saw in the Chicago ruins – the *Great Mausoleum* and the *Tower of Water*, but what's important is that we ran the sorcerers out of there and killed everyone who stood in our way.

No, that's not exactly true. *We annihilated them.* Men, women, children. Hell, any-thing that moved. Killed every last one of them, no questions asked. No mercy. No hesi-tation. No regret.

We were like the hand of God raining down destruction to wash away the land of magic. It might sound terrible to you today, but I have to say, it was easy. There was no malice. There weren't torture or rape or acts of cruelty like you hear about in the recent Coalition-Tolkeen War. We just shot them down like rats in the barn. It was them or us, and they had to go. It was a job and we done what we had to do.

From the Chicago ruins, we went to what the mages called the *Blue City*. You never heard of it because it don't exist no more. We razed it to the ground. I'm told it was once a magnificent place, more beautiful than anything in Tolkeen or Lazlo. Can't say that I noticed.

In the Zone

From there, we just kept going. Every victory filled us with greater motivation and nothing quelled our anger. Before we knew it, we were deep into the heartland of the **Federation of Magic**. It was the first time that most of us had ever travelled that far from the City State of Chi-Town. It was exhilarating and terrifying at the same time.

For miles there would be nothing more than forest, fields and unbroken acres of wild corn and wheat. And then, rising from the landscape like a child's toy cast amongst the weeds, the pinnacles and plateaus of the ruins of the past, or a new city built with magic leering before us. A friend of mine, Corporal Benny Mason, told us with all sincerity that there was ten times the volume of debris below the surface of what we were seeing. We laughed at him, and told him that he had been listening to too many stories told by the old duffers in the Great Library, but dang if he wasn't right.

We repeated the same scenes of destruction over and over again. Communities of magic fell wherever we went. Those who lived were those lucky enough to escape our gunsights or who fled before we got there. When we reached the banks of a large river, the Colonel informed us that it was the Ohio River. When someone asked why it was named the 'Ohio,' he told us that it wasn't important, and to shut up and start digging in.

For the next three months, my life consisted of nothing more than advance a mile, fight some damn army of monsters or evil sons of bitches, sleep, dig in, advance another mile, and do it all over again.

When we entered the ruins of a town called *Harrow Mills,* I smiled for the first time since the Battle for Chi-Town. There before my eyes was my *Emily*. We were about to take on a ring of towns and villages that surrounded the ancient ruins of *Louisville*. Our battalion was to join forces with a combined company of psychics and magic troops. Emily was part of that operation.

Let me tell you, we were damn happy to have them at our side. The dark mages of the Federation of Magic threw everything they had at us as we advanced on the Louisville site, and the only effective weapons we had to counter them were our brethren psychics and mages. We didn't have no Dog Boys back then, their addition to the Coalition Army was still more than half a century away. Our psi-boys and mages made all the difference in the world.

The 9th Special Operations Company, it was called, and we welcomed them as brothers and sisters in arms. They had this *Major Herman* leading them, and there was *Captain Emily Carson* – my Emily – as one of the commanding officers. Major Herman was one of the most serious and bloodthirsty S.O.B.s I have ever met. The old man was all business, guts and thunder. He terrified half the men, but every one of them, mage, psychic and grunt, respected him as if he were Zeus come down from Mount Olympus.

You might not believe it, but our sorcerers hated the Federation of Magic *more* than anyone. They spat as they talked about the Federation and Lord Dunscon. They spoke about how magic was meant to build and protect, not destroy or enslave others. And many acted as if the actions of the Federation was an affront to them personally.

I asked Emily about that one night. We was lying on her cot and just enjoying the glow of being together despite the madness surrounding us. She looked at me in the dim lantern light and said something like, "Most people don't like us, Ian. Ordinary people fear what they don't understand, and they don't understand magic. People accept us because we use magic to help and defend them, but they don't trust us, Sweetheart. Not anymore. Not after what the damn Federation did to Chi-Town. They don't see any difference between us and them. Because of the Federation, they'll never trust us again. So yeah, that makes it personal. Very personal."

She went on to tell me how she and the others were afraid that all of this would haunt them forever. That people would be so afraid and so resentful of magic practitioners that they would condemn everyone who used the craft.

I told her she was crazy. That it would never happen. I pointed out how Chi-Town would have fallen without the help of our mages. I told her how she and her fellow wizards were fighting for the freedom of everyone in the city, and how folks would appreciate the fact that our mages suffered and endured greater losses than any of us. She smiled and ran her fingers through my hair, softly, like she did, and said that was why she loved me so much. I didn't get what she meant at the time, and just enjoyed being with her that night. I would understand later. She was right. Right about all of it.

Emily died three weeks later and I was never the same

Emily lost her life saving her platoon from an ambush by a Necromancer, a Shifter and an army of monsters and animated dead. Major Herman gave me the details of her sacrifice, personally. It was the only time I ever seen him cry.

Seems the rest of the magic squad had been tricked into following a decoy. My Emily and a squad of six other mages and a Mind Melter stayed behind with two platoons of soldiers. She and her squad held off the monsters and undead horde long enough for the rest of the soldiers to get outta harm's way. Only in so doing, she and her squad got cut-off and surrounded. Before the company could regroup and counter, our mages were torn apart. Though not before Emily took down the Shifter with her last dying breath. My girl was really something.

One of the survivors, a skinny kid name Kyle Buscema, told me a twelve foot tall monstrosity composed of hair and teeth and darkness targeted his platoon. The soldiers opened up on the thing, but it seemed to shrug off their weapons fire as if it were no more than black flies in the summer buzzing around its head. He said they were sure they were all going to end up in the belly of this thing when a bolt of lightning crashed down from the sky and nailed the bastard square in the back. Emily came forward muttering to herself and another lance of electric fire slammed into the creature. Saved Kyle's life and every man in his squad. That was just one of the actions she done that day in battle to save lives.

She was posthumously awarded the Chi-Town Medal of Valor, and they even erected a memorial to her and the other mages who died in that battle. The government put up an arch with a plaque bearing the names of all the heroes who died that day in the name of freedom. Half were practitioners of magic. One was my Emily.

A piece of me died that day, but I kept fighting under the leadership of Major Herman and then under General Joseph Prosek himself. Major Herman wouldn't make it out of them dark woods. A lot of people I knew wouldn't make it out either, but we took twenty of those evil S.O.B.s for every man we lost.

I lost count of how many monsters and mages I killed in the Bloody Campaign. Probably hundreds. And I can tell you this, I never regretted killing one of them. Would have kept fighting till one of them bastards dropped me, except the General finally told us we were done and it was time to go home.

Home and heartbreak

When we returned to Chi-Town, I helped man the new battlements erected around the perimeter of Chi-Town. They would serve as the foundations for the new walls that would eventually surround and enclose the city. I stayed in the army for another twenty-seven years and achieved the rank of Command Sergeant Major. I watched as the Independent State of Chi-Town became the nucleus of the Coalition States and we went from a democracy to a benevolent dictatorship. Seemed like the right thing to do at the time, and I was among those cheering when Emperor Prosek took power.

I must admit, I was surprised when the mages were sent away from Chi-Town and the practice of magic was outlawed. They weren't killed or imprisoned as they would be now, and they were given a stipend to begin their new life, but that life had to be away from Chi-Town. Psychics were allowed to stay, but they had to register with the government and were relegated to the status of second-class citizens. A status that was only repealed in the last decade or so.

I never found another to love like Emily, so I have no family to speak of. My brother, Michael, married and raised a sizeable family. They tried to include me in their happiness, but I was always restless. Never felt like I belonged there with the family or in the city. I became the family curmudgeon. Don't get me wrong, I consider my nieces and nephews among the most important parts of my life. I'm glad they are Coalition citizens living in the great fortress city that was once my home. It's my choice to exist out here in the 'Burbs. It was my choice to leave the city and go adventuring in the Pecos Badlands, along the Mississippi, and take a post at Fort El Dorado. For a long time it just felt better for me to be out there in the Wildlands. We still keep in touch, and they know that Uncle Ian would do anything for them, but I can't live a quiet life between them concrete walls.

Maybe I was running away from my feelings, I don't know. When Emily died, it was like this hole in me ate part of my soul, but my heart didn't break till years later. Once every year I'd make a point to come home to Chi-Town and visit with the family. I'd also go and visit Emily at the arch monument in the *Park of Heroes*. It brought me peace and I felt like I could talk to Emily like she was there with me, even though she was atomized with the rest of our fallen comrades back in the Zone.

We'd completely destroy the bodies with our energy weapons, so they couldn't be animated and used against us by Necromancers. There was nothing worse than fighting your fallen comrades. Even though you knew they were dead, it tore you up. Felt like they died for nothing. That dark magic was taking them from us, tarnishing all the good they'd done. Turning them into just another monster we had to stop. Couldn't EVAC them out fast enough, so we'd mist them and send their atoms to the heavens before their dead bodies could be perverted.

My last trip to the monument was 22 years ago. I would put flowers at the base of the arch, rub my hand over her name and start up a discussion. Tell her what I'd been up to the last year, that kind of thing. Only this time there was no name to touch. There was a new plaque without the name of Captain Emily Carson. Without any of the names of the mages who had sacrificed their lives for Chi-Town. They had been removed.

I felt sick and betrayed. How many people even remembered any of them were magic practitioners? It seemed like a pointless act of shame. I understand why the Coalition government did it. They didn't want nobody remembering that mages once fought on the side of Chi-Town. It was hard to demonize all practitioners of magic if magic wielding soldiers were honored in the Park of Heroes. The new regime likes to rewrite history and make it serve their own purpose. I get that, but it turned my stomach and I turned my back on the Coalition State of Chi-Town and walked away, heartbroken.

The Walking Dead

I realize now that was the day I gave up on myself, though I suspect I had become one of the walking dead long before then. I hadn't done much actual living in the days after the Bloody Campaign, but this was the straw that broke my spirit and sent me into a dark place.

I sold my services as a gun for hire and went on a campaign in the south. Probably had a death wish, but I'm a survivor. After that, I retired. That was about 19-20 years ago, when I moved to the 'Burb of Clearview. I was just going through the motions of living. When my savings ran out, I did just enough to get by. I lived in my little shack, one of the hopeless living among the hopeful. One of the human dregs who don't contribute much of nothing to anything.

A few years later I met Jefferson Lancaster and his delightful wife Alice. Jefferson was a good man with a zest for life. I liked him right off and started to come back into the world, a little. Looking back on it now, I wonder if I didn't half live through him and his family – him, Alice, their six kids.

God only knows what he saw in me, but me and Jefferson became inseparable, like brothers. No wonder I fell in love with his life and wife, Alice. I want to make it clear that it was love from afar. I never had no affair or anything like that.

Jefferson always had some new scheme: running contraband books or medical supplies, helping D-Bees in and out of the 'Burbs, going on adventures to scrounge up some extra cash by digging up artifacts or protecting some podunk town from bandits and such. Meanwhile, Alice stayed home with the kids, making extra by selling and trading her baked goods. God, that woman can bake.

It was sad, because Jefferson had made plans to retire from the life of an adventurer and finally settle down. He put all of his money from our last several jobs into a bakery and helped Alice start up a good business. She managed the staff while Jefferson managed the business and handled advertising. It was a smart move, because they did well. It was a good deal for me too, I got all the baked goods I could eat for free, and the pleasure of being part of their family. I think it was Jefferson's idea to start having kids from the orphanages over for dinner a couple times a week. He and Alice were generous people like that. Of course, I was there too. I was always there with Jefferson and Alice. While the kids waited for chow, I'd regale them with stories of monsters and adventures. Nothing too frightening, mind you, fun tales of battle and heroism. Made me feel good. Then we'd roughhouse it a little till Alice would threaten to beat the tar out of all of us, and they'd go back to the orphanage.

I don't know why Jefferson felt like he needed that last adventure. Sure, it promised a big score, but he already had a good life. Maybe if I was alive back then I would have tried to talk him out of it. Instead I was at his side ready to go wherever he wanted to. I remember Alice looked all worried as we rode out of town. Jefferson told me how they was up all night with her pleading for him to stay. He should have listened. We both should have known that there's such thing as a last big score. That line of thinking is for dumb mercs and suckers. We both should have know that if it sounded too good to be true, it probably was. But I was one of the walking dead and couldn't see that back then. I just followed my friend and went through the paces.

I was there when Jefferson caught sick. A bullet would have been kinder. We tried to get him to a proper Healer or Body Doc but a blizzard prevented it. He died from *Black Frog Fever* after only a week. The fever killed a lot of people in Wisconsin that winter. I brought Jefferson home to his family for a proper burial as soon as the snow let up. The second saddest moment of my life was telling Alice her husband died for no good reason.

The next seven years were my darkest yet. I think all that kept me from putting a bullet in my brain or taking one last adventure was watching out for Alice, her near adult children and the bakery. A lot of professional soldiers go out that way. Taking a job they know will probably kill them. They figure that dying in action is somehow better than finding a way to live back in the real world.

The right thing

So there I was, comfortably perched on my favorite bar stool at my favorite watering hole. A quiet joint where a lot of us long in the tooth war hounds hang out. The owner's a good kid. Most of the regulars are nice people and there's seldom any serious trouble. In fact, the last incident was maybe five or six years ago, which is like a half century in the 'Burbs. The kid just took over running the place and was having a big blow out. There was TV and boxing, a band, booze and laughs for everyone. Me and the boys called it a night around midnight or we might have been able to put an end to the trouble before it got started. Two or three hopped-up punks come in around closing and got rowdy. Ended up getting themselves killed, but not till after they've gone and killed good old Bill in a fight. A smart fella that Bill, good with his hands, too. Kept a lot of knowledge in his head, but never used it to make his life better. Reflecting on it, I think he was one of the walking dead too, only he was trying to drown himself the slow way, from inside a bottle.

Anyway, I'm at the bar when we all heard a commotion outside. Most of the younger people raced over to the windows to see what was going on. It's a rare day in the 'Burbs when some fool or another isn't raising a ruckus, so I didn't even bother getting up until my buddy, Brett, calls me over. Said I had to see this little twig of a girl taking on Coalition soldiers in the street outside.

Sure enough, there was this little slip of a girl running down the street. She had already put two Dead Boys outta commission with some kind of magic spell, and was facing down another, when a fourth jumped her from behind. The crowd inside whispered about magic and Dead Boys kicking her ass. A lot of Coalition soldiers liked the term *Dead Boy*. I think it made them feel tougher. Me, I never cared for it much. The name seemed more like a prognostication I didn't much like the sound of. It ain't respectful neither, but it does put the fear of God in most people, and a lot of grunts get off on that.

The Coalition soldier behind the girl knocked her to the ground and jumped on her, pinning her down. You could hear the smile on his face through his voice. Said something about how they were going to hurt her bad before they passed her around to the rest of the boys. Then the one she had been facing walked over and said he gets a piece of her first. The one that had her pinned to the ground laughed, got up, yanked her up and pushed her into the first soldier's arms.

That's when I got a good look at her. Eyes the size of saucers, covered with dirt from the street stuck to her sweat, small scrapes and bruises from the scuffle on her body. Couldn't have been more than 16 or 17. She tried to cast a spell, but these boys are too smart for that, and the grunt holding her let one hand loose, still holding her with his other, and smacked her, hard, across the face. Every time she looked to start to say something he belted her again. Poor thing was probably only going to beg for mercy. Not that it would have done her any good. The other Dead Boy was laughing and said something about 'tenderizing the meat.' Like I said, there are a lot of good men in the Coalition Army, but these two couldn't be counted among them.

Next thing I know, I could hear the people in the bar shouting and howlering at me. That's when I realized I'm in the dang street drawing down on them Coalition soldiers. Don't rightly remember leaving the bar or pulling my weapon, but that's the way it was in battle sometimes. All I remember is thinking, damn, that girl looks like my *Emily*. Her hair was the same style and same shade of red. She had the same body shape, and not much younger than when I met Emily that first time. Though now that I got to see her up close I realized she couldn't be more than 14 or 15. She don't deserve this. And her eyes. Those big, beautiful eyes, pleaded for help without her saying a word.

I ain't senile. I know it wasn't Emily, but there I was, in the street ordering them Dead Boys to stand down and let her go. I'm no City Rat, but I knew these two were the kind of corrupt filth that gave good Coalition soldiers a bad name. I also knew what they had planned for this girl was worse than death and I wasn't about to let it happen.

The one who had jumped the girl from behind turned and spit forth a string expletives. Somewhere buried in them was the question, 'Who the hell do you think you are?' And something about this being Coalition business and to get my behind indoors before I get hurt.

The one holding the girl was laughing and said something about them coming back for me with an ISS squad after he and his platoon were done with the girl.

I guess he shoulda been drawing his weapon instead of laughing, because it gave me time to pump two rounds into his throat. That's the weak spot in Coalition Dead Boy armor, the throat. It's only a viable target in close combat, and you have to be a good shot. He was close and I'm a good shot. He went down with his head rolling off his shoulders.

I think the other one couldn't believe his eyes, because as he drew his side arm I could tell his aim was off and I was able to blast him off his feet with my next shot. Finished him up close with the Vibro-Blade in my bionic left arm. The whole melee was over in less than thirty seconds. Most gunfights are.

I have to admit, I surprised myself at how it all came back to me and went down so quick in my favor. My enhancements may be horribly out of date, but they served me well in that fight.

The girl was suffering from shock. She had dropped to her knees when the fighting started. I told her I wasn't going to hurt her. That she was safe, but we had to go before more troops arrived. She looked up at me with them big eyes, tears streaming down her cheeks, trembling like a leaf. I smiled, reached out my human hand, and repeated that we had to leave. Now. I felt bad, because she glanced at my bionic arm splattered in the dead soldier's blood and then up to my face. I was afraid she thought I was some monster, but she took my human hand and I helped her up.

It wasn't until I had her tucked under my arm and we turned around that I remembered where we were. On a public street. In front of my favorite bar. In front of my friends and about a hundred other eyewitnesses. My drinking buddies and neighbors just stood there silent with their mouths gaping open. It's one thing to hear stories about combat. It's another to see it up close and personal. Probably worse seeing someone you know turn into a killing machine right in front of your eyes.

Brett was the only one to say anything. He shouted, "get outta here, man. Get outta here!"

I grabbed the girl and I ran. Ran as fast as my two bionic legs could carry me. Yeah, I picked up another bionic limb during my last term of service. Don't matter how.

When I finally felt it was safe enough to catch our breaths, I stopped to clean the blood off my arm. Blood splatter is kind of conspicuous even in the 'Burbs.

The girl told me how she didn't mean nothing. That her family was visiting a friend in one of the Shanty Towns and she had run off to play with some other kids. She was showing off her magic at a place where she didn't think anybody could see her. Guess she was new to the 'Burbs or she'd know there were eyes everywhere, especially when you least expect them. Next thing she knew, four Coalition Dead Boys were on them. One bashed in the head of a D-Bee acquaintance and the other kids scattered. The soldiers came for her next, laughed and called after her as she ran. By some miracle she took down two with a Cloud of Slumber. The idiots must of had their face plates off or that spell would never have worked. Those Dead Boy suits is environmental for a reason. The other two only got madder. I knew the rest.

I promised her she'd be okay. That she had to forget about this, get to her family and skedaddle out of town. I took her to a buddy who worked in the 'Burb Underground and paid him the last credits I had to my name to get her to her family in Firetown, and get them all out of town safely before the Psi-Hounds and ISS hit the streets.

And then she was gone.

I found my way into a dark corner of an alley and sat down. I stayed there till morning. Not because I thought the cover of darkness would hide me, but because it all hit me. My life. Being one of the walking dead. Regrets. All of a sudden all these thoughts and memories and questions raced through my mind. The one question I didn't ask myself was why? Why did I do it? Why did I help that girl?

The reason probably isn't what you're thinking. It wasn't that she looked like Emily. I think I was simply tired of sitting on the sidelines while bad things kept happening to people that didn't deserve it. Just like I didn't know when or how I had become one of the walking dead, I don't know why, but I stopped being one and rejoined the human race when that girl was in trouble. I couldn't sit idle no more.

I'm glad I did it. No regrets. Of course, I'm a dead man now. The Coalition won't let something like this go without retribution. They'll find me and that will be that. It all happened so fast, I didn't think about concealing my identity. Everybody saw me. Even if my friends want to do the noble thing and pretend they didn't see nothing, they can't risk their own lives and families for my skin. They can't risk a Coalition Purge on Clearview by hiding me or pretending ignorance. I understand that and I don't hold it against them. They'll have to tell and I.D. me. And even if they don't, there must have been a couple dozen other witnesses who can describe me.

That brings me back to why I'm writing this. The Coalition should come knocking any time and I felt a need to tell my story.

Like I said, I have lived a long life, but not a very good one. I let rage and revenge drive half of it, and I sleepwalked like a damn zombie consumed with sadness and loss through the rest of it.

Funny thing is, now that I *know* it's all going to end soon, I want to live. I want to live, but there's no point of running. When the Coalition authorities figure out who is responsible, they'll hunt me down wherever I go. Especially since I'm one of them gone bad. Yeah, that's how they'll see it. Some crazy Combat 'Borg went off his nut and killed two of his own. Now we have to track and put him down like the mad dog that he is. So I figure I'd go home and make it easy for them. I won't resist arrest and take more lives. I've done enough killing. And because I'm a Coalition citizen, my death will be quick and merciful by lethal injection.

So here I sit, waiting. Spending my last hours reflecting on my life and swimming in regret. Seems all I have left are my regrets: Not doing more for my friends, family and neighbors. Wishing I could say goodbye to my brother and the kids. Wishing I stood up for what's right sooner than last night. Sorry that I closed myself off to life's simple joys and beauty. Regretting I didn't appreciate what was there right in front of my face the whole time. That would be the smell of Alice's baked bread, the embrace of the morning breeze, the laughter of the children when I told them my stories and wrestled with them in play. I regret not having shared my stories with more people. I wish maybe I had written many of them down and told people about the real history of Chi-Town and its heroes. I ain't no Erin Tarn, but I've done plenty of living and seen plenty to tell about. But most of all, I regret never telling Alice how special she is or how much I love her. And I regret that I will make Alice cry at another funeral.

In short, don't make the same mistakes I've made. To my friends, I hope my foolish return to the living has not caused you any trouble or grief.

Respectfully,
Ian Robert Polovich, CS Command Sergeant Major, Retired

* * *

Ian put the pen down and, as if on cue, heard the sound of men moving cautiously outside his hut. He folded his writing, wrote, *'A While Longer'* on it, and put it in his special hiding place with the hope that a City Rat who knew him would come scrounging, find it and take it to his friends at the bar. Then he took a deep breath and turned to face the door.

"Ian? You in there?"

It took him a minute to realize he recognized that voice.

"Brett?"

"Yeah."

"You crazy? Get outta here. You know the storm that's coming for me."

"That's just it, Ian. That storm's not coming."

"What?!"

Ian opened the door wide. There was Brett and Kenny and Allen and some of his other bar friends and neighbors who bore witness to his deed.

"Are you all crazy?"

"No Ian. It's a miracle," said one of the men.

The old Headhunter had given up on miracles a long time ago, but his recent reawakening left room for the possibility.

"One of you better start explaining."

"Those two Dead Boys you killed were rotten to the core. Not only did they treat 'Burbies like garbage, but they were breaking CS laws and had a nice business going with the Black Market."

"So what!" bellowed Ian in frustration. "That ain't gonna stop the CS from seeking retribution for what happened to one of their own."

"No," said Brett. "But Lieutenant Milne did."

"What? Milne?"

"Yeah. About two minutes after you ran off with the girl, six hover cars pulled up and Dead Boys spilled out of 'em. But before they could start asking questions, Lieutenant Milne appeared out of the crowd, stepped forward and took command of the investigation. Said he saw the whole thing. That a wanted criminal with ties to a Tolkeen Retribution Squad had done this. That he even had the man in his squad car. He must have captured him prior to your gunfight."

"It'll never stand up to further investigation."

"That's just it, Ian. The investigation is closed," said Allen.

"You should have seen him," said Brett. "Lieutenant Milne tells the Dead Boys to wait and he disappears back into the crowd. A minute later he returns dragging this beast of a man, gagged and in handcuffs. Milne parades him around for everyone to see. Then he announces, 'This is the dog responsible for the deaths of two Coalition soldiers today.' He drags this guy around a second time, shoving him in our faces without saying a word, and then shouts. 'Isn't that right?' Well, nobody knows what to say. I mean, come on, Ian, we just saw you take down two Dead Boys like it was nothin' and suddenly Milne is there with this brute putting on a show.

"The other Dead Boys are just standing there waiting for a response, Milne tells everyone they have nothing to fear. To tell the truth. And then asks again, 'Isn't this the man responsible for the violence here today?' Only now he sounds pissed off."

"Then a woman says, 'Yes, Lieutenant, that's the madman.' We all turn around and it's Lisa from the bar. I don't think she even saw what happened, but she knew it was you who done it. And then Kenny here bellows, 'That's the dirty bastard.' And then me and a bunch of people all start to shout, 'Yeah, yeah, he's the one.'

"Milne shoves the man toward the other Dead Boys telling them to take this pig away before he loses his composure. He shoves the man again, hard this time, leaning into him with his whole body, and all of a sudden the guy gets free of his handcuffs. Kenny insists he saw Milne unlock the cuffs, but nobody else saw that happen. This bruiser starts to make a run for it. Milne opens fire and we all scramble for cover. The rest of the Dead Boys open up too, and this guy is vaped in six seconds flat.

"Case closed."

"They vaped him?"

"Nothing but pink mist."

"Case closed?"

"Case closed."

"But what about the people who saw . . . who saw . . ."

"You mean your friends? They didn't see you do anything. Were you even there yesterday? Hmm. Nope, I don't think you were."

"I didn't see him," said Allen.

"Me either," grinned Kenny.

"Okay, okay, but what about the other witnesses?"

"They didn't see nothing either. And if they did? They say you stepped on a couple of rats that needed stepping on. They're grateful. And anyone else who saw what happened? You think they're going to contradict Lieutenant Milne and risk Coalition retribution? As far as they know, you could be part of a Coalition operation. Everyone knows you're ex-Coalition Army. Hell, maybe you still are. Get what I'm saying? They're going to go with the *official story*. Incident forgotten. Case closed," announced Brett with confidence.

"What about the other two Dead Boys? The ones the girl took down?"

"Ha, they was sleeping like babies. Didn't see a thing," trumpeted Kenny.

"And Milne?"

"He came into the bar later that night," said Allen. "Says to me, 'Tell Ian he shouldn't lay around his hut all day, missed some real excitement today.' He finishes his drink, pats my hand and leaves."

"Really?"

"Case closed," repeated Brett.

"How could it have played out like that? What are the odds Milne had a perp in his car right then and was even there by the bar?"

"Damned lucky, that's for sure," said Kenny.

"You're not hiding that girl inside there are you?" asked Brett.

"Nah, she's long gone. Just a scared kid," replied Ian.

"Good," said Kenny.

"Case closed," chuckled Brett, happy for his friend.

"Alice!?" said Ian.

"She doesn't know a thing," assured Brett. "And nobody's going to say a word to her about it. As far as she and everyone else who wasn't there knows, this crazy, half-human killer attacked a Coalition squad in broad daylight. Probably part of an ambush that used a girl for bait. The girl and the rest of the Retribution Squad got away. How terrible. Blah, blah, blah."

"Case closed," said Ian softly, with a quizzical smirk. He hadn't realized it earlier, but that explained why Alice treated him like always this morning. She didn't know.

*   *   *

Ian peeked around the back door of Alice's house where he thought she'd be in the kitchen cooking. He could smell a collection of delicious food simmering and baking, but she wasn't there.

"Are those for me?"

Ian practically jumped out of his bioinc limbs. Standing behind him was Alice pointing at the flowers he had picked for her. Good ones he had stolen from a garden in an Old Town 'Burb.

"Geez Louweez, woman! You scared the daylights out of me."

"Why so jumpy?" she asked as she took the flowers and rummaged under the kitchen sink for a vase to put them in.

"What happened to that famous bionic hearing you're always telling the children about? All I did was come back from making sure the bakery was all locked up. Wasn't like I was trying to sneak up on you," she lied. She did sneak up on Ian, like she often did, though this was the first time she ever actually caught him unaware.

"Um, I guess I was focused on something else."

"Must be something important. Is that bit of business still pestering you, Hon?"

"No. That's all taken care of. Worked out much better than I anticipated."

"Oh, good," said Alice, as she put the vase of flowers down on the table and a tray of hot biscuits down with the other hand.

"Alice?"

"Yes?"

"I . . ." Ian stepped up close to Alice and took her hand in his.

"What, Honey? You said everything was okay."

"It is. It's just that . . . I love you. Always have."

"You do?" said Alice, smiling playfully.

"With my whole heart."

She reached up, took his face gently between her hands, and kissed him for a long while. Ian couldn't believe his luck was still holding up. Now he really felt alive.

"Now, wash those hands. The kids will be here any minute and I have to get dinner on the table," said Alice with slap on Ian's rump to drive home the point.

"I'll help. As soon as I wash my hands."

Though there were many fine meals to follow, that one was the best dinner he had ever had, Ian recollected later.

He and Alice wed four months later. When not working around the bakery and helping out at several of the local orphanages, Ian is busy writing his third book to be published by the Black Market. Not that he's an Erin Tarn or anything.

Peddler's End

By Jeffry Scott Hansen and Kevin Siembieda

"A block of cheese, two pounds of bacon, and three loaves of bread, Peddler."

The large man bellowed to Elbav, the old man also known as "Peddler," proprietor of the humble but very popular storefront *Peddler's End*.

Peddler nodded and smiled, opened his cooler and pulled out a large slab of pork. Taking a large cleaver in his good hand, he chopped off a meaty portion of bacon and wrapped it up in paper. Selecting the warmest, freshest bread from his stone oven, old Peddler put three loaves into a large paper bag that was already full of cheese. Looking up at his customer, he flashed his always trusting smile at the man, who pulled out a silk bag of coins and handed it to him. The man walked out of the store and into the busy streets of Tranquility.

Elbav's grin quickly turned into a frown after the man left. If people only knew how sad he really was. One thing he would remember his Grandfather telling him was, "Always smile for the people, because nobody wants to do business with a grouch!"

What he would give to see old Grandfather again, he would think to himself. Grandfather was so wise and kind, but the days of wise and kind old men were gone. The Coalition made sure of that. Saviors of the human race, indeed. His poor Grandfather had been killed by a stray laser blast from a Coalition soldier twenty years before. His parents were killed in a stampede of people attempting to get into Chi-Town when the gates were opened when he was a child. Peddler decided to close up and close his mind to the thoughts of the Coalition and the promises of Chi-Town. No need to brood over a corrupt government anymore today. It was time to relax and have a drink or two. Maybe three.

Elbav closed up his shop and locked the door. He walked briskly down the street to Mel's Tavern and when he entered the old pub, he walked over to his favorite spot and plopped himself down. The tavern was the watering hole for just about the entire *'Burb of Tranquility*. Out of towners, weary travelers and sometimes the Coalition Peacekeepers would stop in for a pint of grog, the house specialty. Peddler's popularity was well established, and he never had to pay for his drinks. He would insist on paying, but the Tavern's owner, *Mel the Mixer*, was so indebted to him from years past, that his credits were never accepted.

Barmaids and customers of all shapes and sizes walked past the wooden bar lined with old and young, adventurer and thief alike. The place had the smell of tobacco smoke and greasy food, with the meats compliments of Peddler's End. Elbav kept mostly to himself and never really had conversations with people. Any verbal gestures towards him were kept to a minimum, especially when Coalition soldiers or police were around. Peddler's friends all knew never to bring too much attention to the old man. That was best for him and everyone he knew. Peddler was not only a dealer in food goods, but of *all things forbidden* by the government of his high Excellency, Emperor Prosek.

Few knew the old man's secret, and those who did were so indebted to him with their very lives and the lives and health of their children, that they would never betray the man no matter what.

After a few hours and a few too many glasses, Elbav slunked off his stool, and took the last swig of his ale.

He waved to his good friend Mel and made his way to the door. Peddler always tried to be aware of his surroundings, and always made it a point to glance at every face in the bar, if only for an instant. He would scan the crowd to see who was there and if anyone was paying him too much attention. This time, as he walked out of the door, either from tiredness or just plain old inebriation, he did not scan the crowd on his way out. If he had, he would have noticed the cloaked young man in the corner watching his every move. Elbav stumbled back to his store and unlocked the door. The cloaked man peeked out of the doorway of the Tavern and quietly observed Peddler as he scooted inside. The man left the Tavern, walked to the alleyway, and disappeared into the night.

* * *

Tranquility. The town's name must have been concocted by either a drunken fool or someone with a bad sense of humor, or maybe just unrealistic expectations. Random shootings, mini-riots and plain old mayhem and chaos fill the day-to-day lives of the folks who choose to live in the 'Burb known as Tranquility. Sleep is regularly interrupted by the barking of dogs, the laughter of drunks, the screams of victims, the bellows of D-Bees, the cry of a monster, gunfire and an occasional explosion or two.

Believe it or not, most people get used to the symphony of chaos. Thus, tonight, like most nights, Elbav slept like a baby. His body and mind immune to the sounds of night-time in Tranquility, his body tired from a long day's work. Elbav's small apartment sat above his shop and had the appearance of being lived in and not cleaned too often. Ever since his wife, Elyssa, passed away from a mysterious illness, Peddler's will to pick up after himself diminished considerably. She was always after him about keeping the place tidy, even if they never entertained guests.

Morning in Tranquility was even noisier than the night, and the rumble of vehicles, clatter of power armor, chatter of people, and bustle of activity called to Peddler like an alluring siren. The old man pulled himself out of bed, and washed his face and hands in hot water from the bathroom sink as he pondered if he *needed* to shave or not today. His morning routine was interrupted by the sound of a crash outside in the street below. He briskly walked over to the window and peeked out to see a vehicle had driven up onto the sidewalk across the street and rammed into the clothing store. He was happy it was not his store, and quickly pulled on his work clothes as he made his way to the front door of the shop. He hung the "Open" sign up and surveyed the damage to the storefront of his neighbor across the street.

Three children dressed in rags were at his door in a split second. Eyes wide and eager to see old Peddler. He smiled at them and gave them each a large chocolate cookie, then shooed them away as he did every morning. It bothered him to see some Coalition police taking notice of the crash across the street. They usually didn't care about traffic accidents or damage to property unless it involved magic, monsters or gunplay, so this was curious. The children ran away and Peddler shook his head as he watched the jack-booted police pull the unfortunate man out of his car and beat him with *zap-sticks,* high-tech maces that could be used as a club or as a stun weapon. The larger of the two police officers looked over at Peddler and waved. Peddler nodded, shut his door and walked into his store. The Coalition cop must be one of his regulars, impossible to tell with his Death's Head face plate in place on his helmet.

It was a clever design, the CS Dead Boy armor. The skull-like face plate was not only intimidating, but provided complete anonymity. Even when they spoke, their voices were electronically scrambled so that you couldn't recognize them. That meant you never knew who you were dealing with, unless you knew the soldier by his number, and you could never be sure if it was him or his newest replacement. This made them seem less human, ethereal, frightening and rather monstrous. Great for scaring the heck out of – well, *everyone* they encountered.

The day went on with two more car crashes on the street and a shootout between a Chi-Town ISS Officer and a Juicer. Peddler was thankful his day was busy but uneventful. He was in the back of his store fixing himself a sandwich when the familiar ring of the door-chime grabbed his attention. Funny, he mused to himself, how it never failed that a customer would show up just as he was about to eat. Bounding around an aisle came *Jeru Benso*, eldest son of one of Elbav's dearest friends, the missing and presumed dead, *Jacoby Benso*. Jeru had taken up his father's business, the lucrative, but very dangerous profession of smuggling contraband in and out of the 'Burbs. A stout fellow, Jeru towered over Peddler by two feet, but always bent down and spoke to him with the utmost respect and humility.

"Hi Peddler. Do you have a minute to talk? In private?"

Elbav motioned him to the back room and made an identical sandwich for his unexpected guest. The two sat down at the small table.

"Jeru, my friend. What business do you have that needs to be discussed in private?"

"Oh, the usual Peddler. I have 'unique things' to show you. They are rare finds indeed," Jeru said, in the lowest voice he could manage.

Elbav looked past Jeru, peeking through the door toward the front of his shop. No customers, but still one can never be too safe. Peddler smiled, stood up and motioned for Jeru to follow him up to his quarters, above the shop. Jeru followed behind as he and his father before him had done countless times in the past. When they were both at the top of the stairs, Peddler turned quickly and grabbed Jeru by his collar and yanked down.

He clenched his teeth and when he spoke, he unintentionally spat in Jeru's stupified face. His voice was whispered but the message was quite clear and angry.

"How many times must you be told to never, *ever* mention the words *'rare finds'*, in my store! Do you want to get us both killed?! Jeru, my most talented dullard of a friend, your father was a great man. A good friend. He would have boxed your ears for such a stupid utterance!"

Jeru, quite shaken from Peddler's words, was equally shaken by his actions. There was not one man in Tranquility, except for a Coalition Officer or two (with backup present), who would ever dare to grab his shirt collar like this. Yet, this frail looking old man was not just anybody. To the Coalition he was just little old Peddler, but to Jeru and most of the townsfolk, he was *Elbav the Wise*. Even though Jeru was a giant both physically and by reputation, when it came to *Elbav the Wise*, he was just a puppy being scolded. Jeru lowered his head and closed his eyes and begged Peddler for forgiveness.

The old man sighed, let go of Jeru's shirt, and patted his shoulder.

"Come show me what 'rare finds' have you so excited."

The pair walked to the sitting area. Elbav sat down in the middle of the couch, Jeru across from him in a large, black leather chair. Jeru reached into his coat sleeve, produced a small burlap sack, and laid it on the end table. He reached into the bag and pulled out a white ball with red stitches around it. The ball had blue writing on one side.

Peddler took the object from Jeru's hand and gave it a most quizzical look. He smiled and faced the writing of the ball at Jeru.

"Let's see how you have done with your studies, Jeru. Tell me, what do the letters on this ball spell out?"

Jeru frowned, shook his head and tapped his feet. He had not been one to study much of anything, after his father's disappearance.

"Come now. Just try. Sound out the words. It will make me happy." Jeru grimaced and scooted forward, squinting to look at the words on the ball.

"OFF ISH AL M-AAAY-JOOR LEEE-GUUAAA BBB-AAASSS-BALLL."

Elbav smiled and said, "Now, all together."

"OFFISHAL MAAYJOR LEEEGA BAASBALL."

"Good work, Jeru! Your father would be proud. Now, do you know what this is? No? Well my boy, I'll tell you. This is an ancient artifact."

That much Jeru already knew, but Peddler always enjoyed talking about the past, so he just looked at the ball and let him continue on.

"It's a baseball, the handwriting marked here on the top reveals that it was owned by someone named RAWL. It is in excellent shape and does not appear to be very worn or damaged, or even greatly discolored. Hmmm. If it's not a fake it's in excellent condition. I have others like it in my vault. It appears that this RAWL fellow had many of them marked with his name, as did a fellow named WILSON. Splendid find, my good Jeru."

Elbav held the ball in his good hand and rolled it around with his fingers. He had some old information discs that explained what the ball was used for. The discs were record-ings of broadcasts from ancient times that showed large stadiums with plush green pas-tures, filled with thousands of screaming citizens. A dozen or so men on opposing teams, throwing the baseball at one another and swinging large wooden clubs in an effort to hit the ball to the screaming citizens as a gift. Very interesting but confusing game, was his conclusion.

Jeru's stomach rumbled, which caused Peddler to look up. He smiled and motioned to the sandwiches they had brought up with them.

"Eat, my big friend. Eat."

They sat and spoke about the other towns Jeru was a courier for and the most recent gossip and goings-on in those towns. Elbav found himself dozing off and looked at the time.

"Jeru, my friend, it is time for me to lock up for another day. Thank you for bringing me this fine artifact. Your usual percentage when I sell it."

"Of course."

"And be mindful of that tongue of yours, young man."

Jeru grunted and smiled weakly at that last comment as Elbav escorted him to the door and filled a grocery bag full of day old bread, and a hunk of cheese for Jeru's crew of couriers. Jeru gave his mentor a hug and went on his way. Elbav was just about to lock the front door and call it a day when a giant of a Coalition Trooper pushed the door open.

The trooper wasn't in full armor, though a pair of tinted goggles obscured his eyes. The man's boots were polished to ebony mirrors. His side arm was a C-18 laser pistol –

old school – and his gloves and jacket were black leather over the standard CS uniform. Elbav's heart pounded for what seemed like forever, and his throat became dry and lumped. Of course, there had been other Coalition Troopers in his store before, but not one so big and so menacing. The trooper stood there grinning and motioned for Peddler to come closer. Elbav stood frozen and was only able to utter a greeting, but just barely.

"Sir, how can I help you today?"

The trooper held his grin and then turned the grin into a scowl. His voice was deep and his tone demeaning.

"Give me a dozen cookies, four pounds of cheese, four loaves of bread, two gallons of milk and a stick of butter. Make it fast, I haven't got all day, old man."

Peddler quickly collected the items the trooper requested and placed them all neatly on the counter. He added the prices in his head and gave the trooper half off. When he told the trooper the price, the man just laughed. Peddler stood still, his face turning beet red. Then his attention quickly changed to the doorway, when a cloaked figure slipped into the store and snuck up behind the trooper. To the surprise of both Peddler and the cloaked figure, the trooper spun around and pulled his gun from its holster in one smooth, quick motion. The sight of the gun pointed at his chest caused the cloaked visitor to freeze in place, arms outstretched, hands empty.

"The store's closed! Get out of here," the trooper bellowed.

The man looked at Peddler and could see that the old man was upset. Then he glanced at the trooper seeming not to know what to say.

The Coalition trooper smiled at the man, pleased that he seemed too scared to make a move or say a word. He collected up his groceries in one big sweeping motion of his right arm, and held the pistol in his left – just in case. Keeping his eye on the two, the trooper headed for the door without paying for his groceries.

"You in the hood, never sneak up on a Coalition soldier. You're lucky I didn't kill you on the spot. And you, old man, Peddler do they call you? You need to show more respect to the men who keep you and this garbage pit of a town safe. You understand? Even think about reporting this, and this shack of yours will burn to the ground."

Confident in his arrogance, the grinning trooper holstered his gun, turned and walked away toward the front door. Peddler watched as the cloaked man turned, ran silently behind the trooper and pounced on him as he turned the corner of the aisle. He lost sight of the trooper and the cloaked man when they turned the corner, but knew exactly what happened next. The sound of electrified metal hitting metal and leather filled his ears and his eyes could see the five to six flashes of light that accompanied the obvious strikes from the stun maces he'd seen the police use just earlier that day.

Not wanting to be a witness for a Coalition Inquiry, he closed his eyes and turned around, praying the young man would run out the door. Then, fearing the lad might not want any witnesses, Peddler ran to his apartment upstairs, locked the door and flung himself into the leather chair Jeru had sat in early. Elbav's heart pounded as he listened for any noise from downstairs. Suddenly, he realized the baseball was still sitting on the table. He reached down to pick it up, but fumbled with it, and it dropped to the floor. Elbav figured he could claim he wasn't in the shop when the trooper was assaulted, but he'd have a hard time explaining why he had pre-Rifts artifacts laying around his apartment.

As Peddler reached down to pick the ball up, it changed colors before his very eyes and turned into a silver ball with a hollow on one side. The hollow was filled with gems of all shapes and sizes and various colors. On the outside of the sphere were strands of multicolored filament.

Elbav's heart fluttered as he realized he possessed a rare and extremely forbidden device. A device that just the mere mention of would send the Coalition on a campaign to the ends of the Earth to find one. And here it was before him, and right under the nose of the high and mighty Coalition Army. He had read a story about the device laying at his feet, and recalled it was created by one of the founding fathers of Techno-Wizardry in North America, Kapan Zo-Tu, rumored to be a Chiang-Ku Dragon. It was a legendary device able to teleport its bearer to wherever they *thought of going*. Unlike other teleportation devices that required the user to be familiar with the target location or having a visual lock on the target location from a distance, this relic would whisk the user anywhere he desired, or so legend had it. That technology died with Zo-Tu and had never been duplicated. Peddler knew this was what he had, because the device also had a magical cloaking mechanism that could make it appear as an ordinary item, such as a ball. It was called the *Orb of Teleportation*.

Three loud knocks brought Elbav's thoughts to the present. In his excitement he'd forgotten about the cloaked assailant beating a giant of a Coalition trooper to his death. Now someone was at his door. Was it the cloaked man come for him next? Or could it be the half dead giant come to exact revenge upon him for not running to get help?

Peddler scooped up the ball and shoved it under the cushion of the black chair.

"Who . . . who's there?"

Silence.

Peddler waited a long time before he approached the door. He thought about calling Jeru or one of his many other connections, but he didn't want to involve them in an assault on a Coalition soldier, who was probably laying dead near the front door of his store.

Then he got a smart idea. He retrieved the Orb of Teleportation and willed himself to appear outside his locked door, behind where he figured an assailant might be waiting. With a blink he was standing on the other side of the door. Alone. Nobody else present.

Peddler frantically looked around to make sure he was, indeed, alone. He shoved baseball in his pocket and crept downstairs. The lights were off, but there was enough light coming through the windows that he could still see. Even from the back of the store he could tell someone had flipped the sign on the door to 'closed.' Slowly, Elbav made his way to the front of the store, one hand in his pocket, clutching the orb.

When he got to the front, he was surprised to find no one there. No cloaked man. No Coalition trooper. A couple people ran past his storefront and he could see several others across the street also running down the same direction. Opening his door a crack and peering down the street, he could see a crowd had gathered on the corner and were craning their necks to look down the side alley. Coalition soldiers suddenly appeared on the scene running towards the alley, pushing bystanders out of their way and beating anyone who didn't move fast enough. Elbav had a bad feeling the body of his trooper was down that alley and wanted no part of that, so he locked the door, turned around, leaned back against it, and let out a big sigh of relief. That's when he saw the bag of groceries the Coalition goon had taken, resting up on a shelf. Walking over to it, he could see it still contained all of its contents. Written on one side in marker was a note that said, *"I hate thieves, here's your food back – a friend."*

Peddler collected the contents of the bag, put them back in stock and promptly burned the bag. A friend, he thought. Let's hope so. Elbav went to the back of his store, still feeling rather shaken and moved the large cooler. Under it was a secret door that led to his cellar. A vault, really. He turned on a light, pressed the code to open the armored door and made his way through the cluttered cellar filled with contraband such as books, baseballs, and medical supplies. He found a velvet bag and placed the Orb inside it, then hid the device in a box under a table covered by old cheese crates. He went back to his room and found himself so excited that it was hard to fall asleep. If the CS didn't come for him in the next few days, he'd be alright.

*   *   *

After a few days went by without event, Peddler started to relax. Word on the street was that someone had beaten a Coalition trooper to a pulp. Broke his jaw in three places and left him in the alley near the clothing store. The poor soldier was beaten so senseless he couldn't remember what happened. The store was investigated, its owner and work staff questioned, but they were cleared by the ISS. If there were any witnesses, nobody was stepping forward, which was typical. There was some fear among the residents that the CS might purge the neighborhood, but that talk soon faded. It seemed Peddler was in the clear.

The old man figured people might start to ask questions if he didn't go back to his routine, so he decided to renew his nightly visits to Mel's Tavern for a few drinks.

When he left that evening, Elbav looked up and down the street before stepping out into it. The trip was uneventful and after calling it a night, the old man returned home. As he approached, he could see a person in front of his shop, walking away from him. As Elbav walked closer to his shop, the Cloaked Man stepped out of the shadows.

Peddler let out a little yelp of surprise. But the Cloaked Man smiled, held up his hands, palms out, and asked if Elbav was okay.

"Yes, I'm fine. Thank you."

"Good, said the Cloaked Man. "Have a pleasant evening." Then he turned to walk away.

"Wait," protested Peddler. "Aren't you. I mean, don't you . . ."

The Cloaked Man turned back to face Elbav, squeezed his left arm gently and said, "It's okay. I don't want anything from you. You might think of me as Tranquility's new guardian angel."

"Guardian angel?"

"Yeah. Let's just say when I can help somebody in trouble, I do. Take care of yourself."

"I . . . I will." And with that, the Cloaked Man walked away and vanished in the shadows.

*   *   *

In the weeks that followed, Elbav saw the Cloaked Man walking the street or standing in the shadows watching. Once in a while, when the Cloaked Man knew he was looking, he'd wave to Elbav, but a moment later he'd be gone.

Reports of a vigilante began to filter through the neighborhood. The descriptions confirmed it was the Cloaked Man. He would appear out of nowhere, seldom said a word to anyone, and asked for nothing in return. Nobody knew who he might be, and he never said anything even to those he rescued from robbery or danger. Conjecture ran wild. Peddler listened to the stories and realized he was the only person the "Angel of Tranquility" – that's what they called him – had ever spoken to. It made him wonder why. It made him wonder if they shared a bond, and it made Elbav feel special and safe.

One night on his way back from Mel's, Peddler saw the Cloaked Man and called out to him and waved. The Cloaked man turned and quickly glanced in Elbav's direction but continued walking. Elbav quickened his pace to catch up with him, but not so fast as to draw attention to himself.

"Hey, wait up," requested Peddler. The man slowed his pace until Elbav had caught up to walk together.

Peddler greeted him with a smile and said, "Hello, my friend. You're making quite the impression on the neighborhood. How are you?"

"It's best if you are not seen with me, in case . . . you know," said the Angel of Tranquility without glancing back at him.

"Yes, I understand, but I can be very discreet. If you ever need a friend . . ."

The cloaked man stopped and stood motionless and silent, then looked across the street. Following his gaze, Peddler realized they were across from his store. The Cloaked Man glanced only with his eyes towards Elbav's store. Elbav took the man's cue and walked toward the Peddler's End. The man followed behind, keeping a distance but pace with Elbav.

The old Peddler unlocked his door and walked in. His mysterious acquaintance was a few steps behind. The man walked into the store and locked the door behind him.

Elbav walked behind his counter and made a hot beverage for his guest and asked him if he wanted anything to eat. The man shook his head no, but took the drink. Elbav motioned for the man to follow him to his upstairs apartment. The visitor carefully surveilled his surroundings and followed his host. Peddler sat down in his chair and requested that the man have a seat on his couch. The man hesitated for a moment, but complied. Elbav was a kind and generous person, but was still very careful around strangers. He had slid his hand on a hidden switch on his chair that would send several thousand volts into the couch his new 'friend' was sitting on, if he had to. One wrong move or anything tricky, and the Cloaked Man would be blasted senseless.

Elbav broke the ice by asking a question.

"Do you have a name? They're calling you the Angel of Tranquility. Did you know that? Um, I never did thank you for what you did with . . . um, you know."

The man pulled his hood down from over his head and gave Elbav a mock surprised look.

"Like I said in my note, I hate thieves. Life is hard enough and thugs make it worse. I was glad I came into your store when I did. I was actually just coming to buy a loaf of bread."

"Well, your actions gave me a start, but it all turned out well."

"Yes."

"So thank you, Mister . . . um, Angel?"

"Kellon. I'm not from anywhere you would know, and my name is Kellon Dirge," the man said as he sipped on the hot drink Elbav had given him.

"Your kindness is very rare in these parts, Mister Dirge. Though I don't think you should be telling people your real name."

"You have a good reputation," said Mr. Dirge. "Seems I'm not the only 'angel' in Tranquility."

Peddler blushed and for a moment didn't know what to say, then, with unusual candor, he said, "Well I'm no hero like you. I just get folks what they need at a fair price, is all."

Kellon Dirge continued to sip his drink and smiled at the old man.

"I think it best if neither of us talk much about our past. Let's just say that *brave act* I did for you was one of my many run-ins with the worms of the Coalition. Only an insect steals food he can afford to buy at a fair price. Rest assured he won't be putting his helmet on for a while, or eating anything besides mush for supper."

Elbav sat forward in his chair and looked directly into Kellon's eyes. He could hardly believe he was saying the words even as they came out of his mouth.

"Mr. Dirge, let me be quite frank with you. I am no friend or ally to the Coalition. I hate them with every ounce of my being. If you are keeping back your true intent for being here in this town out of fear, please understand I am not a supporter of the scumbag Prosek. You can relax a bit, you are with a true comrade."

Kellon adjusted his cloak and pulled it off his shoulders. On each shoulder were tattooed symbols Elbav was familiar with. He was slender but muscular and wore a black tank top and a leather bandolier across his chest. His belt contained several metallic compartments and on his side was the zap staff.

"I could be more trusting sir, but that is not my nature, and you have asked questions of me but have not told me your name," Kellon replied.

"I beg your forgiveness, Mr. Dirge. My name is Elbav Kariskyn. This is my store and home, as it has been for over fifty years. Please be at ease here, I am a sworn enemy to the Coalition and am only biding my time."

"Biding your time? For what? For a great army to come and defeat the pig Prosek? You're wasting your time, kind Elbav. It's going to take many years for that to happen, if ever."

Elbav wrung his hands and looked at the floor. He looked back up at Kellon and studied his tattoos a little closer.

"So it seems that you have spent time in Firetown. Your tattoos are ones that only a few would ever bear on their skin."

Kellon's face grew grim and his voice lowered to a whisper.

"I lived at Momma's Boarding House for a while and I was at the battle of Tolkeen. If you know what the meanings of these tattoos are, then tell me so that we can truly be honest with one another, otherwise I will thank you for your drink and be on my way."

Elbav got up from his chair and pointed to Kellon's right shoulder. "That is the symbol for the Ace Protection Service, and if that is the case then you need to tell me who gave you that tattoo, so we can be *truly honest* with one another."

Kellon smiled and put his cloak back on, stood up, and said, "Fortune favors the brave, kind Elbav."

Elbav laughed out loud and gave Kellon the final code he was waiting for.

He wrote it down on a piece of paper and handed it to Kellon.

Knights are Hard to come by, Enemies Many.

Kellon held out his hand and Elbav extended his and the two greeted each other with a firm handshake.

"You are a brave man to get a tattoo from an Apok, I hear they are not very gentle with the needle when applying their artistry." Then Elbav asked Kellon to remove his cloak so that he could examine the artwork etched into Kellon's flesh. The Ace Protection Service had no business cards, but their members had what would be considered a calling card in the form of a tattoo. An ace of spades playing card with a human skull in the middle of the card.

"Apoks don't use needles, they use the tip of their Vibro-Blade," Kellon added.

Elbav shuddered and changed the subject to Tolkeen and his hatred of the Coalition. The two spoke for several hours, with Kellon confiding to Elbav that he was a merc for hire, and that he was a former member of *Revenge Squad Ragnarok* who decided to go off on his own, though he remained friendly with the Squad and its members.

Elbav saw how late it was and demanded that Kellon stay the night. Kellon, not having anywhere to really stay, took Elbav up on his offer.

One night turned into several weeks of regular visits. All the while, Elbav never confided to Kellon that he was a Rogue Scholar or that his store cellar was full of ancient artifacts and foremost of all, the Orb of Teleportation.

One night, after closing the store, he and Kellon went to Mel's Tavern to have a few drinks. They were minding their own business when three Coalition Troopers walked in. They walked past the bar and one glanced at Kellon and stopped in his tracks. He grabbed Kellon by the back of his cloak and pulled him off his bar stool. The trooper sat down on Kellon's stool and told Mel to fix him a drink and that Kellon would be paying for it.

Elbav glanced at the hero and shook his head. He was warning him not to do anything inside of Mel's Bar. Kellon understood and walked out of the bar and out into the street. The three Coalition soldiers followed. One drew his Neural-Mace, another his Vibro-Blade. Elbav got up and went to the doorway afraid for his friend, but Kellon was nowhere to be seen. The soldiers laughed and called the man a coward and went back to their drinks.

On his way back home, Peddler wondered were Kellon was and left the door unlocked for him. It was an hour later when a powerful explosion shook the entire town. Elbav went to his window and could see that Mel's Tavern was engulfed in flames and that several bodies were lying in the street. Firefighters and Coalition Police secured the area and dozens of citizens were surrounding the scene. Elbav walked into the street and thought it best to stay clear until the crowds went away. When he walked back into his store, he found Kellon standing inside. His face was full of rage and his hands clenched in fists. Elbav walked up to him and took him by his arm. Both men went up to Elbav's apartment.

"Mel is dead, Elbav. Those three Coalition pigs are responsible."

Peddler slumped down in his easy chair and began to cry. Kellon sat across from him, opening and closing his hands into fists.

"Do you know why? Because they believed he was a front for the Revenge Squad Ragnarok. Now, we both know that isn't true, and another thing that we both know is that you've been keeping things from me. I confided to you who I really am and now it's time for you to step up and tell me who you really are."

"I'm a Peddler just like they call me," said Elbav.

"And I'm the tooth fairy."

"No, really Kellon. I sell things. Just some of the things I sell are illegal. You know, books, meds, artifacts. Items that help people mostly or give them pleasure. No guns. No drugs. No magic items. But I have saved my share of lives with medicine. And I don't overcharge either. God, I can't believe they killed Mel on a worthless hunch."

"Believe it, my friend. The Coalition pigs hold no value for the people of the 'Burbs. They do as they please and all we can do is watch, helpless," snarled Kellon.

"You do things that make a difference."

"Do I? Then why is Mel dead and his tavern burning? If only I could make a real difference."

Both men sat silent for a while, each lost to his own thoughts.

Finally, Kellon stood up and said, "I have to go."

"Wait, said Elbav. He grabbed Kellon by his cloak and tugged at him to follow down the stairs. He led him to his secret vault in the cellar. Along the way, Peddler told him how he had taught half the town how to read and that he was going to help as many more folks who wanted to learn. Then Elbav turned to Kellon with tearful eyes blazing.

"Do you really want to strike the Coalition at its heart?" he asked.

"Of course I do," snarled Kellon.

"Then the time has come four us to cut out the heart and soul of the evil Coalition States and kill the Emperor."

"I would only be too happy to oblige, my friend, but that task is impossible," said Kellon in a soft voice.

"Why? Because he hides locked away inside the fortress city? What if you could get to him? Would you do it? Could you kill him?"

"With a smile on my face," trumpeted the Angel of Tranquility.

Peddler knocked aside the cheese crates and brought out a velvet bag. He untied its strings and took out the baseball that Jeru had given him.

Kellon laughed and then apologized. "I am sorry for laughing Elbav, but I'm afraid you are mad with grief. This is but a ball."

"Is it?" And with those words Peddler vanished, only to reappear an instant later behind Kellon.

"This magic device will take you wherever you desire. Including the back of the Emperor. Take it. Use it to shoot him down like the dog he is," implored Peddler.

Kellon looked at Elbav nervously. He'd never seen the kindly old man so angry or upset. Elbav showed him where the hidden switch was and uncloaked the Orb of Teleportation. He told Kellon how to use it. That he had tested it a few times, but that he didn't have the strength or courage to use it to slay Prosek himself.

Peddler placed the Orb in Kellon's left hand and watched and sat down on a crate sobbing.

Kellon smiled and pulled out his blaster.

"My friend," he said. "If this device is real, I can appear before the Emperor like this. With my gun in my hand and with a single shot . . ."

Peddler looked at his friend with disbelief that he had shot him, then slumped to the ground.

Kellon put the Orb of Teleportation in his pocket. He walked back up to the front of the store where he was surprised to see that dawn was already breaking. Several children were waiting outside at the front door. He looked at them all and gave them each a chocolate cookie and told them that Elbav was sick and needed his rest.

Kellon walked out of the front door and around to the alley. Sitting there was a Coalition patrol car occupied by the same trooper who had stolen the groceries from Elbav. Kellon got into the car and shook hands with the trooper.

"Mission accomplished, Major Kravax. The old man wasn't a dangerous subversive. Threat Level Alpha 2, maybe. But he had chanced upon something that made him a Level Omega 10 threat. This magical teleporting orb. From what he told me, it's old magic. Created by one of the pioneers of Techno-Wizardry. Even most practitioners of magic don't know if one really exists or not. Apparently it does."

Kellon produced the orb from his pocket and gave it to his superior officer.

"Another keepsake to lock away in the Black Vault. Excellent work, Lieutenant Johnson."

"Thank you, Sir. Oh, and you were right, killing Mel and torching the bar was what sent the old man over the edge."

"When you've done undercover as long as I have," said Major Kravax, "you get a feel for human psychology. I knew it needed to be handled this way. Besides, that bar allowed D-Bees so it has suffered the consequences of its actions. Wouldn't you agree."

"Yes, Sir," said Kellon with a smirk. "Sir, the cellar at Peddler's End is full, and I mean FULL, of low level contraband. It should be collected or the place should have an 'accident' before it falls into the wrong hands."

"The clean-up crew should be here in another minute," said the Major. "They'll make it look like that gang of D-Bees, I forget their name, killed the old man and ransacked the place. That should win us some sympathy when we move to take the gang down in a few days."

"By the way, it sure took you guys long enough to extract the information out of that smuggler, Jeru Benso. What took so long?" Kellon asked.

Major Kravax smirked, put his hands together and cracked his knuckles. "The big lummox took one hell of a beating, I tell you. We finally broke him when we showed him a video of his father in a Coalition re-education camp. The fool actually believed that his father was still alive and that we would let him go if he told us who he took the baseball to. Isn't it amazing what we can do with digital technology these days?"

Agent Kelly Johnson of the ISS, undercover identity, Kellon Dirge, A.K.A. the Angel of Tranquility, smiled and nodded. He was full of pride with his accomplishment. It's not every day you get to save the Emperor from magic. His sacrifice, being undercover for the last seven months and away from his family was suddenly all worthwhile. He had just saved Emperor Prosek. Amazing. He knew he'd be on cloud nine for a month.

"Kelly, you listening?" snapped the Major.

"Yes, Sir!"

"My hunch turned out to be correct and the outcome impressive," said Major Kravax. "But you made it all come together, Lieutenant. You handled it all just right and should be proud of yourself. You can expect a commendation from the Emperor himself, but your work is not done here, soldier. You need to keep your head in the game. The *Angel of Tranquility* has more pigeons to catch."

The undercover agent Johnson smiled as he leaned over to open the vehicle's door. "Maybe the Angel of Tranquility should be the one to take down them D-Bees," he said. "Let it leak that Peddler was my friend, and that I avenged him. It'd give me more street cred. Besides, it's been a while since I've had the pleasure of killing some slimy D-Bees."

"I like the way you think, Lieutenant," smiled the Major. "Let me talk to Command and make sure we have eyes and shooters in place for your back up. Won't do us any good if the Angel gets himself killed playing hero, now would it?"

"No, Sir," replied Kellon Dirge as he pulled the hood over his head and exited the vehicle.

* * *

When his majesty, Emperor Prosek, was told of the incident, he lifted a glass of wine in a toast to his "brave heroes of humanity."

The Orb of Teleportation was locked away, by General Cabot himself, in the Black Vault for future consideration by the Coalition States.

The people of Tranquility cheered the heroics of their new champion, their "angel," after witnesses reported he single-handedly killed the members of the gang known as "the Terror Boys," and barely escaped the clutches of the Coalition when troops arrived on the scene of the bloodbath. Only the Angel of Tranquility would care about an old man like Peddler and bring his murderers to justice. At last, the people of this New Town 'Burb had a hero they could trust and count on.

The Brothers Perez

By John C. Philpott

When I first meet Phinny he was sellin' snake oil down near Tekakana. Not oil from squashed snakes, mind ya, but that 'miracle cure' stuff what comes in a bottle, an' cures 'bout anyting' stuff.

Must'a been some amazin' juice in that bottle too, because according to him it:

"Cures what ails you, folks! Removes warts and verucas! Gives you health and stamina, and that's the Phinneus Grifter guarantee!"

Now, I was what you might call a *country bumpkin* at the time, bein' just out'a the bayo down near New Mamou, but even I was a bit 'spicious 'bout his claims.

"Now, who this guy an' what he be sellin'?" I asked an Idie in the crowd.

The Idie shrugged. "Him, who know? The stuff he sellin'? Smell like fish oil an' moonshine ya ask me. Ya tink the bass would like it?"

"Naw," I say, "but then agin, my folks farm crawdads, so bass ain't what you call my specialty, ya' know?"

"Yeah, I know."

"Hey," I continued, "where he from? Don't look like no Krak I ever saw 'round here."

"From up north," the Idie said wit' a shrug, convinced that said it all. "Ain't no Krak, though. He's one o' dem Fingahtooth Cahpetbaggers. Watch ya' wallet there, bubba. Dem guys is slicker than a greased catfish."

"I'll watch ma'self," I promised.

Now, I was a bit curious, so I walked up a little closer. I just had to see what that Fingertooth was all about. Dey look a little like us Kraks, ya know. Four feet, froggy skin, big eyes, an' those two mouth fingers look jus' a little bit like Krak mouth tentacles, 'cept dey got them li'l teeth at the end o' them. This guy was on the fat side an' a little taller'n me n' wore one o' them top hats and a vest wit' a watch-chain. Looked a little like my cousin Louie . . . 'cept for the fangs on his tentacles, of course.

"Hey, you!" Phinny the Fingertooth called to me. "You look like a gentleman who could use a pint of Phinneus Grifter's Magic Elixir!" he continued. "It's made with exotic ingredients from the far ends of the Megaverse, like Atlantean Cureweed and Palladian Mugwort! It's got everything a Quartico like yourself needs to maintain his health and vitality!"

"Ah . . . excuse me, sah, but a Quarti-what?"

"You know, son, a Krak! Don't you know your own species' name, son?"

"Ah just though we was called Kraks."

"Nonsense, son! Stand up and be proud! You're a Quartico Cephalopodian, and that's special! And a special guy needs a special elixir."

That there Idie was right, Phinny there *was* slicker than a greased catfish . . . and about as scummy, you ask me.

"A little Magic Elixir will give you the confidence you need for that! Step on up here, son!"

'Spite m'self, I walked on up to his li'l stage.

"Hold on a minute, there!" one human called from the crowd. "D'you know that guy? Y'all look alike. Y'all from the same place? I bet y'all got the same pappy."

"Well," I said, "don't know 'bout him, but I'm from 'round here. Down in the bayo near New Mamou . . . Mikey from Mamou, that's me!"

"No, ain't what I mean there, My-key," the human continued. "I mean from before then! You know, originally?"

"Well . . . momma's side come from Canada, near Perez . . ."

"Naw, man. What Rift?"

"What's a 'Rift'?" Did I mention I was from *waaay* back in the bayo?

Phinny interrupted, "Now, seriously, Mikey did you say? You ever see me before in your life? No, I didn't think so! Now, try a spoonful of this Magic Elixir."

He shoved a spoonful under my mouth-tentacles an' into my mouth. It tasted like cut-bait and sour mash.

"Now," Phinny continued, "can't you just feel the strength and vitality flowing through you?"

Actually, I felt like I needed to bring that Elixir up for an encore, if you know what I mean. But I played along. "Um, ok I guess," I replied, tryin' to be polite. "I do feel a slight buzz. Prolly the cheap booze in it. 'Course 'tween the corn squeezins an' the fish squeezins I bet you could sell it to the Idie as one o' them after-meal drinks."

A chuckle went through the crowd.

"Seriously, son," he continued, nudging me with a bony elbow, "can't you feel the warm feeling going through you?"

"Since ya' asked, yeah, but I thought that was jus' nausea."

Another laugh, louder this time.

"Are you kidding, me? This stuff is pure magic."

"No kiddin'," I replied, "I think it made my stomach linin' disappear."

The crowd laughed. Someone hooted loudly.

"Seriously, kid, you're killing me here!"

"I guess that make us 'bout even then, sah."

Uproarious hysteria broke out. Grumbling like a Bayo Bear wit' his tails tied, Phinny left the stage and I went on my own self, figurin' I'd never see ol' Phinny again. This was down near Tekakana. When I first left out'a the bayo I was a' thinkin' ol' Tekakana be a good place to go. Now, Tekakana supposed to be some big tradin' place wit' a bunch of ah Techno-Wizzies, an' I guess I was thinkin' Id find somethin' to do there other than farm crawdads, but it just look like New Mamou on a bigger scale tah me. 'Course were I to look at it now after my time in Lazlo, Tolkeen, an' the 'Burbs, I'd bet it'd look smaller than a baby bug wit' a leg reduction. At the time, though, it seem *real* big. 'Course Tekakana don' got what I was lookin' for (I didn't really know what I *was* lookin' for, mind you, but I knew it weren't farmin'), so I moved on.

I moved on up farther north, as a matter o' fact. I worked for some Caddo for a while farmin' fields, but that weren't no better than farmin' crawdads. Then I moved on up farther still, skirtin' El Dorado an' Chickasaw turf 'till I got to what I thought was Fed Mag Land, figurin' there must be somethin' for a Krak to do there 'sides farmin'. Now, I was out o' my turf and alone and hungry, so when I saw a light in the woods I risked it bein' a ghost light an' walked up to what turn out to be a wagon train, like a bunch a gypsy circus folk or somethin' though dey talked like local Crull.

Who I see there, but ol' Phinneus Grifter the Fingertooth his own self, tryin' to sell the same ol' snake oil to the circus folk. Now, he's doin' the same speach as in Tekakana and dey ain't buyin' it any more than I did an' he's gettin' desperate.

"Come on, folks," he said, "I'm a performer myself! This stuff gives you the energy to perform or your money back!"

"Really?" a Gracke Tooth in the crowd who look like he 'sposed to be the strong man said. "What do you do? Acrobatics?" There was a laugh at that. Remember when I say ol' Phinny was a li'l chubby?

"I was . . . um, a ringmaster!"

"What about before that? No one *starts* as a ringmaster! Dey start as a *performer!*"

"Uh . . . comedy! Yeah, that's the ticket!" Phinny the Fingertooth said. "I did a comedy act!"

"Well, then," a barely-dressed an' really tattooed human woman called out, "let's hear it!" The performers there chanted in agreement wit' her. Now, Phinny the snake oil salesman doin' jokes I had to hear, so I walked on up.

Phinny began, "Uh . . . so, what's the deal with Joey Prosek? I mean, don't propaganda posters work better when your populace can *read* them?"

Silence from the crowd.

"And how about that Stormspire? That tower is a bit tall, you know. You think K'zaa's compensating for anything *lacking?*"

You could hear the crickets chirpin', I ain't kiddin' you.

"And speaking of Stormspire, did you hear about their new weapon against Dog Boys? It's an electrified TW fire plug! Electrified fire plug!"

Now, even the crickets was havin' a uncomfortable silence at that point.

"Come on, people," Phinny yelled, "yer killin' me here!"

"Don't tempt us," called out the Grackle Tooth. Stole my joke, I swear he did.

"Wait, the, um, problem's that I'm a partner-act, see? And . . . I don't have my partner here with me. Um . . ." he looked around in desperation. Suddenly, he see me in the shadows. "Ah . . . there! There he is!" He pointed to me. "Come on up here, uh . . . Mick."

"Dat ain't my name, suh," I said, an' the crowd snickered.

"Oh, yeah, sorry . . . Mickey?

I shook my head no.

Mark? No, um, Mike! Mikey!! Come on up, Mikey!"

I turned to run away, but a Juicer I didn't see a minute earlier was standing behind me an' growled, "Well? Make us laugh, boy."

Now, I'm not one tah refuse a request from a man who could cut off my arm and quarter it before it hit the ground, so I hesitatin'ly made my way up onto Phinny's li'l stage.

"Ok, kid," Phinny whispered, putting his arm threatenin'ly 'round my shoulder, "you owe me for the Tekakana thing, so let's make this work."

He turned to the crowd of performers. "So, Mikey, my boy!" he said loudly. "What do you think of the situation in Tolkeen?"

"Ah . . ." I hesitated, "Ah think war's a comin'." I guess I should mention here that I'd picked up the latest news in Tekakana, not that I knew where Tolkeen was at that point, mind ya.

"Come on, kid," he whispered. "Where's the funny?"

"Ah . . . well," I replied loudly, "you could always send the Tolkies your elixir."

"To make them strong enough to whip the Coalition, you mean?" he said, placing his thumbs under his suspenders, lookin' real proud wit' himself.

"Nah," I replied. "I figured maybe dey could use 'em as chemical bombs." A strained chuckle moved through the crowd.

"Really, now," Phinny continued. "And I suppose you have an idea how to fight Skelebots?"

Honest, I didn't even know what Skellybots *was* back then, so I winged it: "A robot hound dog could, mebee, dig hisself a big ol' hole an' bury them Skellybots in it like a bone."

"And that's supposed to work?"

"Work better than that electric fire plug joke you tol' earlier." A louder chuckle bubbled up through half the crowd that time.

"Come on, Mikey, that electric fire plug joke was a classic!"

"More like a antique!"

Laughter.

"Well, I suppose you could do better, eh?"

"Can't do no worse."

More laughter, a little more animated that time.

"Hey, now! Where I come from, people have respect for good humor."

"That explains why you're here an' not there, then." The crowd got into it wit' that one.

"Hey, buddy, I suppose you know all about Stormspire, too?"

"Dey make the electric fireplugs, right?"

More laughter.

"Uh . . . You got anything on K'zaa?" asked Phinny wit' a grin.

"Well, if you're right about the whole tower ting," I said, looking smugly below my beltline, "I be tinking mebee I do!"

Howls of laughter moved through the crowd. Even the Grackle Tooth was laughin'.

"That's some good stuff!" laughed an old woman dressed like a voodoo fortune teller. "I'm Maman Maggie and this here is my caravan, and we could use a comedy team. You guys in?"

Phinny leaned over to me and said, "Buddy, you got the gift of gab. What do you say to a partnership? Sixty-forty."

"I get the sixty, right?"

"No."

"Bye, bye."

"Fifty-fifty."

"Sure ting, buddy." I shook his hand. Where else I have to go? I was lost and broke, an' insultin' Phinny for a livin' sounded way better'n crawdad farmin'.

"Glad to be on board, ma'am!" Phinny said, shaikin' Maman Maggie's hand.

"So what do you call yourselves?" Maman Maggie asked.

"Damn," Phinny whispered, "we need a name, Mikey. Where were you from again?"

"New Mamou."

"Hmmm, the Mamou Boys," he said, soundin' it out, quiet like. "Nope. No good. What was that other place, where your mother was from?" he whispered.

"Perez?"

He turned to Maman Maggie: "You may call us 'The Brothers Perez.' Salvador and Pablo, at your service!"

"Pablo?" I asked.

"Go with it, *Pablo*," he said.

And so we became *The Brothers Perez* . . . and so began our great career in comedy.

And so also began a great adventure that took me all the way into the heart of the Coalition War Machine.

* * *

Now, tourin' wit' Maman Maggie's was a whole new experience for me. In addition to Phinny's an' my comedy act there was **Grinnin' Gary the Grackle Tooth** (he *was* the strong man), **The Amazing Floops** acrobatic act, **Lydia** the tattooed contortionist (the men, dey really liked that act), **Saul's Speare-Shakers** (mostly Phlebus, did dah actin'), **Arty the Aarden-Tek** and his *Federation of Music* band, some jugglers an' clowns, an' of course, **Maman Maggie's** voodoo fortune tellin'.

Every day it was a new show in a new place. We toured small towns all through the Magic Zone. An' let me tell you, it get *scary* in dem woods, what wit' all the demons an' all. I done found out all too well what a *Rift* was, an' why dey's a *bad* thing. Some o' the things I seen make a Centaur's toes curl . . . an' dey ain't even *got* toes, mind ya! Sometimes I wondered why I put myself through all that danger, but then again, I started really likin' the performin' business, and wit' the Dead Boys getting' thicker than the back hair on a Bayo Ursine in my home swamps, it weren't like it was any less dang'rous.

The show, it do real good, an' The Brothers Perez got what you call a *followin'*. We honed the act, Phinny-now-Salvador an' me. He play the "straight man" an' I play the "goof," what wit' the delta talk an' all. An' we started to get noticed as the years go by an' soon Maman Maggie's is doin' big gigs all through the Zone.

We knocked 'em dead in **Magestar**:

"Hey Pablo, I just got in from Psyscape, and boy is my Astral construct tired!"

"Tired as that ol' joke, Salvador."

"Hey, wait a minute! I'm talking about my astral construct!"

"Hey, I don' tink the folks here want to hear nothin' 'bout your *Astral nothin'*. There be kids here!"

"Now that just twists my silver thread, it does!"

74

We had 'em rollin' in **Dweomer**:

"Well, Pablo, what do you think of the Magus?"

"You kiddin'? I ain't seen this many people in full-body leather since . . ."

"Watch it there, Pablo!"

"What? I'm talkin' 'bout the Wilderness Scouts' trap meet!"

Even the **City of Brass** loved us, though I must admit I coulda done wit' out that gig. All them guys wit' more eyes than legs and more legs than could possibly do any good make a Krak a bit nervous, since ya' asked.

"So, Pablo, what do you think of the cave?"

"Dey be cavernous."

"They tend to be, yeah. But I'm talking specifically about the features. Like the stalactites and stalagmites!"

"Oh, them? Dey's scary. Which Shifter summoned them again?"

Pretty soon, word spread even beyond the Magic Zone, west to **Arzno** an' up to the big city-states in the north. By this time we had *Lenny the Larmac* on drums backin' us up wit' a timely rim-shot or drum roll.

"Boy, we sure don't envy you hard working Arzno folks. Every day you're fighting the inhuman bloodsuckers!"

"An' them's just the Patent Attorneys!" (rimshot)

We tore 'em up in **New Lazlo**:

"I hear you got a real problem wit' the Xiticix here by the lakes."

"Yea, just ain't bug spray 'nuff to go 'round, Sal." (rimshot)

"I don't think bug spray is going to work, Pablo."

"No kiddin', Sallie. Don't even work on the 'skeeters out here. The drinks is *on me*, you know what I mean?" (rimshot)

"Yeah I do. And here I thought we left the bloodsuckers back in Arzno."

"Nah, *Badger, Bender, and Cajole* got a branch office up here too!" (drum roll-rimshot)

And we really slayed 'em in **Lazlo**:

"Boy, I tell you! That Plato is something else! A dragon on the high council, how about that?"

"Yeah, I hear he got some fiery rhetoric too." (rimshot)

"Now that just *burns*, Pablo. I hear Plato is quite the gentle-dragon."

"He gotta be, the *last* ting anyone want be a pat on the back from the boss!" (drum roll-rimshot-cymbal crash)

Come to think of it, the drums didn't help too good now, did dey?

'Course after a couple ah' years we left Maggie's an' got our own gig in Tolkeen. That was ahfore the war, obv'usly. Lenny the Larmac and the Amazin' Floops came wit' us. The act 'spanded an' we had our own variety show at *Firebird Theater* downtown. We even made films that had good release all through Tolkeen, the Lazlos, the Magic Zone, an' even down in Arzno. **The Brothers Perez Join the Grey Seers** won us wide acclaim. **The Brothers Perez Meet the Prosek Boys** won Best Comedy in '04. I still laugh at that scene where the actor playin' Emperor Karl gets his head stuck in Phinny's pants!

We even had a third Brother Perez for a while: *Francisco*, who was a Flooper (one o' Ferdie's cousins). Francisco didn't talk, mind ya, but he was the *master* of sight gags! He could do more funny without tellin' jokes than anyone I know . . . which was good 'cause he had the squeakiest voice. Man, that ting he did wit' the floopin' into the punch bowl an' floopin' inta people's pants, or floopin' on top ah people's heads. What? No, man. Floopin' mean teleportin'. What's wrong wit' you? Floopin' and pooopin' is two distinkly different tings. And now don' get me started on his famous *Francisco Flop* – that even caught on as a dance craze for a while there in Tolkeen.

Yeah, Frankie was great. I still wonder what happened to him.

Anyway, the **Perez Brothers Follies** was a smash, as dey say, an' money was doin' good . . . at least 'till Phinny blew it all on those dumb investments ("Really, Mikey, dey can't fail!" Guess what, now, *dey did.*). But for the years leadin' up to the war we was on top of the world. My biggest worry was keepin' my bayo accent. It's hard when you're a Krak. You hear people talk an' soon enough you talkin' the same an' actin' the same as dem – ya' can't help it, it's in the blood. Only the bayo accent be part o' the act, mind yah, so I had to watch it. Eventually, we even had to hire a Crull named Boudreaux from down in the swamps jus' to talk swamp wit' me ev'ry day so's I don't start talkin' all Tolkie.

Yea, we done good in Tolkeen, but all that changed wit' the war. When the miss'les flew by we knew it be time to go. Even though the Rift ate 'em, I was shakin' like a Hyperion Juicer wit' epilepsy after twenty espresso shots. Phinny, Lenny, an' I got out on one o' the last flights to Lazlo, but Frankie, he stay behind to fight. Had kin there. When the city fell the messages stopped. We still worry. Phinny say Frankie prolly went west wit' the refugees, but his eyes ain't convinced. We hear about the camps . . . and we worry. Legba, watch over him, wherever he go.

In Lazlo we tried to set up again as best we could. Now, wit' Francisco at war an' the panic that the war spread, an' the political fight in Lazzy-Town over whether ta get involved or not, tings was strained. But folk needed comedy more'n ever, and we try to deliver.

But once you know war, an' once you know what them Dead Boys be doin' to Dee-Bees, it's hard for a Krak to jus' put it out o' his mind. Even Phinny, who never worry 'bout nothin', was gettin' madder than a ten-year Crazy. Our skit got more political an' our act was *def'natly* on the "fight the Coalition" side. I done seen too much a' what the Dead Boys done in the delta, so I more than happy to speak out. It cost us some audience, but gained us another audience. Soon our act included skits like *Danny the Dum-Dum Dead Boy* an' *Joey Prosek and the Four Freehold Floopers*. Dey laugh an' dey cry, an' we all hold on together.

When the war ended the way it did it was a shock to us all, an' what wit' worryin' 'bout Frankie, the act suffered an' we lost the knack. Hard to be funny when you wonderin' how many friends o' yours got sent to the showers. I try to put it in the act, but jokin' 'bout the efficiency of Coalition death chambers ain't funny ta no one save maybe Karlie an' Company. The theater lost money, the movie sales fall off, and Lenny start lookin' for a new gig.

Times was bad. Real bad. You'd 'a thunk it was Lazlo that fall. But as our old theater in Tolkie Town was goin' *up* in flames, the Brothers Perez act was fallin' *down* too.

* * *

When things was at their worst was when Phinny really come through. Sure, our stock in Lazlo was droppin' like a strapless prom dress, an' Arzno was cut off by the CS take-over of Tolkeen, an' we was passé in the Zone what wit' the Three Crazy Magus bein' all the rage there, but we was still pop'lar in one place: a place I swore I'd never be caught dead. Dah 'Burbs.

Yep, Chi-Town. High-C. The cold steel heart of the Coalition. The capital city of the very nation that done turned our ol' city of Tolkeen into burnt rubble.

We was jus' bein' discovered there it turns out, what wit' the delays in gettin' Black Market in town wit' a war on, an' we had a ready-made market. Phinny had a contact who had a contact wit' some Roach Lady or something, and she had contacts to a club called *Sanctimonious* in a 'Burb called *Nightside*, the 'Burb bein' in the afternoon shadow of Chi-Town proper an' all.

Now, it was all Phinny could do to get me to go. I was 'bout havin' 'nuff of the north an' wanted to go home to the swamps an' forget I ever see a Dead Boy. Lay down my burden by the riverside and study war an' all no more. Only them Dead Boys was already there an' wit' El Dorado now a CS State, the neighborhood property values was fallin' like Swamp Sludgers had moved in next door.

But what really sell me on duh 'Burbs was the pictures from the war. A group o' Techno-Wizzies in invisible planes had taken pictures of the Death Camps outside Tolkeen. Now, I've seen a lot in my life, but that? Fryin' innocent Dee-Bees – Kraks like me, Floopers like Francisco, all stacked up . . . sorry, bear wit' me, mind. I guess what I'm sayin' here is I was fightin' mad now. If there was Dee-Bees hidin' out in the shadow o' Prosek I considered it my job . . . hellfire, mah duty, to do what I could to help out. Now, I couldn't fight or cast no magic, but comedy be magic all its own. And we cast like a High Magus right from the start.

Take our dey-byoo night at Club Sanctimonious:

"So, Pablo. How's it feel to get to Chi-Town? The very core of the Coalition?"

"I don' know, Sallie. How's a crawdad feel when he go into the boilin' pot? There be more Black Lobsters here than pimples on Ross Underhill's behind." The crowd, mostly Quick Flex an' Sword Fist, loved that one.

"Now, now, Pablo, let's try to be civil. We're guests here. Have you nothing good to say about the esteemed General Underhill?"

"Well, since ya' asked. No."

"Really? Nothing?"

"Okay. The way I see it he's quite the *philanthropist*. Give all the Dee-Bee children of Tolkeen a free trip to camp, I hear." Dey had a dark laugh on that one.

I continued, a li'l too angry: "The camps must'a been real clean too, what wit' all the big showers an' all. Tink dey got hot tubs, what wit' all the big cookers?" Yeah, I was lettin' my mad get the best o' me, but the crowd, dey really like it. Years o' silent fear must'a been meltin' away wit' each dark laugh.

We got big wit' dark laughs that first night, an' did real well in the comin' weeks. All the Dee-Bee underground show up to Club Sanctimonious, it bein' like a big trendy spot on the underground scene. We play five shows a week an' soon the cash come in again an' we spend it on more elaborate costumes and sets. We hire a band called *The Moanin' Banshees* an' even do song and dance stuff our own self, like we did in the ol' movies. I recall one called, **Another Day in Chi-Town** (with Mel on piano):

(Sal) Oh, it's another day in Chi-Town,
A great day for fun!
Run and jump and hide, my friend
'Cause here comes the gun!

(Me) Yeah, it another day in Chi-Town
An' I'm happy to see,
There ain't no Dog Boys prowlin'
Or lookin' for me!

(Both) Yea we all love Chi-Town,
In the spring or the fall!
And the pillaging and income tax
That paid for it all!

(Me) Fun and drinks and gamblin',
(Sal) Gets our hover ramblin',
To see that Iron Castle in the sky!
(Me) Laser lights a' shinin',
(Sal) Search beams all alignin'
(Both) And party ev'ry nightin' 'till we die!
Yeah, party ev'ry nightin' 'till we diiiiiie! (Take it, Mel!)

Yeah, our fame was back, but this was a whole new world, mind. Back in Tolkie-Town we sometimes had ta slip out the back door of the club ta avoid bein' mobbed by adorin' fans, but for a Dee-Bee in the 'Burbs it's *always* slippin' away an' hidin' – always! Dog Boy patrols come through, Peacekeepers snoop around, even the 'casional hovercycle or tank come by to make sure we's all loyal CS supporters an' all. At least for the humans and near-enough humans.

That said, the 'Burbs might well 'a been in another country from Chi-Town itself. Yeah, the 'Burbs, 'specially Nightside, may 'a been right in the shadow of Chi-Town proper, but it was hardly Coalition turf, 'specially after the sun set . . . an' it set *early* in Nightside! The streets belonged to the City Rats, gangsters and "ladies o' the night when the shadow fall over town. Nightside in partic'lar belonged to the Black Market, as did Club Sanctimonious, but it also belonged to dem undead. Oh yeah, there's vampies there in Nightside. Wit' Phinny an' me in good wit' the Black Market, as long as we makin' them money we was safe from the reg'lar crooks who know not to mess wit' friends of the Market.' But them Vamps a whole diff'rent story now, an' like dodgin' gators is the unofficial sport of the swamps, dodgin' vampies the sport in the city-swamp o' the Nightside 'Burbs.

Yeah, the Dead Boys rule the day there, the Black Market an' Vampies rule the night, an' the Dee-Bees like Phinny an' me run an' hide whenever necessary.

An' Mama Roach, she see it all. Queen of the Bugs, she is. Dey say she's easy on the eyes, despite all the bugs an' stuff that surround her. She has some sort of telepathic link to dem bugs, mind, so she's got the biggest spy network around. Ev'rythin' the bugs see, she see. So you don' want to joke about Mama, at least not in a way that sland'rous or mean spirited, mind, or all yer dirty laundry become front page news.

So yeah, the Brothers Perez was all the rage again in the 'Burbs, but we was livin' like refugees in a war zone, runnin' from basement to basement, gettin' our food second-hand. You don't risk it to go to the store, mind. Luckily Phinny an' I had what dey call *connections* who get us what we need, but it gotta be tough for a Krak on his own in this town. I considered buggin' out a few times, since ya' asked, but I still owed it to my fellow Dee-Bees an' the mem'ry of Frankie.

'Course though times was hard for most, we was taken care of by the Black Market, what wit' the rooms an' gor-may food an' fine booze brung to us. An' even hot young women-folk (my Krakettes, Phinny call them, a bit bitter that Fingertooth women was harder to come by on this planet). The only rule in Nightside was you *don' bite the hands that feed you*. **Smilin' Tony**, he was our *hand*. He work for someone who work for someone who run tings (we smart enough to know not to ask, mind) an' we report to him. He was like our agent, keeper, an' watcher all in one. Like a devil-angel that giveth, but you don' tempt him to taketh away.

He met wit' us after the show one night, Tiny, the Grackle Tooth on one side, Slo-Mo, the Quick-Flex on the other.

"Great job, boys, great show! I about snorted my martini when you did that skit about General Holmes and his army of pleasure-bots escaping certain death in the 'Burbs and sneaking into Chi-Town after curfew through the sewage outlets! Genius! What do you say to a show in Firetown?"

"It'd be a pleasure, my fine sir!" Phinny reply.

"And you, Pablo?" Smilin' Tony said to me wit' his trademark smile. He smile like a gator, I tell you, that scar makin' it even worse.

"M-my pleasure, sah!" Yeah, I shake like a B'an Mic that just swallow a mo-stique whenever Tony talk. Guy jus' *scare* you!

"Great! Then Saturday night The Brothers Perez play the famous *Dry Hydrant club!*"

Now, Firetown quite a diff'rent 'Burb than Nightside. Less glitz, less money, but less *big* crime all said. An' the Dry Hydrant, which was a pop'lar club up and until that night in October, was all the rage. Officially it was a human wat'rin' hole up top an' supposedly named after a fire plug that didn't work an' led to one of the 'Burb's bigger burn-outs (like what give Firetown its name). Now, in reality it had a hidden Dee-Bee club in the basement an' the name, *Dry Hydrant,* was meant to imply that 'Dog Boys didn't make their mark here.' Inside, the place was all neon an' black light an' dance lights. Man, talk about your electrified fire plugs!

It was a thirty minute hover to the club from our digs in Nightside, but we start makin' the trip ev'ry other weekend for the gig. An' we was even more a hit there than in Nightside. Ya' see, Firetown saw more Dead Boys more of the time, seein' as how dey didn't have the Black Market bucks to pay the patrols to look elsewhere like we got in Nightside. So the locals there really cheered at any jokes about dumb Coalition soldiers, hidin' out, an' skits like Danny the Dum-Dum Dead Boy Does the Delta (the news of the day was the CS Army goin' into my home swamps, mind).

For the next few months we was livin' large and laughin' easy, or near enough to considerin'. Sales and attendance were up in both Firetown and Nightside, I met Roxy (who has the cutest Chi-Town accent, though she's startin' to pick up my delta slang, now), an' Phinny was actually learnin' how to make money from Smilin' Tony (though Phinny started dressin' like a pre-Rifts gangster an' that made me a li'l nervous).

All was good till that October when the raid came. We was performin' at the Hydrant to a near-full house when the Dead Boys moved in. Dey kick down the doors and start lightin' up the place. Sev'ral people, humans and Dee-Bees alike, all get vaporized in no time at all. Tiny an' Slo-Mo move in and tear into them Dead Boys. Tiny rip one Dog Boy in two wit' his bare hands. Man, I'm no fan o' Dog Boys, mind, but that yelp will be wit' me forever. I didn't see much else 'cause Tony was draggin' Phinny an' me through an escape tunnel I never knew was there. We escaped in a hover vehicle an' fled to Nightside. Phinny an' I crawl into a bottle and not come out 'till the next mornin'.

Two days later Slo-Mo come back. He was in bad shape and had worse news. Over half the audience was dead, includin' Tiny who die savin' us. Ten Dee-Bees an' human sympathizers caught in the Hydrant were arrested. 'The Dry Hydrant Ten,' as dey come to be called, was set to be executed in public right there in Firetown. An' we was on the CS most wanted list. Our show blacklisted an' outlawed.

*　*　*

Now, I blamed myself for this whole thing. Yeah, in my head I know I can't be blamed for a century of oppression an' genocide, but in my nightmares I see again an' again the people. People there to see me an' Phinny. People who'd not be there were it not for us – dyin' in-mass, an' my heart *know* I'm responsible for it all. I carried that guilt an' I knew if I didn't do nothin' to free the Ten I'd bear that guilt all o' my life.

Now, you remember when I said that the one law in Nightside is 'don' bite the hands that feed?' Part o' that is not exposin' your feeder to undue danger. And raidin' a CS holdin' cell to free prisoners was *def'nately* riskin' exposure for Smilin' Tony an' his folks. I try many times to convince Phinny an' Tony an' even Slo-Mo that we need to do this. Slo-Mo was the easiest to convince, what wit' him wantin' revenge over Tiny who was like his bud. But Tony think I was stupid an' Phinny think I was crazy.

"Mikey, please," Phinny pleaded, "you're endangering more than just yourself and your career. Quit looking at me like that, son, you're endangering *my* life and career, too, you know? But you're also risking Smilin' Tony, you're risking Roxy, and you're risking the lives of every Dee-Bee still hiding in the 'Burbs! I miss Frankie too, Mikey buddy, but killing yourself and risking everything won't help him, wherever he is."

"But Phin, I *have* to do this! I'll *never* get over it ifin' I don't do *somethin'*!"

"Madness, son! Suppose you do succeed? Then what? How do you get them out? Where do you take them? Tony sure as Hades won't let them stay *here*. You'll bring down the Coalition on this entire 'Burb! Giant robots, tanks and soldiers in the streets even more than usual! Purges and witch-hunts! It'll be disaster! Absolute war!"

I feared he was right an' I try to put it behind me an' go on, but I couldn't. Ev'ry night the nightmares. Ev'ry ev'nin' on the Channel Six News there was the Ten, paraded out to show all the might an' power o' the Coalition States. It was three days 'till the execution an' I didn't have no idea what to do. I grew desp'rate an' tried to plead with anyone to help, but Dee-Bees in the 'Burbs, tho' dey know all about oppression an' really wanted someone to save the Ten, dey was all about keepin' their heads down an' keepin' alive. Finally, I see the salvation for the Ten: it was sittin' there in the corner wavin' its feelers.

Yep, I saw me a roach.

Now, not ev'ry roach is workin' for Mama Roach, but I was desp'rate there, so I talk to the roach. Must'a look like a damn fool talkin' to a bug, but I did.

"Now, Mr. Roach," I say to it. "I don' know if you workin' for Mama, but iffen you are, could you please run word to the lady for me? I feel real guilty 'bout them Hydrant Ten seein' as how dey was there to see my act, so if you could please ask Mama for help ta save 'em I'd be forever in her debt, mind."

I guess that roach *did* work for Mama Roach, 'cause it was the next night I get my answer. I'd auto-piloted my way through that night's performance in Club Sanctimonious an' was kickin' back an' just breakin' open the rum when I heard a voice: "So, I hear you want to free the Hydrant Ten?" the high pitch voice say to me. "Well, I have some friends that might help out in that regard." There was a little human-lookin' guy in the corner shadow. He had a white beard and a kindly face that I not trust for a second, but like I say, I was desp'rate.

"Who are you again, sir?" I replied.

"Call me 'The Gnome'. I specialize in going places where I'm not wanted. Now, Mr. Mamou, I'm more than happy to help, but I have my own obligations and need a favor in return."

"An' what's that, Mr. Gnome?" I don't even *want* to know how he know my real name.

"Your employers seem to have a monopoly on, shall we say, the 'import' business in Chi-Town. And my employers seek a stake in the trade, seeing as how their old stomping grounds in Tolkeen are now Coalition-infested ruins. You get me an audience with Smilin' Tony and we'll talk turkey, dig?"

Now, gettin' Tony to agree to meet with this "Gnome" was harder than you'd tink. It seemed Tony knew all about the Gnome and "those flying playboys of his," as Smilin' Tony called 'em, an' that he wasn't interested in meetin' with anyone.

Now, since ya' asked, at the time I was jus' mad, like, so I didn't tink nothin' of what I done next, but lookin' back that was prolly the bravest or stupidest day of my life.

"Sah, I mus' insist here," I tell Tony. "This here Hydrant thing is drivin' me crazier than a short-circuited M.O.M. implant. I can't do the act if I can't keep my mind on it. An . . . an' if I can't do the act your boss can't make no money, an' so this be in your int'rest too, see?"

Now, lookin' back I see I was as replaceable as old jockey shorts, so I could'a been signin' my own death sentence there. But for all Smilin' Tony's ruthless ways (rumors 'bounded 'bout the things he do to those who cross the Black Market, mind), I guess he musta' either admired a person with a big set of ammo drums hangin' with their rail gun or he's got a spot of honor in 'im. So after a long talk, he agreed, an' that night he met behind closed doors with the Gnome.

Now, I don't know what all dey talk 'bout (though I bet Mama Roach do), but in the end I was recruited to come along on the raid to free the Hydrant Ten as a 'representative,' along wit Slo-Mo. Lookin' back I'm tinkin' that if things had gone wrong, Slo-Mo was gonna' plug me an' no one know no diff'rent.

Now, the next night I'm all in black and sneakin' with Slo-Mo to the meetin' point. At the meetin' point we see the Gnome along with a tall human guy in a black coat lookin' all like Baron Samedi (though he ain't, mind), an' wit' dem is 'bout a half dozen commando-lookin' folks, mostly Juicers.

We sneaked along on that overcast October night (an' it was damn cold, I might add) 'till we come to the outpost/jail/whatever. Now, you'd expect what happen next to have all manner of action, lasers flyin', and explosions an' all, but in truth was it not so damn scary I bet it'd be duller than watchin' Idie talk about fish an' fishin', at least for a non-active participant like me.

So I watch the big guy an' all the commando-types go rushin' up t'wards the prison quieter than a padded owl. I see one Dead Boy guard get pulled into a shadow. I see a blur o' movement here an' there. An' I still wonders how that Dog Pack out front just sit there not smellin' or sensin' nothin'. I guess there must be some kind o' magic that hides 'em.

After a long, long few minutes, out trot the commandos with all ten prisoners in tow. We all skedaddle into the alleyways an' run 'long what must'a been a preset path, though I wasn't in on any plannin' an' it all seemed random to me, mind. We was all too scared to talk, well, I an' the Ten was too scared, Slo-Mo an' the Gnome's folks was all silent professional like.

We was pilin' into waitin' hover vehicles just when the alarms go off, screamin' like a scorned harpy. The hover cars all split up and slipped away as the searchlights started.

Now, I was in the hover truck wit' the Ten, Slo-Mo, the Gnome, an' two scary big ol' Juicers. The Ten were all chatty now and thankin' me an' I tell 'em to thank the Gnome an' the folks what got 'em out an' that I just happy to see 'em free an' sorry to get 'em in that cell in dah first place. 'Course dey say dey knew the risk goin' to the club that night an' though some lose fam'ly that night (which don't help my guilt none) dey say it was Prosek's fault an' not mine. But try tellin' that to your conscience, ya know?

An hour later we outside in the country an' we file out of the hover truck to where a group of other commando-lookin' types I never seen ahfore have a radio set up an' are callin' on it. The Gnome walk up and meet wit' 'em an' it seem to me we were expected. Suddenly, I hear the noise of a big buzzin' where it was all silence before – like it suddenly appeared, or un-silenced or somethin'.

Then I see it's an airplane. A big'un with four props. It bounced to a landin' and drive up.

Taxi? No, it weren't no taxi but an aero-plane! A war plane, mind – it had all kinds o' guns pokin' out of ev'rywhere: nose, top, sides, even from a little ball below the belly.

Would ya believe it, a Dog Boy was squeezed inna that li'l gun-ball? Now, since ya' asked I did worry at first 'bout that Dog Boy 'till I find out he a feral an' not Dog Pack.

The big ol' plane – like none I never see ahfore or since – was all shiny silver an' had nose art of a goat standin' on a bomb an' say "Hogan's Goat," which I guess was the plane's name. A door open an' a guy dressed up like a Techno-Wizzy with headphones an' a cap all askew talk briefly with the Gnome an' then say to the Ten, "Welcome aboard, ladies and gentlemen. We'll get all of you to a safe place."

Some argue 'bout family still bein' here in the 'Burbs an' the Techno-Wizzy promises to get der kin out too, so dey all get on. Dey ask me if I'm commin'. Guess I could'a bugged out right then an' lived free, but I say "no" 'cause I got a gig here. But I do tell 'em that I'd be more'n happy to help 'em get others out o' the 'Burbs to safety an' I tell the Gnome to contact me.

So that Techno-Wizzy close the door (hatch? Nothin' hatched, jus' closed) an' the engines rev loud an' the plane speeds up and takes off.

By then the moon had broke through the clouds an' was gleamin' off the big ol' plane as it banked off into the night, takin' the Ten to freedom. An' just as sudden as when I first hear it, it disappear like it never was there.

* * *

Afterwards, like Phinny predict, we all had to hide out while the Dead Boys comb the 'Burbs lookin' for either the Ten or who freed 'em. It got scary, what wit' the tanks an' troops rumblin' on the streets above. We was in the basement, mind. A few days later the Dead Boys give up. Dey gather a few Dee-Bees an' petty criminals an' execute dem instead. Since ya' asked, we 'Burbs folk know how to hide. Ya' got to, mind.

It was a few weeks later dat the Gnome contact me again. He was waitin' in my dressin' room like ahfore – I still don't know how he do that. He had a proposition: I was to find Dee-Bees in the city, find those who want out, and get word to Mama Roach. Mama'd get word to the Gnome, who'd get word to the guy in the big disappearin' plane called Hogan's Goat who'd fly 'em to freedom. I don't know 'xactly what deal dey have with the Black Market, mind, but I can see how a disappearin' airplane'd be as good for smugglin' things in as it is for smugglin' folks out, so I guess dey got somethin' along those lines.

So that's how I become not just a comedian but part o' what we started callin' the "overground railroad," sneakin' Dee-Bees out o' the 'Burbs to freedom in an invisible airplane. Whether dey was goin' north to Lazlo, east to the Zone, west to Arznie, or somewhere else entirely I don' know, but if things get too hot for me dey promise a free ride for Phinny an' me an' Roxy an' all o' us to the place o' our choice.

In the meantime, the Brothers Perez act's still goin'. We're still popular in the 'Burbs an' even gainin' back some popularity in the other cities where we once had a followin'. Rumor say we're even sellin' movies in Atlantis an' across the Megaverse at some place called 'Center,' though who really know, now, eh?

Well, show's on, gotta run. Thank ya' kindly! It was good to talk to you an' I hope your listeners enjoy the interview.

An' remember that the latest Brothers Perez movie, **The Brothers Perez Join the Navy**, is commin' out next week. We play two Dee-Bees who disguise ourselves as humans an' enlist in the Coalition Navy. Hi-jinks ensue, sure 'nuff! Too bad Francisco's not wit' us . . . his sight-gags would'a been *beautiful* in this movie!

"And now, live in their very own 'Comedy Train Theater', The Brothers Perez!" *(Loud cheering.)*

"Thank you, thank you all! Pablo and I are glad to be here and glad to have all you nice folks here in the beautiful Comedy Train Theater here in the 'Burbs! Remember to tip your waiters and bartender, folks. The bartender's a Spinne and has fifty-thousand babies to feed back in the web, so tip well! Ain't that right, Webs?

"Ja, dat's right, dumkopf, fifty-t'ousand no less."

"But enough about Webs . . . Pablo, what do you think about the new demon wars breaking out? Demons against Deevils. Now that's just scary."

"Sounds like your last divorce trial, Sallie!" *(laughter)*

"No kidding, Pablo, my ex-wives are real devils! They deserve the worst."

"As iffen bein' married to you weren't punishment enough?" *(laughter)*

"That's diabolic *there, Pablo! I'm a being of compassion and care."*

"Yeah, that's what you always say when dey told you der problems: 'Yeah, yeah, honey, Like I really care!'" *(howls of laughter)*

"Hey! I thought we were talking about the Minion War! Hell-spawned horrors have been unleashed on the world!"

"Oh no, that's just the Wednesday night comedies on Channel Six!" *(laughter)*

"Please, Pablo! They're using the universe as their battleground! The fight could very well end up here in Nightside! Can you imagine the destruction warring demons and Deevils could visit on this place?"

"Since ya' asked, prolly improve things, Sallie." *(laughter)* *"This place is so dirty the roaches wipe their feet before they* leave*!"* *(shrieks of laughter)*

"Hey! The Nightside health board gave us an 'A' rating this year!"

"Check must'a cleared this time, eh?" *(uproarious laughter)*

"Fine, fine . . . but let me tell you about the time in Firetown when I met . . ."

Truth and Consequences

By Jason Richards

Corporal Ryall Seitz grunted as he squatted down over the first corpse, slung his C-12, and rolled the oversized hulk of a body onto its back. Orange, gelatinous muck oozed out in long strings from the fatal chest wound and stuck to the pavement like warm honey. He silently cursed all D-Bees and their alien anatomies as he dressed down the body and worked it for intelligence.

"Non-human," Seitz began after setting the comm in his helmet to record. "Species unidentified. No armor. Worn clothing, non-uniform."

Try as he might, he couldn't keep from getting the blood or pus or whatever it was all over his flat black armor as he cataloged the items found on the body.

Tucked away in an alley, the *ISS Peacekeper Squad* busily policed a dozen bodies as they quickly ripened in the afternoon sun. Minutes earlier the corpses had been living, breathing proof of the sort of threat that Seitz had dedicated his life to combating. According to a reliable source, the armed insurgency was set to ambush a notable political figure as he returned to the safety of the walls of Chi-Town from abroad. Fortunately this nonhuman resistance group, one of hundreds in the 'Burbs surrounding the megacity, was too loose with their plans and the authorities caught up with them before it was too late.

"Human," came the voice of another Peacekeeper recording his check-over of a body a few feet away. Seitz felt nearly pushed over by a wave of revulsion at the thought of a *human being* throwing in with the extremist group's assorted alien membership, now scattered amidst the twisted steel and debris. Seitz hurried through the final checks of his first subject, then stood up with his arms held awkwardly away from his body and looked around futilely for something to use to scrape the goo from his hands.

"I don't believe it!" cried a trooper from the edge of the combat zone. Seitz and a number of others looked up from their work and in the direction of the voice. "Sergeant! Live one!" The entirety of the squad grabbed their rifles and ran to the origin of the report.

Behind the hollow husk of a burned out car a Peacekeeper trained his weapon on a lone, live fugitive writhing uselessly amidst the scrap. He was on his belly trying to pull himself free from the jagged, overturned frame, but Seitz could tell just by looking that the bones in one arm were shattered and unable to support him as he struggled. Bits of shrapnel and glass protruded from his side and he was bleeding more and more heavily with each exertion. He was clearly in shock, oblivious to the growing number of soldiers standing around him.

The sergeant walked through the gaggle of onlookers and stood over the whimpering man. "Secure this prisoner," he barked, then reached down with an armored hand and grabbed the bleeding, broken arm. With a jerk, he pulled the man free and was rewarded with a new octave of painful shrieks. "Another traitor," the sergeant growled to anyone close enough to hear him as he turned his back and left the man to be gathered up. "Makes me sick."

The sight of a captive human turncoat, so badly wounded and in obvious pain, brought a certain type of satisfaction to Corporal Seitz as he watched two troopers bind the prisoner's arms and legs with metal cuffs, then lift his head off the concrete to gag him. Tears of pain and fear traced tracks down his soot-covered face as he sobbed. As Seitz moved to return to his own work, the restraint muffled the last pathetic, slurred cry from the prisoner's lips. "Mother, save me."

Seitz froze as a bomb went off in his brain. He turned back to look at the figure lying on the ground, then was gripped by a violent shudder inside the shell of his armor that nearly buckled his knees. He was faintly aware of the sergeant giving instructions about moving the bodies, but Seitz wasn't listening. He was transfixed by this hopelessly struggling, near-dead prisoner sprawled on the pavement in front of him.

He was shocked awake from his nightmare by the sudden realization that someone had walked up beside him. The lieutenant stood, arms folded, looking down on the bound captive.

"A prisoner, Sergeant?" he asked.

"Wounded, Sir," answered back the sergeant, who walked past Seitz and stood over the shaking man, and nudged his bleeding side with the toe of his boot. "Not sure he'll even make it. Should we just finish him off?"

Seitz felt his heart sink and the bile rise in his throat.

"No sense in that," stated the lieutenant, more as an order than an issuance of opinion. At his wave, the two Peacekeepers standing by stepped up to take charge of the man still writhing in his shackles.

"Finish policing these bodies and then we'll head back home. Well done."

As the officers walked away, Seitz turned his back, raised his faceplate and hurriedly found the nearest trash bin to be sick.

* * *

Ryall looked up from his second drink as his grinning brother slid into the booth across from him. It was seven o'clock in the morning and Travis already had grease all over his coveralls. Even so, he looked a sight better than Ryall in his wrinkled ISS uniform and baggy eyes. The only other patrons in the establishment were those finishing off all-nighters or those just getting on with their day and looking for relief in the form of hair of the dog. None of the assorted local color paid notice to the two men as they sat alone in the back corner, clearly wanting to keep their conversation private. Still, Ryall guardedly leaned over the table toward his confused brother and said in a low tone, "I called as soon as I got off duty. We're in big, big trouble."

He hadn't stopped shaking since the afternoon before and even now his quaking hand set loose the bubbles clinging to the side of his mug, which floated to the top and added to the foamy head of his brew. He took a big gulp and gasped as he set the mug down again. "Big, big trouble. I'm not sure what we should do."

Travis, usually so glib, had a face of stone. "What are you talking about?" he asked, now leaning in and lowering his own voice.

Ryall began his story with the events of the day before. The raid on a nonhuman supremacy group. The firefight in the alley. The policing of the human and D-Bee bodies. As his voice weakened, his shaking hand clumsily put the sweating mug back up to his lips and he drained it.

"So?" asked Travis, trying his very best to be reassuring, as if he could stave off whatever inevitable upshot came from the story to give his brother such a scare. "Good work. Job well done."

"No," stated Ryall as simply as he could. "One lived. He was hurt pretty bad, but they took him back for processing and questioning." He took a deep breath.

"It was Devan."

Ryall waited, and watched his brother's ever-changing reaction to the mention of a name so long shut out of memory, but yet never forgotten. Confusion, recognition, and then horror; all familiar sensations to Ryall, just like he experienced at the discovery, hours before. Then, Travis's face went blank and his eyes dropped to the table.

"No. Impossible."

"Travis . . ." Ryall desperately tried to cut short the dismissal he knew was coming.

"It couldn't be. He's still back home. Probably dead before we ever even got out." He shook his head and tried to toss loose the images that came so unbeckoned to the forefront of his mind.

"It was him."

"No, Ryall, it couldn't have been."

"It was."

Travis continued to shake his head, glaring at a knot in the worn, polished wood table, and said nothing else.

"I'm telling you that it was Devan." Ryall swallowed hard and fought to keep his stare directed at Travis's downturned gaze.

"He called for mom when they took him in, just like . . ." His voice suddenly wouldn't rise to finish the sentence. He swallowed and cleared his throat. "You remember."

They both remembered. Try as they might to convince themselves it was only a nightmare, or that it had happened to somebody else. Both sat envisioning a terrible night, shackled to one another at the knees and slaving under the watchful crimson eyes of an alien taskmaster. It was their home gone to Hell, toiling in a work camp to help their masters fuel their war machine. Devan had been there too, tethered to their father. Their dad was an old man and unable to take so much anguish, so much loss, and died there on his feet in that assembly line. Those red-eyed monsters dragged that 16-year-old kid away along with the corpse; screaming, clawing at the concrete slab and begging for someone to help him, still chained to the limp body of their father. No one could do anything but watch, and nobody ever came back from wherever the living were taken with the dead.

Months later, Ryall and Travis got lucky, along with a few others. A Rift, much like those that had brought their usurpers in sheep's clothing to their Earth generations before, had opened randomly in their camp. A handful of human slaves managed to cross through into a relative paradise that they were surprised to discover was Earth. Whether another time or place or dimension they could never know, but it was home in a sense, and freedom.

Now, years later and arguably a world away, an ISS Peacekeeper and a local mechanic spoke about a past that they could not keep behind them.

The time spent reflecting on that life seemed to steel Ryall. "I have to go and try to see him," he said after a long while of sitting in awkward silence. "He's our brother. We have to help him. I can explain things to the Inspector." His voice and hands were steady.

Travis was visibly horrified, mouth agape and eyes wide. Slowly his jaw closed and set and his eyes narrowed to a glare.

"Do you not understand?" he grimaced through clenched teeth. "Have you not been listening to yourself? We're as good as dead already! I don't even know why we're still sitting here when we should be out, on the run, this second!" Travis's lip turned up into a scornful sneer of disbelief as he glanced at his watch. "It's been fourteen hours since he was taken in. I'm surprised they haven't come looking for us yet. It's only a matter of time."

Now it was Ryall that stared down at the table, refusing to meet his brother's reproachful look. "He doesn't know that we're here. He didn't see me. It could slip through and we might still be okay, especially if I go in now and talk to the Inspector and lay it out on the table."

"You listen to me," said Travis in a slow, cold, clear tone. "This is not your decision to make. This affects *both* of us. I didn't escape from that Hell just to die here like *this*. There's nothing that we can do for Devan now. From what you said, he might have bled to death." He lowered his voice further and tried to be calm. "We have got to get out of here. Right now."

Ryall raised his head to meet his brother's eyes. "No. Run if you want. I'm staying."

The scene was familiar. Travis was the older brother convinced that he was right; Ryall, the obstinate middle child unwilling to budge. Every second that passed without a response caused an uptick in Travis's frustration.

"Ryall, he has been taken in as a sympathizer. He's being processed right now. You and I are both in the database and they'll run his sample. It'll take half a second for it to be linked to us as family. Brothers to a nonhuman-sympathizing D-Bee."

"Hey!" yelled Ryall suddenly as heads turned toward them around the sparse bar. Travis looked at his brother and then sideways at the staff and patrons of *A While Longer*, who all quickly resumed minding their own business. Ryall's voice lowered again but lost none of its intensity.

"Don't you call me that," he hissed menacingly. "We're human. Both of us. All *three* of us. Down to the last cell." He was rabid, beyond outraged at being compared to such filth. His mind raced from images of red glowing eyes of years gone to a gray-skinned corpse not yet a day old.

"It doesn't matter if we're human," said Travis as he leaned on his elbow and rubbed the bridge of his nose, searching for a way to make his brother understand. He sighed. "You know better than anyone that Psi-Net will have already had some Sensitive crawling around in his brain, sorting through memories and collecting information. They'll know how he got here and where he came from."

"*You* don't even know how he got here or where *any* of us came from," Ryall interjected, leveling a finger across the table.

"How else?" asked Travis, dismissively. "They'll know he's not one of them. They'll use DNA and the memories they pluck out of his head to independently link him to us, and then – we're as guilty as him."

Ryall was still resolute. "It won't be like that. We're as human as the Emperor, himself. Look at me." He prodded himself in the chest with his finger, punctuating each word. "Poster child for humanity. Corporal Seitz, decorated member of the ISS. I signed on because we've seen what allowing these freaks to take hold means for all of us. I did this for Devan. I can't abandon him now."

"That uniform will not protect you from this," Travis stated plainly, certain of the truth of it. "If anything, it makes it worse. If he's some alien subversive, that makes you a *spy* and a traitor and you'll get yourself executed just after Devan."

"Like I said, we're all humans, not aliens."

"How do you know that Devan thinks so? What was he doing there in the first place?" asked Travis. "Are you going to go in there and defend him for being a member of this group that you raided yesterday? Social underminers? *Terrorists?*"

Ryall looked blankly at the condensation on his mug and searched for an answer. He admitted to himself that he hadn't considered that, caught up as he was in his little brother's sudden and miraculous reappearance. "I don't know," he said, finally. "But who knows what condition he was in when he came over? He might not know any better. To take the side of these monsters over us doesn't make sense. Manipulation. Brainwashing. Voodoo hocus pocus. Who knows for sure? And how can you rest not knowing?"

"You're stretching."

"I'm *not*. The bottom line is that we're not one of those 'others.' For all we know we could have stepped through that Rift and traveled 100 miles, or 100 years! Or both! We're from Earth, Travis. Same sun. Same moon. We have no reason to assume that we're from some other world, and neither will the Inspector if I'm honest about what we *do* know."

A heavy pause settled between them and grew for several minutes before Ryall finally broke it. "Do what you want. I'm going in for Devan."

Travis stood up with resolute determination. The discussion, for what it was worth, was over.

"Then I'm leaving. Take care of yourself if I don't see you again." He stuck out his hand to his little brother who stood and shook it mechanically. Ryall had suspected this might be how the talk would end, but his heart sank all the same. The two stayed locked for a moment until Travis let go.

"I hope you're right, Ryall." With nothing left to say, he turned and quickly walked out the door to his waiting car, hit the ignition, and didn't look back as Ryall watched him drive past the row of smudged windows and away from the shadow of the looming megacity.

"Me, too," thought Ryall as he walked toward the door.

* * *

Corporal Ryall Seitz triple-checked his fresh uniform as he hurriedly walked through the hallway of ISS Precinct 12 headquarters toward the Chief Inspector's office. His pace slowed as he got closer to the outer door and he again weighed the balance in his mind as he thought about his two brothers. He stared at the door handle as he slowly reached for it like it was a burning coal. It was all or nothing. No half measures. "But then," Ryall thought, "I know who I am, don't I?"

Ryall squeezed his eyes shut, grabbed the handle, turned it, stepped inside, and closed the door all in one chaotic motion. The Chief Inspector's aide looked up from his desk with a befuddled expression at the Peacekeeper who had just so unceremoniously entered the room. Before either of them could speak, the door ahead to the inner office opened. Seitz's commanding sergeant and lieutenant, followed by the Chief Inspector, stepped out. All three stopped short and stared at the corporal, then looked at each other with grave faces.

Seitz felt his face burn to the tips of his ears as he saluted. "Good afternoon Sirs, Sergeant." There was silence in the room and the aide looked back and forth between Seitz and the officers as the space between them seemed to expand with each pounding heartbeat. The Chief Inspector casually returned the salute, and Ryall dropped his hand to his side. "For Devan," he thought.

"Chief Inspector, I have something to report regarding yesterday's raid that I believe may interest you."

The officers exchanged stoic glances again. "I wondered if you might, Corproal Seitz. Please come in and have a seat." The Chief Inspector nodded his gray head at the concerned sergeant and lieutenant, who looked at each other and again at Seitz as they put on their service covers and walked past Ryall and left the outer office. The Chief Inspector held the door for the corporal, followed him inside, and then closed it behind them. The aide scratched his head and turned his attention back to his paperwork.

Casualties of War

By Mark Oberle

William and his parents had moved from their small rural home in southeastern Missouri to the 'Burbs of Chi-Town when he was just a toddler. Will's father, Jonathan, had wanted to provide a higher standard of living for them by moving them into the walled mega-city that served as the capital of the Coalition States. The massive fortress insulated its inhabitants from the hardships of post-Cataclysm life, a haven of tranquility in a world gone mad. Unfortunately, this was a goal that many citizens of the CS strove for, leading millions to apply for a spot within the titanic arcology. Jon had been informed after filling out the necessary paperwork that it would be at least five years before their application came up for review due to the size of the waiting list.

But Jonathan Alder was not one to give up easily. Rather than return to his home town "with his tail between his legs," he had found a small home in the 'Burbs surrounding the capital city and settled his family in to wait. After a few years, Will's little brother Charlie was born, prompting a change in the application. That meant the family was placed back on the bottom of the list, which had grown even longer by that point. It appeared that William would be grown by the time the family was finally given Chi-Town citizenship.

The spring of 105 P.A. proved to be unseasonably warm, allowing Will to take his new bike out in the back alleys of New Colfax, the 'burb in which the Alders had settled nine years before. As one of the older communities, it was much more stable than the newer 'burbs further out from the city's walls, and practically heaven compared to the Shanty Towns that bordered them. Despite the fact that the 'Burbs were not officially recognized as communities by the Coalition, they had been allowed to be built for almost a century. Some of the oldest, like *New Colfax*, had grown into relatively stable pseudo-cities unto themselves. New Colfax and a couple others even provided valuable services to the fortress city, like the food processing plant where Will's parents worked that produced field rations for the Coalition military.

After a few hours of racing around the jumbled streets, Will had noticed it was nearing dinner time. Returning home, he had found his family gathered around the vid-screen rather than the kitchen table. One of the announcers for the government was on the screen giving the details of a new recruitment drive initiated by the CS military. They were offering any resident of the 'Burbs special consideration for their application if they signed up for a six-year tour of duty. Will's father was on the edge of his seat, eager to hear every last detail. Once the announcement concluded, he turned to Will's mother, Hillary, and said, "That's it, that's our ticket in!"

"I dunno, Jon," Will's mother hesitated, "six years is an awful long time for you to be away from us."

"But Hil," Jon replied, almost pleading in tone, "if it gets you an' the boys into the city then it'll be worth it. Just think, we could get the boys into school an' my pay'll get you by so you kin' stay home."

Hillary opened her mouth as if to say something more, but merely dropped her shoulders and sighed instead. She had been with him long enough now to know that once he got an idea like this in his head, it would take a twister with a crowbar to get it out again.

"But what if . . ." Her voice trailed off as she turned to look at Will and Charlie. She couldn't help thinking about them without a father. "It's the army, Jon," said Hillary, finally mustering the energy to respond. It was apparent she was working hard to hold back tears as she tried to stop a range of horrible scenarios playing out in her head.

"Hillary, honey, don't think like that. I'll probably end up assigned to some outpost in the middle o' nowhere makin' sure the corn don't get outta hand and chasin' away Fury Beetles." Jon tried to sound as reassuring as possible and even cracked a thin smile. "You trust me, don't ya?"

So that was that, Will's father signed up for the Coalition military the very next day. He would be trained as a "Dead Boy," and wear the skull-faced helmet for the next six years. The Dead Boys were the pride of the Coalition States. The heroes of humanity, the Emperor called them. Soldiers charged with retaking America from the nameless horrors that had swarmed over it after the Great Cataclysm.

Will and his little brother were actually excited about Daddy being a soldier – "a knight in shiny armor," – the little one would say. For the next few months they would lie awake in their bunk beds at night and talk about what exploits their father might have. Would he be sent to fight the rabble-rousing Pecos Raiders in the south? Or maybe the evil sorcerers of the reviled Federation of Magic? Or maybe the bug men in the North. Certainly he would became a famous hero, they both decided, who would take them to meet Karl Prosek, Emperor of the Coalition States!

That summer, the children's fantasies came to an abrupt end. As the pair laid on the floor watching the new vid-screen their father's first salary payment had purchased, the kind and caring Emperor of the Coalition States appeared to make a speech about the future of the CS. When the Emperor spoke, the people of the Coalition listened, even those in the 'Burbs. Especially those people living in the 'Burbs.

"War," that's what the speech was about. Emperor Prosek had announced a "Campaign of Unity" to rein in the rebellious city-state of Free Quebec, and a "Crusade for Humanity" aimed at wiping out the kingdom of Tolkeen in what was once Minnesota. Tolkeen, he said, was a nation that had been corrupted by magic and consorted with demonic beings from beyond the Rifts, the very forces that many believed caused the Great Cataclysm and brought the horrors to Earth in the first place. Tolkeen was the antithesis to everything the Coalition believed, and now the time had come to *destroy* them. Jonathan Alder and his entire division would be part of that war effort.

The Alder boys were ecstatic! Daddy was going to be a war hero! Their mother simply hugged them tight and held them close to her. It was obvious now that the recruiting program of the last few months had been for this war, this "Siege on Tolkeen," all along. She would beat herself up with recrimination for months to come. Why? Why didn't she do more to stop him from joining the Coalition Army?

Jon's last video-letter to her had shown him with his unit, gearing up for moving into the field. Hillary could tell, despite his location being censored out of the video by CS Intelligence, there had been a number of Psi-Hounds (genetically engineered, humanoid dog-soldiers that could literally sniff out the supernatural – they prowled the 'Burbs, these "Dog Boys") drilling in the background. The family said a prayer over dinner that evening, and prepared for the country to go to war. Everyone, except Dad's friend, Ian, an old Headhunter from a neighboring 'Burb, insisted it would be a short war, maybe six months, maybe eight, before the CS troops would route the enemy and claim victory.

Tolkeen would "fall under the crushing weight and technology of the Coaltion war machine," was the word on the street.

Six months slipped into one year. One year into two, and two years into three. The enemy was more devious and resourceful than originally imagined. The CS propaganda machine made certain the daily Video reports always seemed positive, lifting the spirits of the people in the Coalition States, they it painted the enemy as monsters and zealots.

Other than the reports and the absence of their father, life hadn't changed much for William or his brother. They played, ran around, went to school, helped around the house and imagined their father the war hero. Their mother could have stayed at home since the family was receiving Jonathan's military pay, but she had chosen continue to working at the plant. It meant she could save almost her entire paycheck and she said it was her part in the war effort, but mostly, it kept her from worrying about Jon and thinking about the war at Tolkeen. William, following in the footsteps of his father, did his part to support the Coalition too, by getting a job with the Propaganda Department. That included tacking up recruitment posters around New Colfax and participating in youth rallies with his younger brother in tow.

The family received video letters from Jonathan at least twice a month. Whenever one arrived, they would get together and watch it after dinner as a proud family. Jon always appeared to be in good spirits, joking with his men even as he recorded the videos. He had been promoted to Corporal in short order and his unit had seen some heavy fighting in the border towns of Tolkeen. William and his brother would sit quietly through their father's tales of pitched battles with spell-flinging menaces, horrific aliens, man-eating monsters, and every kind of extra-dimensional nightmare imaginable. He'd leave out the strategic details such as locations, times and the names of his enemies, of course, but they got enough to be proud. That seemed to be the if father's purpose too. To make his family proud and to assure them he was okay and doing his part to "keep humanity safe," as William's posters touted.

One tale inparticular stayed on the boys' minds for weeks. Jonathan recorded the message shortly after returning to his unit from a short stint in the field hospital. "I'm doin' just fine," he explained with a smile on his face. "Damn dragon breath is hot enough to melt even stout armor like ours. But you shoulda' seen the look on that slimy scaleback's face when I snatched up one of our rocket launchers and gave em' a face full of high-explosive for his trouble. Rest o' the boys finished the monster off while I hunted up a medic to treat the minor burns I got on my chest. We're told there is an entire city of dragons in the Kingdom of Tolkeen, so you know why this place is so dangerous and why these forces of magic must be stopped. Don't worry, my darlings, them overgrown lizards ain't so tough."

Will and Charlie began referring to their dad as the "Dragon Slayer" until their mom became so annoyed with the name she threatened to ground them both for a month if she heard it again. "Enough is enough," she scolded. "I'm just glad your father is safe, and I pray he never locks horns with another one of those beasts again."

The videos all ended the same way, "Hillary, please don't worry. I'm doing this for you and the boys. So we can become Coalition Citizens and never have to live in fear again. Don't forget to check on the status of our Citizens App. Oh, and vid me the second y'all get the papers and are admitted into the fortress city. You boys be good an' mind your mother, now. Keep your chins up and I'll be home just as soon as we send these monsters back to the pit they crawled out of. I love ya' guys, take care of each other."

Then the screen would go dark, leaving the family to sit and chat about what Jon had said, how nice it would be when he got back home, and what life would be like in the fortress-city.

Always the dutiful wife, Hillary would check on the application after every vid-letter, but their citizenship papers always seemed to be somewhere in bureaucratic limbo. She'd say a prayer for her husband and family on the way back home, and thank the gods that life was stable in New Colfax.

Yeah, compared to so many others living hand to mouth in the 'Burbs, the Alders had it okay, and the slow process toward Coaltion Citizenship was not unusual.

By the fall of 108 P.A., William had begun talking about joining the Coalition Army himself. After all, he had just turned sixteen and several of his friends had already joined up. He hadn't brought it up to his mother yet, as he knew she would be against it, but he had been working on his sales pitch. "Ma, if Dad and I are both in the army, it should speed up our chances of making Citizenship sooner. Don't you want to live in the walls of Chi-Town? Don't you want two war heroes in the family? Charlie is old enough to watch himself now, and I'll send most of my salary home like Dad so we can afford a really nice place when we get inside Chi-Town!" It all sounded carefully reasoned and sound to him.

These thoughts had been on William's mind when he walked through the door to find mother and Charlie huddled around the vid-screen. At first, William was angry that they would watch a vid-letter from Dad without him, but then he realized it wasn't his father on the screen. A government war correspondent relayed what was known about a massive counterattack launched from the heart of Tolkeen. The Coalition Army had been forced to beat a hasty retreat, and tens of thousands of troops were missing in action. The war correspondent called it the "Tolkeen Massacre," and used words like "shocking," "unprecedented," "unrelenting," and "savage." He talked about the courage of our fighting forces and how the "heroes of humanity" would rally and triumph. Mother was sobbing, and that made Charlie cry too."

"Don't worry, Ma. I'm sure Dad's okay," said William with sincere earnestness. Hillary just gave him that look mothers give their children when they want them to sit down and be quiet. All William could do was stand in a shocked silence while his mother and Charlie wept.

The streets were buzzing about the Tolkeen Massacre too, only they called it "The Sorcerers' Revenge." Coalition television said it was a last-ditch effort to drive the CS from Tolkeen, and that even now the battle groups had rallied and prepared to push back into the kingdom with fresh troops and supplies to crush the villains and rescue any survivors. On the streets though, D-Bees, outsiders and those soured on waiting to become Citizens of the CS laughed and talked about how the champions of Tolkeen had handed the Coalition Army its first and greatest defeat. How tens of thousands of soldiers had been killed in a single, massive offensive, and how thousands more were on the run like dogs with their tails tucked between their legs. In the gambling halls, the odds for Tolkeen winning the war went up. Some filthy traitors went so far as to praise the massacre and spit on the Coalition Army and the name of Emperor Prosek. It made William angry and want to join the army more than ever.

A month later, the Alder family received the vid-letter they had hoped they'd never get: Sgt. Jonathan Alder was one of the many MIAs. The family kept a silent vigil hoping that the Dead Boys would find Jonathan alive and bring him home safe. William tried to keep hope alive by pointing out that Missing In Action was *not* dead.

A few weeks later, William finally steeled his nerves and locked eyes with his mother.

"I want to enlist, Ma."

The room grew eerily silent as his mother and brother froze in their seats.

"I want to enlist so I can find Dad and bring him home."

Hillary sat, the few gray hairs amongst her blond ones suddenly seeming much more prominent. Her expression never changed as she uttered her single-word response.

"No."

"Mom, I . . ."

"You what?" she practically spat. "Want to end up like your father? Do you want to never see your brother and me again? Do you want to leave us alone and not come back?"

"That won't happen to me, Ma."

"That's what your father said and . . . and just look at him now! Gone!" she said in tears.

"Dad's not dead!" William retaliated. "He's not dead! I know it. And if you let me enlist, I promise to bring him home so we can be a family again."

"Oh, Willy," his mother moaned. "I know you mean well, son, but I can't give you my blessing. No. I won't allow it."

"I can't just sit here and do nothin' when Dad may be alive out there, I have to go and help him, Ma. I have to bring him back!"

His brother Charlie was crying now, too.

"No Willy," the lad chimed in. "I don't want you to go either. I love you."

Tears streamed down both of their faces as mother shook her head, "Your father is gone, William, do you understand me? Lord knows I should've stopped him from going, but I won't make that mistake twice. I won't lose you too."

*   *   *

The sound of the front door closing snapped Will back to reality. How long had he stood there, lost in thought? He moved away from the commemorative plaque and cautiously peeked around the discolored plaster archway that separated the living room from the front entryway. It was his mother, coming in from her day at the processing plant with an armful of groceries she had picked up along the way.

"You need any help with those?"

Hillary started at the sound of William's voice, nearly dropping one of the bags.

"Will, you scared me half to death. Yes, you can carry these into the kitchen for me," she answered in a relieved tone. Will grinned sheepishly and took the three largest bags of groceries from his mother's arms and transported them to the kitchen counter.

It had been nine months since their argument about him joining the service. He didn't blame her for not wanting him to enlist. He had finally given up the notion, though he sometimes still fantasized about having become a soldier, kicking down the door to some shack in Tolkeen where his father was held captive and rescuing him. He would blast his captors to oblivion, his father would weep for joy, and the two of them would return home as heroes to live happily ever after.

While William's daydream had a happy ending, he woke up every day to a nightmare. The war was over. The Coalition forces did regroup and overcome the enemy. Tolkeen fell in spectacular fashion. Thousands of Coalition soldiers remained missing. Thousands more had died. The horror stories of soldiers being torn to shreds, blasted to atoms, or eaten by Brodkil, Gargoyles, dragons and other monsters and demons that had composed Tolkeen's inhuman army filled the streets. William had prepared himself for the worst ever since the Sorcerers' Revenge and thought he had dealt with the loss of his father reasonably well. Still, it was painful and sad to know that there would be no new, happy memories to share with his father. The man he loved would never return home.

The family had fallen on hard luck. Dad's severance benefits were tied up in bureaucratic limbo, the savings were gone, and Mom's salary from the processing plant was barely enough to cover the bills. William found part-time work to help out.

Then one day Mom brought home *the Monster*.

*   *   *

"You need to move your bike Hon, you know how he hates a mess, and he'll be home any minute."

Will's voice lowered, and through clenched teeth he responded, "I'm tired of being ordered around by him. That man is not my father."

His mother sighed, and looked into her son's angry eyes. "Will, you have to accept that things change. We've been through this before," she said in a disappointed tone. "Look, it's been a rough day. Can't we just sit down and have a nice dinner as a family?"

"He is not my father!" Will shouted. "He's nothing like Dad was, so don't expect me to treat him the same."

William's mother called after him as he grabbed his jacket, stomped out the backdoor, and slammed it behind him. As he kicked over the engine of his beat-up, black and silver dirt bike, he wondered, "Why can't she see the man for what he is? Why does she stay with a monster like that?"

A split second later, he was slinging a tail of dust and gravel behind him as he tore out of the back lot. *The Monster* – that was what he and Charlie called the man – was a decorated veteran of the war. He had survived the Sorcerers' Revenge and suffered greatly at the hands of monsters who had captured and tortured him until the fall of Tolkeen. He said he was one of the lucky ones, because he lived. When he was discharged from the military he came to the 'Burbs, scarred in more ways than his body and cybernetic eye would suggest.

Will had felt uneasy around him since the first day his mother brought him home. At first, the Monster didn't seem so bad. He was still recuperating from injuries sustained in the war, but managed to land a job at the processing plant and tried to take responsibility in the support of the family. He wasn't a father, mind you. There wasn't a nurturing bone in his body. He criticized everything Will and Charlie said or did. Called them fools, stupid, and lazy. He dealt out harsh discipline and treated them like they were grunts under his command. The Monster grumbled about how many good men suffered and died in the Siege on Tolkeen, and how fools like Jonathan Alder sacrificed their lives for a dream and an empty promise. Diatribes like that cut William to the bone and made him hate the Monster all the more.

Mother did ever everything she could to please the Monster, even to the extent of ignoring her children to win his favor. That hurt, too. Especially when the Monster treated her like a whipped dog. At first, the Monster showed the occasional flash of kindness, and responded to their mother's care with some measure of appreciation. That changed when the Monster's meds stopped and the drinking began.

Things had gone downhill quickly after that point. The drinking got worse. So did the browbeating, complaining and Mother's tears. Then, one night after the Monster had been drinking, the unthinkable happened. He had been yelling at Charlie for not rinsing out the sink and leaving the towel crumpled and uneven after he had washed his hands for supper. The Monster snarled and fumed. Charlie said something like, "so what," and the Monster grabbed the boy by the shirt. When Hillary tried to get between them, the Monster slapped her across the face and told her to stay out of his business. That he was the man of the house now and the boys needed to learn to show him respect. Especially after everything he suffered in the war. It was always about the war and how much he suffered, and for what?

William hadn't known what to do that night. He wanted to hit the Monster for daring to strike his mother, but his thin teenage frame couldn't do much to a heavily-muscled ex-soldier. So he stood by and did nothing, except hating the Monster for coming into their lives, hurting his mother and little brother, and hating himself for being unable to protect them.

It was a process that would become a daily routine. In retaliation, Will became more and more defiant. The more the Monster demanded his respect, the less he showed it. That worked quite well, because Will learned to draw the Monster's rage away from Mom and Charlie, and to himself. Somehow it wasn't as bad when the Monster attacked him of instead them. Making himself a target kept his mother and brother safe, at least for that night.

It made Will sick to his stomach when Mom would blame herself or blame the war, or used any excuse she could think of to justify what he did to them. When did Mother become so weak and scared, he'd wonder to himself. Why wouldn't she throw the Monster out? They were fine without him. They survived just fine when Dad was away.

William didn't return home that night until well after sunset, figuring everyone would be in bed and he could avoid having to deal with the Monster lurking inside his home. Despite the chilly night air, he killed the bike's engine a half-mile before his neighborhood so he wouldn't wake anyone at home. He propped the bike up against the back shed and crept toward the back door. He froze in his tracks when he realized the light was on in the kitchen. Mom always turned it out before she went to bed. It was then that he noticed the screen door was torn and hanging half off of its hinges. Glass littered the ground beneath a broken kitchen window.

William rushed through the back door and into the kitchen, where everything was in a state of disarray. The table had been overturned, chicken dinner laid scattered on the hardwood floor. One of the chairs was broken and there were deep marks in the wall as if something heavy had been thrown into it. Fearing the worst, Will picked up one of the chair legs and crept into the hallway leading to the bedrooms.

The bathroom light was on, revealing the contents of the family's first-aid kit scattered across the counter. There was blood in the sink, and some bloody towels wadded in the bathtub. Will's heart sank and he was almost too afraid to keep investigating. The overpowering smell of rubbing alcohol burned his nostrils and it felt as if a bottomless pit was opened in his stomach. The teen's heart raced as he moved toward his Mom's bedroom. He turned the handle with one hand and gripped the chair leg with white knuckles in the other hand.

As the door came open with a soft creak, William could hear soft breathing coming from a short distance within. He readied his makeshift weapon and pushed the door open just far enough to slide into the darkened room.

In the wan light, he was able to make out his mother's bed a couple of feet in front of him. The blankets lay in mounds on the bed, with the source of the breathing lying beneath them. As his eyes began to adjust to the relative darkness, he could make out a human form, its face protruding just above the edge of the blankets. As the details of the face came into focus, a pit opened in Will's stomach.

Before him lay his mother, though he could hardly recognize her through the bruises and abrasions. The entire left side of her face was swollen and her nose looked as if it were leaning to the right. William's breath caught in his throat as he realized what must have happened. He should have stayed, maybe if he had been here . . .

Something stirred in the corner of the room. Drawing the club back, he spun to meet whatever it was face-to-face.

"Will?" His brother's voice sleepily whispered from the darkened corner.

God, in his shock he had forgotten all about Charlie. Now a fresh wave of concern shot through him.

"Charles, are you alright?!" asked Will in a hoarse whisper.

Will dropped the table leg and almost tripped over a displaced night stand as he fumbled around in the dark until he located a lamp that had been toppled from its place by the door. The light sputtered as he switched it on, but after a couple of tense seconds burned steadily to illuminate the ghostly appearance of his little brother. Charlie shied away from the sudden light, wincing and shading his eyes as quickly as his drowsy reflexes would allow.

"Will," the young boy whined, "are you trying to burn my eyes out?"

"Sorry, I just wanted to make sure you're not hurt."

"I got a black eye and a sore back, but I'm not gonna die or nuthin'."

Will reached out and gently seized his little brother's chin, and turned his face toward him. A deep purple halo surround his right eye, but what stopped Will cold wasn't the bruise. The look in Charlie's eyes made Will remember that void in his stomach. Somewhere along the line this had all become routine and they just took it. They had become resigned to a life of violence and brutality, of anger and blood. Here they were again, just another family night in Hell.

"What happened?" asked William.

"Whadda you think, Will?" Charlie responded while pulling back from his brother. Suddenly, Charlie seemed older than his eleven years. "He blew up like usual. I don't even know what it was about this time. Something about dinner I guess. The next thing I know the table was flipped over and he had Mom by the throat. I tried to get in between them, Will, I did, but he hit me hard enough to knock me off my feet. Before I could get up he picked me up off the floor and threw me out the back door." Wincing and rubbing his back, he added, "And he didn't open it first."

"That had to be when Mom threw the frying pan at 'im, cause I know I heard the window break. I gathered myself as quick as I could, but when I got back in I found Mom in a heap on the living room floor with him storming out the front. I helped her into the bathroom and got her cleaned up best I could, then helped her into bed. I been sittin' with her since."

William's face had contorted as he listened to Charlie's recounting of the night's events unfold.

"Charlie," said Will his eyes beginning to water, "I'm sorry I wasn't . . ."

"Dammit, Will," Charlie interrupted, "don't. If you were here you'd have gotten beat up too. The way you two go at it . . . I'm glad you weren't here. I did all there was to be done. It's okay."

Will straightened, startled at the authority in his little brother's voice and shocked by the statement that it was okay. It was, most definitely, *not* okay. He realized for the first time just how much he and Charlie had been forced to grow up since their father went to war. In that one blurry-eyed moment, Charlie seemed more a man than William could hope to be. A man in the image of the kind Jonathan Alder they had loved so dearly. After a moment of stunned silence, William squared his shoulders and said, "You're right, little brother, the time for talking is long gone."

"What's that supposed to mean?" Charlie questioned, visibly concerned.

Will knew what he had to do. His father was gone, and if he had accepted that months ago and accepted his responsibility as the man of the house, then maybe he could have spared his family all of this pain. Maybe he would have never allowed the Monster into their lives. This was not the time to wallow in guilt, however, it was time to take action. Not all the monsters were out in Tolkeen or the Wildlands, and it was time for William to take responsibility to protect his family from the one that had invaded their home.

Will placed his hands on Charlie's shoulders and calmly said, "I know you've had a rough night, Charlie, but I need your help."

"I'll do whatever I can for you, Will. You know that."

"I know, Charlie," he responded in a soft tone, "but right now I need you to lock the front door and make sure all the windows are shut and locked too.

"I'll be out to help you in a sec," said William, "but I have to talk to Mom first."

Moving as quickly as he could, the young boy limped out of the room to fulfill William's request.

William moved to his mother's side and stroked her hair.

"Jonathan?" Hillary mumbled in half-conscious blurr.

"No, Ma, it's Will."

"Will? When did you get in? I was worried . . . I'm sorry I got mad at you, honey."

William choked back tears and said, "It's okay Mom. I'm not mad. Are you feelin' alright?"

"I'm alright, just a little sore . . . it's not as bad as it probably looks."

Before she could begin to make excuses for what had happened, Will said, "I need to know where Dad's medal is."

"It's in the night stand drawer, the one by your leg there." As Will jerked the drawer open and began to rummage through it, Hillary became a bit more lucid. "What do you need with it, Will?"

"I have an idea. I'll explain everything later, right now you need to rest," said Will as he put the box with the medal in his pocket and moved toward the door without bothering to close the drawer.

"Stop right there!" came Hillary's voice, sounding as if she were on the verge of tears. "Just because he can get away with pushing me around on occasion doesn't mean I'm going to let you walk all over me too. I am your mother, so start showing me a little respect, young man. Now I asked you a question and I expect you to answer me."

Will froze in his tracks. He wanted to wheel on her, to tell her that he would respect her just as soon as she started respecting herself enough to stop letting the Monster slap her around. But he gritted his teeth and turned to face her. She had managed to push herself into a reclined position and glared at him with her one unswollen eye.

"You don't need to worry, Mom, Charlie's gonna be here with you until I get back, and I shouldn't be more than a couple hours."

"That still doesn't answer my question, William. What exactly are you planning to do?"

"Whatever I have to, Mom. You need your rest. I promise I'll fill you in when I come back. Just rest."

Will could tell she wasn't happy with his answer, and under different circumstances she'd have stopped him, but as it was, she was beaten half to death and slumped back on her pillows and let out a defeated sigh.

William turned to leave the room, but paused in the doorway, and looked back at his mother. Although he was sure she couldn't hear him, Will said, "I'll be back soon, I promise. I love you, Mom."

He met Charlie in the living room as he was returning from the kitchen.

"The house is all locked up, Will, but he has his keys and the kitchen window is broken. The back door ain't too solid, either."

"That's why I need you to help me get the couch in front of the door, and we can take care of the window."

After they had barricaded the front door, William retrieved some spare lumber from the family's shed and nailed a few planks across the outside of the shattered window. "That should be enough to keep out most of the cold and . . . " Will's voice trailed off, but Charlie knew who he meant.

Donning a heavier jacket, the boy showed Charlie how to wedge one of the unbroken chairs beneath the knob of the back door to hold it shut. Hopefully, their fortifications wouldn't have to be tested, because that would mean he failed in his mission.

"I don't want you to open this door unless it's me, got it Charlie?"

"Yeah, I've got it. But where are you going, anyway? What are you going to do, Will? I'm worried about you."

He could hear the fear and concern start to creep into Charlie's voice, so William knelt down and took hold of each shoulder just like Dad used to when he had something important to tell them.

"Charles, you've done an excellent job taking care of Mom tonight. You were here while I was off being mad, and you did good. Now I need you to let me take care of the rest. Can you do that, buddy?"

"You can count on me, Will, but what are you gonna do?" asked Charlie as he straightened and nodded.

Allowing a smile to cross his face for the first time all night, William responded, "Just sit with Mom and I'll be back before you know it." He then stepped out the back door, nodded one more time at his little brother, and closed the door behind him. He stood a moment until he heard Charlie wedge the chair beneath the doorknob before he hopped on his bike and hammered the kick-start.

"Just promise me one thing, Will," shouted his little brother through an opening in the boarded up window. "That you'll come back to us. Come back whole. Promise me, Will. I mean it."

"I promise, Charlie. I promise."

* * *

"One way or another," Will thought to himself, "things change tonight."

An eternity had seemed to pass since he had set out from home. In reality, he had only been gone for an hour. He had ridden like a madman out to the Newtown 'Burb of Tranquility to see an old friend, narrowly avoiding wiping out on several occasions. His short stint as a runner, or "Maze Rat," for the Gutterpunks street gang had at least taught him how to navigate the twisted streets of the 'Burbs at speeds only select City Rats and maybe a Juicer could handle without crashing.

It hadn't taken too long to locate Jake, despite the chaos that was Tranquility. He and the gang had set up shop in a run-down apartment building on the outer edge of the 'Burb that the last tenants had vacated to escape the latest purge by the CS military. The crumbling three-story building looked to be on the verge of collapse, but was a far sight better than the tent-cities of the Shanty-Towns just a little further out. To Will, it was just another reminder of how good he and his family had it by comparison.

Upon arrival at the gang's new hideout, Will was almost jumped by a few of the new members who served as lookouts. Luckily, Jake and a few of the older members were around to vouch for him before he ended up as just another red stain on the concrete. Jake was what was known as a "Pack Rat," a rough-and-tumble character who had joined the Gutterpunks crew when he was only Charlie's age. He was the toughest person Will knew, and had survived this long because of his determination and sharp wits, two good reasons for William to seek his advice on the current situation.

Just as Will had expected, Jake put things into perspective rather quickly.

"So he beats up on you, your mom, and your little brother?"

"Yeah, just did it again tonight," said Will.

"How bad we talkin' here?"

"Well, Charlie's alright I guess, but Mom was pretty banged-up and half out of her head. Probably won't be getting around much for a couple of days, at least."

A look of admonishment crossed Jake's face. "And you're just comin' to me with this now? I know we jumped you out and all, but dammit, fool, you know I told you if you needed somethin' . . ."

The dark-skinned tower of anger that was Jake seemed to loom over the entire room as he processed what Will had told him.

"Where is this dung heap, now? Me an' the boys will take care of your problem for you. You and your mama will never have ta worry about him again. Get me?"

"No Jake, you can't do that," Will interrupted. Ignoring the incredulous stare he got from everyone in the room.

"How'z that?"

"I have a different solution."

"Can't say that I agree, but seein' how it's you and all, me and the boys can just have a little 'chat' with him and break a few parts that'll heal. But your first option is the permanent solution, you know that, right?"

"I hope not . . ." sputtered Will. "I . . . I've got to handle this myself. That's all."

"Still dreaming about being a hero, or you finally decided to step up to be a man?" asked Jake with grin. "So the Newtown boy has something to prove, huh? A'right, I can respect that, a man has gotta be able to solve his own problems. One of the only things my old man taught me before I left home."

"That's kinda funny, my Dad used to say the same thing."

"Okay little man, so how you gonna take care of this?" asked Jake as they both sat down on the decrepit furniture across from each other.

"That's why I'm here. I've got a plan, but I need a little help from you . . . insurance of sorts."

"Can't say I'm in the insurance business, Newtownie. What kind of insurance we talkin'?"

"If something happens to me, I need to know that my family will be safe."

"Is that all? Shoot, I offered to have me and the boys do that in the first place."

"Yeah," agreed Will, "but I need to do this my way. Okay?"

"Consider it done, brother. The Gutterpunks take care of their own."

"Thanks, Jake."

"No problem. That washed up Dead Boy will wish the Xiticix ate him alive before we get done with him."

"Good. Then there's just one more thing," said Will.

A look of mild disbelief crossed Jake's face. "Now I knew you'd gotten a bit big for your britches, boy, but ain't you askin' a lot for a punk who ain't no longer a part of this gang? I think you should know that your leverage is getting a little thin and this sure as hell ain't no monastery."

"Do I look like I'm stupid? This is the kind of help I can afford to pay for," Will stated confidently.

Jake relaxed his posture and put on his best impression of a sales rep. "Well then, young man, how may we be of assistance?"

* * *

The chilly night air combined with his nervousness caused William to shiver no matter how hard he tried not to. He was standing down the block from the Monster's favorite haunt, a bar named *A While Longer*. There were several nights a week where the Monster would go and drink for hours with the few people who tolerated him, former members of his infantry unit that fought in the war on Tolkeen. The place was out of the way and not everyone there liked him. From what Will had heard, the Headhunter Ian, the owner of the bar, and a bunch of the regulars didn't care for the Monster at all. All William could figure was that he kept going there just to spite them. Ian was well known in the community and a friend of his Dad. A nice fella who had recently become something of a local celebrity by seeing his war stories published in book form. Mother and the Monster said he was a fool just asking to get himself killed writing books under his real name. Ian just laughed it off and insisted he "never wrote nothin'. That he'd told them stories a thousand times and some S.O.B. was writing them down and publishing them through the Black Market." All Will knew was that Ian was a good guy. Likeable and kind. Someone his Dad had approved of. Of course, Will and Charlie had heard plenty of those stories first hand from the old fella. He even tried to comfort them when their father went MIA. He had advised them to keep hope, but to be realistic. He warned them that war changed the people who lived it, soldiers included, and that this war would have lasting ramifications. He had even brung them rolls and muffins on a few occasions, claiming to be in the neighborhood. Ian's visits stopped when the Monster moved in, but their altercations didn't stop there.

The Monster must have angered Ian considerably one night, because he came home with a black eye, fractured jaw and a mashed lip. He woke up the whole house, and screamed about 'who the hell did that old man think he was trying to tell him how to live? Of course, since he couldn't beat up an 'old man' like Ian, he beat up Mom instead that night. Another reason to hate him, William thought to himself.

After a night of boozing it up, the Monster would walk the few miles back to the house. Those nights were the worst, as he would come in drunk and riled up after reminiscing with his pals. For the first time ever, though, Will hoped he'd stick to his routine.

Before crouching in his current position between some makeshift trash bins made from wooden pallets and a parked hover jeep, William had screwed up the courage and walked past one of the windows of the bar to make sure the man he sought was still inside. Sure enough, there he sat at a booth with two other men around the same age. Luckily, he also had his back turned to the window and didn't notice the young man spying on him.

That had been two hours ago, and the wait was beginning to take its toll on Will's confidence. Much to his chagrin, he had become aware that he hadn't eaten dinner. Of course, his stomach was tied in knots from his nerves, so anything he would have eaten would have probably just come right back up anyway. Alone in the dark, cold and hungry, waiting to come face-to-face with his greatest nemesis, Will continued to think about all the wrongs the Monster had done to him and his family since coming into their lives.

As William argued the merit of this plan to himself, for no less than the eighth time, the volume of the noise coming from the bar spiked, signaling that someone had opened the door. Will's heart skipped a beat as the Monster was silhouetted in the doorway and stumbled out into the street.

All at once, William's anxiety was washed away by the anger welling up within him. This was the man responsible for all of his family's misery. The beast they all hated and feared. And it was time to put a stop to his tyranny.

Will waited for him to walk past his hiding place and shuffle a couple of blocks down the street before he dared to move to follow him. He muttered a prayer under his breath that the alcohol would dull the man's senses enough for him to follow a short distance unnoticed before what William hoped would be the final confrontation. At least the cold would keep most people indoors for the night.

After almost twenty minutes of moving from shadow to shadow, building to building, trying to stay out of sight, the man Will was tailing crossed a well lit section of road. It was apparently colder out than it felt to the adrenaline-fueled teen, because it had begun to snow. Will stood for a couple of seconds watching the flakes swirl about in the lights, blown about by the ever-increasing wind.

A sense of dread fell like a weight upon his chest as Will surveyed the surroundings. There were no good hiding places for at least forty feet, no cover even for a young man who was teased about being able to hide behind a corn stalk. He couldn't simply sprint across the patch of illumination either, as some of the snow had already melted into shallow puddles, dotting the street like a minefield. This one section of simple electric light could prove to be the undoing of the last few hours of William's work.

"He can't see me here, not here. Too many people around that could get in the way," Will thought. He did his best to steady himself, waiting for the Monster to trudge just a little further on. Taking a deep breath, the young man stepped into the pale yellow light. He did his best to move quickly and yet quietly around the growing puddles to make it to the safety of the shadows beyond. He was almost there, had almost made it across . . . and a shout echoed through the street from somewhere off behind him. Will froze in his tracks like a spooked white-tail deer. Surely his target would turn to investigate the noise and see him standing there like some toddler caught stealing cookies from his mother's counter.

Whether it was the alcohol, the man's sullen attitude, or perhaps sheer blind luck, the Monster continued on as if nothing had happened. It took Will a few of his rapid heartbeats to realize the man was still going and allow himself the luxury of exhaling. He finished picking his way through the gauntlet of water and light to the embrace of the darkness beyond.

Another fifteen minutes brought the Monster and his would-be stalker to a side road running through an industrial section of the 'Burbs. On one side of the rapidly-whitening path was a row of darkened, nondescript warehouses. On the other side, a lumber yard, where stacks of boards sat partially shrouded by the blowing snow. The only light came from flood lamps positioned to light up the lumber yard as a deterrent for thieves, though they only shone dimly on the street. This was it, the place William had been waiting for. It was secluded enough that it should keep others out of the way and let him do what needed to be done. Without a moment of hesitation, Will lowered his head and sped up his pace to close the gap between himself and the man who had ruined his family's life. His mind worked furiously over what he would say. How would he get his attention? Would the man even listen to what he had to say?

As thoughts spun through his mind, William lost track of how close he was getting. At about twelve paces from the man's back, Will realized he was almost on top of him.

"Hey!" his voice sounded louder than he had intended. The Monster spun and assumed a defensive stance to face what he must have assumed to be an attacker. His reaction time suggested that his reflexes weren't as slow as Will had hoped, and that could be bad news if things got ugly.

Shielding his eyes with one gloved hand, the Monster seemed to burn holes into William with his gaze. "Will?" the man called out confusedly. "What in Hades are you doin' out here?"

All at once, the bravado left Will. It vanished like morning dew under a midday sun. He was once again William Alder, a scared sixteen year-old boy who thought himself capable of standing as an adult and protecting his family. As he fumbled for the words, the man took a couple of steps closer and questioned him again, "What're you doing out at this time of night, in this weather?"

Will immediately took two steps back as his mind registered the threat the Monster posed if he got within arm's reach. Perhaps the fear is what jump started his mind again, but whatever the case, William once again felt the anger seething through him like boiling tar. "I came out here to find you."

"Me? Why, what's wrong, Will?" he asked, almost seeming concerned.

"What's wrong?" Will repeated, the words seeming to have the acrid taste of bile. "What's *wrong*?!" he exclaimed. Now the anger was boiling, and Will practically exploded.

"You have the nerve to ask me what's wrong, you son of a bitch?!"

The Monster's head rocked back at the outburst, and then his face changed to the callous expression Will had become quite familiar with. "This is about your mother, huh?"

"No," Will's voice was practically dripping in venom, "this is about my family, and about you." Will made sure to pause between the two, making it clear that the word "family" didn't include the Monster in the young man's definition. "I want you out of our life for good," he stated bluntly. "Get out and stay out of our lives."

The man raised a single eyebrow and let out an incredulous chuckle. "Don't you think you're being a little dramatic here, boy?"

"I'm not going to let you hurt them anymore."

"And who the hell are you to be making demands of me, little boy? You know what I think, I think that you got too used to not havin' a man around the house during the war. So when I set foot in that door it ruined your lil' world. Now you've grown a couple hairs in the right places and you think you can boot me back out the door because you don't like how I run things? An' just what made you think I'd pull up stakes on your say so? Huh?"

Will gritted his teeth so hard it felt as if they might shatter any second. But he managed to maintain his composure and fish a small black box from his jacket pocket. He tossed the box into the slush at the man's feet. The box popped open, disgorging a small metal object onto the ground beside it.

"The man who earned that medal was a decent man, a soldier, a hero. My father, Jonathan Alder. I'm hoping that somewhere deep down inside you is something that at least resembles the kinda' stuff he was made of. That maybe you'll have the sense to hear me out and do what's right."

The Monster was obviously taken aback at this display. He stood slack-jawed for a moment and wobbled in the breeze as he stared at the *Coalition States Cross for Bravery* lying on the snowy ground before him. After a long silence, the man's face contorted into a sneer as he snarled, "Why you ungrateful bastard! You have no idea the sacrifices I made on the battlefield, do you?! Fighting for years in that God-forsaken country against all manners of evil. Putting my life on the line to defend this entire country from those that would love nothing more than to slit the throat of people like us just for the pleasure of it. And you have the gall to try and get righteous with me?! You don't know what pain is, you pathetic little punk!"

The man lurched forward at William with malice burning in his eyes like red-hot coals. Will hardly had time to react before the Monster was practically on top of him. Stepping back and fumbling in his other jacket pocket, he managed to produce the second favor he had asked from Jake just in time to give his attacker pause. The enraged man skidded to a halt about three feet from Will as the teen brought the antiquated Colt .45 pistol up to chest level, grasped firmly in both hands with his finger on the trigger. He quickly thumbed the safety off with an audible click to let the man know he was deadly serious.

"I'm not just some punk kid throwing a temper tantrum." Anger and venom dripped from William's voice. "I'm gonna suggest you take my offer real serious, because I don't think you're gonna like the other option you've got."

The Monster appeared to recognize the gravity of the situation, because he appeared to relax his stance and acknowledge that William was in control of the situation. Unfortunately for William, that's exactly what he wanted him to think. Just as Will was about to speak again, the Monster's hands shot forward and seized the young man's wrists.

The ex-soldier's vise-like grip felt as if it were going to crush Will's wrists to a pulp. A resounding crack split the air as he inadvertently squeezed off a round. The Monster took the opportunity to throw the teen's arms to one side, forcing the pistol from his grip to clatter across the pavement. At the same time, Will was thrown off balance and hit the frozen ground. The impact knocked every last wisp of breath from his lungs, and Will had to fight to keep from blacking out.

The next thing Will knew he was being lifted back up. The Monster put him back on his feet with a grunt, only to deliver a right hook to his jaw, sending him sprawling into the chain-link fence that surrounded the lumber yard. Will managed to catch himself on it, not even having the presence of mind to consider whether or not it might be electrified. The good news was that the fence didn't deliver a high-voltage shock to the young man, the bad news was that he found himself being forced back into the metal barrier with a thick forearm across his throat. William tasted blood as his vision began to tunnel on the face of the man about to kill him.

The Monster practically foamed at the mouth now and was saying something. However, to Will it seemed as if his assailant were yelling from the bottom of a well, and he could barely make out the words as consciousness slipped away.

"Promise you'll come back, Will." He heard Charlie's words ring in his ears as sharp and real as day. It gave him strength. He couldn't give up now, he had to protect them.

As Will fought to keep from passing out, he looked for some way, any way, to break the man's hold and get free. If he could only breathe, he would have a fighting chance.

As luck would have it, he had been thrown into the fence with such force that it had partially dislodged the upper support rail on his right side. With a last-ditch effort, he flung his hand for the metal tubing and managed to catch hold of one end. Jerking forward with all of his might, he wrenched the piece of fencing free. A combination of a dull ring and muffled thud indicated that the makeshift weapon had found its mark as it impacted the side of the man's skull.

And just like that, Will was free. The Monster stumbled sideways, lost balance in the wet snow, and fell in a heap on the ground. William could do nothing but fall forward onto the ground, where he coughed and gasped for air. He knew he had come close to being killed. His head rang, his jaw ached, his back was already stiffening, and his wrists felt like they were on fire. He kneeled there in pain, trying to force his exhausted body to move again, knowing that a matter of a few feet away was a trained soldier who could finish him off at any moment.

Slowly, William managed to push himself up from the ground. The Monster groaned and gathered himself as well. As the Monster began to rise, Will remembered the pistol a short distance away. This was it. His life depended on getting to that gun before the Monster got to him again.

Time seemed to slow down and he felt as if he moved through molasses. Then he heard it: The heavy, sloshing footsteps of the Monster behind him. He feared he wasn't going to make it, but he had to try, just a little further . . .

Will snatched the gun from the ground and turned to see the Monster standing there in front of him. Smiling, unafraid. This time William stayed out of his reach. "I'll kill you where you stand," he choked out between gasps of the icy air.

With blood streaming down the side of his ashen face from the ragged cut the boy had delivered to him above his eye, the Monster growled, "No, son, I don't think you will. Like you said, your father was a decent man. As the son of such a respectable war-hero, are you really capable of killin' me? Killing anyone? No, I don't think so, especially not dear ol' Dad."

The truth cut him deeper than a Vibro-Knife ever could. Will raised the muzzle of the weapon and aimed it at the man he had once loved so fiercely. He forced himself to think about what that man had become.

"Dad, what happened to you?" William pleaded.

"Life happened to me, Son. Life ate me up and spit me out to come back here. To a place where everything reminds me every single day of what I lost. Of the fool I was and the world that left me behind."

"But we love you, Dad. We were so happy when they told us you were alive."

"I ain't feelin' the love right now," said the Monster who was once Jonathan Alder with a sneer and a sinister chuckle.

"Dad . . . it's the booze. If you stopped drinking and saw someone," pleaded Will.

"Ain't seeing no Fixer in a psych-ward. An' it ain't the booze. I need to drink to dull the pain, Willy Boy. Need it to make living with your worthless bitch mother, your pathetic cur brother, and your smart mouth tolerable. You understand, Willy Boy? Smart, smart Willy Boy? And now you think you're so smart you can tell your ol' man what to do. Is that it?! You tellin' me what to do?! ME!? Is that it?!"

"Dad . . . I . . . I . . ." was all Will could utter as sorrow consumed him. The boy's body shuddered with grief.

"Oh, boo hoo," chided the Monster as it chuckled at the boy's agony. "That's right, Willy Boy, cry. Poor baby, Daddy's come home a different man than you remember. Cry me a river, you worthless puke. I done all this for you . . . fer all o' ya, and you treat me with not one ounce of respect. Not one ounce."

"Dad, please stop. You're tearing us apart. Hurting Mom . . . Charlie . . ." weezed William, tears pouring down his face.

"You don't know what hurt means, boy," roared the Monster. "You don't have a clue about feeling loss."

"You're wrong about that," said Will with a snarl of his own.

"Oh? And what have you lost, Willy? A stupid toy? Your virginity? Puh, you think it's hard. You challenge me because I mighta slapped your worthless mother once or twice? Grow up, boy. Loss? Suffering? You don't know the meaning of the words. You all make me sick. You think you've suffered? You think you sacrificed?" bellowed the Monster as it gnashed its teeth and spat blood. "I'll give you something to cry about, Will. I'll give you all something to cry about when I git home."

That's when William realized the truth. Suddenly, his body stopped shaking, and the tears dried up. A weird calm fell over him. He looked at the Monster and almost felt sorry for it. Almost. It was like a wounded animal that snapped at anyone that came near it. That made the Monster dangerous, cruel and murderous. One of these days, lashing out in pain, it was going to cripple or kill Mom or Charlie. That's why they put mad dogs down, to prevent them from hurting anyone. It seemed so simple, now.

"So tell me, Will," taunted the Monster, its one inhuman eye glowing eerily in the dim lit, its fetid breath rising like steamy brimstone from its mouth and nose. "What is it you've lost that hurts you so bad?"

William shook his head and drew in an unsteady breath.

"My father died in the war."

Three rapid-fire shots rang out in the darkness. Hardly worth noticing in a place like the 'Burbs.

The Monster's face contorted into an angry scowl and blood spat from its mouth as if it was trying to spit out one last barb or curse, before it crumpled to the ground, its blood staining the fresh snow red.

The body wouldn't be found for two days. By then the scavengers of the 'Burbs had plucked out the bionic eye and picked the body clean. The murder was written off as the work of Cyber-Snatchers. The man's wife would mourn his passing and lament that the war had changed a good man and loving father into something cruel and best not spoken about. The elder son would try to comfort her and his brother as best he could. He'd encourage them to remember the good times before the Monster and appreciate the life they had. However, the death of his father had seemed to change the boy in ways his mother couldn't understand, and it made her sad. Something was gone from his eyes.

Though the official report told of one man's demise, there were two deaths that night. One of a man who had lost his soul. The other the lost innocence of his son, who strove to be the man his father had taught him to be. Sad proof that not all casualties of war are to be found on the battlefield.

Me and Mr. Choke

By Taylor White

Herbert Snyder sat at his desk, having just returned from his mid-morning coffee break. It was now ten-fifteen. As per his usual routine, Herbert planned to spend the next ten minutes staring at the unsorted files and paperwork that had filled the shelf behind him the night before. He had perfected a technique where his fingers would peruse the files automatically, leaving his mind to wander freely. He could only get away with ten minutes of staring; that was his record. The average was seven minutes, before someone would notice and comment.

An hour later, Herbert got into an altercation with Beverly, an older woman who sat in the cubicle across from his. The altercation had to do with the colored stickers they used to number their files. Beverly accused him of pilfering from her supply, which was not true. Herbert had simply asked for more stickers and they were given to him by Lenny Rogers, the daytime manager of Floor Twenty Medical Records Department. Arguing with Beverly would be the first exciting thing to happen in the office for weeks, though it would not be the last exciting thing to happen.

At exactly noon, Herbert always broke for lunch. He had his lunch break timed precisely so he could make it out of the office and to the street level, where a number of food vendors hawked at passers-by. He had just enough time to grab a hot dog or sandwich, eat it on his way back inside the office, and hide in the office restroom for five minutes, in which time he would either stare at the inside of a stall, or consider killing himself. When Herbert had to work on the weekends, there would be no vendors, and he was forced to eat in the Floor Twenty Hospital Cafeteria, where the long lines would offer him little time to daydream of taking his own life.

Herbert was scheduled to leave at seven in the eening, and to assure that, he would clean his workspace at six-thirty, and hide in either the office restroom (where he would daydream, not of suicide, but of dinner and the basketball game), or in the loose filing section, an immense depository of unsorted and largely unnecessary paperwork.

At six-twenty, a large file was dropped onto his desk by Lenny, his boss.

Lenny Rogers was much younger than Herbert, and much better educated. Lenny was fresh from a Chi-Town Business Management Program, and ended up in the glamorous world of Medical Records. He was also a smug little twerp, never passing up an opportunity to flaunt his credentials. He especially enjoyed picking on Herbert, for some reason. It seemed every week that Lenny would call him into his office with some sort of reprimand regarding some minutiae in his work. 'You used the wrong colored sticker on this record, Herbert.' 'That font isn't approved by management, Herbert.' 'You're using too many manila folders, Herbert.'

"Look who it is, Herbert. Your old friend, Mr. Jackson," Lenny said, obviously taking joy in tormenting him.

Herbert's heart sank as the enormous volume slammed on his desk. Alex Jackson was scheduled for three more radiology tests this week, and Herbert would need to prepare his chart by making sure the paperwork was up to date and complete. Once the chart returned, it would have to be sorted, analyzed for errors and then sent off to another department for digital entry into the department's data servers, and finally filed away into permanent paper storage. The process would add at least another hour and a half to his day.

Herbert knew Alex Jackson's chart, nearly by heart. He was no one special, a mid-level citizen just like Herbert, who had developed some sort of alien cancer when he was younger. Mr. Jackson had "slummed" a lot as a teenager, venturing outside the confines of the Chi-Town fortress city to seek excitement in the *'Burbs,* the squalid mass of humanity and D-Bees that surrounded the city. The virtual army of doctors who had seen him in agreement that he was exposed to something unnatural during one of these jaunts, which left him in his current condition. They were not in agreement over the exact cause, however. Perhaps it was something he ate. Perhaps it was a venereal disease. Perhaps it was a magical curse put upon him by a demon, evil spirit, or insane wizard. They speculated a lot, but no one ever really figured it out.

When he had to work on this chart, Herbert was always reminded of the controversy when Mr. Jackson had first been diagnosed. The *Chi-Town Internal Security Forces* wanted him isolated from the citizenry, afraid that his sickness might spread. Mr. Jackson's doctors were convinced that the cancer was not infectious and going to "leak out," as they put it. In the end, no one knew what to expect, but it had been twenty years now, and Mr. Jackson was, fortunately, the sole recipient of his own unique sickness. A sickness that left him in a near-vegetative state, unable to speak, and mostly too weak to even move.

For twenty years, doctors and scientists poked and prodded Alex Jackson with every kind of test imaginable, even bringing in geneticists, xenobiologists, and oncological specialists from as far away as Lone Star. Mr. Jackson was a test monkey, living his life from one painful, debilitating test to another. Herbert liked Alex Jackson because he knew there was at least one person in the world who was more miserable than he was. Nevertheless, he groaned when Lenny sat the chart in front of him, suspecting that Lenny had held onto it all day just to drop it on him at the last moment.

Herbert left the office at eight-forty, and arrived at the train station at eight-fifty. If he had been able to get out of work on time, he could have simply taken a cab home, and stopped at a local pharmacy on the way. He could have been home in fifteen minutes, enjoying a beer and watching the Level Twenty basketball team mop up the floor with Level Seventeen. The Level Seventeen team had no defense, and wouldn't stand a chance against the most aggressive basketball team in Chi-Town. Instead, Herbert had to take a train down to a twenty-four hour pharmacy in the lower levels of the city. The whole trip would take another hour. He was going to be late coming home, but he would have his wife's medication. At the very least, she wouldn't be able to yell at him for forgetting that.

The train ride going to Level Six was quiet, having almost no passengers aboard. Herbert would sometimes look at the other people on the train and imagine why they were heading down to the lower levels. You could sometimes guess by the way people looked what their business was. Most were business people or laborers on their home, but a few were interesting characters.

The young man with the green Mohawk and skull tattoos was a City Rat, probably on his way back from a drug deal or running numbers, or maybe he was on his way to a rumble on one of the lower levels. Yes, City Rats were found inside the fortress city as well as in the 'Burbs. He was always surprised at how may Topsiders, 'Burbies and out-of-towners didn't know that.

The strung-out blonde with the faded red dress and make-up to cover the bruises was a call girl, probably on her way to meet a client or hook up with her pimp or drug dealer.

The old woman in old clothes pushing a shopping cart was probably just a poor Downsider coming back from visiting a family member higher up in the city, or she might be a wandering street person.

The muscular guy with the intense eyes, who kept tapping his finger was probably an undercover Internal Security Officer, or maybe someone who didn't belong in the city, an Outsider. They sometimes found their way in, with a forged Day Pass or as a limited time favor or via bribery.

Thankfully, the pharmacy was only two blocks from the train station. If Herbert walked fast, kept his head low, and avoided eye contact, he could make it there and back in time to catch the next train and avoid any harassment from the locals. The faster he moved, the less he would have to deal with the smell of the lower level; a pungent pot-pourri of sewage, stale air and desperation.

Just as luck would have it, there was a long line at the pharmacy. It was the first Monday of the month, so all the dregs were cashing in their tickets for government medication. It was no secret that the Chi-Town government handed out drugs to keep the oppressed, hopeless masses on the bottom levels sedated. A medicated populace was a docile populace.

Herbert sighed as he stood at the back of the line. In front of him, the scum of Chi-Town, the disgusting, unwashed, ignorant bottom-feeders, waited for their government-sanctioned fix. They hacked and coughed and spit yellow phlegm onto the floor, windows, or each other. An old man vomited on the person in front of him, who slugged the guy, dropping him to the floor. As the line moved forward, people simply stepped over the man. One even snatched his medicine ticket.

At ten-fifteen, Herbert made it back to the train station, his wife's anxiety pills in hand. He was alone on the platform, with only the sounds of the street outside breaking the silence. He checked his watch. Ten-eighteen. A rat, nearly as long as Herbert's arm, came out of the darkness behind a smashed-up vending machine. It sniffed the air, met eyes with Herbert, then crossed the platform and disappeared down the stairs to the street. Herbert nervously checked his watch again. Ten-nineteen.

'The train is late,' he thought. 'It is supposed to be here at ten-twenty. It's going to be late.' Fear started to grip him like a vice. His heart sped up. His hands became clammy and sweaty. He rubbed them on his jacket. He started considering alternate routes home. He could take a cab, but these lower-level cabbies would take one look at him and rob him blind by taking the long way. He could walk, or maybe steal a bicycle. Maybe he could call Margaret and she could send a car. She would be angry, but at least he could hand her her pills to lessen the verbal abuse.

At ten-twenty-one, Herbert turned and started to go the same way as the giant rat, back onto the street to find a payphone. Just then, he felt a familiar gust of wind coming from the tunnel, and his fear melted away. A few seconds later, the growing roar of machinery and lights beaming from the tunnel signaled the arrival of the train. Desperate to leave Level Six, Herbert rushed through the door as soon as it was open enough for him to fit and threw himself into a seat. He checked his hands, they were still clammy and shaking. He set the bag of pills on the seat next to him and feverishly rubbed his hands on his pants leg.

Herbert failed to notice, in his mad dash into the safe confines of the train, that his car was occupied. Herbert usually peered through the windows of the cars at the other passengers to gauge which car would be the safest. If he had checked this time, he would have noticed the four City Rats at the far end. If he had noticed these particular 'Rats, he would have climbed aboard a different car, or even waited for another train. It was only after the doors closed and the train started up that Herbert realized he was suddenly in a compromising situation. He looked around the car and saw the 'Rats, and immediately shot his eyes away, snatching up the bag of pills as he did so and tucking it into his coat pocket. The 'Rats saw this as a sign of fear and apprehension. Two qualities they always looked for in a victim.

"Whatcha got there, old man?" one of the 'Rats asked him, swaggering over to Herbert. He couldn't have been more than seventeen, though the scars and needle marks, visible through his black mesh shirt, spoke of a much longer life. The kid stood directly in front of Herbert, tall and lean, decorated with metal spikes. Herbert stared at the floor. When he spoke, his words came out in a voice raspy with fear.

"Nothing. I don't have anything."

The other 'Rats surrounded Herbert, one on each side, and a third, a girl, standing beside Black Mesh Shirt. Herbert mentally named the one to his left No Hair, and the one to his right Metal Teeth, and the girl was simply The Girl. Herbert couldn't help but give names to people and things that stressed or scared him. It was his only way to bring order to a situation that was quickly getting out of his control.

"We saw the bag, Lofty," Metal Teeth hissed.

"Do you know where you are, man?" asked No Hair. "We're the Six Sixty Sixers. We own every train that passes through Level Six."

"That's right. And you owe us a toll, old man," said Black Mesh Shirt.

Metal Teeth reached into Herbert's coat. Frozen with fear, Herbert could do nothing. He felt the liner and pinched the material.

"Nice coat," Metal Teeth said, his breath smelling like the spray stuff you use on squeaky door hinges.

"Forget the coat. I want what's in the bag," The Girl finally spoke up. Her voice was harsh, tired, strung out. Herbert briefly glanced at her face. Her sad eyes poked out, contrasted against the grayness of sunken sockets. She rubbed Black Mesh Shirt's arm affectionately. "Get it for me, baby."

Black Mesh Shirt produced a black hard plastic wand from behind his leg. He flipped a small switch on the handle and Herbert could hear a small whine of energy as the wand activated. The 'Rat raised it high and brought it down on Herbert's head. Not hard; just hard enough so the device would discharge a shock into Herbert's neural system.

Stunned and disoriented, Herbert was still keenly aware of the 'Rats kicking and punching him in the head and chest as he lay on the floor, unable to get up or even call out for help. As the train pulled into a stop on Level Ten, Black Mesh Shirt snatched up Margaret's anxiety medicine, and the gang ran out of the car onto the platform.

Passengers boarded after the 'Rats left, stepping over Herbert to get to a seat. Although the effects of the Neural Mace wore off by the time the train got to Level Fifteen, Herbert continued to just lie on the floor of the car.

Herbert arrived home at around ten-fifty. He swiped his key card into the door of his apartment and let himself in. The apartment was dark, and mostly quiet. The only sounds were coming from his bedroom; the unmistakable rhythmic "squeak-bump-squeak-bump" of his wife having sex with Corporal Dwayne Lee. Herbert, without stopping, crossed over to the tiny kitchen and grabbed a beer from the refrigerator.

The basketball game was over, but at least the news was about to come on. Herbert sunk onto the old brown sofa he and Margaret had been given as a wedding present. He turned on the television. The rhythm of the couple in the next room skipped a beat from the sudden sound, and then started back up again. Herbert had to sit through a used car advertisement, two propaganda spots proclaiming the glory of the Coalition Army, one more propaganda spot detailing figures of how many humans were killed by demons last month and asking 'What are YOU doing to secure humanity's future?' and finally a commercial for government medication.

As the Eleven O'Clock News came on, the noise in the bedroom became more intense. The squeaking was louder, the bumping faster, and the sounds of Margaret and Corporal Lee grunting, screaming, and swearing started to drown out the television. Herbert turned the volume up.

Right as the newscaster finished the first story of the night, one about a successful raid on an illegal operation on Level Twenty-Five selling books and other 'Educational Contraband,' the rancor in the bedroom rose to a high point, punctuated by a stream of verbal obscenities from Margaret, and then fell silent. The next news story was about how the price of gasoline was going to rise again due to bandit attacks on Chi-Town's refineries. Herbert groaned; that meant cab and bus fares were going to rise as well.

The bedroom door opened and Corporal Lee walked out, wearing only a pair of black boxer shorts. He came in and sat next to Herbert on the couch.

"You startled me out here," he said.

Herbert didn't respond. Although he had learned to accept Margaret's extramarital activities, that was no reason to interact with her suitors. He hoped Dwayne would find the situation awkward and leave.

"Level Twenty lost. I don't know where they were at tonight. I had two hundred credits on that damn game," he continued. A small pang of anger pricked Herbert. The bastard told him how it ended.

Margaret stormed out of the bedroom in a bathrobe. She snatched the remote control from Herbert's hand and lowered the television volume to half of where it was.

"Herbert, can't you keep this damn thing at a reasonable level? I swear, if I have to hear from the neighbors one more time about you playing this thing loud, I'll divorce you."

Herbert emptied the rest of his beer into his mouth and swallowed. "Sorry, dear," he said flatly. She was lying. She enjoyed Herbert's money too much to divorce him. Without him, she'd have to get a job, and that would leave little time to sit around, pop prescription pills, screw other guys, and get fatter.

"Alright, well, I gotta run. I'm pulling Border Patrol in the morning," Dwayne said as he rose up off the couch. He and Margaret went back into the bedroom and dressed. Five minutes later, Dwayne was on his way out. He patted Herbert on the shoulder, as if they were old chums, saying what a good guy he was, and kissed Herbert's wife long and hard by the doorway. Herbert tried to pay attention to the television, but instead watched his wife and this other man make out with a dull anger.

"I don't suppose there is any dinner left," Herbert assumed.

"It's in the fridge. We didn't eat much of it. You're welcome to what's left."

Taking a second look at her husband in the glow of the television set, Margaret turned on the lights. "What happened to you, Herbert?" she asked, the same way you would ask a child who had tried to fly by tying a towel around his neck and leaping off the top of the staircase.

"I was mugged on the train today. It hurts like a son-of-a-bitch," Herbert replied, with a shred of hope that she would fetch him an ice pack or some salve.

"Did you get my pills?"

"I'm sorry, dear, the guys who beat me senseless took them," Herbert said with hurt in his voice.

"Don't take that tone with me," Margaret scolded, "You should know better than to go to that pharmacy on Level Six. We can afford the extra few credits to go to the good place. If you weren't so cheap you wouldn't have been attacked, and I wouldn't be five pills away from a stress-induced heart attack."

"I'm sorry, dear. I'll call the doctor tomorrow and get a new prescription."

"Good. Well, I'm very tired. I spent all day cleaning up around here, by myself, so I'm going to turn in." Margaret made sure to accentuate "by myself," even though Herbert knew from looking at the condition of the apartment it was more likely she spent the whole day with Corporal Lee.

"By the way," she yelled from the bedroom. "A package arrived for you today. By courier, too. I think it might be from your grandfather. Don't let that crazy old coot pass off any more garbage onto you. Remember what happened after his last package didn't make it through customs?"

Herbert remembered. His grandfather, Artemis Snyder, had tried to sneak a crate full of magazines into Chi-Town as a gift to Herbert. Grandpa Snyder was probably the only person in the world who genuinely liked Herbert, and the feeling was mutual. Of course, the crate was discovered, and seized by the city's border guards. Herbert was held in a cell for a week for questioning, where he was interrogated mercilessly. For a year afterward, Herbert was under surveillance by Chi-Town Internal Security Inspectors. Herbert sent his grandfather an audio message asking him to please never send any more packages. Not only did Herbert fear for his own safety, but he was worried that the Coalition Army would use the packages to track down Grandpa Snyder.

"And keep that damn T.V. down!" Margaret screeched before closing the bedroom door.

Herbert picked the package up off a nightstand by the door. It wasn't very big, and had already been opened and resealed. A red stamp reading "Chi-Town Customs Office: Approved" was next to his name and address. He didn't recognize the handwriting on the package. Herbert had gotten proficient at recognizing handwriting through his job. Many of the Doctors, Cyber-Docs, and Body Fixers at Level Twenty Hospital had very sloppy penmanship, some signing documents with a squiggly line decipherable only by the trained eye.

Inside the box was a small digital audio recorder, a set of earphones, and a typed note that read 'PLAY ME' with a picture of a green triangle. Never one to disobey an order, Herbert did what the note said. He fastened the earphones in and hit the button with the small green triangle.

A man's voice came on. A voice Herbert had never heard before. He checked the running time of the digital file; it would last a few minutes. Herbert grabbed himself another beer, opted not to eat the cold meatloaf in the fridge, and sat on the couch.

"Mr. Herbert Snyder, I hope this message reaches you in good health. I apologize for the odd manner of delivery. I do not know if you are literate beyond your experience with medical terminology. My name is Clyde Westphal. I am a colleague of your grandfather's. Well, I was, anyway. I'm afraid I have bad news for you. Artemis recently passed away. He died peacefully, in his sleep, at the site of our most recent excavation."

Herbert's heart sank at the news of his grandfather's death. He set the bottle down on the coffee table and held his head in his hands, full of sorrow.

On the recording, Clyde's message continued, "His passing is a tragedy, Herbert. Artemis was a good man. A noble, honest man, and a salesman like no other. One of the finest excavators out here. I consider it an honor to have worked with him. He taught me much about how the world was before the Great Cataclysm. It was a world he was truly in love with. I realize how hard this must be for you, but there is a bright side. Artemis often spoke of a collection of artifacts he had stashed away in the 'Burbs. I think he sensed that he was not long for this world, because soon before he died, he divulged to me the location of this stash. There was one condition, he said. He made me promise that I would share his artifacts with *you*, his last living heir. I am a man of my word, Herbert, and I am contacting you to uphold my end of the agreement."

His grief briefly abated by curiosity and a small twinge of excitement, Herbert perked up and listened intently.

"I need you to come to the 'Burbs tonight. There is a bar about ten blocks south of the South Gate. It's called *A While Longer*.

"Your grandfather told me about a book he gave you as a child. He said you used to love listening to Pre-Cataclysm music, and you own a book of songs. I hope you still own this book, because I need you to bring it with you. If I don't see you by two in the morning, I'll assume you aren't coming at all. I'm afraid I won't be able to wait any longer than that. Otherwise I look forward to meeting you, Herbert. Goodbye."

The audio recording ended, and Herbert removed the earphones. He checked his watch; it was only eleven-twenty. Herbert moved swiftly into the hall closet and dug through a box tucked way in the back. He was feeling almost rejuvenated. He was still very sad about his grandpa passing away, but there would be plenty of time to grieve later. He very much wanted to meet this man, Clyde Westphal. He wanted to ask him about Grandpa Snyder, and see this amazing collection of artifacts.

It mattered little to Herbert what the artifacts were worth monetarily. He had never understood Grandpa Snyder's passion for digging up the past and selling it off for a profit. Herbert had been propositioned by Black Market Excavators and historians before. They had nothing but a truck full of old soda cans, crumbling magazines, scratched DVDs, and photographs of people and places Herbert had never known or cared about. There was no doubt that his grandfather's collection was similar useless trash. Nevertheless, he wanted to see it, to hold it, to try to get to know his grandfather better through his treasures.

At the bottom of the box in the hall closet, Herbert found a dusty book full of sheet music. The music had been intended to be played on a piano, something Herbert had never seen before, and had not heard since he was a child. He flipped through the book, reminiscing about singing along with his grandfather so many years ago.

Herbert snapped out of his nostalgia when he looked up at the hall clock. Eleven-twenty-five. Herbert ran into the kitchen and rummaged under the sink. He pulled out a brown paper grocery bag and slid the book into it. Then as quietly as possible, Herbert crept out of the apartment and walked briskly to the sidewalk to hail a taxi.

The whole time he walked to the street, and during the taxi ride down to the South Gate, Herbert held tightly onto the book, shoving it deep into his coat. The last thing he wanted was to be seen by Internal Security carrying 'Educational Contraband.' If they caught him smuggling a book through the city, he'd be imprisoned, interrogated, he'd lose his job, his apartment, and his wife. And he really liked that apartment. It was clean, rent-controlled, and in close proximity to the grocery store and train station.

It was five minutes after midnight when Herbert arrived at the South Gate. He tried to bribe the cab driver to take him out to the 'Burbs, but the guy didn't want to deal with the hassle of getting his cab back into the city. If the Border Patrol even suspected him of suspicious activity, they would impound the car, tear it apart, and detain the driver for a week. If he was lucky, they would let him tow it to a garage to be rebuilt.

It wasn't so bad getting out of Chi-Town. There was a quick examination for the presence of magic or psychic abilities, inhuman qualities, strange mutations or any other abnormalities. Then, a quick criminal background check. The examination occurred swiftly; those leaving the city were more or less shoved out the door while Dog Boys sauntered up and down the line, sniffing each person for an indication of illegal activity while another Border Guard inspected identification cards, snapping headshots for identification via the face recognition Citizens and Criminal Record Database (CCRD). This time of night, hardly anyone was looking to get outside the city; mainly rich teenagers looking for a wild night in the 'Burbs. Herbert was in and out of line in less than five minutes.

Herbert was positively terrified he would be frisked before leaving the city. His heart pounded in his chest and his hands and face sweated. He kept his eyes low and tried his best to look sick. He figured maybe if he sweated enough, shook enough, and his skin went pale enough, they would let him pass through quickly and not wish to touch him. One of the Dog Boys sniffed at him, the mutant's nose trying to smell through his lie. The mutant's eyes narrowed slightly, but then it moved on without making a sound.

Herbert and the others in line with him were ushered down a metal corridor, through a large blast door, and finally out the South Gate. Herbert's feet touched the soaking wet mud, just barely sinking in. He looked up at the night sky, the stars barely visible against the lights of the 'Burbs and the massive Chi-Town fortress city behind him. A small drizzle of rain hit him, cooling his face. The cold night air filled his lungs, the flavor of fresh air saturating him. Inside his chest, his heart pounded with the exhilaration brought about by unrestrained freedom and the unknown dangers of the 'Burbs. It was the first time in thirty years that Herbert Snyder had set foot outside of Chi-Town.

* * *

It was easy to find a cab in the Old Town 'Burb near the fortress wall. Here the 'Burbs looked like a sprawling modern city, but within minutes the buildings began to shrink and the neighborhood began to look shabby. The driver knew exactly where he wanted to go, and got him to the general location in what Herbert imagined must have been record time.

Herbert's initial reaction to this part of the 'Burbs was that it was very much like Chi-Town's lower levels. It was dirty – and not the grit of an inner-city, nor the boiler-room atmosphere, nor the streets reeking of sewer stench – the 'Burbs had a much more natural filth to it, if the distinction can even be made. Here in the 'Burbs, the Chi-Town government had little control. This decadent New Town 'Burb, barely more than a Shanty Town, was beneath their radar. This meant the inhabitants were free to think and live any way they wanted. Well, almost. And as he walked through the streets after midnight, he saw only a few people outside, but could peer into homes and bars and gaze at the multitude of faces inside. There was a lightness to their expression. Nothing like the crushing despair he felt or the cattle call expression of the worker drones he saw every day on the faces of citizens in Chi-Town. Herbert felt he could relax, as if no one was watching over his shoulder, waiting for him to slip up.

He checked his watch and saw it was a quarter to one. He had been wandering for nearly ten minutes before he realized he didn't really know where he was going. Herbert stopped, looked around, and surveyed his surroundings. There was nothing but crumbling old buildings and the occasional passer-by. He had no way to tell where he was or in what direction he was going. The cabbie who had dropped him at the edge of this 'Burb told him he'd be able to catch a local taxi to get the rest of the way, but he hadn't seen a single one yet.

"Hey there," a voice said behind him. Her voice was soft, and smooth. It was actually rather soothing. Herbert turned and saw a young woman wearing a green mini-skirt and stockings. She was thin, and only a little dirty. Her make-up was liberally applied, tricking Herbert into thinking she was more attractive than she really was.

"Hi. I'm looking for this bar. It's called *A While Longer*. Do you know where it is?" Herbert asked. He felt he should have been apprehensive, meeting a strange woman in the 'Burbs, in the dark, alone. For some reason, though, he did not. She made him feel strangely at ease.

"Sure, Honey, it's about a block that way, and two more that way," she replied, punctuating her directions by pointing her fingers.

"Thank you, I have to be going."

"What's your hurry, Honey? I know what you've come here for. Just to see me, right?" she whispered. In Herbert's mind, that suddenly seemed very true. He had come to the 'Burbs to meet her. He had been waiting all day in anticipation of seeing the girl in the green mini-skirt. When the girl came closer, he could see something he had not noticed earlier. It had been hidden from him before, due to the dim, flashing street lights, but the girl's forehead was a road map of large, bulging, red veins. They pulsated under her skin sickeningly. Herbert was shocked out of his spell at the horrific sight. When he recoiled, the veins pulsed faster and more intensely. Herbert felt the need for the girl's body rise up inside him, even stronger. Only by screaming a string of vulgarities was he able to stop himself from throwing the girl against a wall and ravishing her wildly.

"D-Bee! D-Bee! Mutant! Monster! Get away from me! Help! Someone help! There's a D-Bee here!! Get away, monster!" Herbert screamed as he tore away from the girl and ran off down the street, the mud and filth splashing his coat and pants.

Herbert ran, and ran, and ran. He ran as fast as he could. His lungs burned like fire. His legs felt like jelly. His saliva tasted like acid. His head pounded as hard as his heart. Finally, he leaned up against a wall to catch his breath. He could not remember the last time he had run like that. Once the fear subsided, he laughed a little. He could also not re-member the last time he laughed, at all. His body screamed at him, suddenly alive after decades of disuse.

Herbert stood there, against the wall, wondering what Margaret was doing. Was she still asleep? Was she with another man? Had she woken up and noticed her husband had left? Did she think he had left for good, or just gone to buy her a Black Market perscription? Herbert suddenly remembered he had not left her an audio message explain-ing where he was. He found himself hoping she figured he had left for good. Maybe she would pack up and move out and disappear. Maybe he would never go back to her. Maybe she could just keep the apartment.

Remembering where he was and what he was supposed to be doing, the Coalition Citi-zen looked around. There was a building across the street with its lights still on, and oc-cupied with people. This one had three floors, and was carefully constructed from brick and concrete, instead of hollowed out vehicles, rusting patchwork sheet metal, or rotting wood. Above the door was a sign, and a graphic of a cartoon beer mug.

Herbert concentrated hard on the sign, trying to read it. He recognized each letter; he had seen them before at work. He tried to relate the words on the sign to words he had seen at work. He knew the first letter, it was an 'A', by itself. The last two took some time for him to figure out. He ran through the names of doctors he knew, diseases and medical maladies he had read about, and though the extrapolation took a few minutes, he did figure it out. Of all the luck, he had run straight to it: *A While Longer*.

Unsure of how to approach the place, Herbert crept up to one of the large storefront windows. He wiped the rain off the glass and peered inside. He could only see a few 'Burb Folks, as Herbert had come to dub them, drinking alcohol, sitting quietly. It actu-ally looked rather warm and inviting inside, not at all the seedy dive he had expected. Herbert hoped they accepted credits, because he surely wanted a drink of something deli-cious.

Something in the corner of the room caught Herbert's attention. It was an older gentle-man, wearing a dark khaki jumpsuit. He was waving and smiling at Herbert, motioning for him to come inside. Herbert opened the door and stepped inside the cozy bar.

It was much warmer and dryer inside, and the aroma of food from the kitchen tickled his nostrils. Herbert scuffed his feet on a mat by the door, and noted, for the first time, how muddy his shoes and pants were. A couple of 'Burb Folks in the bar looked up, and seeing nothing of interest, only a city person wiping the mud off his shoes, went back to their drinks and conversation.

Clutching his old songbook against his chest, Herbert walked through the bar area to a table in the corner where two men sat. One was the gentleman in the khaki jumpsuit. The other seemed to be about the same age, but was dressed all in black. His white hair was matted and unkempt. His white beard was the same. In front of them both was a tall, clear bottle of some kind of brown liquid.

The older gentleman motioned for Herbert to sit. Herbert did, keeping his songbook close. "Welcome, Herbert," he finally said. "I'm glad you were able to make it. It's good to finally meet you."

"Thank you. Are you Mr. Westphal?"

"I am. But you can call me Clyde."

"Um, thanks Clyde, but how did you know what I looked like?"

"Your Granddad had a couple of vid-letters from you."

"Oh. Yes, of course. Uh, nice to meet you too. Who is this?"

"A local. Job and I were just discussing . . . what were we discussing, Job?" chuckled Clyde.

"All those who provide free drinks for old preachers are blessed by God."

Herbert's face twisted in confusion.

"I know," Clyde agreed. "I can only talk to him for so long. He's really very drunk right now."

"I brought the song book. I want to know about my grandfather," Herbert said, hoping that changing the subject would remove the smelly old prophet.

"Of course. We'll discuss this shortly. My colleague is making use of the restroom. Once he returns, you and I will talk. In the meantime, can I offer you a drink?"

Unsure of whether he should allow the semi-transparent brown juice in the bottle to touch his lips, but not wanting to appear rude in front of this man, Herbert searched for a response. He did want a drink, but things were different in the 'Burbs. The contents of this bottle might be too much for him. "Well, I don't usually, I mean, I haven't in a long time. It's not that I don't want to, but . . ."

"It's perfectly fine, Herbert. Just have a little, to calm you down and warm you up." Clyde poured a small amount of brown liquid in a glass. When the light hit it just right, it had a golden sheen to it. Calming down seemed like a fantastic idea to Herbert. He took the glass and poured it down his throat.

Although the golden-brownish juice was no warmer than the rest of the room, it burned Herbert's throat intensely. It's not that Herbert never drank, it's just the fact he had never drank 'Burb Whiskey before. Or 'Burb Bourbon. "Burbon." Herbert smiled to himself at his own cleverness.

"You like it? It's the best in the bar," Clyde said, as if he had distilled and bottled it himself.

"It's very strong," Herbert replied, "Margaret . . . my wife, she usually buys the government stuff. It's terrible, but it gets me drunk."

"I see. Well, have as much as you like."

Herbert poured a little more in the glass and raised it to his lips. Out of the corner of his eye, a man of incredible stature approached. Fearful, Herbert sat the glass down and turned to take in this titan.

"Herbert, this is my assistant and bodyguard, Charles. Charles, this is our man, Herbert."

Charles was nearly seven feet tall, Herbert estimated. He was dressed in camouflage pants and a grey tank-top. Herbert could only stare and admire Charles' physique. It was as if the man was carved out of marble. Seven feet tall and all muscle. Over the shirt, Charles had a harness and neck brace which connected to a device which he wore under his clothes. Herbert could only guess what the purpose of the harness was, but he reasoned it had something to do with his impressive size.

Charles smiled, took Herbert's hand, and shook it vigorously. Herbert took his hand back and examined it to make sure it had not been crushed. Charles probably could have crushed Herbert's head in with his bare hands, he reckoned. Hell, he could probably crush anything in those hands.

Remembering his manners, Herbert said, "It's a pleasure, Sir." His voice sounded weak and mousy. His hand felt like it had been run over by a car.

"Same here," replied the giant. He turned to Clyde and added, "Check this guy out. Acts like he's never seen a Juicer before."

"He probably hasn't," chuckled Clyde.

Charles took the seat next to Clyde, ushering the drunk old preacher away. Job stumbled across the room and slid into a stool at the bar.

"Having a rough night?" asked the Juicer of Herbert.

"What do you mean?"

"Somebody did that to your face."

In all the excitement, he had forgotten he had been attacked early that evening.

"Oh yes, I almost forgot, I was mugged this evening."

"Almost forgot, eh?" grinned the Juicer. "I like that."

Herbert came back to his senses and took his drink. What a strange world it was outside Chi-Town. Strange, but exciting.

"Charles, I need you to stand watch outside while Herbert and I talk. Stay discreet, but I want to know the first sign of the authorities."

"Yes Sir. You got it," said Charles with a grin. The Juicer stood and patted Herbert lightly on the back. "Relax, pal. It's not so bad outside the city, now is it? You should enjoy this. Live for once."

Herbert tried to smile at the giant, but his back felt like it had been gone over with a jackhammer. Charles snickered at Herbert's pained expression and walked outside, where the rain had started picking up and a cold wind had started to blow.

"Do you have the book, Herbert?"

"Yes. I really want to talk to you about my grandfather."

"Herbert, I'm afraid we don't have much time."

Herbert looked at his watch. It was ten minutes after one. "What are you talking about? You said you could only be here until two. We have plenty of time."

"I shouldn't be in the 'Burbs at all, Herbert. Even as we speak, there are Coalition Soldiers prowling the streets, looking for me."

"Why? What did you do!?"

"I smuggle books. I teach people to read. Worse in the Coalition's eyes, I teach non-humans to read. I hold seminars on how the Coalition government is distorting and perverting history. I educate, and I try to make a little bit of money from it. That makes me a very dangerous enemy of the State."

"Is that what my grandfather did? You said you worked with him."

"Oh no. Artemis was no educator. He was a businessman. He helped me spread the truth, but only if he felt we could make a profit. Artemis was a practical man. A clever man. He was always two steps ahead of everyone, even me."

Clyde and Herbert sat in silence for a moment. Herbert's thoughts went back to his grandfather, who he recalled was quite clever. He was also quite secretive. Herbert recalled how CS troops came to Granddad's flat in the 'Burbs once while he was visiting. The Coalition soldiers kicked in the door and tore the place up looking for them, but Grandpa was too smart for them. He had everything prepared, bags packed, motorcycle gassed up, hidden under a tarp in the alley. The two of them were out of the house before the soldiers even knew they were gone. Grandpa was never afraid of Dead Boys. He out-smarted them every time.

"May I see the book, Herbert?"

"Oh, of course. Forgive me. This whole thing is just . . . well it's all moving very quickly for me." Herbert handed the book to Clyde. Clyde thumbed through it, reading each line carefully.

"Do you read music, Herbert?" Clyde asked, licking his finger as he flipped each page, taking care not to damage the book.

"I used to. As a child. I haven't sung since I got married. My wife doesn't like it. She threatened to turn me over to Internal Security if I didn't get rid of that book."

"Well I'm very glad you didn't. We're going to need this to access Artemis' fortune."

Herbert looked at him quizzically. "I'm afraid I don't understand."

Clyde closed the book. "Do you mind if I hang onto this?" he asked, already placing the book into a messenger bag he had on the floor.

"I suppose not, but . . ."

"We have to leave, Sir," Charles said only a few feet away. Startled, Herbert jumped from his chair. He hadn't heard the door open, felt the cold wind come in from outside, nor heard Charles approach.

"I will explain when we get there, Herbert," Clyde responded as he gathered his be-longings and pointed to the corridor at the back of the bar. Charles led the way, his move-ments extremely quick, and somewhat jerky, as if he moved in intentional spasms. Herbert was then ushered down the hallway by Clyde, who produced a pistol from his messenger bag.

"A gun?" Herbert whispered loudly as they hurried towards the back door. "What are you doing with a gun?"

"Trying to get you your share of Grandpa's inheritance. Now move."

Charles pressed on the bar on the back door and swung it open. He leapt into the driver's seat of a hover car that had been parked next to the exit. Herbert was shoved into the back seat by Clyde, who jumped in right after him. "Keep your head down. Don't do anything and you'll stay alive."

The Juicer started the engine and they took off through the back alleyways at an in-credible speed.

"How many did you see, Charles?"

"Four. No Dog Boys. I don't think they saw me," replied the Juicer.

"Good. Now, let's get to Artemis' flat."

"Yes, Sir."

Clyde leaned back and grinned at Herbert, who was curled up on the floor of the back seat, his heart pumping and his hands shaking. 'How could this old man do this all the time?,' he wondered, staring up at Clyde's face. He wondered if this is what life is like for everyone outside the city. He wondered if this is what Grandpa had to deal with.

"How are you, Herbert?" asked Clyde.

"Perfect."

Clyde laughed. "Not so scared you can't crack a joke? Glad to hear it. For a moment back there I thought you were going to completely lose it. Shoulda known you were made of sterner stuff."

Herbert got up off the floor and sat in the seat. He was getting in deep, he knew it. He did almost lose it, and wished he really was made of sterner stuff, but knew he was not. Were there Coalition soldiers looking for him now? What if they contacted the city's Internal Security? What if they went to his home and arrested his wife? What if they trashed his apartment, or laid an ambush? He could lose his job over this! Then what would he do? He might have to move down to the lower levels and take government medication to keep himself from trying to revolt. Herbert wrung his hands in worry.

"Would you relax, Herb? You're making me nervous acting like that." Clyde reached into his messenger bag, grabbed the song book and handed it to Herbert. He flipped it open and turned it to one particular song. "Here. I want you to read this. Try to remember how it goes. Try to get your voice back."

Herbert read the book. The song was called *Angel Eyes*. It was his favorite as a child. He recalled how Grandpa would sing it softly to Grandma. Herbert sang it to Margaret on their first date. That was thirty years ago. It was the last time he sang anything. Scribbled in the margins of the song was Grandpa's handwriting. Herbert had read the notes a hundred times, but never really paid any attention to what it said. Most were incomprehensible ink scratches.

On the second page, a note, circled heavily in black ink, commanded Herbert's attention. Cryptically, it simply said "The Choking Man's Favorite Song."

Choking Man? Whatever could he mean by that!? And why was that important? And why was this song important to Clyde? Oh, this was too much excitement. Herbert saw the time on the dashboard of the car. It was nearly one-thirty. He was starting to wear down. Too much excitement. He wanted nothing more than to go home and pass out on the couch.

Herbert studied the notes of the song. He recognized them pretty quickly, testing out each one by humming to himself. They were like old forgotten friends. People his wife did not want him associating with.

"That's very good, Herbert. Do you remember the words? Can you read them there in the book?" Clyde was starting to sound impatient. He had lost the friendliness and class he had displayed earlier. Now he was sounding more like . . . well more like Margaret or Lenny at Medical Records.

"I think so. I need a few minutes. I haven't recalled most of these words in years."

"Well hurry. We're not going to have a lot of time once we get to your grandfather's place. They will be looking for us."

Herbert did as he was told.

At one-forty, Charles stopped the car and barked, "This is it." He unlocked the doors and Clyde and Herbert climbed out of the car and stepped onto a muddy street, someplace deep in the 'Burbs. Clyde told Charles to take the car around back and hide it out of sight.

Herbert and Clyde stood in front of a dilapidated old building, surrounded by other old buildings that hadn't seen paint or maintenance in years. The entire street was lined with empty buildings and no one seemed to be around at all. There were no lights, no street-walkers, not even a fire burning in a barrel. It was empty and quiet.

Off in the distance, Herbert could see the great Chi-Town fortress city, towering above the 'Burbs, lighting up the night sky. From here it seemed so small. He had spent nearly his entire adult life inside that little thing over there. That little thing contained his whole world.

"I remember this neighborhood," said Herbert, conjuring up images from his childhood, "There used to be a flower shop right there. And over there, that was a liquor store. Most of the rest of these were apartments." Herbert then noticed the building which they now stood in front of. "And this was Grandpa's place. He lived in the basement. What happened here?"

"This used to be a nice part of the 'Burbs," Clyde explained, "It was all residential. New buildings, new stores, newly paved streets. Mostly humans lived here, but then D-Bee families started moving in. The people in this community accepted them. Humans and D-Bees really cared about what was happening here. They started to build a school, and they formed a neighborhood watch group to get rid of the drug dealers, pimps, bandits, and mercenaries. That's why the Coalition Army purged it a few years back. Six. Seven, maybe. Charles would know."

Clyde looked up at Grandpa's building, his face wrenched in pain and anger. He closed his eyes, pushed out a deep breath, and relaxed. He turned to Herbert and added, "Let's go. I'll explain the rest inside."

Over the concrete steps, they went into the crumbling building. The place stunk of mildew, mold, and urine. The floor was littered with broken bottles, dirty syringes, and the bones of either a large rat or a small dog. Sections of the wall had been torn down or broken out. A large section of the floor above them had collapsed.

As they stepped carefully over the wreckage, making their way to the basement through an old stairwell, Clyde continued his story.

"It worked really well for a long time. Crime was a fraction compared to the rest of the 'Burbs. It was safe to walk the streets here. People were happy, and hopeful that their success would spread throughout the 'Burbs. D-Bees, mutants, humans, everyone lived in peace. I mean, it was no utopia, but nobody was getting gunned down in the street just for being different. Not here."

When they reached the basement, they found that the door leading to Grandpa's apartment was swinging freely. The locks had been burned completely out of the door. The burns were clean and precise, as if with a laser. The inside was in no better condition than the upstairs. All of the furniture had been thrown about, overturned, or smashed. Silverware and dishes had been callously dumped on the floor. Every drawer and cabinet was open, their contents spilled out among the mess. A heavy layer of dust and soot covered everything.

"No one really knows why, as the reasons are rarely explained to us poor, ignorant unclean, masses, but one day, nearly a hundred Dead Boys rolled into the neighborhood, blocked it off with giant 'bots, put tanks in the streets and stationed a squad of SAMAS on every corner. Everyone was too shocked and scared to do anything. The Dead Boys wouldn't let anyone in or out. And then, without saying a word to us, they opened fire. They burned down the school first, then a few of the shops. They killed anyone with a book or computer. They shot any D-Bee or mutant on sight. Just killed them like they were lambs to slaughter. The normal people among us, they corralled into the street, chained us up, and led us away."

"Clyde, you were here? You saw it happen?" croaked Herbert in disbelief.

"Yeah, I was here when the purge took place. Hauled us to a holding cell and let us ripen for a week before they released us. They never told us why. Never asked us a question. We had worked so hard for something good in this life and they took it away, just like that. I half suspect just to be mean."

Herbert just stood, stunned. Clyde was a combination of sad and furious now, the last few sentences coming out in a loud roar, a statement of pure anger and hate. A small wind blew in from outside, and Charles was then standing behind Herbert.

"Maybe you want to be a little louder? I don't think the guys chasing us heard you." Charles put his hand, his huge hand which could crush a man like a grape, on Herbert's shoulder. The two men were now on either side of Herbert, and he started to become nervous.

Clyde took a deep breath and slicked his hair back, which had become as frazzled as his disposition.

"Well, we're all here now, I may as well be honest with you, Herbert," he said, drawing his pistol once again from his messenger bag. "You see, that day, I watched all of this happen. I was on my way back from a dig where Artemis was working. We were in a place called *Madhaven*. Well, we weren't exactly in it, we were camped outside. Madhaven is a haunted city. The haunted ruins of a city. One that collapsed centuries ago during the Great Cataclysm. It was supposed to be the grandest city of the pre-Cataclysm era. A magnificent place that served as the hub of all civilization. Artemis, the old fool, was following a dream he had about that place. He said someone came to him while he slept and spoke to him of a great treasure buried deep in the ruins of Madhaven. It's insane, I told him, to go chasing after this. Madhaven is a waking nightmare, Herbert. Going to that place is like being confronted with the darkest parts of the human soul, and then having them shoved down your throat. Full of ancient ghosts that deliver insanity and death. Nevertheless, Artemis was dead-set on digging there. He assembled a team, gathered the resources necessary, and we started digging."

Clyde turned away from Herbert, and as he did so, Charles put his meaty paw around Herbert's neck. One tiny movement, Herbert feared, and his neck would snap like a toothpick. Clyde moved to the center of the basement. He picked up the pieces of broken furniture and tossed them aside. Underneath the mess was a large rug, partially burnt and corroded with age. Herbert recognized it. He once tried to peek under it, and was subsequently berated by his grandfather. 'Not until you're older. You wouldn't understand,' he had said.

Clyde flipped the rug over, careful not to produce too much dust. Underneath was a large concrete slab, barely discernable from the floor of the basement.

"Ah. Here we are, Charles. I'll watch our friend. If you please," Clyde said, almost returning to the friendly tone he expressed earlier. He pointed his pistol at Herbert, who had not moved an inch, tightly clutching his songbook. Charlie released his iron grasp on Herbert's neck and went to the concrete slab.

With tremendous strength and power, the Juicer sunk his hands into the concrete and slowly started to lift the slab. Herbert watched in amazement as the superman lifted it up and, swiveling at the waist, set it down behind him.

Underneath the slab, there was a small hole and ladder.

"Check it out down there, Charles. I have to finish my story," Clyde said. Charles did as he was told, unhooking a flashlight from his belt and climbing down into the darkness.

"Anyway, we started digging," Clyde continued. "We dug for six weeks, and we found nothing. Nothing but ancient street signs, broken bits of pre-Rifts vehicles, and other assorted garbage. There was no treasure. We started losing the cooperation of the men. They complained of nightmares. They saw things in the darkness. Horrible things. Some of them, I don't know. They just snapped. They ran off. They attacked their comrades. That place was seeping into our minds, driving us all to the brink of madness. And through it all, Artemis pushed us on. 'Just a bit further,' he said. After six weeks, we were at the breaking point. We had to turn back. We traveled south, and made camp in an old trading post called *Trenton*. Artemis sent me back to Chi-Town to buy more supplies, recruit more workers, and try to gather more information on Madhaven. That is when I saw the Coalition soldiers tear apart my home and kill my friends. If I had been here, where I was supposed to be, I could have done something. I would have heard something. I could have stopped it. Instead I was off on some fool's errand with your goddamned grandfather, digging for something that we didn't even know if it existed or not."

Once again, Clyde was having trouble controlling himself. He shook the pistol at Herbert, threatening to end his life with each word. He breathed out once again, trying to calm down. Quietly, he asked, "Do you want to know what I did next?"

"You killed my grandfather," Herbert finally spoke up.

Clyde laughed. He was genuinely amused. "You're really quite astute, Herbert. You take after Artemis, no doubt. Yes, I did kill him. Oh, I had not intended to. It was that place. That terrible place that did it. Madhaven. It gets into your system. It takes a hold of your soul and it plants something evil there. It wraps you in darkness until it chokes everything good out of you. But you know, he deserved it, Herbert."

"How did he deserve it?"

"He lied to me. He *had* found the treasure he was after. As he lay on the floor, beaten and bloody, begging me not to kill him, he told me what he had found. The truth was, he had found it years ago. Years ago, Herbert. Can you imagine that? He lied to me for years about that treasure. And he brought us out there again. For what? For the delusions that ancient ghosts planted in that old man's head. For nothing! He found something horrible in that place, and it was trying to get him to return. I tortured him until he told me everything about the treasure. What it was, what it did, and most importantly, how to get to it. That's why you're here, Herbert."

Herbert was barely listening. Fear gripped him like a vise. Clyde's emotional state kept switching. He would start out calm, then rise into a full rage, then settle down and become darkly cynical and evil. He was all over the place.

Charles called up from the darkness, "It's clear down here, Boss. Safe to come down."

Clyde motioned Herbert to the ladder. "Be my guest," he said wryly.

Herbert tucked the songbook into his coat and descended into his grandfather's vault. Luckily, it seemed to have survived the purge untouched. Charles lit a couple of flares and laid them on the floor of the vault. Their light bathed the room in a red glow.

The first thing Herbert noticed was how small the vault was. He measured it out in his head, and estimated it was only about as large as maybe nine of the cubicles he worked in, arranged in a perfect square. A small iron grate on the ceiling provided ventilation from somewhere up top. The walls and floor were concrete slabs, and there were shelves drilled into the walls which held priceless pre-cataclysm artifacts. At least they used to, it seemed.

"I don't understand," Clyde said to no one in particular. "Where are the artifacts? Artemis' collection; where is it?"

Clyde took Charles' flashlight and shined it around the tiny room. All he saw were shelves, covered in ash and bits of melted slag. He put his fingers into the ashes and examined them.

"Burned. Everything has been burned," Clyde explained to himself.

"It doesn't make any sense," said the Juicer. "The walls aren't burnt. There's no marks on the ceiling. There's nothing down here to start a fire. It doesn't add up."

"Artemis, you tricked me, you son of a bitch," Clyde swore loudly.

Herbert could see they were right. Nothing remained of Grandpa's collection. He would never be able to see them; to know what kind of person Grandpa really was. It was all gone. Then, something in the corner caught Herbert's eye. Something that wasn't ashes or unrecognizable trash. Something small and shiny.

"Look there," Herbert said, pointing to the thing he saw.

Clyde shined the light over. He sifted through some charred remains of books and singed papers and found a little music box. The thing was dirty, and very old, but at one time, it must have been beautiful. It seemed to be constructed out of porcelain. It was trimmed in intricate, golden designs. Painted in the same gold on the sides were the words: *To My Darling Wife on Her Birthday – September 1st, 2087.*

Clyde examined the thing over in his hands. He leered at it greedily. "This is it. The one thing that wasn't destroyed is exactly what I came here for."

"Don't you suppose that is a bad sign?" Herbert asked.

"Oh, finally Mr. Snyder speaks up. You actually formed an opinion on your own. I'm very proud of you," Clyde said cynically. He pointed his pistol at Herbert. "Now climb. Let's get some fresh air."

Once they were back up into Grandpa's apartment, gathered around an old wooden table, the music box in the center, Clyde finished his story.

"I brought you here, Herbert, because you are the only one who can break the seal on the box. Your grandfather knew some powerful people. Psychics, sorcerers, people who are attuned to the saturation of magical energy in our world. He told me that there was something unholy inside this box. A force of incredible destructive power. To keep anyone from using it, he had it sealed by a spell caster. The only way it can be opened is for you to sing to it."

"That's insane. It's impossible," Herbert contested.

"Yes, yes, I know. Listen, Herbert, you must put aside your ridiculous Chi-Town doctrine for a moment and pay attention. I would not have gone through the trouble of luring you out here if I did not really need you. Trust me. The magic sealing this box is real. And in order to unlock it, you have to sing to it. The song your grandfather marked for you as a child. The song you practiced on the way here. That song and your voice are the key. And you will open this box for me. Because if you don't, I'll torture you, and then I'll kill you."

"And if I do open it for you?"

"Then I will take my new weapon and leave the 'Burbs. I will go and take my revenge against the Coalition States for what they did to my people. You can go back to Chi-Town and continue your miserable, mundane, little life, sealed up nice and safe inside the fortress city. I was going to let you keep all of Artemis' artifacts, just to show that I'm not a bad guy, but as you can see, that won't be possible."

Herbert took out the old songbook and laid it on the table between the music box and himself. He opened it to *Angel Eyes*. He took a deep breath, tried to relax, and started to hum the notes of the song.

"Sing it, Herbert. Don't hum."

"I don't remember the words."

"Christ, do I have to do everything?" Clyde got up and stood over Herbert, looking at the lyrics of the song. "I will say them, and you sing what I say."

As Clyde read off the song, line by line, Herbert sang along. The music flowed back to him easily. He reached down into a part of him, maybe it was his long-undernourished soul, or maybe just a slice of his childhood memories, and found the music he needed.

"Try to think that love's not around

But it's uncomfortably near.

My old heart ain't gaining no ground

Because my Angel Eyes ain't here."

At the end of the first verse, Charles noticed the box moving. Just a little bit, the ancient hinges moved and the box began to open. As it did, the air in the basement became a little thicker with heat. He noticed he had started to sweat from the rising temperature. Clyde and Herbert were too, though they failed to notice.

"Angel Eyes, that old devil sent

They glow unbearably bright

Need I say my love's misspent

Misspent with Angel Eyes tonight."

Herbert found himself enraptured in the song. A million memories and emotions flooded back to him. He recalled who he was as a youth – a talented singer who would entertain his grandfather's workers while they sat around a campfire. He had dreams of leaving the Coalition States entirely, making the trek across the vast wilderness to one of the Free Cities and singing professionally. That was, until he met Margaret.

Somehow she seemed sweet and beautiful back then. Only, Margaret didn't want to live away from the Coalition States. "We can be safe in Chi-Town," she said. "There are monsters out here. Demons. D-Bees. Wizards. You won't find any of that in Chi-Town. We can live safe and be happy there." She was right, of course. Chi-Town was blissfully free of otherworldly and supernatural horrors, but living happily?

Inside Chi-Town, they started a new life together. Herbert got a job, they moved into an apartment, and they planned a family. That was thirty years ago. Over time, he let the joy of life be sucked out of him. The Coalition, Level Twenty Medical Records, and Margaret especially, had drained every ounce of passion and love out of him. But now, here in this dark basement in a ruined part of the 'Burbs, with a gun pointed at his head, he was gaining a little bit back. If even for just a minute.

"So drink up all you people

Order anything you see.

Have fun, you happy people

The drinks and the laughs are on me."

The box creaked open further. Clyde, leaning over Herbert's shoulder, was close enough that he could peer inside. At first glance, he saw the mechanism that played the music box; a tiny metal cylinder with notches covering it, with metal strips raking along the outside of the cylinder. As each strip struck a notch, a note would play. Only the box was producing no music. It played along with Herbert, hitting each note at the same moment he did.

As Clyde looked deeper into the box, the mechanism faded away. Inside, he could only see a great and infinite blackness. Small wisps of swirling smoke began to rise from inside the box. Clyde could smell something terrible. The room was filled with it. Burning wood, and cooked flesh.

"Pardon me, but I've gotta run

The fact's uncommonly clear

Got to find who's now number one

And why my Angel Eyes ain't here."

The box on the table swung open forcefully and emitted black smoke billowing from inside. The smoke shot up to the ceiling and hung there. Bits of black ash rained down, lightly dusting the room. The heat of the room became completely stifling. Clyde and Charles could barely breathe. Only Herbert, still locked in the hypnotic sounds of his own voice, seemed calm and relaxed. If he noticed the cloud of smoke, he did not show it.

There was only one line left, and Herbert knew it without it needing it to be read to him. *"Pardon me while I disappear."*

"I'm done, man. I'm freaking done!" Charles yelled, "You can keep the ten thousand creds. It ain't worth this shit!" And the Juicer ran for the staircase back up to the street, when the door slammed shut, barring his way. He began to push on it, but even his massive Titan Juicer strength was unable to move it. Frustrated and scared, he kicked the door repeatedly, to no avail.

In desperation, Charles leaned in on the door, pushing with all his might. Suddenly, it burst into flames and the Juicer found himself unable to pull away from the door as it immolated. He screamed as his flesh began searing itself to the wood, his hands and face melting from the intense heat. Finally, with one last yank, Charles freed himself from the door and collapsed onto the ground. The skin on his hands was melted into goo, and portions of his face had been peeled off. Seared to the door, it shriveled up and burned away. Underneath his skin, only cooked meat was revealed.

Charles' screams snapped Herbert out of his trance. He stood and looked around him wildly, unsure of what to do or where to go. Just as the door had done a second ago, the cabinets burst into flames. Then the couch, then a moth-eaten recliner in the corner. Anything flammable in the room was igniting.

"What's going on?!" Herbert yelled to Clyde over the roar of the flames.

"I don't know! We did everything Artemis said! Why is this happening?" Clyde screamed in terror.

The music box began to shake and rattle. From out of its infinite blackness, a hand crawled forth. Followed by an arm. Then another hand. Then, a face.

"Artemis, what in the name of all that is holy did you find in that accursed city?" Clyde whispered to himself, almost like a prayer.

The man in the box began to crawl forth, sinking his bony fingers into the table and pulling himself free of the darkness within the music box. His mouth hung open and his eyes were wide. They were missing eyelids and lips. It was only a blackened skull face.

Herbert knew it was a man because of its height and body structure. He had seen pictures of people disfigured by all manner of means; shotgun suicides, subway car accidents, car crashes, mauling by mutants and monsters. Herbert found it quite disturbing in his early days of work, but now he was far desensitized to those sterile medical photographs. This was different. This was real. Herbert knew from experience that the man in the box was some sort of horrible burn victim. His entire body was blackened, melting. His flesh seemed to still smolder in places, like the end of a cigarette. When he opened his mouth, maybe to speak, maybe to scream, maybe to beg to be put out of his misery, he could only cough up ashes, smoke, and bits of charred lung.

The man-thing in the box was now there, in the room. It crawled off the table and onto the floor, reaching out to Clyde and Herbert. Charles lay screaming on the floor behind them. His hair and clothes had caught fire from the door and he was desperately trying to put it out.

"Do something!" Clyde pleaded to Herbert.

"Do what?" Herbert whispered, his speech staccato with terror. "This is your thing. You wanted the box. You wanted the weapon it contained. YOU do something."

Clyde pointed his pistol at the Burning Man, who was crawling towards them, inching ever closer, leaving a trail of ashes and flame behind him. He pulled the trigger and a beam of coherent light shot forth from the weapon, hitting the Burning Man in the shoulder. Sparks flew from his body and there was a short burst of light. There was, however, no effect to the target.

The Burning Man crawled forward still, and as Clyde stood, mortified at his worthless attempt to kill the creature, he snapped his hand forward and grabbed Clyde's gun. Almost immediately, the pistol began to melt, the metal of the gun fusing with Clyde's own flesh and blood hand. Somehow, he managed to yank his hand from the weapon, but twirled about the room, holding it out, screaming in agony before he finally fell against a broken chair and sat there in shock.

The Burning Man crawled, now on his knees, towards Herbert, but then turned his attention to the Juicer, Charles. Herbert scooted to the side, taking care not to get too close to the burning furniture behind the smoldering corpse, relieved that the Burning Man ignored him in favor of the beefy Juicer.

"OH GOD NO!!" Charles screamed as the Burning Man crept towards him, "GET AWAY FROM ME!"

The Juicer flailed his one good arm wildly, and struck the Burning Man across the face. His arm instantly burned up like a dry leaf. One moment, it was a living appendage, full of muscle, skin, and bone, and mere seconds later it was little more than a dried out husk. One more second later, and it crumbled and disintegrated into a pile of ash. The Juicer simply watched in disbelief and horror.

The Burning Man inched closer and closer. Charles could do nothing but scream and stare into those wide, murderous eyes burning like red hot embers. The Burning Man opened his mouth to unleash a stream of smoke in a thick plume. It went right into

Charles' mouth and nose, clogging his lungs and throat. Over the flames, Herbert could hear a horrible choking and gagging sound as the Juicer gurgled and vomited, thick and black, like tar. Next his eyes bugged out of his head, threatening to explode.

The Burning Man and the Titan Juicer stayed locked in this sick embrace for a full minute before Charles fell to the ground, his soot blackened body locked in convulsions. Finally, he shuddered and died, his body turning a dark grey like a lump of charcoal.

The Burning Man renewed his interest in Clyde and turned in his direction. Herbert couldn't help but notice that the monster seemed stronger and now stood firmly on two legs as it turned towards Clyde.

From where he stood, Herbert could see the dead Juicer's face, all burnt and blistered, with black, viscous ooze pouring from his mouth. Herbert had seen faces like this before, from photographs of drowning victims and people who had asphyxiated from smoke inhalation or strangulation. In Charles' face, however, he saw something worse: the unmistakable look of a person who had been scared to death. Frozen in a grimace of pure, raw terror.

The Burning Man walked now, over to Clyde in a low and limping gait. With every footstep, bits of black flesh dropped off the bottom of his foot and caught fire behind him.

Clyde was losing consciousness from his injury and the lack of oxygen in the room by the time the Burning Man reached him. He gazed up at the smoldering creature and started to weep. He held his mangled hand close to his chest and pleaded with the horror leering down at him.

"Please. I'm sorry. I didn't want this," Clyde gasped between sobs.

The Burning Man grabbed Clyde's throat with his hands, and lifted him effortlessly up to his own eye level. The flesh on Clyde's neck began to smoke and smolder. His face became red as the blood rushed to his head. The pain brought him out of shock, and he was suddenly all too aware of the torment and death that awaited him in the monster's grasp.

"Herbert! Herbert, please help me!" were Clyde's last words.

Too scared to do anything, Herbert watched and prayed that his end would come more quickly.

Again the Burning Man opened his mouth and once more, the black smoke billowed from his mouth and into Clyde's mouth and nostrils. Clyde coughed and gagged, as black ooze gurbled from his lungs and bubbled out of his mouth. He tried, in vain, to scream, a last defiant expression of pain and fear, but all he could manage was a choked gurgling noise, after which he fell silent. The creature held onto Clyde a little longer, scorching his face, singing his hair, until only a blistered, burning mess remained.

When the Burning Man dropped Clyde's lifeless body on the floor, Clyde's face seemed to stare across the room, directly into Herbert's eyes. His expression matched that of Charles, his mouth unnaturally wide, black goo seeping from every orifice onto the floor.

The Burning Man turned and stared directly at Herbert. The mousy clerk sank to the floor and shut his eyes, knowing that his turn had come. He could not look at this horrible creature, this ghost, or demon, or whatever it was. He could not face his own death like this. Herbert remembered all those times in the last fifteen or twenty years in which he had wished for death. Hopeless and lonely, he wanted the sweet release of leaving his life behind. Sometimes, the only thing that got him through his workday was knowing that someday he was going to die, and it might have been that day. Somehow, now that death was literally staring him in the face, Herbert did not wish to die. He never really had. All he really wanted was release from the suffocating life he had made for himself. The only thing he ever really wanted was some measure of control over his own life. Stepped on every day by his boss, his wife, the Chi-Town police, and his glorious fellow citizens of the Fortress City, his spirit had been trampled, but now with the specter of death lumbering toward him, he wanted to live more than anything in the world. And if he lived, he vowed he'd stop being a floor mat and take control of his life once again.

Even with his eyes closed Herbert could feel the heat of the Burning Man, standing over him. He could smell the carbon in his breath. There was something else he could smell. It was hate. Hate and anger. He could feel it, radiating from the creature like a light bulb. It was not fire and smoke that consumed the monster and his foes, it was rage.

'Rage, but from what?' Herbert wondered.

As if pulled from the ether, the choking man issued answers in a stream of consciousness. "Betrayal. Hurt. Fire. Chaos. Love. Choke. Death."

Each word was punctuated by an image. Not a visual representation, but an emotional one. The Burning Man had been alive once. He was betrayed and crushed by those around him in much the same manner as Herbert. Then as the world collapsed into the chaos of the Great Cataclysm, he was consumed by fire. Someone he had loved very dearly had left him to burn. While his body was reduced to ashes, his fury and anger burned with such intensity, it refused to die. It hid, instead, inside a music box, a treasured gift, and waited. It waited, searching the dreams of the living for someone, anyone to come and find it, to dig it out from the ruins of a haunted city. Herbert felt every emotion, pounded into him by the poor, tortured creature. He felt its agony undiluted over three hundred years.

A normal, well-adjusted person might have been overcome by the emotions presented by the Burning Man. A normal, well-adjusted person might have been driven to the very brink of madness. But for Herbert, these emotions were nothing new. He had felt everything this ghost had felt, and understood its agony and sympathized. Herbert remembered the first time Margaret brought another man into their bed. He remembered the first time she said she hated him. He remembered the first time she threatened to divorce him. The first time she demanded pills to calm the anxiety she blamed him for bringing on. The first time she threw away his grandfather's gifts. The first time she shut him out of their bedroom, consigning him to years of sleeping alone on the couch. He remembered, every single hurt she had inflicted upon him. The pain was fresh in his mind – a thousand memories, busting down the walls he had built around his heart. The scars re-opened, as fresh as the day they were made. Everything came back to him in a torrent of nightmares, anger, sorrow and regret!

When Herbert opened his eyes, the Burning Man was gone. The smoke and fire were also gone, though Clyde and Charles were still there, and quite dead. A pair of charcoal corpses. The walls and the ceiling of the basement were scorched black. The furniture was in cinders. Ashen footprints marked where the ghost had been. They stopped at Herbert, then disappeared completely. The music box was still on the table, though now it was shut.

Herbert checked his watch. It was almost three in the morning. He stood to run from the basement, but something pulled at him. He turned, looked at the music box, and felt the music from within.

*   *   *

As Herbert walked quickly through the streets of the 'Burbs, he held onto the music box tight in his hand. A couple of times, he tried to pry it open with his fingers, but quickly gave up when it refused to give. He decided the ghost he had encountered needed a name.

Fire Ghost? No.

Harmful Ghost? No.

Burning Man? No.

Choking Man? No, but close.

He decided on the name *Mr. Choke*. For some reason, it seemed more respectful of the wraith now tucked away in his jacket pocket.

Mr. Choke was a name, not a title. It put them as equals, in Herbert's mind, as if you would say, "A pleasure to meet you, Mr. Choke. I am Mr. Snyder. What a lovely music box you live in."

Trapped in their own respective prisons, full of hate, Herbert felt they had some things in common. At least he found someone he could relate to. Herbert chuckled to himself at that last part.

At three twenty-five, Herbert found himself at Chi-Town's South Gate. He looked at the long line of people waiting to gain entrance into the city and estimated it would take at least ten times the amount of time to get back in to the city as it did to leave. Chi-Town doesn't care if you want to leave. "Go ahead, there's nothing out there but peasants, lowlifes, Juicers, D-Bees and monsters. There will always be someone to take your apartment when you're gone." That was their motto, he imagined.

Herbert remembered how scared he was earlier, when he left the city. He was so afraid they would find his book and arrest him. The book, he no longer had, but there was something on his person now that was much worse. Surely the Dog Boys, with their heightened sense of smell, would detect the scent of death and smoke that Herbert was caked with. They would find the box, and he would be executed as a traitor for trying to smuggle in a dangerous demonic entity hidden inside a magic box.

Herbert had to get back into the city. He just had to. The 'Burbs were no place for a man like him. He was better suited to city life. He had to get back to work in three-and-a-half hours. He had to let Margaret know where he was all night, if she even cared. The apartment needed to be cleaned, there were bills to pay, and laundry to do, and there was still that meatloaf in the fridge. It didn't sound too appetizing at the time, but Herbert had not eaten since lunch earlier that day, so right now meatloaf sounded damn good.

Herbert ran through his options as fast as his mind could calculate them. He could try to sneak in when no one was looking, but that would never work. The Border Guards were vigilant and dedicated. No one got in without the proper papers and an inspection.

Hmmm, he could let the ghost out of the box and get in during the confusion. No, they would probably slam the doors shut and shoot anyone who got too close. Then he would either die in the crossfire or as a smuggler of demonic magic.

Bribery. Maybe he could buy his way back in. No, that was no good. He didn't have enough money to bribe these guys; he barely had any money on him at all.

Just toss the box away and walk in as normal, he thought with firm resolve for a fleeting second, but Herbert couldn't bring himself to do it. His grandfather wanted him to have it. It was a family heirloom. Beside, what if some child found it and figured out a way to open it? Kids these days were good at figuring out stuff like that. The poor child and his playmates would be burnt to a crisp.

No, it was best that Herbert kept the box and looked after it. Surely he would figure something out by the time he got to the gate.

Three hours later, and Herbert was closer to getting back into the city but nowhere closer to figuring out what to do with the music box. The line had shrunk down considerably, with the majority of people being turned away. "Sorry, your papers don't check out. Try again tomorrow," is what they said, time and again. And then the poor 'Burb Folk would wander off, in no particular direction, with nothing in particular to do. A few hopefuls were even arrested upon their inspections, being carried away by armed Border Guards. Herbert wondered what crimes they had committed, and if they were lesser or worse crimes than the one he was about to commit himself.

Herbert began to panic. He was about to attempt a very perilous task, sneaking into Chi-Town with a demon in his pocket.

"Herbert?" a Border Guard asked from behind him, his voice tinny and metallic from behind his facemask, "Herbert Snyder?"

Herbert turned and was face-to-face with the grinning skull and red glass eyes of a Coalition soldier.

The soldier removed his helmet, revealing a perfectly non-threatening human being underneath. The two men looked at each other curiously. Herbert fumbled with what to say. It was quite awkward to be caught here, outside the city, his clothes covered in mud and ashes, his face unshaven, weary, and exhausted.

"Corporal Lee. I don't quite know what to say?" Herbert was too frightened and too tired to be anything but completely honest.

"Please, call me Dwayne," the man, who only a few hours ago had been plowing Herbert's wife in their wedding bed, sounded sincerely embarrassed and pitiful.

"Okay. Um, Dwayne."

"What are you doing out here? Especially at this time of night?"

"My grandfather died. I went to pay my respects."

"Really? I'm sorry to hear that." Dwayne looked Herbert over, noticing how rough he appeared. "Are you okay? You look a little messed-up."

"Yeah. I was accosted at some dive bar." And then, in a stroke of brilliance completely uncharacteristic for Herbert, he added, "They mugged me, took my papers, my identification, my driver's license, my credit card, and threw me in the mud. All I have left is this little box with my grandfather's ashes in it."

"Really? Oh, that's terrible. I'm sorry to hear about that."

The bastard. He sounded genuinely concerned.

There was a moment of silence between them. Herbert watched Dwayne's face. The gears were turning inside the man's head. Glancing around cautiously, he leaned in to Herbert and said quietly, "Step out of line. Come with me up to the gate. But don't look at anyone. Keep your head down. Pretend I'm taking you away for questioning."

Herbert did as he was told. Dwayne led him up to the Main Gate and inside the processing area into a tiny white corridor. Herbert tried to remain calm, but the knowledge of what he held in his pocket and the consequences of his lies were nagging at him mercilessly. However, if the Dog Boys sniffing around at the Main Gate took notice of Mr. Choke, they did not raise any alarms.

Once they were alone, Dwayne the Dead Boy led Herbert down the hall.

"Look, I feel like a real asshole for what me and Margaret have been doing. I know she doesn't give a shit about you, and really, neither do I. But I also see the way she treats you, and . . ."

Dwayne paused, trying to sort his thoughts out. "No one should have to deal with that. Especially for so long. I guess I just really pity you. Not enough to stop seeing her," he said with an arrogant smirk. "I mean, she's wild in the sack . . ."

Herbert frowned and Dwayne started to stumble over his words.

"Sorry. Anyway, here's my point. I'm going to let you into the city without an inspection or anything. If you stay in that line it could be hours before they let you through. Your grandfather died, you got mugged, twice in one day, you look like hell, you deserve a break. The least I can do is let you get home and grab a shower before work."

Herbert grinned widely. That was exactly what he had been hoping for. "Thanks, Dwayne, I . . . I really appreciate this."

"Look, don't mention it, alright? I mean that. If anyone finds out I did this they'll shoot us both."

"The secret dies with me."

Dwayne gave Herbert some quick directions and sent him on his way. Once back inside the walls, Herbert was slammed with the sensations of Chi-Town's interior. The smells of machinery, stale air, and smog rushed into his lungs. All around him were throngs of people, rushing off to catch cabs and trains to take them to work. An enormous digital sign played a looping video welcoming visitors and new citizens to Chi-Town, promising them safety and security from the nightmare of the outside world. Smaller signs and videoscreens, scattered on the sides of buildings, warned of the dangers of involving oneself with wizards, demons, psychics, and educators.

At the train station, Herbert compared his watch with the schedule. He groaned out of frustration. There was no way he could make it to work on time, much less go home and shower first. Lenny was going to chew him out again. He would probably dump more work on him as punishment.

On the train, Herbert briefly dozed off. He was so very tired, and this was the first time he had been able to relax all night. He even managed to dream a little. The kind of dream you have when you're only barely asleep, hanging on between the world of the living and the world of the sleeper.

In his dream, he was on the train, and it started to catch fire. People, bits of litter, billboard advertisements, one by one they spontaneously combusted. The dream-Herbert looked outside the window and all he could see were the burning remnants of Chi-Town. Empty, smoking buildings and twisted, blackened metal stretched out as far as he could see. When he turned back around, he could only see his friend, *Mr. Choke*, in the faces of every person on the train, staring back into him with hate-filled eyes and wicked smiles.

The dream stuck with him all morning.

*　*　*

By eight o'clock in the morning, Herbert had hurried into work, typed his passkey into the security door and walked into *Floor Twenty Medical Records Department*. He kept his eyes low, but the first thing he saw was Lenny, standing by the receptionist's desk and flirting with the very attractive new woman handling the position. Lenny leaned up against her desk, coffee cup in his hand, playing with his tie. The girl at the phones flirted back, no doubt looking for some upward mobility. Herbert almost made it past them.

"Herbert," Lenny called out loudly, obviously looking to embarrass him for his truancy, "I believe work started at seven. It is now eight-oh-two. Where have you been?"

"I'm sorry, sir, I was mugged . . ." Herbert started, searching for a good lie.

"Never mind, I'm not interested in your lame excuses," Lenny interrupted. He turned to the receptionist and laughed loudly. She giggled to him in return.

"It won't happen again, Mr. Rogers," Herbert replied humbly.

"Get your ass to your desk. And for Pete's sake, do some laundry. Clean clothing is part of the dress code. Do I need to get you an employee handbook video?"

"That won't be necessary," Herbert said, quickly making his way over to his desk. For a split second, he wondered what Lenny would do if his tie suddenly burst into flames.

Herbert sat at his desk and removed Mr. Choke's music box from his coat. He set it next to his stack of paperwork, overflowing from his lost hour. He took the top medical chart from the stack and immediately set into it and tried to put out of mind his adventure from earlier that morning.

At five o'clock the work day was drawing to a close, when his phone rang. It was Lenny on the other line, asking Herbert to come to his office. Herbert tucked the music box into his pocket. The last thing he wanted was nosy old Beverly trying to report him for non-work-related items on his desk. The hypocrite, her desk was full of photos of her ugly children and stupid dog.

"Have a seat, Herbert," Lenny said. He pointed to the chair directly across from his desk. Sitting in a metal folding chair, next to Lenny was a very fat woman who Herbert recognized from Human Resources. Herbert could see where this was going before either of them said a word, and took the seat.

"I'm going to be blunt, because I have a massage appointment I have to get to, and frankly, you're not worth the effort of tact or diplomacy," chided Lenny.

"You're fired, Herbert. You have a serious attitude problem, and the quality of your performance has only gone down the longer you've been here."

"Serious attitude problem," Fat Woman echoed.

Lenny continued, "And now, look at you. You show up late. You're covered in mud. It's like you don't care about your appearance at all."

"Don't you care about your appearance at all?"

As they took turns verbally abusing him, Herbert switched his eyes from Lenny to Fat Woman. The rage started deep and dull inside him. All he could do was finger the music box, caressing its corners lightly.

"I've watched you taking extra-long breaks. You stand there and finger the shelf files while daydreaming, as if no one notices. We all notice. You sit in the restroom, taking up valuable space that someone else could be using – someone who actually needs the facilities."

"Someone might need to use the facilities."

"And worst of all, Beverly tells me you've been stealing supplies from your coworkers."

That was it. He couldn't take it anymore. Not from these worthless dung heaps. They couldn't do this to him. He had worked here for too long. Given too much of his life to this place. They couldn't betray him like this.

"Well? What do you have to say for yourself?" Lenny barked.

Herbert removed the music box from his pocket and sat it on Lenny's desk. Lenny and Fat Woman looked at it, then each other, then at Herbert, confusion crawled across their faces. He closed his eyes and started to hum to himself. He didn't need the songbook anymore to remember how this one went.

"What is this?" Lenny asked. "Some kind of joke?"

He stood up and started to yell, pointing his finger accusingly at Herbert. "You get the hell out of my office . . ."

The music box swung open and a pleasant tune started to play, harmonizing with Herbert's humming. Lenny stopped yelling, startled at the box's autonomous action. The Fat Woman was equally silent.

The music stopped. For a moment, no one uttered a sound. Then, emanating from deep within the darkness of the box, a low groan boiled to the surface. Then rose to a roar. Black smoke poured forth from the box. Soot and ash rained down, covering the room. The heat rose tremendously, curling papers and melting Lenny's expensive computer into plastic slag.

Fat Woman starting screaming, and Lenny shoved her aside to break for the door. His hand touched the doorknob and almost instantly fused to it as his hand melted. Herbert sat in his chair without a word. He let his boiling anger speak for him through Mr. Choke. The release of his repressed emotions was the greatest high he had ever felt. Better than drugs. Better than sex. This outpouring of pure rage was euphoric.

Out of the smoke on the ceiling, a figure descended, face-first, slowly lowering itself above Lenny. It was Mr. Choke, his mouth gaping open, his eyes wide and fixed on the cruel supervisor. Lenny, horrified by what he saw, desperately reached around for anything he could grab for help. The doorknob held him firmly, however. The phone was out of reach. His keys were out of reach. The letter opener was out of reach. Wildly, Lenny lashed around, screaming at Herbert and crying out for help.

As Mr. Choke slowly descended, Fat Woman started going into some kind of seizure. She shook violently, her eyes rolling back into her head. Her large body began steaming and blistering all over. Pustules rose and busted, some as large as coffee cups. Boiling yellow fluid oozed from them, releasing a foul odor. All the while, Herbert sat back and watched as she was cooked in her own lard. Her melting flesh fell off her body in clumps, hitting the floor and sizzling sickeningly. Finally, black tar gushed from her open mouth, covering her "business casual" jacket and skirt that were now starting to smolder.

Mr. Choke reached out with his skeletal, steaming hands and grabbed Lenny's face. Lenny's entire head caught fire, causing his hairpiece to burst into cinders. Mr. Choke opened his mouth wider and coughed a stream of black smoke and soot into Lenny's screaming lungs, caking them. Lenny gagged violently, then vomited black tar and fell to the ground, a burning hunk of flesh and bone, one hand still stuck, welded to the doorknob.

Herbert watched Mr. Choke, wondering if the ghost had changed his mind about their friendship. He was pleased to see that he had not. Mr. Choke, his eyes on Herbert and a smile on his face, rose back into the cloud of smoke. The cloud was sucked back into the music box as if it had never existed, and the box slammed shut. The door to Lenny's office unlocked and swung open by itself, swinging Lenny's burning corpse like a rag doll.

Herbert stepped out of the office, gazing around at his coworkers, who looked at him in confusion, apparently not hearing the screams and roar of flames from inside the office. Herbert held the music box out in front of him, and it opened once more. This time, there was no smoke; only flames. The fire shot out in a great pillar, hitting the ceiling and rolling through the entire department. Medical records and paperwork of all kinds caught and spread the fire even further.

"Burn everything," Herbert said to his friend, Mr. Choke, "Let it all burn."

With the entire department an inferno, Herbert left the office. The fire alarms blared all around him as Hospital Security ran past, fire extinguishers in their hands. Herbert made it out onto the street just as fire trucks arrived. He walked past them and down the street.

With the waning blares of sirens behind him, his rage was replaced with a sense of satisfaction and calm. However, as he replayed the event in his mind, his hands started shaking, his breathing became short and rapid, and he could feel himself ready to break into sobs. He sat on the street curb, holding himself, rocking back and forth. What had he just done? What insanity gripped him that he would kill his coworkers and burn up the Medical Records department? What was the demon in the box doing to him?

Suddenly, more sirens flew past him. Internal Security police cars, one after another, drove past in a series of blurs. Herbert stood and fled the scene. He ran to the only place he could think of, the train station.

They would catch him, he thought to himself. They would put out the fire and launch an investigation. They would see the horribly burned and mangled bodies of Lenny and Fat Woman and know right off that it was unnatural. People don't just die like that for no reason. They would bring in psychics, Dog Boys, and experts on the supernatural. They would know it was him. Or figure it out soon enough. They would know, and they would come for him. He probably wouldn't even get a trial. They would just shoot him in the street like a rabid dog. Afterward, for months to come, his pathetic, worn face would be plastered on every news video and propaganda poster as another dangerous madman brought to an end by the heroic ISS.

Herbert ran up the stairs onto the platform and into the first open train car he saw. He didn't care where it went or who was on it. He only wanted to get out of Level Twenty. He needed time to think; time to calm down and collect himself.

Oh, what was he going to do now? Where could he run to? How could he fix this? He could toss the music box out the window. No, that wouldn't help. They would find it. Dog Boys or psychics would hunt it down. It was an evil box, full of horror and magic. They could smell the evil. They would find it, and then they would find him. No, it was best to keep the box.

Herbert took the music box out of his pocket and held it in his hands, staring at it. "What do you want from me?" he asked Mr. Choke. "I don't want any of this. I don't want to hurt anyone. My life is over, do you understand that? They will find me and they will kill me."

Deep within his wilted soul, Herbert could feel Mr. Choke, reaching out to him with an answer. "Your life was already over. You must consume everything with hate. Fill your empty shell with anger, and burn all that has hurt and betrayed you. Only then will you feel whole again." The message came to him, not in words, but in emotion. And in a way, it made sense. The spirit of pain spoke truth.

No, that was insane! thought Herbert. He was no killer or insane avenger. He was unhappy about his life, but he could change it. He had the strength, at least he used to. Before he married. Before Margaret. Before this city and that woman stomped his spirit into the concrete, grinding him beneath their heels. But maybe he could find it again and become someone better.

"What's in the box, Lofty?" a voice asked.

Herbert looked up, torn from his wild musings. He had not even noticed that once again he was surrounded by a gang of sinister City Rats. Not all City Rats were criminals, thugs or punks, but as luck would have it, it was Black Mesh Shirt and his friends from yesterday.

"More pills, I hope," said The Girl, standing behind Black Mesh Shirt. She looked even worse than she did the day before; even more strung out and miserable. She was also sporting some new bruises on her face and arms, compliments of her boyfriend, no doubt.

Metal Teeth and No Hair stood on either side of Black Mesh Shirt. They snickered. "Yeah. We had a real good time with the candy you brought us yesterday. We really appreciate it," No Hair said.

"You don't want what's in this box," Herbert said quietly. "It's not pills. It's not money. It will bring you only pain."

"What's that?" Black Mesh shirt said, pulling out the black wand he hit Herbert with before. "Is that some kind of threat, joker? You want a little repeat of what we did to you before? Hand it over now."

Why wouldn't they just leave him alone? They had already taken so much from him. He didn't deserve this. He had never hurt these people. And yet all they wanted was to hurt him. Fine, if they wanted the box, he'd let them have it. When Internal Security came and tracked it down, they would find it in the hands of these punks. Maybe the heat would be off of Herbert. Who cared if they arrested or even executed this street trash?

"Here. Take it," Herbert said. "I don't even want it anymore."

Metal Teeth snatched it from his palms. "Yeah, that's more like it." He started to pull hard on the latch. Struggling, he pulled and pulled, but the box would not open.

"Here, let me see that," said Black Mesh Shirt. He took the box and started to pull too. One by one, they passed the music box around, each trying to open it, and each failing. They threw the box across the train car. They stomped on it, they tried to pry it open with knives, but they could not even scratch it.

"What's the deal, old man?" Black Mesh Shirt asked, threateningly prodding Herbert with the black wand. "You trying to be funny? You better open it up before I open you up. Understand?"

"Alright," Herbert said quietly. "Give it to me."

Herbert sat the box on the floor in front of him, with the City Rats surrounding it. They watched him, suspiciously, as he went about this little ritual. When he started to sing, they snickered.

Towards the end of the song, Black Mesh Shirt began to get impatient. He raised the black wand high. "Quit screwing around. Forget the stupid box, just give us your money or I swear I'll beat you to death."

Herbert, not missing a beat, motioned with his finger for Black Mesh Shirt to come closer, as if he were about to tell him a secret. He lowered his voice to barely above a whisper.

Black Mesh Shirt leaned in, raising his wand even higher. He was about two seconds from popping Herbert in the skull and throwing him off the train.

"*Pardon me while I disappear*," Herbert sang softly into the ear of the thug. As the last words were uttered, the music box swung open and a blast of hot volcanic smoke and fire spewed forth, catching Black Mesh Shirt directly in the blast.

The other 'Rats watched in horror as their leader was incinerated in seconds. Metal Teeth yanked him from the plume of smoke, and then they recoiled at his burnt remains. Black Mesh Shirt's upper torso, head, and arms were completely burned up, leaving nothing but a black charred skeleton. The Girl fell to her knees next to her lover and started wailing.

Herbert knew what would come next. This time, he could not watch. He held his head in his hands, trying desperately to shut out the sounds of screaming and flesh burning by singing Mr. Choke's song over and over. Try as he could, he could not ignore the ghastly sounds of each thug choking on their own scorched lungs.

Like a genie from a lamp, Mr. Choke rose from the box and killed the City Rats one by one. He was a raging demon of fire, lashing out with his unquenchable hate at the living. The City Rats were gutter trash, picking on those weaker than themselves, so they never had a chance against Mr. Choke. Inside each of them, however, was the fire of life that Mr. Choke sought to extinguish. Each died a horrible death.

When the noise of the carnage stopped and the smoke disappeared, Herbert opened his eyes. The metal subway car was warped and twisted from the incredible heat. The plastic seat cushions, melted. Four smoldering bodies lay on the floor of the car. Leaking from their open mouths was the black, tar-like ooze. On each of their faces, expressions of absolute terror and agony.

When the train stopped and the doors opened, Herbert ran from the station as fast as he could. Behind him, he could just barely hear the screams of people as they discovered the grisly scene in the car. Herbert ran and ran and ran, heading for the one place, the only place he thought he would be safe.

He reached his apartment without further incident. He didn't know how much time he had before the authorities followed the trail of bodies to his doorstep. He didn't even know what time it was anymore. He had stopped paying attention long ago. He didn't care anymore about being caught. He only wanted to rest. To take a shower. To have a hot meal. And to see his wife one more time before it all ended for him.

Again, regret fueled by fear caused Herbert's mind to race. Mr. Choke was no friend. Mr. Choke was a curse. He would take this damned box and bury it in the back of the closet. He would leave a note that no one should ever try to open the box. No one should ever sing around it. Clyde may have been right, it may only open when Herbert sang to it, but when Herbert died someday, either by execution, old age, or by finally taking his own life, Mr. Choke might choose someone else to be his partner in murder.

Inside his apartment, Herbert dropped his mud-covered coat and removed his shoes. He sat the music box down on the coffee table and went to the bathroom door. Inside, he could hear the sound of someone in the shower. He assumed it was Margaret and instead went to the kitchen, where he removed the meatloaf from last night and slid it into the oven.

"Where the hell have you been?" Margaret yelled from the bedroom door. She wasn't in the shower. Margaret was in her robe. Her hair was messed up.

"Who is in the shower?" Herbert asked dryly.

"Dwayne. He came over after his shift ended this morning. He told me he found you outside in the 'Burbs. The 'Burbs, Herbert. What the hell were you doing in the 'Burbs?"

"You know that package I got last night? It was a message from a man who worked with my grandfather. Grandpa died, and I went to pay my respects."

"Good. Maybe now they'll take you off that watch list since your loser grandfather won't be sending you anymore illegal items."

Herbert simply stared at his wife. A slow simmer of anger stirred in his belly. How could she disrespect Grandpa Snyder like that? The man was dead. How could she say such a hurtful thing? Why did she always have to be so damn cruel and hurtful?

"Don't you remember how grandfather helped pay for our wedding, Margaret? He helped me get into Chi-Town. The only reason I'm here in this stinking hell-hole with you is because of him!"

"Oh well, he should have died years ago so I wouldn't have wasted my life with you!"

It was unlike Herbert to stand up for himself against his wife. He hoped his sudden defiance would shock her into listening to him for once. No such luck. She only screamed louder, and nastier than ever. Herbert could do nothing. He was powerless against this woman. He had also lost his appetite, and now he was too angry and frustrated to sleep. Any comfort he had hoped to achieve by coming home was now completely denied him.

"You're so goddamned worthless, Herbert. Just like your worthless grandfather."

Defeated, Herbert sunk into the couch and turned on the television to watch the news. Margaret berated him the whole time, standing over him, her nagging needling its way into his ears and tearing out pieces of his mind.

"I should have married a man like Dwayne. A Coalition Soldier. A Real Man."

Herbert rolled into a ball on the couch, pulling his blanket over his head and wishing she would be quiet. Please be quiet. I'm sorry. Please just stop yelling at me.

"And I bet you didn't get my pills again today, did you? I swear if you forget one more time I'm divorcing you and I'm taking everything you own."

Please just go away, thought Herbert.

"I'll take everything. You'll have nothing because you are nothing. You're like a dead person, Herbert. My husband is a dead person."

Later that night, Herbert lay awake on the couch, crying softly into a pillow. He couldn't sleep. The events of the past two days ran over and over in his mind. They seemed so long ago, like they weren't even real. The evening news, however, reminded him just how real they were. The office fire and the subway fire were both top stories of the night.

Herbert wondered about Alex Jackson, the controversial patient, sick with an alien virus. Were his charts burned with the rest of the office? Would it even matter? Could anyone save him, or was he doomed to a slow, painful death? And did it even matter? In a way, everyone in Chi-Town was doomed to a slow death. They were all trapped. Trapped and dying. Alex Jackson, in his hospital bed. Margaret, in her selfishness and laziness. Mr. Choke, in his unwillingness to let go of the past. Herbert, in every facet of his entire life. It seemed to him that each and every citizen of Chi-Town was trapped in some way. Everyone out there was being kicked around and put down by someone else. Everyone was living in someone else's filth.

In the other room, Dwayne and Margaret had started to go at it again. Margaret was extra loud tonight, no doubt to further punish her husband. Herbert, long having grown accustomed to the sounds of his wife's faked orgasms, was able to brush it off. He simply lay on his side, staring at Mr. Choke's music box.

From deep inside the box, Mr. Choke whispered to Herbert a quiet, wordless nagging. "No sleep," he said. "Things are not finished."

"What more do you want from me?" Herbert said, barely audible. It was useless to ask. Mr. Choke never spoke with words, only with emotion that spoke to Herbert's heart. Herbert already knew the answer to that question. It was obvious what had to happen next. It was simply a matter of following intent with action. Herbert knew that he could not do it, however. He simply did not have the courage. He would need to set it up so that it would happen on its own.

Herbert went to the medicine cabinet in the bathroom. Inside were a variety of pills Margaret used for a variety of imaginary ailments. Most of them had unpleasant side effects. Herbert knew these medications, almost by heart. He remembered each one and the side effects it had on his wife. He picked one that had made her very tired. There in the bathroom, Herbert swallowed the entire bottle of pills, one by one. Unsatisfied that they would achieve the desired result, he swallowed another bottle, these with a similar drowsy effect. He then swallowed another, until finally he was confident that the job would get done.

Herbert then took the audio recorder, the one delivered to him by Clyde, locked himself in the bathroom so no one would hear, and recorded a new message. It was a short message, as Herbert had little to say, but it would get the point across nicely, he felt.

Taking the audio recorder and the music box into the bedroom, he placed them on the night stand next to Margaret. She slept soundly, with Dwayne shoved off to the very edge of the bed. She was hogging all the covers as usual.

Herbert took one last look at his wife and tried vainly to remember a time when they were in love. He remembered being in love the way you remember reading a book from a very long time ago. He remembered the fact of being in love, but not what it was really like to be in love.

Was it even her fault that she was like this? Herbert vaguely recalled a time when she wasn't such a horrid witch. When they were young, she was different. Even then, however, the foundation was laid for what she would become. With each pleasant memory, Herbert remembered a hundred more where she screamed at him, threw things at him, degraded and ridiculed him mercilessly, and finally shut him away from his friends and family and everything he used to enjoy.

Even if Margaret's degradation into darkness were not inevitable, it was forced upon her by the confines of Chi-Town, Herbert reckoned. Many people simply could not live for so long cooped up inside the city. Some citizens went their entire lives without seeing the sun or feeling the cool breeze on their faces. It was no matter. Herbert would have his revenge against Chi-Town as well. Anyone who dared to enter the apartment after this night would meet the man with the burning skin. No music box, no singing. All who entered would be consumed by fire and rage.

Before bedding down on the sofa, Herbert locked the door to the apartment, unplugged the telephone, and threw it and the door keys out the window onto the street below.

At two in the morning, Herbert drifted off to sleep. He would never awaken. His autopsy report would indicate that he expired at approximately eight thirty-five. The cause of death would be asphyxiation from smoke inhalation. There would be no pain, and no terrified visage frozen on his face. He had gone quietly. The autopsy would also report that he had a massive amount of medicine in his stomach, which most likely led to his inability to be roused when the apartment had caught fire.

At eight thirty that morning, Margaret awoke from her sleep. She reached over to the night stand to check the time on the digital clock and found an old music box and audio recorder. Next to the recorder was a small card with some indecipherable words and a small green triangle. There were no headphones to the recorder, so Margaret simply hit the button with the small green triangle and it started to play through the integrated speaker.

Herbert's voice came on the recorder. He sounded very tired, and his voice was shaky and nervous. Margaret sighed, wondering what ridiculous message he wished to waste her time with.

"Margaret, this is a message from your husband. I don't have much to say, so please just listen for a moment. On the night stand I have left a present for you. It was something that my grandfather found on one of his digs in a place called *Madhaven*. Apparently Madhaven is filled with wonderful treasures of the Golden Age. This box is not valuable, but I thought you would like it anyway. It plays a beautiful tune once it is opened."

As Margaret listened, she toyed with the music box. It was an old and fragile-looking thing, as if it would fall apart if she touched it. Surprisingly, it was quite heavy and durable. She couldn't even get the stupid thing opened. She was getting fed up with it and about to simply toss it in the closet.

Herbert's message continued, "There is a special way to open it, you see. You have to sing to it. I know you don't approve of my singing, but this box plays a special song. I simply could not wait until our anniversary to give it to you. Here, I'll sing now so the box will open. I think you will be quite surprised."

Herbert cleared his throat and began to sing through the recorder. The sound of his voice, a little scratchy and weary, but not unpleasant, brought back a small sense of nostalgia to Margaret. She hadn't heard this song for years. What an odd coincidence that it was the very same song that opened the box.

"Try to think that love's not around

But it's uncomfortably near.

My old heart ain't gaining no ground

Because my Angel Eyes ain't here."

The box opened slightly. Only a crack. Margaret ignored it, paying attention to the sudden waft of smoke and the scent of burning wood. Where was that smell coming from?

"Angel Eyes, that old devil sent

They glow unbearably bright

Need I say my love's misspent

Misspent with Angel Eyes tonight."

On the opposite side of the bed, Dwayne awoke. "What's this?" he asked.

"Just some stupid thing Herbert gave me," she responded.

The box opened a little more. Small trails of smoke rose up from the inside, going unnoticed by the two lovers, greeting each other with entwined bodies and a good morning kiss.

"So drink up all you people

Order anything you see.

Have fun, you happy people

The drinks and the laughs are on me."

The box opened completely, and a volcano explosion of smoke and flames erupted from it. Margaret kicked the box and the recorder off the bed and into the corner of the room out of shock and fear. The box lay on its side, and flames raced across the carpet, igniting the drapes and sheets she bought by pilfering money from Herbert's credit card. Dwayne's uniform, lying on the floor in a pile, went up in flames.

"Pardon me, but I've gotta run

The fact's uncommonly clear

Got to find who's now number one

And why my Angel Eyes ain't here."

The walls ignited. Fire completely surrounded the two adulterers. Margaret tugged violently on Dwayne's arm, ordering him to take some kind of action to save them.

Across the room, a figure crawled forth from the box. He rose to his blackened feet and stumbled to the bed. His skin was charred flesh and smoldering ash. His face was gone, replaced by a crispy black skull. His mouth hung open, coughing thick smoke. His eyes stared forward, never moving from Margaret's wide white orbs with black pupils. His hands, bony burnt twigs, reached for her, lusting to burn the life from her. His rage could be felt; a physical, palpable force, threatening to envelop and consume their souls.

"Pardon me while I disappear."

The figure stood only inches away from Margaret. She could not scream. She could only choke.

Going Home

By Josh Sinsapaugh

He would slip into the bar in the same way that he had slipped into town: at night, like a man hurrying to get out of the rain. Those who saw him enter that first night looked on the stranger with a sense of familiarity and ease.

Months later, even after they had gotten to know him, they regarded him in the same light. They would chuckle, too, each time he stepped through that door, as he would run in from the rain even when it wasn't falling. Otherwise, when he was making his way around the bar or the 'Burbs, he would walk as if to music, with a happy little bob in his step and a shrug of his shoulders. His voice flowed easily and effortlessly, like a mountain stream after the first thaw, as if everything he said had been written by Dylan, Silverstein, Yeats or one of those other famous poets from antiquity. Sometimes, when he was more laid back than usual, it would seem like he was reciting poetry or singing a slow song. Yet, despite his manner of speech, he rarely said anything sophisticated or deep, except of course when he was addressing his favorite topics. Ironically, when he did sing, his voice was substandard, though everyone listened anyways just to hear him strum on his guitar and sing songs from foreign lands and times of myth and legend.

His appearance threw many off, as well. A Bayou Ursine, he was a bear-like D-Bee with six eyes, four ears, and two bushy, fox-like tails. The fur that covered his body was a scattershot of brown and black, with a lone white tuft on his chest that looked sort of like a stolen diamond that had never been recovered. As if that wasn't odd enough, he was fond of putting the fur on the top of his head into cornrows, a subtle bit of styling that often went unnoticed unless one was standing right above him. He always wore the same old hooded sweatshirt – a tattered blue mess with multiple stains that, as he would say, "not even God has counted." Coffee, wine, bleach, pine pitch, oil, and other classic colors laid splashed across the blue canvas, turning it into a Cubist masterpiece with a broken zipper, installed above a sparkling clean pair of cargo shorts or slacks.

Castor Berb was the name he was currently going by, and it was clear that he had given it to himself, although no one ever called him on it. Even up in the 'Burbs, where his kind were rare, they could tell the name was made up, borrowed, or maybe even stolen. Bayou Ursines didn't name their children "Castor," or any other hard sounding names. They preferred names from their home dimension, like Budkiss, Groland, Marisol, or Saluush, or names from the Good Book such as Job, Josiah, or Tobit. "Berb" was not the surname of any Bayou Ursine family that ever lived, either, as it flowed too easily off the tongue. No, the Bayou Bear Men of the South had last names that fooled the tongue, names that either went on too long or stopped abruptly, like Dracklinn, Morkinivian, and Rablanacumlai.

"Does he honestly believe that name is fooling anyone?" someone once asked.

"Do you honestly think he cares?" someone immediately shot back.

He probably didn't care, either.

In fact, to the casual observer, it seemed like he didn't have a care in the world. They were wrong, of course, as he cared a lot about a great many things: booze, music and baseball were all at the top of his list. The latter he could talk about for hours and hours, spinning lengthy yarns that stretched from home plate to the foul pole and back again.

The 'Burbs were full of baseball teams, with each 'Burb and even some neighborhoods hosting their own ball club, and Castor knew each and every one, what they hit, and what their chances of winning were. If he cared enough, he probably could have been a bookie, though he always figured that he was too busy keeping track of earned run and batting averages to memorize who he owed or who owed him. Baseball was a funny thing in the 'Burbs, because it hadn't caught on until 6-8 years ago, and many old timers still couldn't get the point of the game.

There was only one thing he adored more than sinking fastballs and bloop singles: home.

Home was miles and miles away, nestled up in the back of beyond, a little place called *Black Bayou* that was hidden away somewhere in the Deep South. To Castor, this was the greatest place in the world, and he wouldn't let anyone forget it. Every night, whenever the talk of baseball died down, he would begin to weave stories about his youth in Black Bayou and the adventures that he'd had there. Always up for a story after a hard day's work, he spun his yarns about a place that might as well have been on another planet. If the listeners let him – and sometimes even when they tried not to – he could go for hours, his tales broken only by a song on his guitar when he remembered to bring it.

"It was then that I saw him," he once noted in one of his stories. "That alligator was twenty feet long and ready to tear down the wall to get to me and my sister, and it almost did!"

"You're full of crap, Castor," someone would usually interject in disbelief.

"No I'm not," he would shoot back with a smirk. "But that alligator would have been if he had gotten a hold of my sister and me."

It was always like that, and thus Castor quickly became a likable facet of the bar scene. He would show up a little after eight o'clock, down some whiskey, and start right in with baseball talk. When the conversation lulled, and sometimes when it didn't, he would start in on his stories about Black Bayou. His tales of home would last into the wee hours of the night, sometimes until last call. Their source of alcohol cut off, Castor Berb and the remaining bar patrons would all disperse like rats into the night, and would either seek further entertainment or simply return home to their beds. The next evening, they'd return and Castor would begin where he left off the night before.

After weeks and weeks of this, someone finally noticed something out of the ordinary about Castor Berb. It was a Sunday night, and Castor arrived like he always did, bounding into the tavern with a smile on his face and a song on his lips. This time he arrived with a hookah he had just purchased from a local shop. It wasn't long before he stopped showing off the hookah and started in with talk about the afternoon's baseball game. The Firetown Red Dogs had lost to the Staunton Heights Highlanders, and were in danger of being swept, much to the Firetown fans' chagrin. One of the Highlanders players, the catcher, was seemingly hitting everything, batting an impressive .350, and thus dominated the conversations on that particular night.

"He's a monster," one of the Firetown fans stated rather bluntly. "He's got twelve home runs already and there's only been twenty-two games so far!"

"He's got to be cheating somehow," grumbled one Highlanders fan.

"Magic, he's using magic," another person suggested.

"I don't know about that," one of the more levelheaded Firetown fans admonished. "All that I do know is that there is no one else on the Highlanders who scares me more than him."

"Really?" Castor interjected finally, a hint of surprise woven into his cool voice. "I would think you would be more scared of the third baseman. After all, he's batting .380 on the year with fifteen homers and an absurd number of RBIs." The levelheaded Firetown fan simply shook his head.

"Look Castor, I honestly don't care about Mr. Three-Eighty, he's inconsistent," he noted dryly. "Sure, he has hit two walk off home runs and one grand slam already, but he is in no way as clutch as . . ."

"The Highlanders' catcher may be clutch," Castor said with a smile as he rocked his new hookah back and forth. "However, he does hit into double plays a lot."

"Not when there are runners in scoring position."

"Still, the third baseman is batting .380," the Bayou Ursine began, only to be cut off by the levelheaded fan.

"And he was batting .210 last year." The Firetown Fan's words hit the mark, cutting through the sports talk like a knife through warm butter. "The monster of Staunton Heights bats over .320 every year. *That* is consistency and *that* is why I'm scared whenever he comes to bat."

Castor simply smiled, as if he knew what the fellow was going to say all along and was simply playing along so that he could talk baseball. All eyes turned on the D-Bee, but before anyone could accuse him of playing Devil's Advocate he leaned back in his chair and downed the rest of his whiskey, letting out a long and satisfied sigh once the glass left his lips.

"The Highlanders' catcher reminds me of a catcher I knew back home." Castor's words caused many to smile, though a few rolled their eyes at the setup. Oblivious to how anyone felt about hearing a yarn about Black Bayou, Castor immediately set in weaving a tale about his friend *Josiah Dracklinn*, another Bayou Ursine who could hit in the clutch as good as any player in the 'Burbs.

"Of course, baseball wasn't all he was good at," Castor went on to note, at length, after going over Josiah's godly exploits on the field. "In fact, he was mighty good with an energy rifle, and even knew his way around a Triax Predator. I believe he joined some mercenary outfit a year or two after I left. He was going to put the spurs to the Coalition, and according to my brother he did exactly that on one occasion."

The hours stretched on as he wowed them, first with the tale of Josiah's duel with a SAMAS, and then with a tale about how he and Josiah had stolen some rum from the Black Bayou distillery when they were only twelve. The onslaught of hayseed tales didn't stop there though, and Castor was soon diving headlong into other tales and stories about his swampy homeland, from the awkward story of a male Bayou Ursine cub with the misfortune of being named *Marisol*, to the frightening stories of the malignant River Gods who made him think twice about going into the water after dark. He had them laughing, he had them cringing, he had them questioning if anything he said was real, and he was loving every moment of it. He stopped though, like he did every night, around midnight, so that they could all step outside for some "fresh air" and return for last call.

Once outside they all broke out cigars and cigarettes – whatever their pleasure might be – striking up yet another baseball conversation beneath the massive cloud of acrid, yellow smoke that was soon collecting above them. Castor threw in some insightful points every now and again, though he otherwise kept quiet during the debate, saving his two cents for when they were most valuable. The few there who found him to be annoying were thankful for the silence, while the rest didn't think anything of it; Castor always spoke less when he was smoking. His voice did regain the spotlight though, fifteen minutes into their smoking break.

"Well, I think I'll be taking off early," said the Bayou Ursine, pretending to peer at the invisible watch on his wrist with a goofy grin, and looking up at the others as he did so. "It's getting late and it has been a long week, so I better get a jump on the one that lies ahead."

"We're not going to beg you to stay, Castor," someone laughed, smiling as the boisterous D-Bee turned his gaze toward her.

"I know," he shot back, "you're probably all going to pray that I stay." He flashed his pearly whites again, this time with a grin that was a hundred times goofier than the one he made before. They all laughed, and so did he, and with that he stumbled up the street, nonchalantly waving off the murmur of goodbyes as he went. The conversation shifted after his departure, turning to talk of a recent Coalition purge of a Shanty Town. Twenty people had been killed, countless wounded – though it wasn't long before the topic changed to the odd D-Bee fellow who had just left their company.

"Did you ever notice that Castor leaves early every Sunday?" asked the woman.

"Your point being?" said one of the men, following up his query with a long drag on his cigarette.

"He didn't leave early every week when he first got here."

"And?"

"Well, just what is he doing?" she asked, her tone inquisitive, her cigarette dangling from her lips. "If he really wanted to get a jump start on this coming week then he wouldn't come out drinking with us, right?"

"We're talking about Castor," someone noted dryly, causing everyone to erupt into laughter. "He's all about routine," the man added after the laughter died down. "What's so different about this Sunday?"

"I still say there has to be a reason he leaves early," the female patron sighed after the laughter wilted, her voice trailing off with the yellow fog. One or two of her fellow patrons murmured in halfhearted agreement, causing her to scowl a bit. "Guess I'm being too curious," she mumbled, and almost everyone marked that as the end of the matter.

The next two weeks passed like all those before them: an inebriated time warp where the nightly barroom ritual was as much a part of existence as the sunrise. During this time, everyone's favorite Bayou Ursine started to bring his guitar every night, and thus every story was capped off with some ancient song about the Southland. He said they were all folk songs from antiquity, songs whose authors were not granted the same immortality as their lyrics or melodies. No one cared if Castor was lying though, and instead they just enjoyed the music, treating it as a simple escape from the harsh realities of the world around them. Reality was overrated as far as they were concerned anyways, and luckily, it could be diluted with alcohol and good music.

A Tuesday at the beginning of May found them in the bar once again, a night that was shaping up to be a repeat of all the Tuesdays that came before it. The baseball talk was heated as usual, with batting averages, earned run averages, and on base percentages thrown up into the barroom air just as often as profanity and calls for another round. Castor had brought his guitar once again, and the wooden instrument rested at his side, its neck caressing his own as he slouched in his chair and threw back shots of whiskey. He wasn't participating much in the conversation, though no one seemed to notice, and he only offered the occasional correction for batting averages or other stats.

"The Monster of Staunton Heights is down to .300," one of the Firetown fans jeered. "He's finally in a slump."

"Three-oh-one," the D-Bee stated with a yawn, absentmindedly rocking his guitar back and forth as he offered up the adjustment.

"What?"

"His average is down to .301, not .300."

"Oh, yeah, you're right," the fan acknowledged, though he still leapt headlong into a ruthless character assassination of the Highlanders' catcher. He was not alone, either, and soon other Red Dog fans joined in on the impromptu roast of the man they never met.

"It's nice to see that smug jerk get his reward," one of the patrons noted sarcastically.

"I hope he enjoys swatting air and chasing knuckleballs for at least another two or three games," someone else added.

"I hope his house gets knocked over in the next purge!" one of the more overzealous Red Dog fans shouted with a laugh.

"Enjoy the slump," another sarcastic voice cried out, speaking as if the Highlanders' catcher was in the room.

"He's not in a slump," Castor spoke up once again in a cool voice, causing everyone within earshot to fall silent. "Yeah, it's no slump, he's just not hitting." The absurdity of the statement hung in the air for a few seconds, drifting over their heads like the grin of the Cheshire Cat, and disappeared just as quickly. Once it was gone, it not was long before the sarcastic laughter and heated tension melted into a series of cool chuckles, and eventually full on laughter. No one knew that Castor had just paraphrased a man who was long dead (or if he had done so intentionally), and no one cared, either. Someone ordered another round with tears in his eyes, and Castor picked up his guitar, smiling as he ran his fingers up the neck. "I was in a hitting slump back home once . . ." he began, most of those in attendance recognizing the weak segue all too well.

"I had just returned home from a long journey and my old pals wanted me to play some baseball so I could unwind. I couldn't hit the side of a barn though; my mind just wasn't in the game. Why? Well, I guess I was away for too long, or maybe my mind was still out on the open seas. Heck, I got into a fight with Josiah within hours of returning home – and we haven't been friends since. Baseball was the last thing on my mind, and my life was falling apart with every swing of the bat."

Something was different, something was not right. Castor's stories were usually happy ones, and yet this one was shaping up to be sad, very sad. The smiles that ringed the table started to fade, and the D-Bee's friends began to nurse their beers. The Bayou Ursine seemed oblivious though, and continued onward.

"Home just wasn't home anymore, whether it was Black Bayou or the plate in front of the backstop. It seems silly to compare what happened on the field to what was happening off of it, but hey, that's the way things were. I almost hit a home run during that slump, only to have it caught by an outfielder at the last second – and then when the game was over I found out my grandmother had died. I was batting 1.000 when it came to bad luck, and it seemed as if the whole world was on the opposing team. Hell, the pitcher, both on the mound and in Heaven, might as well have been throwing bowling balls toward me. Though I was home, I just couldn't get home – if you catch my meaning."

He paused for a moment to down another shot of whiskey, raking the neck of his guitar with his free hand as he slammed the glass down. All eyes were on the Bayou Ursine, and all ears were on his story. He swallowed hard – memories or whiskey, no one was sure – and then continued.

"A few weeks before Halloween I got my first hit: a bloop single. It felt good. I was finally coming out of the slump, or so I thought. That night, all the strings on my guitar broke, letting me know clear and well that the slump was still on. I thought about ending it all, but couldn't find a way that suited me, so I decided against it. I hit the bottle hard, and hit it harder still when I found out that my girl was cheating on me with my brother. I thought about finding some Houngan or maybe even a Bokor – someone that I could pay to lay some mojo on me. I didn't have any cash though, or anything worth trading for that matter. So, I did the only thing I could do to break out of that slump . . ."

He let his words trail off into the barroom haze, causing his companions to lean forward with anticipation. Seemingly ignoring them, he started to tune his guitar, his many eyes avoiding theirs. He plucked a string and the resulting note rose like a calamity through the drunken silence. He plucked another string and got the same result, causing a few of his comrades to rock back and forth in an attempt to dispel the tension. He opened his mouth, though it was only to suck in some air, and when he exhaled some of them had had enough.

"And?" one of the assembled patrons asked.

"What did you do to break out of the slump?" another spoke up.

"The only thing I could do," Castor replied without looking up from his guitar.

"Which was?" someone at an adjacent table asked, a bit of anger framing his words.

"I did the thing that baseball players have been doing for over five hundred years to get out of a slump," the D-Bee elaborated, a sly smile snaking its way across his face. He made as if to strum a few chords on his guitar, but stopped when his hand was halfway there – choosing instead to down another shot of whiskey.

"Castor, come on, what did you do?" the man seated closest to the D-Bee begged, his hand gripped tightly around the handle of his mug both from anticipation and annoyance.

"The only thing I could do," Castor noted once again. "The thing that baseball players have been doing for five hundred years to break slumps." He paused once more, and took the smallest deep breath that bar had ever seen: "I spent the night . . . and I mean *all* night . . . with . . ." He raised his head, as slowly as he could, and took a long look all at those sitting around him who cared to hear the story. He smiled again, broadly this time.

"I spent the night with a fat chick."

A few groans rose from the assembled company, like the first drops of rain after a drought, and like those raindrops they were soon joined by a torrential downpour of groans, sighs, and the occasional laugh. Castor had them, he had them good, and they all knew it by the way the D-Bee laughed and slapped his hand against his knee.

"Why did I expect a serious story out of you?" one of the patrons laughed.

"Because you're a drunk fool that doesn't know any better," the Bayou Ursine replied in a sly tone, his pearly whites displayed for all to see in a grin that was half amused, half mocking, and every bit triumphant. He barely paused though, and instead seized the opportunity that rose from the mixed commotion that he had caused only a few moments ago. With a flick of his wrist, he kept control of the room, sending a few notes reverberating into the ether from his guitar strings.

"A song?" he asked.

"A song," some of his comrades answered, raising their mugs to the sky, and for a second it seemed as if the glasses of beer were conductors' batons, signaling the orchestra to ready itself. There was only one musician in the orchestra though: a sly storyteller with too much whiskey in his gut, but he heeded the "conductors" nonetheless, starting his song as soon as the mugs hit the table.

With the first note reality faded away, with the second they were in a distant land, and with the third they were in a distant time. The music flowed easily out of the guitar, and quickly rambled on across the table, past the patrons, and out over the hills and far away. He sang a song that must have been about the Dark Woods, as it made mention of Alabama, though they were clueless as to *which* Alabama that he sang of: past or present. It wasn't important though, as *any* Alabama, ancient, modern or otherwise, was as foreign to them as Europe or Atlantis. Likewise, whoever the hell Neil Young or the governor of Birmingham were supposed to be was irrelevant, as was Watergate, though they knew the latter didn't bother Castor any (so why should it bother them?). No, none of those things mattered to any to them, nor did the fact that they were clueless to much of its meaning. All that mattered was that it was music, and escapism at its finest.

The odd D-Bee stopped singing, the lyrics had run their course, and the music followed suit a few moments later. As the relative silence rushed back into the void he removed his instrument from his lap, placed it at his side, and spun it around as if it was his dance partner. Once the dance was done, the guitar's neck met his once again, and together the two slouched in rest like tired lovers. Realizing that Castor wasn't going to sing another song (at least not yet), a flutter of drunken claps spiraled up from the table like butterflies taking wing after a storm. If he had been on the stage he would've bowed, but because he wasn't he simply threw back another shot of whiskey and smiled.

"I love that song, it reminds me of home, even though home wasn't in Alabama," the bear man sighed happily as he slammed the shot glass back down. "It also reminds me of . . ."

"Castor, shut the hell up!" one of the patrons bellowed, cutting Castor off and slamming his fist against the table. "Every Goddamn night you drag your sorry ass in here and you talk about home as if anybody but you gives a crap!" The D-Bee only smiled though, and shrugged his free shoulder, the one that didn't have a sleeping guitar on it.

"I sure hope that none of you will give me crap, after all . . ."

"No, I said shut the hell up!" the patron shot back. "No, you ain't wisecracking this down, you had this coming for a long time! You're pathetic, Castor, don't you know that there is a reason they call it the past? It's because the past is in the *past*." He took a swig from his beer in hopes that Castor would take the opportunity to defend himself – the D-Bee didn't, so instead he continued: "Hey Castor, remember the time that the pissed-off drunk reported you to the Coalition because he was tired of hearing your damn stories? No? Neither do I, but wouldn't that be a great story to remember?"

The drunk's words rippled across the table like rolling thunder, silencing everyone. Normally, a punch would have been thrown or the mob would have taken over – not this time, though. No, the situation was far too surreal for them, especially considering that they knew only happiness before he opened his mouth. Thus, the painful absurdity of the scene left them motionless like deer caught in rushing headlights, anchoring them to their seats stronger than any ropes ever could. They were expecting a punch from Castor, but the D-Bee wasn't the kind to throw them, at least not over words. Besides, he would much rather cut somebody down with a cleverly worded insult instead of with a crushing blow if given the chance. Yet, no insults came either. Only silence flowed from the lips of the bear man, the loudest silence that any of them had ever heard.

"What, no witty retort?" the man mocked. "No anecdote? No story about the boonies?" He took another swig of his beer, though this time it was out of triumph rather than to give Castor an opportunity. "So, Castor," he continued, speaking in a smooth tone that was dripping with sarcasm. "If home is so great, why the hell don't you go back?" He didn't expect a quick reply from the D-Bee, not this time, and it was doubtful that anyone did. That didn't deter the patron's celebration though, a fact that was clear in his smile: a twisted crescent of unholy yellow teeth that glittered like gold in the light of the bar. Silence gripped their little world once again, though it was quickly shattered by four simple words.

"I *am* going back."

The five syllables slipped into the tense nothing so quickly that no one could believe that Castor had uttered them. Instead, the absurdity of the twelve letters hammered their eardrums like hail – unexpected intruders that might as well have slithered out of some dimensional Rift rather than out of their friend's mouth. They swiftly scrambled to reaffirm their sanity by asking themselves all manner of questions, ranging from the simple "did Castor really say that?" to the desperate "am I really that drunk?" Few could find satisfactory answers in their drunken states, while those who did found themselves proven wrong only moments later.

"I *am* going back," Castor repeated, this time emphasizing his words with a few notes from his guitar so that no one could doubt that they were his own. The notes faded and a smile etched its way across the D-Bee's face, even as the yellow crescent on his (former) friend's face disappeared behind bewildered lips. Castor's grin left the man silent, knocking the wind out of his sails as he watched a very different sort of smile replace his own. Neither yellow nor malicious, it was a clear parade of pointed white teeth that seemed to both mock and reassure as they made their way across his jaw. It wasn't the glowing smile of a drunk though; rather it was the sharp smile of a man who had his wits about him – a man who *still* had control over the situation.

"Yes, you heard right, *friend*, I said that I am going back."

Confusion slowly turned into disbelief as the intensity of the stale barroom air shifted into a feeling of odd relief – like a spring breeze rattling the Venetian blinds at three in the morning. Those assembled around Castor, friends and acquaintances alike, collectively exhaled, the wind from their mouths scattering a dozen questions into the still air.

"Are you serious?" one asked.

"Yes, am I ever not serious?" came the answer.

"When are you going?" someone else asked.

"In the next few months, once I save up the necessary credits," came another answer.

"Why are you leaving?" another asked.

"So I can stretch my legs." Again, Castor answered, and it was an answer that many of them felt they should've expected. Why the bear man was leaving was going to remain a mystery and they knew it, and the only way that was going to change was at Castor's convenience. So, they assaulted him with yet more questions, though the new salvo was about the destination, rather than the how or why, the kind of questions that the D-Bee was always happy to answer. A few even acted as excellent segues into the bear man's familiar anecdotes, though none of them led easily into another song, much to his chagrin.

The impromptu Q&A session stretched on toward closing time, and as it did two events simultaneously occurred, though they went unnoticed by Castor and his group of friends. First, the man with the yellow smile backed away from their table, out the door, and into obscurity. He had been defeated, as all bullies eventually are, and thus he had fled their barroom reality for another. Where he went – another bar, town, territory, or dimension – they never knew or cared, though none of them doubted for a second that he found some other scuffed up table to darken with his beer stained shadow. Second, and more importantly, a new period in Castor's contribution to the bar scene had been ushered in. He was going home, eventually, and he never let any of them forget it, beginning (and ending) many of his whiskey addled sentences with four simple words: "when I go home."

*　*　*

"When I go home to Black Bayou I'll be able to drink real whiskey and not this sewer water," Castor sighed as he slammed his empty glass back onto the table. Two months had gone by since he had revealed his homeward plans to his friends, and some of them were beginning to expect that he was never going to leave. Of course, none of them intended to call him on it, and there were worse things in their lives than a drunk friend talking about returning home.

"The whiskey here is not *that* bad," the man across the table from Castor interjected. "Heck, it's a damn sight better than what you can usually expect from a dive like this."

"I hear that there are places in the Magic Zone with really good whiskey," someone else added.

"Yeah, if you don't mind getting turned into a newt in the process," another pointed out.

"Nah, Zone Whiskey is safe to drink," Castor reassured. "It's the girls that you have to watch out for." He smiled devilishly as he poured himself another glass. "If only you could be so lucky as to be turned into a newt after running into one of them."

Smiles and a bit of laughter made their way around the table, skipping a few members of the fairer sex as they went. Whiskey and jokes about whiskey were merely a distraction though, or at least more of a distraction than usual. The Coalition had leveled a Shanty Town earlier that morning, killing hundreds in the process and destroying twice as many dreams, and the specter of that event drifted over the 'Burbs like some noxious gas, stealing the life from every *real* smile outside of the Old Towns. They tried to keep it at bay the best they could, which was the only way they knew how: with alcohol and camaraderie. It was a losing battle though, and the black fog always seemed to find a way back into their reality, as if they were falling in love with the wrong girl over and over again.

"There was a good little whiskey cart out *there* in the fringe," someone noted as soberly as he could, leaving no doubt in any of their minds as to what he was talking about. "Of course, it was always a risk to go out that far into the Shanties . . ." It was a poor choice of words and he knew it, they all did, so he let the sentence die, drowning it mercifully in a flood of beer.

"It was good," Castor agreed, knocking back some more whiskey. "Some of the best damn whiskey I ever poured past my teeth."

"I wonder where they got it," another patron thought aloud.

"Maybe New Paducah?" someone offered, though she sounded very unsure of herself.

"Wouldn't surprise me if they were getting it from this little operation down in the Dark Woods . . ." Castor interjected, his words trailing off as if in a dream.

"Really?" one of his friends asked as casually as possible, expecting another story – anything to take his mind off the harsh reality of those dark days.

"Just this little hamlet I found once, deep within the ivy . . ." he began, only to have his words trail off again. Apparently, even Castor couldn't divert his mind away from the present for long, even with prompting from a friend. Yet, despite the fact that the Da Vinci of distractions had just failed, they all tried to escape the long shadows by telling stories of their own. Of course, they all failed one by one, toppling like gravestones on a hill or floundering like dying fish caught at low tide. The air had been sucked from their lungs by the pressure, and thus they couldn't swim, tread, or even paddle away from the desolation. All they could do was sit at their table and fight to keep the sinking conversation afloat, though they all knew the boat wasn't going anywhere.

"The Coalition can go to Hell," someone hissed at last, dropping all pretenses from the bloodied air. "We're just waiting to get in because that's what we have to do. That's all we can do." He downed the rest of his beer and slammed the mug back onto the table with a resounding thud, leaving the glass on its side as if it was some great, wounded beast. "All that we want is safety, to live the dream of paradise in the fortress cities, and yet they refuse us and blow us to bits."

"It ain't right," someone else cried.

"It doesn't make no sense," another sobbed.

"This is exactly why I want to get into New Waukegan as soon as possible," yet another noted, though it seemed as if he missed the point.

"What the hell is wrong with this world?" another patron asked, grasping for straws. "I mean, come on, we're on the freakin' doorstep of Chi-Town. Even Tarn called this place the un . . ." She seemed to have trouble pronouncing the words in her drunken stupor. "The undisputed hubbub of North American civilization!"

"Hub," Castor corrected, signaling for another bottle of whiskey with his free hand.

"Hub of North American civilization," she repeated.

Castor's fresh bottle of whiskey arrived in short order, plopped down into the center of the table by the barkeep. This time though, they all partook, including the lightweights – it wasn't a time for tangling with reality, and they all knew it. Instead, they fell for their own weaknesses and ushered away the haunts of that terrible existence with the booze, replacing the friendly sights of the familiar bar with a blurred, surrealist smear. They were abusing themselves, and deep down inside they all knew it, though none said it. In fact, no one said anything, the conversation replaced with the clinking of glasses and the thud of the bottle on the table. Later that night, or the next morning, many of them would look back at the conquest of that bottle as a mistake, though it never occurred to them as they flitted through the moment.

"Things were much happier when I lived in New Chillicothe, why did I come here?" the whiskey asked, though it spoke in the voice of the man sitting across the table from Castor. "I guess New Chillicothe is my Black Bayou."

"You shouldn't regret moving," the whiskey noted, though it spoke in Castor's voice. "Even if in the end you come to find out you failed, never regret trying."

"I was a Coalition citizen in New Chillicothe though!" the whiskey admonished, again in the man's voice. "I had security, and I gave it all up for a chance at real security in one of the fortress cities! I'm an idiot, I've doomed my whole family!" The whiskey's voice wavered, and began to sob, placing its head in its hands.

"Castor, why did you leave Black Bayou?" The whiskey spoke up again, though this time with a female voice to Castor's left.

"I had no reason not to," the whiskey answered, speaking in Castor's voice. "Home is great and all, but sometimes you just have to get away so that you can get back."

"But why here? Why the 'Burbs?" the whiskey continued to prod, still in a feminine voice.

"Why not?" the whiskey asked back with Castor's voice. "This place isn't *that* bad. Sure, it has more than its fair share of hardship, but it is as good a place as any."

"But Black Bayou sounds so much nicer!" the whiskey protested using another voice. "No purges and no Coalition!"

"I hate to break it to you . . ." the whiskey sighed, using Castor's voice once again. "The Coalition are down in the South as well, and they occasionally purged *a whole village* or two." The whiskey paused for a second, a forlorn look sketched across its face. "Even without the Coalition it's no paradise. Yeah, sorry to say, but every place on this planet has its fair share of sour points."

"Come on now, you have to be joking!" the whiskey cried, using the feminine voice from before once again. "Are the Coalition everywhere?"

"No," came the whiskey's simple answer with Castor's voice. "They're in a fair amount of places, but they ain't everywhere. They bring death wherever they go though, though it's not like death isn't in those places before they get there anyways."

"So what the hell are we supposed to do?" the whiskey asked, speaking in the voice that it spoke up with in the first place. "If none of us humans can get inside Chi-Town or New Waukegan, then what are we supposed to do?"

"I don't know," the whiskey admitted, sounding like Castor once more. "What I do know though is that tears won't put out a fire. So, eventually, we have to accept things the way they are and hope for the best, and maybe even move on."

"So you're telling us to do nothing?!" the whiskey all but yelled, speaking angrily in a voice that sounded like it belonged to someone on Castor's right. "Are you really telling us to grin as we take crap to the face over and over again? What're you trying to say?"

"I'm not even sure what I'm trying to say," the whiskey admitted in Castor's voice.

"How's that even possible?" the whiskey asked in another voice.

"I don't know the answer to that either," the whiskey admitted, once again in Castor's voice. "All I know is that tears won't put out fires, and neither will alcohol."

"So where do we go from here?" the whiskey asked in its New Chillicothe voice.

"I guess that we just have to keep going without any regrets, taking victory and defeat as it comes," the whiskey replied in the bear man's voice. "And on the way, you cry when you need to, and drink when you want to. Just keep in mind that neither solves anything."

A few moments later many of them came to the realization that strong drinks weren't going to make the night any shorter. Truth be told, they were having the opposite effect, so they took matters into their own hands. Taking the initiative, someone tipped the empty whiskey bottle onto its side and called for a round of black coffee. No one ordered any more beer or liquor.

Eventually, the hangovers of that sad night faded, as did the terrifying strength of the memories and the secondhand hardship that came with them. Jokes, smiles, and baseball talk returned to their little barroom world, as did Castor's hayseed anecdotes about Black Bayou. Up in the relative North, in the Chi-Town 'Burbs, it was an alien place to be sure – yet those who had heard the Bayou Ursine weave his stories during the previous months started to reflect on it as if they been there. It was almost as familiar to them as their nightly excursions to the bar, the lights of that humble establishment reminding them of the blazing southern sun that they knew only through Castor's colorful yarns. The bayou bear man's lover made additional appearances as well, stretched across his lap playfully as he pulled her strings, causing her to sing beautifully in apparent ecstasy.

Life, at least as it applied to the bar scene, was back to normal. Thus, each night was once again a repeat of the last: a temporal flux fueled by cheap alcohol and camaraderie. They were in a rut, though no one noticed or cared. Instead, time became an expendable commodity that no one paid much attention to, the days and nights rushing away like beer from the tap. Even the Dog Days of August, which are often long, almost excruciating ordeals in North America, passed by as easily and flippantly as a drunk knocking back a shot of alcohol. Soon, the temperature and leaves began to drop, omens that heralded the exit of baseball (until next spring) and the return of hard wintertime liquors.

The word "surprise" had lost all meaning by the time September was drawing to a close, and thus none of them ever expected that Castor would suddenly up and leave them like he was about to. Looking back a few months later, once they realized that he had left their lives forever, it seemed rather clear that he was going to leave them when he did. If they had been paying attention, they may have noticed that *that* night was special, especially when compared to the army of mediocre evenings that had marched before it. Hindsight is 20/20 though, so they couldn't fault themselves too much – Castor wouldn't have.

The last Sunday of September was a miserable day by all accounts. It even started miserably, with thick fog and light rain, and ended equally as miserably with a weak thunderstorm. Thus, expectations were set incredibly low for the night that was guaranteed to follow, so much so that many in Castor's party considered breaking tradition by staying home. None of them did, of course; the lure of friendship and forgetting, for a time, all the world's troubles was far too great to ignore. So, at about seven o'clock they began to file into their house of worship, calling out to the bartender, who quickly answered their prayers with a flick of his wrists and a freshly filled glass.

By eight o'clock it was still raining, though they had long since forgotten about the storm. Raindrops did not concern them anymore, their focus drawn instead to the never-ending supply of amber liquid before them. Their attention diverted by their life's blood, they didn't see Castor when he entered the bar, carrying his guitar with him. If they had, they might have noticed that, despite the fact that it was *actually* raining this time, he didn't run into the bar like he always did so many times before. Instead, he seemed to walk apprehensively, like a stranger in a strange land – each footstep chosen with the kind of care and precision that is usually reserved only for minefields. There was no bob in his step either, the unseen music that normally accompanied him falling as flat as the dull thuds of his sandals.

His friends finally noticed him when he slumped down into his chair with a satisfying sigh, the bear man acknowledging each and every greeting that came his way with a smile and a simple nod. No one had seen him enter, and thus no one noticed that the Castor who sat in front of them was a very different Castor than the one who had just strolled in from out of the rain. Indeed, there was no weight on his shoulders as there had seemingly been only a few moments before. Instead, the professional drinker who sat before them was as lighthearted and carefree as anyone could ever hope to be, a broad grin etched into his face as he signaled to the bartender for a glass of straight whiskey. He continued to smile as they dove into the small talk, throwing in his two cents every once and a while, though he seemed content enough just to listen and tune his guitar.

For once they didn't talk about baseball, the terms "out of the park" and "batting a thousand" showing up only as euphemisms in their alcohol addled discussions. As an alternative, they talked about everything else: the old times of only a few months before, what potent potable they had yet to try, and even what the cryptic writing that had been scratched into their table meant. As far as they were concerned, "Jenny is a Bitch" had to be some code, though who left it – pre-Rifts Free Masons or perhaps the fabled Vanguard – was up for debate, while a carving of a stick figure taking a whiz just had to be some Atlantean hieroglyph revealing the way to Xanadu. However, most intriguing of all were the words "Lisa and Eric Forever," which were undoubtedly the proclamation of two lovers who had uncovered the alchemic recipe for everlasting life.

"That reminds me . . ." Castor said at length, after a half hour of translating the Voynich Manuscript that had been scrawled across their table. It was a segue that they all recognized, and this time it was met with an enthusiastic cheer from all those sitting around him. Smiling, he continued, weaving tales about his home of Black Bayou – stories that they had all heard before. Yet, although they had heard each tale at least once before, they still paid attention with the same visceral intensity that they would have lent to a Rogue Scholar revealing the treasured secrets of the ancient Americans. If any of them had remembered the cold rain outside up until that point, they quickly forgot it, finding themselves awash in a foreign sun that knew only comfort and simplicity.

At the end of one of his stories, the ursine bard paused to let some whiskey loose down his throat, an opportunity that was quickly seized upon by one of his fellow patrons.

"Play a song, Castor!" she shouted from across the table, her head crooked and lit with a radiant glow and an equally radiant smile.

"Yeah, a song would be great," someone else noted in agreement, his words slipping from his lips lazily and with the greatest of comfort.

"Sure, a song *sounds* like a good idea," Castor answered with a smirk, though nobody caught his pun. "What should I play though?"

"Something grand!" came the enthusiastic answer from someone sitting to Castor's left.

"Play a song that you really like!" came another answer, which seemed to agree with the first.

"Sounds good to me," Castor admitted with a smile, fixing his lover onto his lap much to the delight of his fellow patrons. Slowly, he began to pluck the strings, and after a few slow notes the "edge" faded away, leaving them all in a relaxed state, and after a few chords they were instilled with the notion of being a part of something that was bigger than them all. Without seemingly any effort, but with all of his love, he played something that he said was called "Stairway to Heaven," and laid the Universe out at their feet, and then he followed it up with what he said was called "The Son Never Shines on Closed Doors," pulling them through a familiar green country that they had never been to. They were ensorcelled by every note and chord, and even by his admittedly substandard singing voice, swaying pleasantly back and forth through existence like a leaf caught in a whispering breeze. It wasn't music, it was more like magic, and at that moment, they couldn't have been happier.

"Those songs seem kind of sad," one of Castor's fellow patrons noted sometime after the final notes faded into the ether. "Sad but beautiful," she quickly added, causing many of her fellow barflies to agree with her.

"I can kind of see what you are saying," the D-Bee admitted, kicking back in his chair with his old lover caressing his neck with its own. "However, I don't think any song is really ever sad from its core to its chords." He ran his fingers gently along his lover's frets and smiled, taking his own actions as a cue to make his point: "After all, a smile can be sad, can't it?"

Murmurs of agreement rippled away across their table, as if Castor had dropped some enlightened pebble into the pond that connected their minds. However, few of them were drunk enough to talk philosophy, and thus one of them spoke up against the current: "Castor, what do those songs mean?"

"You'll have to take that up with their creators," the D-Bee answered with a smile, knowing that such a feat was impossible. "No," he added without taking a breath, "I don't know what either song *truly* means, and I don't want to know." The bear man didn't stop there though, probably because he thought that a "why" was inevitable, and quickly added: "I like guessing what they mean, but never knowing is so much better."

"Why is that?" the man to Castor's right asked, unleashing the "why" anyways, despite the bear man's best efforts.

"Well, that's the point of most poetry and music, isn't it?" the musician from the southern marshes replied. "You can say things without exactly saying them, communicating feelings instead of ideas. So, if you don't like the message, you can just enjoy the way the message is told." He ran his fingers gently along his lover's frets again, his free hand retrieving a shot of whiskey from the table. "At least, that's the way it is with good music."

"Well, what do you think the songs mean?" one of the other patrons asked as Castor made the shot disappear quicker than any stage magician ever could.

"What does that matter?" he asked with a bit of a sigh once the devil brew was done burning a trail down his throat.

"You're the one that sang the songs . . ." she replied. "So I just thought it would be interesting to know what you think." Castor sighed again and threw back another shot, shaking off the burn as his free hand tapped lightly on the neck of his guitar.

"If you must know . . ." the bear man began, his words immediately trailing off into nothing, though they weren't sure if that was out of reluctance or because of the alcohol. "If you must know," he began again, "I think that both songs are about returning home, if only eventually."

"You think *everything* nowadays is about going home," someone noted with a chuckle, apparently believing that the D-Bee was setting up a joke or yet another anecdote.

"Yeah, that's true," the storyteller confessed with a bit of a smirk. "This is *different* though," he quickly added. "I've *always* thought that those two songs were about going home."

"Fig . . . fig . . . figuratively or literally?" someone asked from across the table, a man who evidently *was* drunk enough to philosophize.

"I guess, both and neither at the same time," Castor shot back, causing everyone (including himself) to smile. "We're always trying to go home," he continued (much to everyone's amazement), "whether it is home plate, where we rest our head, or some indefinable place in our mind. And of course, there is the other home . . ."

Instead of finishing his thought he startled them, rapping his shot glass back against the table as if it was a judge's gavel, or (more appropriately) a shovel striking the top of a metal coffin. He had not put it back down after his last shot, though none of them had noticed, and thus it was a bigger surprise than him going "deep" with his explanation. The barkeep shouted something about being careful with the glassware and the D-Bee smiled mischievously, leaving everyone wondering if they had just been set up or if anything he had just said really meant anything at all. Of course, he cut them all off before they could accuse him of playing a prank or using a defense mechanism, retaining control of the situation.

"Kind of reminds me of something from back home . . ." he noted with a big goofy grin.

"A story about home?" one of his friends asked, her pleasant smile slack-jawed by one too many mugs of beer.

"Nope," he slyly replied, pausing for a moment as he drank in the surprised expressions on his fellow patrons' faces. "A story that someone told *me* years ago, a folk story from back home."

"So it's a change of pace?" another friend asked, his excitement and attention masked by a long yawn.

"Yup, a change of pace," Castor answered with yet another smile. "It's a story that my mother told me long ago. When I go home to Black Bayou, she'll probably tell me it again just for old time's sake."

"Well heck, let's hear it!" one of his drunker friends cheerfully demanded, raising his whiskey sour toward the ceiling.

"Alright, here goes . . ." Castor began as he too lifted up his glass, all of them following in the impromptu toast. "L'Chaim," the Bayou Ursine all but shouted, and then he began:

"Long ago in the quiet of the world, when things were a bit simpler, before the Coalition came to the Delta, there lived a musician that was as horrible as a musician could ever be. He was the kind of man that hoped for mediocrity, and dreamt of stardom – the kind of man that was horrible at singing the blues but knew them all too well. Some say he was human, others say he was a Bayou Ursine like myself (at least that is what I've always been told), while others say that he was some kind of half-breed that came out of the wilderness. Whatever or whoever he was, he was probably the worst musician that ever lived.

"He really had no reason to complain though: he had a good childhood, and life in the South was generally good despite all of its hardships. He wanted something more though, and in that regard, he was selfish. He believed, almost religiously, that his life was not worth living without good music as a spice. He wasn't content to listen to others play good music either, and as you may or may not know, the South has always created the greatest musicians; it's been that way since antiquity. No, he wanted to *play* good music himself so that he could have good music whenever and wherever he wanted.

"He realized though that he would never be able to play good music all on his own, and thus he put his feet to the pavement and followed the road. He went to a certain place, one of those legendary locales that even time has forgotten: a crossroad near the Old Miss, and it was there that he rested his feet. Then, at about midnight, that man that regards darkness as a virtue came sauntering up the road and hailed the poor musician. Upon seeing him, he knew that he was a monster in human skin, a creature that was devoid of form only a few moments before. He smelt more than a bit like burnt matches, and was wearing the most dapper black suit that the poor musician had ever seen. 'Play your guitar, boy!' he demanded, and the poor musician obeyed immediately.

"He played some old folk song about the levees breaking, and the man that smelt like burnt matches wrinkled his nose at him, sending a chill up his spine. So instead, the poor musician played 'When the Saints Go Marching In,' and again the man who smelt like burnt matches didn't approve – though he appreciated the irony of the poor musician's choice of songs. 'Play something good, boy!' he demanded, and the poor musician, at a loss for what to do, tried playing the folk song about the levees breaking once again.

"This angered the man who smelt like burnt matches, and he stamped his foot at the center of the crossroads and shouted at the poor musician. 'Give me that guitar, boy! It's out of tune!' Of course, the poor musician immediately complied, handing the guitar over to the man. At once, the man who smelt like burnt matches set about tuning the poor musician's guitar, creating unearthly sounds with the strings as he tightened them one by one. A few moments later, though it felt like an eternity to the old musician, the man who smelt like burnt matches handed him his guitar back, and the instrument was warm to the touch.

"Then that man in the dapper black suit that smelt more than a bit like burnt matches smiled, and it was the biggest smile that poor man ever saw. 'Play that song about the levees breaking again, boy.' He demanded. 'It's my favorite song.' Once again, the poor musician complied, though he was a poor musician no longer, as the music that flowed from his strings was as beautiful as the light of a firefly amongst the twilight of June. He played on, and the man who smelt like burnt matches was so pleased that he tapped his left foot to the beat and hummed along.

"After the song was done, the man who smelt like burnt matches gave his approval: clapping his hands heartily, which made the air smell like gunpowder. 'Well done, boy!' He praised the formerly poor musician. 'See what you can do with a properly tuned guitar? Now, you do know the price I charge for music lessons, don't you boy?' The good musician simply nodded, and handed over his everlasting soul to the man in the dapper black suit that smelt more than a bit like burnt matches. Then, once the deal had been done, he walked back up the road and faded into the night like automobile exhaust, his laughter and foul smell lingering long after him.

"Able to play music, and play music good, the man began to wander the wilds. First, he crossed the Old Miss and played many a good tune under the western sky, though he did not stop there. Instead, he kept wandering and playing music until he found a place where the stars all had different names, and after that a place where the stars were strange and unfamiliar. He wandered to the End of the World, where the bison shamans play with blue flames, and where an impenetrable wall of ice progresses slowly forward forever. Elsewhere, he saw manmade mountains that were more ancient than the Old American Empire, and wandered beneath jungle canopies traversed by ancient gods. He saw it all, and filled the air with music as he went.

"Eventually though, he yearned for home, so he returned from his travels. However, some of his friends and some of his family rejected him for the choice he had made, rebuking him for trading his everlasting soul for a 'little bit of music.' It was then, as his world crumbled around him, that he realized that without his soul, he could never be happy – everything else was a diversion, and people would only come to blame him for his musical talent. So, he did the only thing he could do: he set out on to the road once again, though he never stopped looking back. His soul was gone forever and he knew it, so he decided to search for a new one along with a new home.

"He never found a new soul or home, though he came close a few times, and thus he wandered on forever until he too became a creature void of form like the man who smelt like burnt matches."

Upon finishing the story, Castor made a bit of an informal bow and smiled, finishing off the last of his whiskey soon thereafter. He twirled his guitar around on his lap, leading many to believe he was about to break into another song. That did not happen though, and instead the neck of the instrument came to rest on his own once more, the two lovers basking contentedly in the afterglow.

"Heh, interesting folk story," one of Castor's fellow patrons complimented as he finishing off his beer. "Do you think it has a kernel of truth to it?" His face was as wearied by fatigue as it was palsied by alcohol, causing him to squint across the table in search of the bear man bard.

"Heck if I know," the D-Bee answered, running his fingers up and down his lover's frets. "Though I bet it's allegorical, and the real meaning is probably not as plain as the story itself." He smiled and yanked a cigar out from somewhere within his hooded sweatshirt. "Let's forget that for now though, I think it is about time that we step outside to get some fresh air." Everyone agreed, and soon they were stumbling out the door, looking every bit like some warped religious procession as they went.

Once outside they all produced some form of nicotine from their pockets, or bummed one from a friend, and were all soon sucking down a fog of carcinogens. The rain had finally stopped, and thus, as they sucked on their cancer sticks, they couldn't help but comment on how the already great night just kept getting better and better. It wasn't long before their conversation wandered back to old times (that were really only a few months old), causing half of the group, Castor included, to recall one by one – in excruciating detail – an event that they had all experienced. It was Sunday though, and thus, as always when midnight rolled around, when the chain smokers in the group were busy sucking down their third or fourth respective cancer sticks, Castor noted that it was time for him to go.

"Well, I think I'll be taking off early," he said as he pretended to peer at the invisible watch on his wrist with a goofy grin, looking up at the others as he did so. "It's getting late and it has been a long week, so I better get a jump on the one that lies ahead."

"Ain't nobody gonna beg your sorry butt to stay, Castor," someone laughed, smirking as the boisterous D-Bee turned his gaze toward him.

"Hey, don't say what's not true," Castor laughed back. "You'll be crying yourselves to sleep tonight when you realize that you won't see me until tomorrow." He took an especially long drag from his cigar and smiled, raising all six of his eyebrows at once. "Hell, when I leave for Black Bayou, to go back home, you'll probably cry for three weeks straight."

"Yeah, you're probably right," the nearest man to Castor noted with a sarcastic chuckle.

"I always knew you were a bunch of sissies," Castor shot back with a smirk, knocking the ash off his cigar as everyone erupted into laughter. "Anyways, like I said: I got to go." He twirled around slowly and began to walk up the block with that same old happy bob in his step, his guitar hanging upside down at his side. "Don't do anything I wouldn't do," he called back.

"See you tomorrow, Castor," they all called after him, the Bayou Ursine waving off their farewells without even turning around. They stuck up a conversation about last night's baseball game moments later, giving some of them reason to marvel at the fact that they had yet to talk about the sport that night. It wasn't an exciting game by any standards, a six to four loss for the Highlanders, with substandard pitching *and* batting performances on both sides. Thus, without his stat keeping and pointed insight to spur the conversation, it was no surprise that their conversation quickly turned back to the D-Bee who had just left early like he did every week.

"Just where the hell does he go every Sunday night?" one of them asked, trying her best to keep quiet and hoping that the Bayou Ursine was out of earshot. No answer came though, her question met with an uneasy silence. Determined, she asked once again: "Where does he go every Sunday?"

"His mother's grave," one of them answered at last.

"That's not very funny," she admonished.

"Who said it was a joke?" he shot back as gently as possible.

"But I thought . . ."

"No."

"What about . . ."

"Destroyed by the Coalition ten years ago."

"And when did you guys find this out?" she asked, a bit angered that they hadn't informed her sooner, especially considering that she was the one that first posed the question all those months ago.

"Does it really matter?" they all answered.

"I guess it doesn't," she admitted, knocking ash off her cancer stick while simultaneously thinking of Black Bayou.

The wisps of cigarette smoke curled up into the night air, dancing to some unseen beat as they joined above the bar. Beneath the waltz of nicotine, the patrons watched quietly as Castor faded further and further into the distance. Eventually, he turned the corner and disappeared from sight, and out of their lives, the smoke from his cigar lingering long after him. Illuminated by the streetlight, it drifted sadly up into the air and past the rooftops, and on again toward the heavens.

Strangers in Paradise

By Kevin Siembieda

Nora knew to go home whenever something was going on in the streets of the 'Burb, especially if it involved the Coalition Army. She didn't know what was going on, but it had to be big. Sky Cycles, Rocket Bikes and SAMAS flew overhead, and Coalition soldiers seemed to be searching every street.

A Dog Boy crouching on all fours sniffed the girl as she stepped out of the narrow alley and onto the street. Nora smiled. It tickled.

"Hi, Doggie," the little girl said.

The mutant canine smiled and sprang down the street, eye-balling and sniffing at other people. Mama said Dog Boys scared her more than Dead Boys, but Nora didn't understand why. They liked people, especially little kids. Mister Ian always said he 'never met a Dog Boy he didn't like,' but then Mister Ian said a lot of things Mama didn't agree with. All Nora knew was that Dog Boys were always nice to her and the other kids, and most of them would even let you pet them.

Nora ran across the street and down the next narrow alley. She dropped to all fours, slid under a heavy-gauge cyclone fence that only a 40 pound, bean pole of a child could fit under, and continued toward home. Down every street she saw Dead Boys looking inside vehicles, peering in the windows of storefronts and homes, and asking questions.

Finally, Nora came to the narrow, cobblestone street just around the corner from home. The street was barely wide enough for a car or pickup truck, so hardly anyone used it, 'cept for City Rats on bicycles, scooters and hovercycles, and even that wasn't very often. The street was almost always in the shadow of the two and three story buildings that lined it, and the doors were always locked tight. She guessed the lady nervously trying the doors didn't know that.

Nora watched as the lady moved from one door to another in a zigzag pattern, trying the knob and then moving on. She ducked into a doorway as a trio of Sky Cycles flew by overhead. Nora waved to them because sometimes they waved back, but they must not have seen her.

The woman stepped out of the shadows and walked up to the little street urchin. "Baby," she said in a concerned tone. "You shouldn't be out on the streets. You should go home, Honey."

"I'm not a baby," said Nora, stomping her foot for emphasis. "I'm six and a half."

The woman pulled down the hood of her cloak to reveal gentle eyes and white hair. "Of course, you're not a baby. How foolish of me, but you must still go home, Dear. The streets aren't safe right now."

The woman practically jumped out of her skin when a large grey cat leaped out of a garbage can, knocking it over.

"Don't be afraid," Nora giggled. "That's only Whiskers, he's Mrs. Linda's cat. He's always gettin' into the garbage and makin' a mess. Mama says he's a nuisance, but he don't mean nothin', he's just lookin' for breakfast."

The white haired lady with the gentle eyes smiled and began to look around. In the distance they could hear the sound of a large vehicle coming down the street. Soldiers, probably. Nora reached up and took the woman's hand.

"Don't be afraid. Follow me."

Nora pulled the woman to a wall of planks that sealed the alley from the street. One of the planks slid to the side like a secret door. The slip of a girl slid through it like a mouse, but the woman had to bend and wiggle her way through the space. The two squeezed down a space between two buildings so narrow that the lady had to go sideways, stumbling over garbage that littered the ground.

Suddenly, they popped out of the dark passageway and into a field of light and color. The woman shaded her eyes from the sunlight with one hand while the girl still had hold of the other. They stood on the edge of a large, open courtyard filled with flowers and light. It was surrounded by the walls of the other buildings. Only one building had a few windows looking out on the wonderful garden, the rest were solid brick. The woman speculated that a building once stood here but was destroyed by fire or some other disaster. The space was left empty and forgotten between the other buildings.

"Oh my," said the woman in a soft voice. "Is this your secret hiding place?"

"Nah," said the girl as if the woman should have known better. "It's my backyard."

"It is?"

"Well, sorta. Mama calls it her secret paradise."

"I can see why."

"Nobody was using it, so Mama started planting flowers to make it prettier. Just a few at first, an' well, now it's all ours. There's a vegetable garden too, with strawberries and grapes. Wanna see?"

"Yes, Child."

As the little girl walked with the lady through the garden, her visitor told her the flowers had real names. Nora liked the idea that the flowers had full names like people. There was chamaemelum nobile, convallaria majalis, rosa centifolia and dozens of others – not that she'd remember any of them.

"Mama says you can find beauty anywhere if you try hard enough, an' sometimes you haveta make your own beauty, like here."

"Oh yes," the stranger agreed. "She's right, but this . . . this garden is so beautiful. I haven't seen anything like it since the wildflower fields of New Brunswick."

Nora nodded and figured the lady was talking about one of the Old Town 'Burbs. She had heard they had pretty gardens in the Old Towns.

"Mama says life is what you make it."

"Smart lady, your mother."

Nora beamed, "She is. She's smart and pretty and works hard."

"And what about your father, Dear?"

"Oh, he's been away for a long time. Since I was little, but he'll be back one day."

"Of course," said the kind woman.

"So, why are you hiding from the Dead Boys?" asked Nora out of the blue.

"What makes you think I'm hiding from them?"

"Are you a dragon?"

"What?" chuckled the lady.

"Mr. Ian says them dang dragons kin make themselves look just like everyday people. So I was thinkin', the Co'lishion don't like dragons, an' you're afraid of the Co'lishion, an' maybe all them flower names are what you dragons call 'em."

"Oh my, what an imagination," said the woman with a smile. "Would you have invited a dragon to your home and garden, Child?"

"Um, probably not, but you seem like a nice enough dragon, if you are one. Mama would be pretty sad if you ate me, so I hope that don't happen," teased the little imp of a girl.

The woman smiled and asked if they had any tea in the house. Nora took her to the kitchen, where they had gallon jugs of bottled water next to the refrigerator and a wood burning stove. She climbed up onto a chair and opened a tin on the kitchen counter. The room, like the rest of the home, was simple, but neat and clean.

"Oh, I guess not. Mama's going to the store after work."

The lady explained she had some tea of her own and asked for the tea kettle to boil some water. When she was done making tea for them both, the woman put the rest of her tea inside the tin and produced a small bottle of honey that she put next to the tin after adding some to their drinks.

"Yummmmmm," smiled Nora. "I like honey in my tea."

"So do I," said the lady. "Child, can you read?"

"No ma'am. Mama says there ain't no good that has ever come from readin'. Co'lishion don't like it none either, you know."

"Oh," frowned the woman. "I'll have to disagree with your mother on that one." She hated the fact that the Coalition had put the fear into so many people about reading, but she understood.

"Mister Ian and Miss Alice at the bakery sez Mama should let me learn to read, but you know, like you said, Mama's smart, so I listen to her."

The kindly woman smiled and stroked the sweet girl's cherub-like face and long, blonde hair.

"Child, would do me a favor?"

"Yes, if it ain't illegal."

The woman hesitated for a minute because, strictly speaking, what she was about to ask was illegal, at least in the eyes of the Coalition States.

"I'm here to visit a friend," said the lady. "He's your Mister Ian at the bakery, but I don't think I'll be able to go there after all."

"Because of all the dang Co'lishion soldiers lookin' for you?"

"Something like that, yes," said the woman, admiring the girl's awareness. "I was hoping that you'd give him something for me in a day or two when the Coalition soldiers aren't patrolling the streets."

"What?" asked Nora.

The lady pulled out a note pad, tore out a sheet, wrote something on it, and tucked it inside a book she removed from her leather bag. Nora wasn't afraid of books like her mother, but she knew enough to keep them hidden from people, even her friends.

"I was wondering if you'd be kind enough to give this book to Mister Ian," asked the lady as she opened it and wrote two things inside. "This other book is for you."

"But I told ya I can't read," groaned the girl.

"I know, Honey. Take it to Mister Ian and ask him to read it to you when he can. He can hold on to it for you and he can read the stories to all the children. This book is written by a girl who reminds me a great deal of you, Dear. It's called *Little House on the Prairie*, and I think you'll love the stories."

"Okay, but I think this transaction should be 'tween you an' me. Mama, won't like me haulin' books around. Oh, and I do like stories. Mister Ian has a zillion of 'em."

"Listen, Dear," said the lady. "This book I'm giving you is very old and is worth a fair amount of money. If the need ever arises, I want you to sell it. Mister Ian will know how and to whom."

"Hey!" said Nora loudly. "Is that your picture on the back of this other book? The one you wrote in?"

"Yes," chuckled the woman.

"How come?"

"Because I wrote it."

"Mister Ian has written some books too."

"I know. I read them and enjoyed them very much. Would you tell him that for me?"

"Sure, but Mama says he's askin' for trouble writing books."

"He probably is," said the lady. "But maybe he thinks what he has to say is worth the trouble."

Nora shrugged and moved on to a new subject. The two sat, drank tea, and talked about a million things into the late afternoon. Then a man peered through the window, came to the back door, stepped in and said to the woman, "It's clear. We should go now."

Nora could barely believe her eyes, a knight . . . a Cyber-Knight with golden armor and long braids of black hair was standing in her kitchen. The kind lady leaned over, kissed Nora on the forehead and thanked her for her fine company and hospitality.

It was only after the lady had left and Nora ran through all the things she wanted to tell her mother, that she realized she didn't know who she was.

An hour later, Nora's mother came in the front door, her arms so filled with groceries she could barely see around them.

"Mama! Mama," shouted Nora as she sprang off the couch and got underfoot.

"Nora Kathleen Roberts," scolded her mother as she narrowly dodged being tripped by her daughter. "I swear you have more energy than a Hyperion Juicer."

"Mama, you'll never guess what . . ."

"It can wait," said her mother as she fumbled to put the bags on the kitchen counter before dropping them.

"But Mama, you won't believe what happened today!"

"I said it can wait," growled her mother. She hated being short with her daughter, but she had been up since four in the morning, prepared Nora breakfast for later, made a sandwich for her lunch, got to work by 5:00 A.M., and had been working in the hot bakery till four. Then she had to buy groceries and juggle them home. She was hot, tired and wanted to put away the groceries in peace, so she could collapse on the sofa for five minutes before having to deal with her sweet chatter box.

"DANG!" shouted Nora, pointing to the paper in her mother's fist. "Who's that?!"

"Language, young lady," scolded her mother.

Nora scowled. Mama had no tolerance for foul language. Not even 'dang,' 'holy cow,' or 'for the love of heaven.' The argument that Mister Ian used all them words and a whole lot worse never held up.

"Ma, who is that?!"

"It's nobody, Sweetheart."

"No mom, who is that? I need to know."

"I said, nobody. Just something the Dead Boys were passing out. You know how it goes."

Nora knew, alright. It was a *wanted poster*. The CS soldiers would post them in places and hand them out sometimes when they thought a fugitive was in the area. You didn't have to be able to read to recognize a face or see the numbers of the reward at the bottom. Everyone new 661 was the Hot Tip Reward Line to the authorities. And this reward had a lot of zeroes after it. More importantly, it was the same picture of the lady that was on the book she had to be given to Mister Ian.

"Ma! I gotta know who that is?! Is she a dragon?"

"What? No, I told you, she's NOBODY," said her mother forcefully. She crushed the paper circular into a ball and tossed it into the wood burning stove.

"Have you been using the stove, young lady?"

"No, Mama."

Then her mother noticed the honey and the two washed cups in the sink.

"Oh my . . . someone was in the house. Who was here, Nora? Are you okay?"

"Yep, I'm fit as a fiddle, Ma." Her dad used to say that.

"Who was it?"

"Oh," said Nora with a mischievous grin spreading across her cherubic face. "It was Nobody."

A Juicer's Tale

By Carl Gleba

Chapter 1 - Worse than a Hangover

Rex's hands trembled as they tap danced across the arm of his chair. He hated to wait. He especially hated waiting for a Cyber-Doc. Body-Chop-Shops made him uncomfortable. Made him feel like a steer who had walked into a slaughterhouse. Silly, he knew, but still . . .

The longer he waited, the faster his fingers tapped out their maddening dance. He wouldn't be here at all if it wasn't a matter of life and death.

Damn, he thought to himself, why did his Bio-Comp dispenser have to go on the fritz? He rubbed the device positioned in his chest under the drug harness that it was connected to. This was the device that delivered the drugs that made him a superman, a fabled Juicer.

Without skipping a beat, his hand shot out to grab and crush the annoying fly that had been buzzing in a figure-eight orbit around his head. Rex wasn't even aware of his bug squashing attack. He was too preoccupied by the drums throbbing in his ears from last night's drink fest. He wasn't feeling so super this morning. His vision was slightly blurred; he was feeling groggy and lethargic, and angry with himself about actually having a hangover. As if on cue, his fingers stiffened and his entire body shook for three seconds. That wasn't right, either. Not right at all.

Where the hell is that Cyber-Doc, Rex thought to himself as he stood up and began to pace. Two minutes had crawled by since he last looked at the clock on the wall – felt like twenty to the hyper Juicer.

Trying to distract himself, Rex began looking around and taking in the lobby of the small doctor's office. Doc Young was well known in the north part of the 'Burbs. His clinic was clean – immaculate compared to most – he asked few questions and the Dead Boys usually left him and his establishment alone. That's why most modified men like Crazies and Juicers to Headhunters and 'Borgs visited the Doc. Today it seemed like a whole merc crew was waiting in the lobby.

Rex happened to be in good standing with the Cyber-Doc. During his first visit a couple of Headhunters tried to skip out without paying the bill, and he interceded on the Doc's behalf. They didn't realize how good he was with a *Neural Mace* and the next thing they knew, one of them was hitting the floor hard after being zapped by the stun baton. When the other one went to pull his ion rifle on Doc Young he considered disarming the guy, but being a Juicer, Rex had considerable time to think about it and decided to use his Vibro-Sword to cut the guy's arm off at the elbow. Rex apologized for the mess and the doctor just chuckled. That little incident ingratiated him to Doc Young. From that point on, Rex would stop in from time to time just to check on the doctor or to shoot the breeze usually, about their families.

Rex paced the room, looked at the family photos and diplomas the Doc had hanging in his office, and sat back in the waiting room chair. A whole other minute had passed. Where the hell was the Doc?

Despite the throbbing in his head, Rex thought about his beautiful wife and two boys. They always brought a smile to the Juicer's face. Lost in his thoughts and the thrum of his headache, Rex didn't hear the nurse calling his name. He was too busy dwelling on his family. Most people who became Juicers either did it for the power or for revenge. Not Rex, he did it to give his family a better life. His wife and two kids lived in a nice apartment in one of the south-side Old Town 'Burbs where it was safe. Rex had lost his job when a Coalition sweep leveled the small metal forge he worked at. The Coalition's paranoia of magic had somehow shined a light on his place of employment and it was destroyed by a squad of Dead Boys, even though the place had nothing to do with magic. From what he had heard, the owner tried to tell them that before they beat his head in and destroyed the place. Rex only knew what was said on the street about the raid, because he was late for work that day, and missed getting turned to ash by plasma fire or cut in half by rail gun rounds. They killed everyone in the building. No one escaped.

Without his income at the forge, he and his family would have to leave and probably move to a shanty on the edge of the 'Burbs. Rex wouldn't have his family living hand to mouth and having to associate with D-Bees and the worse dregs of 'Burb society, so he did the only thing he could do. He had a friend with the right contacts hook him up to get Juiced. The Black Market was always looking for heavy-hitters as enforcers, and they seemed to prefer Juicers, so that's what Rex became. For a two year contract, they would do the conversion, provide on the job training and even provide a modest pay. After that two-year stint, you could go independent and stay with them as a contractor or go off adventuring or getting work as a merc. Either way, the money would be excellent. And of course, Rex planned to detox after he made a mountain of creds to keep his family set for the next couple of decades, maybe for life. It seemed liked a win, win situation to Rex. He could provide for his family, hopefully make a big score or two, enough for him and his family to live off of for a long time, and all he would have to do is survive detox, and he was a survivor.

Rex had got through his two years with the Black Market and last night he and his comrades were celebrating, and not just having survived being a Juicer for two years. Now Rex was now a free agent, no longer beholden to anyone but his family. Independent Juicers working as mercenaries made good cash in the 'Burbs, and that's what Rex was looking forward to.

"Rex . . . Mister Rex!" said the Nurse, looking around the waiting room. Not only was Rex known to the Doc and his staff, but he was a big guy at six feet, two inches tall, well defined muscles (thanks mostly to the steroids in his Juicer cocktail), sharp blue eyes and a blond Mohawk that looked as if it were slept on. Normally Rex saw his environment in slow motion and could often react twice as fast as normal opponents. Today with his dulled reflexes, for the first time in two years, he was actually startled by the nurse's touch when she walked over and put her hand on his shoulder. Rex nearly jumped out of his skin.

"About damn time! I feel like I've been here all day," Rex said, trying to regain his composure. Without a further word he staggered into the doctor's office. The fog returned to Rex's brain and his legs began to feel as if they were weighed down by lead weights. Each step took a considerable amount of effort. The room began to spin and Rex had to steady himself in the doorway.

Doc Young's examination room had that typical smell of antiseptic. Aside from the smell, everything else was a blur. There was some kind of sound that Rex couldn't make out . . . a voice, perhaps. The only thing that Rex could focus on was the exam table where he collapsed in a heap, his vision having finally faded to black.

Chapter 2 - Business and Revenge

Due to the Juicers' enhanced metabolism, plus the constant influx of adrenaline, hormones and other chemicals, they rarely slept, and when they did, it was only for a few hours. In order for Juicers to truly sleep, they needed a special cocktail called K.O. Juice, which was usually delivered by the Bio-Comp and drug dispenser when the Juicer was ready for sleep mode. A typical dose knocked a normal man out for 8-10 hours. Juicers take four times the dosage and if they're lucky they get four or five solid hours of true REM sleep. That's what Viper managed to slip into Rex's drink the night before. Being the "buddy" that he was, he even helped Rex get to his room. Rex accepted the act of kindness and was not aware that Viper had sabotaged his Bio-Comp while he was asleep.

This act of sabotage was a mix of revenge and business. Revenge, because Rex trained Viper and led him on missions. Business, because he always felt Rex was holding him back. Rex never allowed Viper to mix with the "upper management" with him, plus Rex always seemed to get the larger bonuses, somehow always managing to find the target first and for the most part, always had their employer's favor. The final straw was the offer to join a merc crew led by a Juicer named *Slasher*. Rex was offered a position as a Sergeant while all Viper was offered was a position under Rex. Enough was enough. Rex had gotten in the way for the last time.

Viper intended to hand him over to his benefactor, *Blood Reaper*. Viper owed him a *living Juicer* in his prime, and felt no remorse at handing over Rex. If all went according to plan, Rex would be delivered and Viper's debt paid off. Once Rex was out and the Bio-Comp disabled, Viper arranged to have Rex delivered and had a vehicle outside waiting.

Viper was five feet tall but as wide as a tank. His heavily muscled body was covered with various serpent tattoos. He had a thing about snakes, which is why he took the name, and even his shaved head had serpents tattooed on it. He wore the typical Juicer Assassin Plate armor and carried a JA-11 laser rifle strapped over his back. Unlike Rex, Viper favored knives, which he referred to as his fangs, and always had several on his person.

It was early morning and the first rays of the sun were just coming over the horizon. Viper walked down the hall of the still dark inn. There were no lights. Those went off hours ago when the generator was shut down, but there were a few glow rods that made the hallway an eerie green with lots of shadows. He whistled a tune, and was dismayed when he realized it was Chi-Town's national anthem. They played the damn music all the time on the radio, news programs, public service announcements, State announcements and State programming, so it was no wonder it had been burned inside his skull. Viper chuckled that he was whistling it absentmindedly. What the heck? He felt giddy excitement at the prospect of selling his arch-rival, Rex, down the river. That glee turned into anger in a microsecond when, as he approached Rex's room, he noticed that the door was ajar. The whistling stopped and in the blink of an eye two Vibro-Blades were drawn and in his hands. There was dead silence save for the slight hum of the twin energy blades. Viper readied his two 'fangs' as he peered into the room without touching the door. Nothing but darkness. He listened hard for a moment before sheathing one Vibro-Blade in exchange for a glow rod, and walked into the room ready for anything.

"Hey buddy, you up?"

There was no response. Just as he feared when he saw the door ajar, the room was empty and Rex was gone.

Damnit, Viper thought to himself. That Rex was nothing but a pain in the . . . He wasn't sure he had completely disabled the Bio-Comp dispenser on his rival when he did it. It was a simple enough procedure, but there was something hinky – different – about Rex's Bio-Comp unit. It was an old model that looked to have been custom modified at some points. Some of the component elements were unfamiliar to Viper so he had taken his best guess at shutting it down. Obviously, he did not succeed at doing so.

Now he had to think fast and find Rex before he put two and two together and came looking for him. To get the job done, Viper knew he'd need help.

Faster than most people could think, let alone move, Viper descended down the hallway and stairs into the inn's dining area to meet a comrade. *Goliath* was a variation of Rex and Viper, who were both standard, run of the mill Juicers. Goliath was a Titan Juicer. The combination of drugs and hormones altered his physiology to give the Titan Juicer superhuman strength and girth over speed and agility. Although a Titan Juicer was still faster than a normal man, they were ponderous compared to most Juicers. Then again, a Titan Juicer didn't have to be as fast as a traditional Juicer, all he had to do was get his hands on his opponent to rip him in half or pound him into paste. And like most Titans, Goliath loved being a human tank able to take apart even power armored opponents with his bare hands.

Goliath was a giant of a man. He stood seven feet tall and had a full head of fiery-red hair – just like the Titans of myth, the Juicer had always contended. Like most Titan Juicers, Goliath wore a pair of protective gloves, padded and reinforced in such a way as to protect the hands from injury when punching through hard materials, duking it out with super-tough opponents or blocking and parrying Vibro-Blades and magic weapons. Goliath also had a pair of red gloves that matched his hair. The knuckles and tops of the hand and forearm sections of the gloves were dotted with spikes for added protection, damage and intimidation. He completed his look by having a splash of red on his heavy armor, and even his C-27 Heavy Plasma Rifle stowed on his back was painted red and silver.

This morning, Goliath had a table full of food and he was wolfing down everything in sight. It wasn't just that Titan Juicers had voracious appetites, Goliath had a condition known as *Metabolic-Induced Voracity,* compelling him to devour large quantities of food. He was right where Viper had expected to find him, eating as usual. Goliath looked up with a mouth full of food.

"Mornin' Viper," said the red-haired giant.

"Hey man, you wanna have some fun?"

"Doing what?" asked Goliath as food fell out of his mouth.

"I thought you and I would do a little hunting for a Juicer with a price on his head. You in?"

"I want at least fifty percent!"

"Oh, don't worry, I'll make it worth your while, big guy. How would you like to be an independent agent?"

"Works for me," said the eating machine accepting the lie.

Viper knew that last enticement was probably necessary. Goliath only had loyalty for himself, but the thought of being a free agent should keep him on the up and up. Independence was always good motivation for anyone beholden to the Black Market. With the short life of a Juicer, getting out from under the thumb of your sponsor and going independent as soon as possible was always desirable.

Chapter 3 – A New Debt

The room was a spinning blur to Rex, so he kept his eyes closed. All he could hear was the sound of electronics, kind of like a dentist's drill, he thought through his haze.

There was also a distinct smell mixed in with the antiseptic, ozone perhaps?

Damnit . . . must'a passed out! Rex thought to himself in disbelief. It was like his whole body was failing him and shutting down. He was on the verge of panic. It felt the way old timers in their late twenties or early thirties talked about *Last Call*, only it was way too soon for that to be happening to him. Waaay too soon.

Forcing his eyes open, Rex gripped the sides of the exam table in an effort to push himself up into a sitting position. The effort was easier than he had anticipated, but a moment later he went crashing back on the table. Rex's hands darted to his chest and neck. It was gone! His Bio-Comp and drug harness were gone. He was so upset by this revelation that he didn't care that his body armor was gone too and he was naked on the gurney. The drug harness could be removed, even if only for hygienic and medical reasons. The Bio-Comp, however, was an *implant* in his chest that regulated all of the drugs that made Juicers superhuman. Instead his chest appeared to be connected to a series of cables and tubes coming from a device on the side of the exam table. Damn, he was hooked up to some kind of machine! What was going on here?! Where was he? The last thing he could remember was . . . what? Getting drunk. Being helped to his room, and then . . . a blank.

Rex took a deep breath and tried to collect his thoughts. Okay, things couldn't be all bad, because he could feel life and strength returning to his body. Limbs that felt as if they had been weighed down only a minute ago were feeling light and limber. The world was coming back into focus, too. Rex heard a familiar voice cursing about something. Hey, it was Doc Young! Doc could make even a hardened merc blush with a string of profanities that included several from different languages, some not even native to Earth.

"Doc . . . wha . . . what the hell is going on?" asked Rex in a raspy voice.

"It's a good thing you came to me when you did, my boy, else you would've checked out for good," said Doc Young.

Rex leaned to his right to see the Cyber-Doc examining his Bio-Comp under a high-powered micro-viewer and not bothering to look over at him while he talked.

"Rex, your Bio-Comp unit must be over 150 years old. Where did you ever get an original Golden Age military unit?"

"Dunno, Doc. Black Market boys juiced me up. Who knows where they get their gear? Hey, I don't need to tell you that," replied Rex, still slurring his words.

"There are at least four different micro-bypass mechanisms to the central processor, the osmotic pump is shot and the interface leads to the drug harness are all severed. Rex, I don't know how much more life this here Bio-Comp has, I'd suggest a new one, unless you're ready for detox. Your vitals are strong, your organs seem mostly intact with little damage, heck, you've got a good chance of surviving detox and being back to normal in a few weeks. Eight weeks, tops."

Rex started to speak, but suddenly felt weak.

"What about the one in my head? Can't that sustain me?"

"Its just a back-up unit and is meant to communicate through the primary Bio-Comp unit. Even if I restored the connection leads, it wouldn't last very long. It's an early death sentence, if you ask me you're better off going through detox."

Rex considered the doctor's words carefully. That had been his plan, but the Black Market had kept him busy doing their enforcer work. He got a few good bonuses, but nothing that the family could live long term on. He wasn't ready. Hell, he was young by Juicer standards. Had years before it was time to detox. If he toxed-out now, the last two years would have been for nothing. He was finally out of debt to the Black Market and had an "in" with a fellow Juicer who wanted him to join his merc crew. All he needed was a couple of good scores, a couple more years, and then he could detox and be back to normal spending time with his family.

"What's a new Bio-Comp gonna cost me, Doc?" asked Rex without missing a beat. He could feel his strength starting to return and things were starting to become clearer. The Doc must have hooked him up to another Bio-Comp, or some kind of Juicer life support system.

"I have a brand new unit straight from Newtown, but its 150k!"

Rex winced at hearing the price tag. "Got any used units?" he asked, a touch of desperation creeping into his voice.

"Nope. Sorry, nothing that's in working order, anyway."

"Can you fix what I got?"

"I can do something, but I can't guarantee how long it will work, Rex. I'm a doctor, not an Operator. My patchwork might last you a year, or might last you only till tomorrow. You'd be playing Russian Roulette with your life. I can't recommend it."

"I appreciate your concern, Doc, but I don't have much other choice. Just patch it up as best you can and get me up and running," groaned Rex.

He didn't have 150,000 credits. He'd just have to pray that the Doc's repairs lasted long enough for him to score the cash to get this unit replaced. He hated the idea, because it set back his plans for the family and his retirement from being a Juicer, but what else could he do? His family didn't live ostentatiously, just comfortable enough to live a decent life in the 'Burbs. That was good enough until he could get a new Bio-Comp and make that big score or two.

As Rex thought about it, he knew that the Doc's time was going to cost him some serious credits; perhaps there was a way to lower the cost.

"Hey Doc, what's this gonna cost me?"

"Well, I still have work to do on the Bio-Comp. With time, parts, plus it looks like you need a new supply of chems, probably 25,000 creds. But don't worry about that now. I know you're good for it. Let's get you back on your feet, eh?"

Rex winced again at hearing the estimate. That was almost half of his operating capital, and he would need that to buy equipment.

His mind having finally cleared the cobwebs and his migraine now down to a dull ache, Rex was finally thinking more clearly. The first thing to come to mind was the Doc's statement about the chems. He had at least two months left on his six month supply. Knowing that the Doc wouldn't screw him over, he figured the chems must have been pumped into his system as a result his Bio-Comp's malfunction. It seemed to make sense, but what to do about the money? Maybe there was something he could do for the doctor? Something short and sweet, and then he could get back to completing his plan.

"Hey Doc, look, I'm in a bind here. Maybe there's something I can do for ya in trade rather then shelling out the last of my creds?"

Doctor Young stopped looking into the micro-viewer and stared at Rex, clearly thinking about something. It was also the first time that Rex noticed that the Cyber-Doc's face was covered in bruises and scrapes. Plus, where at one time was a cybernetic eye, was now covered with bloody gauze and bandages.

"Doc! What happened to you?" asked Rex, suddenly more concerned about Doc Young than himself.

Whatever the Doc was doing for him was working, because he was starting to feel a whole lot better and many things were becoming more apparent to him. For instance, looking around the exam room he noticed several broken medical instruments and blood smeared against one of the walls, which was out of place, as Doc Young ran a clean shop. The Cyber-Doc started to speak, but Rex could tell by the look on his face that it was difficult for him to talk about. Taking a moment to regain his composure, Doctor Young grabbed a handkerchief and blotted sweat off his brow and took a long swig of water from a nearby bottle.

"With the recent tightening of the Coalition borders, the supply of bionics and cybernetics has started to dwindle. Maybe that's the reason. I don't know. All I do know is that *Cyber-Snatchers* are becoming a serious problem. Innocent people, mostly those who are just simple workers and have cybernetic or bionic prosthetics, are being victimized and having their implants stolen.

"A group calling themselves the *Hammer Fists* tried to unload a truckload of used cyber-gear and bionics on me last night. Oh, they tried to clean them up, but you could tell they pulled the parts off people while they were still alive. I even recognized some of the parts as units I've sold and installed! As you might have guessed, I refused to buy what they were selling. They didn't like my answer and worked me over a bit. When I still refused, that walking tank, Vulcan, pulled my multi-optics eye right out of its socket!

"I'm surprised they didn't kill me. I think I'm supposed to be an example in the 'Burbs of what happens when you refuse to deal with Vulcan and his Hammer Fists."

Doctor Young stood up and limped over to a cabinet, where he pulled out a new roll of gauze and a fresh bandage. Rex watched as he took the bloody bandage off and cleaned around his empty right eye socket. Placing a fresh piece of gauze in the eye socket and wrapping the bandage around his head, the doctor continued with his tale.

"They took a few million creds' worth of my best merchandise, and my doctor's bag. If you can get my doctor's bag back, we'll call it even."

"What's so special about this bag?" asked Rex, figuring the Doc would have asked to get his stolen inventory back.

"The bag is pre-Rifts, and goes back in my family several generations. It even has some medical instruments from the Golden Age, before the Great Cataclysm, that are irreplaceable. My father gave me that bag, and someday I want to pass it on to my children. To me it's priceless and worth more than anything, including the gear they stole, not that I wouldn't love to get it back, too."

Doctor Young sat back down at the micro-viewer, picked up some delicate instruments and started to work on the Bio-Comp.

"I'll get your bag back, Doc, you can count on it. I'll see about the other gear, too. I'm already feeling a lot better thanks to you."

Chapter 4 - Quality Family Time

Rex was back on his feet in a few hours. Doctor Young had managed to repair most of the damage to the ancient Bio-Comp. Turned out the old Golden Age units were better than the junk they sold today. Military grade, the Doc had said. Most of the damage was to the interface to the drug harness, and the Cyber-Doc was able to replace it along with restocking the Juicer's drugs. The cost was bit more, 30,000 credits or his medical bag, and the Doc still worried about how long or well his repairs would last, especially under the stress of combat. But like Rex had said, he didn't have much choice in the matter.

The world was back in perfect clarity for Rex. From the front of the Body-Chop-Shop, Rex took in the sight of the Chi-Town 'Burbs as the sun rose over the horizon. The 'Burbs surrounded a massive arcology where only Coalition citizens lived. Ever since the city was established, all kinds of people from all over the North American continent traveled to the city in the hope that they could join the fabled paradise inside. Inside the fortress city, its citizens were said to live carefree lives and didn't have to worry about their next meal or protection from the monsters or alien raiders that often emerged from the Rifts. Plus Chi-Town was the capital of the Coalition States.

The Coalition included several other mega-cities that ran from Chi-Town in Illinois to as far north as Free Quebec in Canada. The Coalition had a formidable army of troops and technology. They claimed to be the salvation of humanity, but that's where it stopped. Monsters weren't the only things that came out of the Rifts. Thousands upon thousands of misplaced dimensional beings known as *D-Bees* had come to Earth since the apocalypse, two to three hundred years ago. Some were hostile, but most were just as lost and confused as the last remnants of humanity. D-Bees lived in the 'Burbs as well. For at least the last hundred years the 'Burbs had been a melting pot for D-Bees as well as humans. However, it was decided long ago by the upper echelon of Chi-Town that Earth belonged to humanity, and anyone or "anything" that wasn't human was a scourge to be destroyed. So it was that only humans were allowed to apply for CS citizenship and the chance to live in the safety of the mega-city. Nonhumans . . . death at the end of a gun barrel, or worse.

The 'Burbs varied greatly, from tall skyscrapers and clean neighborhoods, to the tent cities of the Shanty Towns that extended out from the arcology for several miles. Pure filth with nothing more than shacks for houses and buildings, the gutters overflowing with human waste and garbage. Still, even the worst 'Burbs were better places to live than the uncertainty of the Wildlands.

Rex stood in one of the more decent neighborhoods. Not all of the 'Burbs were garbage heaps or squalid masses of humanity. Some sections had real buildings, while the more affluent sections actually had electricity and running water, the streets were clean and most of the people in the area weren't looking to rob you. This morning, people were everywhere. Some heading to work, others trying to look for work, some just begging for food. Still others waited in long lines, hoping to get an interview with one of the Coalition's Citizenship Liaison Officers. People across the land held out hope that they would be accepted into the arcology and live a comfortable life as a Coalition citizen. Yeah right, Rex thought to himself. It often took years before anyone was let in, and most of those people had some kind of advantage, managed to have enough credits to buy their way in, or just lucked out.

After nearly losing his life, Rex realized he was famished. Looking around, he decided to have a bite to eat before heading off to an appointment he had at noon.

After a hearty meal, the Juicer cleaned himself up. His appointment was personal and not business, so he left his JA-11 Juicer Rifle, Body Armor, and Vibro-Sword in the room of the inn he was staying at. Rex also wanted to hide the fact that he was a Juicer. He and his wife decided before his conversion to not tell their children. Many kids idolized Juicers, and as parents they didn't want their kids following in their father's footsteps. So Rex put on a flannel shirt and a pair of extra large jean overalls. They were bit baggy, but did the job of hiding the drug harness, collar, and his chiseled musculature. Rex looked in the mirror, having combed his Mohawk to just lie flat on his head, and smiled. The last thing to do was dial down the dosage of drugs. The Bio-Comp was equipped with a small manual controller that hung from the bottom of the drug harness. The controller had several pre-programmed settings like sleep mode to full out combat mode, which is where most Juicers kept it. Rex set it to conservation mode. This was a rarely used setting needed only when a Juicer might not be able to restock his chems anytime soon. Small amounts of drugs would still course through his body, keeping him from going into detox shock, and keeping the warrior fit and combat ready, just not at maximum levels. For a few hours he would appear "normal" and not hyperactive. His wife and kids were everything to him, and it was important to Rex what they thought of him. Looking in the mirror Rex's smile widened, and he felt a surge of joy. Seeing his wife and kids always reminded him that what he was doing was worth the price. Any price.

Today Rex was meeting his family at a small park in one of the southern 'Burbs. It actually wasn't much of a park, just a place where a building had been cleared long ago, the site abandoned and grass and wildflowers grown over it. One of the neighbors cut the grass and weeds, another put up some bleacher seats and there were nine soccer teams and four baseball teams that used the field on a regular basis. Including peewee games for children under seven and another game for the older kids, ten to 15. Both his sons played and it was something both he and his wife encouraged. That meant it was in addition to numerous impromptu games and play by the local children. Surprisingly, the local inhabitants had managed to keep thugs and criminals out of the makeshift park, in large part because several bands of City Rats had declared it a "free zone." That meant it was nobody's turf and everyone could use it without crossing any sort of line of rivalry.

Walking the perimeter of the field, Rex looked for his boys. Todd was the oldest at 10, and would be playing in the older kids' game, but at present it was the two peewee soccer games on the field, one for the girls, one for the boys. Rex could see his youngest, Jason, running from center field with the ball. Jason was a runt compared to the other boys, but had speed and heart. Lots of heart. Rex could feel his own heart begin to race as his son lined up for the goal, took the shot, and watched as it was deflected back by the goalie. Rex had gotten lost in the moment and was just another cheering parent when his son took the kick on goal. Even though his drug dosage was dialed down, the proud papa jumped five feet in the air with excitement. His little boy did not score, but it did not diminish the pride Rex felt for his boy.

"You know, if your son sees, you jumping that high he might get a little suspicious," came a pleasant female voice from behind the Juicer. Rex recognized the sultry voice instantly, and whipped around to embrace his wife in a bear hug and planted a kiss square on her lips. Rachel hated when he did that, he was so fast that she could barely catch her breath before being pulled into his arms. Rex held on for several long seconds until his wife kissed him back. He let her down gently and looked her over. She was a woman of small stature standing only 5 feet, 2 inches tall, with chestnut brown hair, brown eyes and glasses which, for some reason, Rex found very alluring. While holding her he could feel the notebook under her windbreaker and also noticed the pencil in her left hand.

"Still writing?" he asked as he admired her smile.

"No, lesson plan for the boys. Todd has taken a shining to archeology, and I'm coming up with a spelling test for Jason, who by the way is already reading better than you!" she said in a half joking, half scolding voice.

Literacy was scarce around the Coalition States, mostly because it was discouraged. Information was tightly controlled by the Coalition government, and reading was not a necessity when there was a constant stream of State provided news and entertainment on the video and Internet service provided by the CS. Anything not approved by the Coalition States – which was most everything written or published outside the CS – was treated as contraband. Even historic books from before the Great Cataclysm, heck, especially ancient books, were outlawed, because they might give the people ideas. Ideas about freedom and free thinking and individual rights. Consequently, anyone found with books or even writings of their own was harassed and questioned. If they were lucky, they would just get away with their reading material confiscated, a mild beating and a warning. The unlucky were beaten and taken away, usually never to be seen again, or summarily executed on the spot as a traitor to the CS or smuggler of dangerous contraband. Coalition Peacekeepers commanded that much authority in the 'Burbs.

That always worried Rex. He knew that Rachel's obvious education would rank her as a *Rogue Scholar* and enemy of the State. If she was ever arrested she'd be marked for death. All educated scholars were. His wife was exceptionally smart and versed in several disciplines including archaeology, anthropology, physics, and history, plus she was fluent in five different languages and could read and write in three of them. Her father had raised her as they traveled the country, trying to discover more about the past and preserve what precious knowledge was left before the CS could destroy it and whitewash history. Her father actually knew Erin Tarn, and Rachel had met the infamous historian on two different occasions. She had tried to teach Rex to read and write, but he didn't take to education like she did. His last lesson was over two years ago. Rex might not have even tried to learn to read at all if it wasn't for his children. Rachel would always read the boys a bedtime story. One night, Jason was being fussy and wanted his father to read the story. Rex had explained to his son that he couldn't read, and for the first time ever, Rex had felt embarrassed by his inability to comfort his son. That night, after his wife had helped him get through the bed time story, he started his reading and writing lessons.

"So, read any good books lately?" Rachael teased with a smile.

"Well hey . . . um . . . you know it's not like I have time to read Traversing our Modern World or anything," Rex tried to retort, even though he knew his wife was just joking at his expense.

"So I hear there was a bit of a celebration last night at the tavern?" she asked in a more serious tone.

"Well, you know, it was my last day, and the boss wanted to take a few of us out for some beer and . . ."

"And you didn't think to come get me? I see how it is, Mister, you and the rest of your augmented buddies have to have a drinking contest to see which of you can get drunk, for what? Five minutes before the buzz wears off? You know, I haven't had a cold beer in ages. Oh, that sounds good," lamented Rachael.

Rex could hear the crowd of parents on this side of the field start to cheer. His son's team must have had the ball again. As gently as possible he picked up his wife so she could see over the crowd and turned towards the field. Rachel had picked up on the crowd's enthusiasm, too, and watched intently as one of the boys kicked the ball to Jason who, this time, positioned himself closer to the goalie. The ball whizzed across a quarter of the field too fast for Jason to kick, but he did manage to stop it. Three six year olds ran over to protect their goal and take the ball away from seven year old Jason, but the young boy was just too quick. With a big wind-up, he kicked the ball and sent it between the legs of the goalie, scoring a point for his team. Both parents hooted and hollered with excitement, as did many of the families of Jason's team. Halftime had soon come and one of the parents refereeing the game banged on a metal drum indicating the end of the second quarter. Rex and Rachel moved toward the side of the field as their son ran looking for his mother, only to be surprised to see his Mom floating above the crowd, held up high in his Dad's arms.

"Daddy, Daddy! Did you see? I scored another goal!" yelled Jason, his arms held high for his Dad to pick him up. Rex scooped him up in one arm while continuing to hold his wife in the other.

"Another goal?" asked Rex with excitement.

"Yes, it's his fourth this season," said Rachel with pride in her voice.

She slipped out of her husband's grasp and led the two to the end of the field, while Jason told his dad of his various games where he scored his goals. At the end of the field were a group of six boys all wearing the same jersey. A bald, middle-aged man with several metallic studs sticking out of his head commanded them. Each of the boys held a soccer ball and was trying to kick it into the goal that the man was guarding. Six balls would come in at a time, and with a swiftness to rival a Juicer, the bald man would block them all. He kicked three of the balls back while flipping to get the remaining three, and coming up from the flip he blocked two of the balls with his hands and sent the last one back with a head butt. The boys would repeatedly try to stump the man, but his quickness and agility were so finely tuned that the boys would just giggle and laugh, knowing that they would eventually get a ball in. Todd was among the boys trying to kick the ball past his uncle Bruce. Rex watched with a grin. Bruce was another type of modified man known as a *Crazy*.

From what Rex understood, there was no longer a need to use the giant metal studs, but they were the mark of a Crazy and few would get the conversion without them. Their form of augmentation involved sticking special magnets and nanites in their brains. These, in turn, enhanced a Crazy's reflexes, increased his strength and speed, sharpened all of the senses and even provided a few minor psionic abilities, but it all came at a terrible cost. After only a few years insanity would result, everything from phobias to multiple personalities. Some Crazies had their personalities so altered that they were completely different men. Even Uncle Bruce had changed since his augmentation. For some reason he wouldn't talk anymore, instead he uses sign language and sometimes Telepathy. And while he was always one of the sweetest men Rachel had ever known, sometimes a rage would overcome Bruce that would turn him into a caged animal. Fortunately the rages were infrequent, and only when his alter ego, *Shadow*, was in a fight. Seeing Rex, Rachel and Jason walking over, Uncle Bruce collected all the balls and started to juggle them. The boys began to complain that he was teasing them again when he tossed one of the balls towards Rex. The Juicer caught it with his free hand and smiled. Todd turned around to chase after the ball and was delighted to see his Dad walking towards him holding Jason in his arms and Mom walking at his side. Seeing his parents, Todd ran over towards his Dad, embracing him in a big hug.

"Are you going to stay for my game, too?" he asked, looking up at his Dad.

"I'll be with you guys all day. And tonight after dinner, maybe we can kick the ball around a little," Rex replied, happy to be with his family at last.

Today was going to be better than he thought, Rex decided as he and his family walked back to the soccer field, where halftime would be ending and Jason would be finishing his big game.

* * *

Viper and his fellow Juicer had spent the better part of a day trying to track down Rex. How could you miss the guy, he thought, it's not like there were that many Juicers in town, especially with a blond Mohawk. He had finally resorted to using one of his City Rat contacts called Stags.

Stags was a D-Bee kid, and from appearances looked like a large, humanoid rat man. He was tall and lanky, had a long, pointed, pink rat nose with hairs sticking out like a mustache. He had matted tan fur and smelled like he lived in the sewers. The City Rat was wearing torn and faded jeans, and a leather vest for a jacket. He also wore some kind of bag around his neck, which he claimed was his good luck piece. Viper had seen the contents once, which consisted of bones from a small rodent, two glass marbles, a piece of copper and a wad of string. The D-Bee was now leading Viper and his partner Goliath through a series of burnt out buildings towards the center where there was an open field. From a distance, Viper could see a man a head above the rest cheering and waving. The hair was neater than usual, but it appeared to be Rex.

"Damn," Viper muttered out loud.

"Sees, I tolds yous I wass heres ands hes lefts the Cyber-Docs likes a news mans," responded the D-Bee, opening his palm towards the Juicer. "Nows yous pays Stags as promiseds."

Viper couldn't stand the way the D-Bee spoke. Everything he said practically ended in an "S." The anger in Viper was swelling and he would have loved nothing more than to disembowel the rat man. In fact, his hands had moved toward his Vibro-Blades when he noticed something. Rex wasn't alone. He and some cute chick were talking to one of the rug rats that Viper could see running all over the place. Could Rex be a family man? thought Viper. No, it couldn't be that easy.

"Good job, Stags. You did so well, in fact, that I'm gonna give you a bonus." The rat man's nose twitched and his mouth opened to reveal a toothy grin as he put his hand out again. However, before any money was placed in the D-Bee's outstretched hand, Viper moved at lightning speed in two quick movements. Stags' eyes looked down to see blood on his hand and the Juicer cleaning his Vibro-Blades on his leather vest. Insults leapt to Stags' tongue, but never materialized as his rat-like head separated from his neck and his body fell limp.

"What kind of bonus was that?" asked Goliath.

Viper smirked and shrugged his shoulders.

"He didn't suffer, I guess," replied the Juicer as he began to chuckle. Goliath chuckled too.

"So what's the plan?" he asked.

Viper's smirk turned into a toothy grin.

"Tonight, my friend, we party with Rex and his family."

Chapter 5 - A Little Night Work

April nights were chilly in the 'Burbs. By nightfall, most good and godfearing people were indoors. Everyone knew that danger lurked in the night, from giant serpents, deranged sorcerers and D-Bees, to Cyber-Snatchers, street gangs, criminals and Coalition soldiers on patrol. It was best to stay inside, and if that wasn't possible, you didn't want to draw attention to yourself. That didn't stop plenty of people from going out at night, but most were scoundrels, out-of-towners, the desperate or the dangerous. Viper and Goliath fell into the last category.

Rex had put the boys to bed after telling them a bedtime story. It was inspired by one of the jobs he had a few months back, out east in Dinosaur Swamp. Rex and his fellow Juicers had run into Splugorth Slavers. Rex embellished the story a bit about a damsel in distress, hungry dinosaurs and a Cyber-Knight coming to her rescue. The boys hung on every word until finally they couldn't keep their eyes open anymore and had drifted off to sleep. Rex kissed them both on the forehead and as he had done many times before, he swore a quiet oath to them:

"My sons, the world is a crazy place. Both of you and your mother are the only things that make any sense to me. The choices I've made, I know in my heart are the right ones for us. The man that is your father will return to you, I promise."

Rex felt a lump in his throat and felt as if he was on the verge of tears. He could hear his wife coming up behind him and she embraced him.

"Why do you say that to them all the time, Rex?" asked Rachel, looking up into his eyes, seeing that something was different this time.

"I need to remind myself who I am," he said and returned her embrace. "The power coursing through my body, the feelings of being superior, stronger, faster. I can't escape them. Sometimes I feel lost and not the man I once was. If only you knew, just for a second, how I see the world, the crystal clarity of it all and how sometimes the world seems to stand still while I move through it like an observer."

Rex paused to take a breath and just hold on to his wife.

"I can't help but think that once I go through the detox process I'll be a shell of the man I once was. That . . . I'll be nothing."

Rachel's body stiffened and her face took on that stern look when she disciplined the boys.

"You're their father! You're my husband. Is that nothing?"

"No, it's not that, it's just that . . ." Rex stammered, trying to find the words.

"That's all that matters, Reed Honey. It's you I love, not the power you feel coursing through your veins. Never forget that."

Rex knew Rachel meant what she was saying when she used his birth name.

"You don't need chemicals," she continued, "or technology to be strong for your boys. You have the strength I love and admire inside of you. You always have. I've seen it. I've known it since the first time I met you."

Rachel was right, of course. Rex had gone all day with his Bio-Comp dialed down to its lowest setting. Before that he had the problem with his Bio-Comp unit and it was an eye-opening experience. He knew what he felt were some of the withdrawal symptoms that he'd experience when he'd finally go through detox in two or three years.

"Now why don't you come tell me a bedtime story?" said Rachael with a purr in her voice. Rex hadn't realized that other than her bathrobe the only other thing she was wearing were her glasses. Regret tore at Rex.

"What is it? she asked."

"I have to go, sweetie. I have to do something for Doc Young. He fixed me up before coming over today."

"What happened?" she asked.

Rex didn't want Rachel to worry that something might be wrong with his Bio-Comp unit, so he lied.

"It was nothing. Just a little check up and restock, if you know what I mean. The Doc's letting me pay in trade so I have to head out and do some work tonight. I promise though, I have a week before I have to go anywhere and, I will be here every second of every day for that entire week. That's why I want to take care of this tonight. After that, I'm all yours."

"Oh well, your loss tonight," she said playfully as she turned to walk towards their bedroom.

"Wait!" commanded Rex as he slipped past her with lightning speed. "Does your brother still keep his hovercycle stashed in the same place?"

"Yeah, but I don't think he'll be too happy if you borrow it again. Last time when you pissed off those Dead Boys he was patching laser holes for weeks and then he had to do the paint job twice!"

"It's black, right?"

"Nope, not anymore. For some reason he keeps calling it his 'Countach' and he painted it a bright banana yellow with some black racing stripes."

Rex looked perplexed. Uncle Bruce had a thing for pre-Rifts cars, really old ones from back in the twentieth century. Maybe it was named after one of those.

"Not a scratch, I promise," said Rex as he started to head toward the front door. "And if all goes well, you'll be making me breakfast in the morning," he added, sneaking into the living room, where Uncle Bruce was meditating in a corner behind the couch. Rachel threw Rex a kiss as he slipped out the door. Resigning herself to another lonely night, she grabbed a candle, her writing tablet and her pencil. Trying not to disturb her brother, she crept down the hall and carefully closed the bedroom door.

Uncle Bruce's right eye opened and looked around. He couldn't help having heard all of Rachel's and Rex's conversation. Despite their hushed discussion at the end of the hallway down by the boys' room, he had heard it all very clearly. His Crazy enhanced senses allowed him to hear a fly fart in a tornado. There was more, however. Bruce's empathic senses had felt something else coming from Rex and his thoughts betrayed him. Something was bothering his brother-in-law and he had some apprehension about his task tonight, and the feeling he might be facing serious danger. Bruce was very protective of "his" family. Rex, Rachel and the boys were his charges. Normally, Rex could easily take care of himself and the Crazy would never have given it a second thought. However, if Rex wasn't operating at full capacity and he was heading straight into trouble, then Bruce would have to help out. Besides, he thought, Shadow wouldn't appreciate anyone else driving his Lamborghini Countach. Rising from his meditative position, the Crazy back flipped over the couch, landing on a nearby kitchen chair with hardly a sound. Bruce had to reach up into the false ceiling to gather his gear hidden there. Looking at his watch, he knew he didn't have long to catch the Juicer. Bruce slipped over to a window and looked out from the tenth story. With no one watching, he jumped!

The apartment building that Rex's family lived in wasn't the best by modern standards, and power failures happened all the time. At least it had indoor plumbing, clean fresh water, and electricity most of the time. All of which really raised the price of rent, but it was worth every cred. The surrounding buildings we're also apartments, but not as tall as the one his family lived in. Rex vaulted from rooftop to rooftop until he got to a burnt out shell of a building.

At one time the building must have been some kind of mechanics shop. Littered all around the area were pieces from hovercrafts, limbs from robot vehicles and even pieces or busted up body armor. All the good salvage was taken years ago, plus the place was a haven for D-Bees so most humans stayed away from the shop. One of the garage stalls was actually sealed shut; apparently the metal door was welded to the steal frame and the remaining entrances were blocked off by rubble. The stall was only accessible from above, the ceiling having caved in a long time ago, and Rex had to vault in from a nearby rooftop. The hovercycle was right where Uncle Bruce stored it, except this time, Bruce was sitting on the bike with his feet resting on the handlebars. Being a Juicer, Rex was rarely surprised, but the fact the Crazy had gotten ahead of him and was waiting for him caused Rex to stagger when he landed next to the bike. The Crazy just smiled and waved his finger at Rex indicating that the Juicer was being naughty.

"Damnit, Bruce, I hate it when you do that!"

The Crazy just smiled even wider in response.

"I was just going to use it for a little while, I promise, not like last time."

The Crazy just shook his head no.

"C'mon man, I got to get this job done and I have to run around half the 'Burbs to do it! Can we make a deal, or something?"

Bruce sat up on the hovercycle, putting his feet on the foot controls, threw his helmet on and patted the rear passenger seat indicating for Rex to sit down.

"You're coming with me?" asked Rex.

The Crazy's head nodded in the affirmative.

"Dude, I can't be seen with you! People will talk, seeing a Juicer and a Crazy . . . both of us working together. Think about your reputation, if not mine!"

Uncle Bruce fired up the hovercycle. The engine was so well tuned that only the swoosh of the air jets could be heard. The bike gently rose in place. Seeing that he had no choice in the matter, Rex hopped on the back.

"Head to the *Rusty Cup* and for Prosek's sake, let's keep a low profile."

The hovercycle's engine purred a little louder as the bike rose from its storage area. Bruce maneuvered the bike so it was facing in the right direction. Looking back, the Crazy grabbed one of Rex's hands and pointed to his waist. Even with his strength the Juicer could still be thrown from the bike. He reluctantly grabbed the Crazy just as Bruce gunned the engine, sending the bike careening down the street at over a hundred miles an hour. Rex had no choice but to hold on for dear life.

Rex and Bruce made good time and arrived at Rex's temporary residence on the opposite side of the 'Burbs. Rex went in to change while the Crazy stored the hovercycle in a safe location. When Bruce entered, Rex was already wearing his Juicer Assassin Plate armor, with his Vibro-Sword over his back and his JA-11 laser rifle slung in place. As Bruce climbed through the second floor window, Rex was in the process of clipping on grenades to his belt harness. The last thing to do was to dial up the chems. Instantly, the power returned to Rex. The flame in the nearby lantern flickered in slow motion, as did the shadows in the room. The drip from the nearby sink was drawn out and even Bruce seemed to move slower now. The rush of power was back! It was an instant high that he knew would be difficult to break some day.

"Hey, you ready?" asked Rex. The Crazy just nodded in response.

"Good. We need to find some Cyber-Snatchers that belong to a gang calling themselves the *Hammer Fists*." Uncle Bruce frowned and gave Rex a disapproving look.

"It's not what you think! I'm not going to waste them." The expression on Bruce's face changed to indicate that he was listening. Rex filled him in on the events of that morning and how he owed Doc Young a debt. Bruce seemed satisfied with that answer and donned his black ski-mask, assuming his Shadow persona. Shadow responded by nodding and climbing out the window of the inn. Rex followed behind the Crazy, heading to the roof where the hovercycle was stashed.

*   *   *

Chi-Town consumed many natural resources to sustain its enormous population each day. With the rediscovery of nuclear fusion, the city's need for coal had dropped over the years to practically nothing. Several of the original coal plants were located outside the arcology. Despite being some of the more advanced plants that could burn the coal cleanly, there was still smog and pollution that would not have made the plants practical inside a contained city like Chi-Town. Once the coal operations were abandoned, many residents of the 'Burbs leapt at the chance to have electricity and many people did their best to restore them to deliver power throughout the 'Burbs. Today, there were two functioning power plants in the 'Burbs and coal was constantly being trucked in. Mining was not a safe occupation, and as a result, many of the miners would sustain injuries that could easily be repaired with cybernetic prosthetics and implants, or even the more advanced cybernetics known as Bio-Systems. They were one of the few groups of people in the 'Burbs that could afford them. Given the hour, many of the miners would either be heading to work, or leaving a drinking hole drunk off their ass, an easy target for a

Cyber-Snatcher. It would be pot luck at best, but in the shadier part of town where some of the miners drank, Rex and Shadow learned where the Hammer Fists liked to grab their prey. All they had to do was watch and wait.

As much as Rex tried to occupy himself, stakeouts were boring. He chewed his gum slowly, he chewed it faster, he blew bubbles, but after thirty seconds of that, he spit the wad out. Being a Juicer always meant having an overabundance of energy, and sitting doing nothing was like pulling back on a rubber band that would eventually snap. The only thing Rex could do to relieve his boredom was to keep watch on three bars at once. They were all within a half klick of each other. Rex would use his inhuman speed to run from various vantage points, keeping an eye on the ground while Shadow watched from a higher vantage point. Thanks to the Crazy's enhanced senses he didn't even need binoculars. However, there was still the problem of it being dark, and Shadow had to resign himself to wearing a set of night-sight goggles. There were a few times when they thought they saw the telltale signs of the Hammer Fists, but they turned out to be roving gangs of City Rats. After a couple of hours, Rex caught sight of a pair of miners leaving the bar and both singing a song together. One of the miners, by his gait, clearly had a pair of mismatched cybernetic legs. From the looks they might even be bionics. Bionics were the heavy-duty version of cybernetics and had a much higher price tag. Rex felt a glimmer of hope as he pulled his walkie-talkie off his belt.

"I'm following a pair of potential targets east towards the Old Town 'Burb," reported Rex to his partner.

Shadow responded with a double click from his radio. Rex kept to the shadows and was a blur to most who saw him. He stayed behind the miners as they headed deeper into the 'Burbs, towards the mega-city of Chi-Town where the oldest and nicest 'Burbs were located. The pair were making fools of themselves and attracting a lot of attention with their horrible singing and staggered movement. After a good couple of kilometers, Rex was ready to give up when ahead of the two miners he noticed a red glow about a man's height in the air. He recognized the glow as coming from a cyber-eye. It was looking over the area in the infrared spectrum and was following the two drunken men. This was it, Rex thought.

Always looking for an advantage, the Juicer ducked down an alley and leapt at the wall. As soon as he hit it he sprang again, bouncing up between the alley walls until he was on the roof of a building three stories in height. There was a scream from one of the miners. Rex would have to be quick. He felt a measure of responsibility to the miners even though they were strangers to him. If he could get the info he needed without the two falling to the Cyber-Snatchers first, all the better.

Rex rushed to the edge of the building to assess the situation. Cyber-Snatchers almost always attacked in pairs and packs, because most were cowards at heart. Six men surrounded the two miners. One had been knocked to the ground and by the looks of things, was missing a few teeth, but both were alive. The other one with the mismatched mechanical legs was in a defensive stance and was reaching into a compartment that was opened on his right leg.

Damn, Rex thought, they'll cut him down first and then just take the parts. Rex leapt into the air from the three story building and could feel the rush of adrenaline as it was pumped into his body. His focus became sharp and the world started to move in slow motion. Rex took in the scene below, analyzing the situation and formulating a plan of attack on the way down. By the looks of it, the standing miner was drawing a C-18 laser pistol to defend himself. The Cyber-Snatchers were already responding. The lead Snatcher had a bionic arm with an assortment of implements, and one looked like some kind of energy blaster. The bionic arm rose in response and from what Rex could estimate, it would kill the miner before he even got his gun pointed at one of his attackers. The others were starting to fan out. Three of them had Vibro-Blades, which meant they were the butchers of the group. The other three were the muscle.

In addition to the thug with the bionic arm, the other two guys appeared to have similar enhancements. Another one had a pair of bionic arms and cybernetic eyes, while the last one seemed to have just a pair of bionic wrists and hands, but that's all Rex could make out, as he was wearing an oversized poncho. The Juicer targeted the big guy with the blaster on the arm as the immediate threat if he was going to try to save the miner.

As the ground rushed up at him, Rex grabbed and swung his Vibro-Sword just before his feet touched the ground. The blade bit deep into the arm of the Cyber-Snatcher, knocking off the trajectory of his blast and causing the energy beam to miss its target, which reminded Rex about the miner hiimself. Not feeling like getting drilled in the back by a laser pistol, he spun around with a kick, sending the now raised laser pistol of the miner into the air. The act of spinning around allowed Rex to take in the faces of each of his opponents. The Juicer always loved to see the look of surprise on people's faces as he appeared out of nowhere and moved with lightning speed. He could also read their expressions and determine if they were frightened, angry or about to attack. Rex, however, wasn't always the fastest in combat, and the Cyber-Snatcher with the poncho responded by throwing it over his shoulders to reveal a mechanical torso.

Great, Rex thought, one of them is a partial conversion cyborg, who could be as fast as a Juicer with their wired reflexes.

From his opponent's arms, a pair of Vibro-Blades slid out of concealed compartments in the wrists and the cyborg thrust both blades in Rex's direction. The Juicer simply turned sideways, allowing the blades to pass on either side of him.

Before the cyborg could react, Rex brought his sword across his attacker's face. Normally, such a blow would sever a head, but the reinforced composite saved the Cyber-Snatcher's life. Rex already knew that, which was why he had targeted his opponent's eyes. When his blade completed its arc, Rex leapt clear while the cyborg clutched his eyes and screamed.

Even at a great distance, Shadow had observed Rex leaping off of the building and suspected the action was commencing without him. He was bounding across the rooftops, but not as fast as the Juicer, and instead of leaping right into the middle of the action he opted to fire a small grappling hook affixed to the armor on his right forearm. The grappling hook was aimed at a nearby billboard that had been defaced months ago, with red spray paint spelling out, *KS is godly*, not that even the few people who were able to read it, knew what that meant or who KS might be.

As soon as the wire went taut, the Crazy jumped. This caused him to come right down the middle of the street, heading right toward the now defenseless miners. Shadow could see Rex had engaged at least three of the Cyber-Snatchers, leaving the three with Vibro-Blades. The punks were still trying to move in for a quick kill on the miners, figuring their cyber-augmented teammates could handle the Juicer. And if not, they would snatch what they could and make a run for it.

Using the last of the momentum, Shadow landed right behind the miners. He quickly disengaged the magnetic lock on the grappling device from his armor, reactivated it and slapped it on the miner's bionic leg. Pressing a green button, the motors in the tiny mechanism whirled loudly as they lifted their load out of the battle scene. One down, one to go, thought Shadow.

However, he didn't have time to marvel at his plan as the miner was lifted to the billboard above. The three Cyber-Snatchers, having lost one of their quarries, moved in on Shadow and the last miner like a pack of hungry wolves. Two of the Vibro-Knife wielding thugs charged in at the Crazy. He simply responded by grabbing their wrists and flipping them over his shoulders. There were two bone crunching snaps and the clatter of the Vibro-Blades as they hit the ground. Both Cyber-Snatchers grabbed at their broken wrists and screamed in agony. The last knife-wielding stooge decided to run and fight another day. The Crazy could have easily chased him down, but decided to make sure the miner was safe. The miner, who had been punched by a bionic fist and knocked to the ground, was finally up on his feet. He looked at the Crazy with a confused and exasperated expression, and then at the two Cyber-Snatchers on the ground. Shadow gave him the thumbs up and nodded that he should get going. Shadow broke out the duct-tape and moved in on the two squirming Cyber-Snatchers he had incapacitated. They didn't put up much of a fight as he wrapped them up like Christmas presents, sans the bow.

Rex had blinded one of the Cyber-Snatchers. He was busy grabbing his face and screaming a series of curses about Rex's lineage. The one Cyber-Snatcher with the energy blaster moved a distance back from the whirling Juicer, kneeled and let loose with his energy cannon.

One blast hit Rex as he flipped behind the blind Cyber-Snatcher. For the moment, Rex used the cyborg as a makeshift shield, while he assessed his own damage. From what he could tell he had all his limbs, so his armor must have absorbed the shot. His shoulder was feeling a bit warm and was probably blistered from the residual energy from the blast, but he would be just fine. His Cyber-Snatcher shield, however, received the brunt of the remaining shots. Sparks were flying as some of the cyberware began to smolder and servos and motors were melted to slag. Rex snap kicked his human shield right into the sleeze bag firing the energy blaster. The now lifeless body crashed into the gunman, giving Rex time to deal with the last of the three Cyber-Snatchers with bionics. While Rex was dancing with the other two, this guy had time to slap an energy clip into his forearm to power a bionic mini-gun that Rex hadn't noticed earlier. All Rex could do was react as he watched the projectiles leaving the mini-gun at high velocity. He flipped aside and in mid-flip, launched his own attack by throwing his Vibro-Sword. The Cyber-Snatcher, so intent on gunning Rex down, didn't react nearly as fast and only realized his mistake as the blade slid through his neck, killing him instantly and pinning him to the wall of a nearby abandoned building.

Rex had to move fast. The Cyber-Snatcher with the forearm blaster had thrown off the body of his dead friend and was getting up quickly. Rex had decided enough was enough and brought his JA-11 energy rifle to bear.

"Don't be stupid, just tell me what I want to know and you can walk away from here."

The Cyber-Snatcher wasn't yet ready to give up. Instead he pointed his energy weapon at the Juicer. Rex, of course, already had his rifle drawn and fired a single shot, vaporizing the Snatcher's hand and forearm, including most of the weapon. For good measure, Rex fired a shot though the Cyber-Snatcher's foot, which appeared to be flesh and bone.

The villain fell to the ground writhing in pain and disbelief. He wasn't used to anybody getting the best of him, but then, he had never faced a Juicer before. 'Street punk,' thought Rex as he looked toward Shadow to see how he was doing. The Crazy had duct taped the two poor souls back to back and dragged them against a wall when he noticed that Rex had finished with his own combatants.

"We need to get out of here. No doubt some Dead Boy patrol heard the whole thing and is moving our way." Shadow nodded in response and pointed at the two duct taped prisoners, shrugged and shook his head.

"Yeah, you're probably right," Rex said in response. "They probably don't know anything, if they have to do the dirty work."

Rex tossed the Cyber-Snatcher he had been tangling with over his shoulder and began moving out. Shadow began to follow when he heard a cry from above. Looking up it was the miner right where he had left him. 'Don't move, I'll be right back,' thought the Crazy as he chased after the Juicer and forgot about the poor fellow he had saved.

* * *

Rachel had kept a journal for years. First it was to take note of her observations as she traveled around North America and to document all that she had learned. After she settled down with Rex, the journal became a more personal account of her life and the things she observed and experienced in the 'Burbs. Nobody had ever done a sociological study of this unique urban environment, and she fancied she would be the first.

She knew from her studies of the Golden Age of Man that some families would video document everything from the child's birth and all subsequent events until they left for a college or a university. Rachel and Rex didn't have the luxury of a video camera. Instead Rachel opted to write it all down for her boys and she kept a private journal for each of them, as well as her sociological studies.

Tonight she was focusing on Jason's soccer game and how proud she was of him. She was finishing the last part of the entry when she heard noise from the front of the apartment. Normally Bruce didn't make noise, at least not in the last two years he had lived with the family. Neither did Rex. It wasn't the boys, because they were much louder and usually woke her up or came to her room. Something wasn't right. Putting pen and pad down, she reached for a Neural Mace she kept in a nearby chest. It was a very effective, non-lethal weapon originally created by the Coalition Army for riot control and policing the 'Burbs, but the Black Market had been selling their knock-off brand for years.

Rachel's heart quickened as she heard heavy boots coming down the hall. Something was wrong, very wrong. Flicking on the mace, she raced to the door, panic welling up in her chest. Before Rachel could reach the door, it was already flying off its hinges and through the air right at her. The next thing she knew, she was on the ground with blood running down her forehead, and a Juicer covered in serpent tattoos was standing in the doorway. Before she could utter a sound, the Juicer picked her up by the neck and slammed her into the wall. Rachel could feel at least two of her ribs crack and she began to gasp for breath as the Juicer's grip tightened. Seconds passed as the Juicer just eyed her up and down, his tongue darting in and out of his mouth like a snakes. Her vision began to fade and her lungs felt like they were going to burst. Finally, Rachel couldn't keep herself conscious anymore and her body went limp.

When Rachel woke up, she found her hands and feet bound and her entire body hurt. Something, probably a sock, was stuffed into her mouth and was being held in place by duct tape. Before she even opened her eyes she could hear the whimpering of her boys. By the sounds of it they were right next to her. Opening her eyes, she had hoped to at least reassure them that all would be ok with her eyes and facial expressions. Thus, Rachel was dismayed to see two trembling sacks made from the boys' bed sheets and held closed by duct tape. Her boys were in sacks like kittens, waiting for an uncertain fate. She wanted to lash out like a lioness to protect them, but she knew she had to stay level headed. If the boys heard her trying to scream or lashing out it would frighten them all the more.

There was also a large Juicer, Titan by the looks of him, sitting on a bench, looking down at Rachel and the two white sacks that held the boys. She could make out the inside of a truck and could feel the bounce of movement along a gravel road. The Titan Juicer bent forward, putting his face right next to hers.

"Don't worry, Sweets, we're gonna have some fun, as soon as we take care of your man." Goliath could see the surprise in Rachel's eyes as she began to put it all together.

The giant, red haired Juicer smiled as tears began to well up in Rachel's eyes. Blood and tears began to drip down her face, and Goliath licked at the wound on her forehead and laughed! They were going to use her and the boys to get to Rex, and there was nothing she could do about it.

* * *

Rex and Shadow had interrogated the Cyber-Snatcher for over an hour. Eventually it took strong-arm tactics to get him to talk and reveal where the *Hammer Fist Gang* stored all their stolen cybernetics.

With the information they needed in hand, all they had to do was dispose of their prisoner. Something the Black Market used to always preach to Rex was to not leave any enemies behind. While Rex had killed many men in his career as a Juicer enforcer, he would never do it in cold blood. Instead, they decided to leave the Cyber-Snatcher for the Dead Boys. The prisoner's bionic limbs were all incapacitated, and with a few hits from Shadow's Neural Mace, the prisoner was out cold. All that was left was an invitation for the Dead Boys. Shadow took care of that. Earlier he grabbed from a nearby telephone pole a Coalition recruitment poster like those found all over the 'Burbs. This one, however, had been defaced and had a red circle and slash through it over the visage of Emperor Prosek. Coalition soldiers were adamant about taking these defaced posters down and putting up new ones, and if the perpetrators were ever found they were arrested and, at the very least, interrogated for days. Rex and Shadow taped the poster to the Cyber-Snatcher's chest. In all likelihood the thug had unregistered bionics and cybernetics, which would land him in a Coalition prison far away.

Leaving the trussed up Cyber-Snatcher in the middle of a street where CS patrols were known to go, Rex and Shadow went on their way. Now, all they had to do was recover Doc Young's medical bag, and maybe some of his other cybernetics for good measure, and call it a night.

Shadow and Rex sped through the 'Burbs. It was still a few hours until dawn, and if Rex was lucky, the rest of the Hammer Fist Gang would still be out looking for victims or partying in some dive. Most vermin like Cyber-Snatchers only worked at night and slept during the day. Rex hoped that meant there would only be a few to deal with when they arrived at the hideout. As graceful as most Juicers were, one false move was all that would be needed for someone with amplified hearing to detect them. With only a few present, the odds of slipping in and out unseen improved dramatically.

Their destination came into view. A place designated by the CS as *Off-Limits: Foundry Number Four*. It was one of the original metal foundries used in the construction of Chi-Town's fortress walls. It was abandoned long ago when the foundries were moved into the city proper. The structure was too large for the Coalition to just raze, plus it could always be used in an emergency. It was also conveniently located just under a mile from the city's walls and was part of an Old Town 'Burb involved in industrial manufacturing. The foundry was huge and surrounded by a barbed wire fence which wasn't much of a deterrent. Coalition troopers in SAMAS power armor and Sky Cycles would often go through the foundry on their patrols. They were mostly high speed passes providing the bored troopers with an obstacle course to run through. Given the amount of machinery still inside, a small army could hide in there and the CS would be none the wiser.

Rex and Shadow watched the foundry from a distance to observe the timing on Coalition Peacekeeper patrols. According to their source, the Cyber-Snatchers were using the underground sewers to get in and out of the foundry undetected. There were just too many miles of sewers to figure out how to get to the foundry, so Rex and Shadow decided it would be easier for them to slip in from above.

Waiting until the most recent SAMAS patrol finished their flyby around the foundry, the two men made their move as soon as the powered armor patrol disappeared around the corner. The patrols this close to the city were as regular as clockwork, so Rex and Shadow knew exactly how much time they had between flybys and how quickly they had get in, get their prize and get out. They also had to be quick and careful just in case there were any observers on the ground. Shadow doused the headlight on the hovercycle to rely on his night-vision goggles. Rex just closed his eyes and hoped the Crazy didn't miss his mark.

The cycle burst forward at full speed and even Rex felt his stomach in his throat for a few seconds. The duo had been observing from a rooftop one mile away, which meant when the hovercycle dropped to the ground, Shadow had to weave through the street, dodging the occasional D-Bee, drunk, and vegetable stand along the way.

Coming to the barbed wire fence, Shadow cranked-up the vertical jets to make the hovercycle leap up into the air and over the fence, before landing inside the yard of the old foundry. There was still a good half mile to go and Rex could see a trio of Sky Cycles off in the distance, and by the looks of it, they were heading towards the metal foundry as well. Damn, Rex thought, CS being paranoid as usual, must have doubled their patrols. He nudged Shadow and pointed towards the inbound vehicles, which had to be less than a mile away and closing. If not for Shadow having doused the lights and piloting by the seat of his pants, the Sky Cycle patrol would have no doubt spotted them by now. If they didn't get inside soon, they would still be spotted. Shadow's current course through a series of large cargo containers and various other obstacles on the ground outside would intercept with the Sky Cycles', so instead he did the unthinkable.

Only seconds ahead of the patrol, Shadow gunned the hovercycle, entered the metal foundry barely ahead of them, jetting up a sharp incline toward the only visible entrance some 300 feet up! The main body of the structure was long and hollow, allowing the patrol to enter and exit, but inside there were still all kinds of hanging machinery like giant crucibles, various cranes and other equipment meant to pour hot steel into the crucibles. As Shadow and Rex entered the foundry, the hovercycle was aimed for one of the crucibles. Just as the CS patrol was entering the foundry, the hovercycle jets were cut and it descended with a loud clang into a giant metal pot! The patrol flew overhead roughly four seconds latter. Rex waited 15 more seconds before popping his head up to make sure they didn't turn around. They hadn't. The pair had flown their formation in and around the old foundry like they did every night, and continued on their way.

"Damn, that was close, you maniac!" said Rex, clapping the Crazy on the shoulder. Shadow responded by pointing to the paint that had chipped on the hovercycle's jets.

"Hey dude, don't look at me! I would have parked it outside where it would have been safe." Rex could see Shadow's right eyebrow raise behind the ski-mask, more or less saying, yeah right!

"C'mon, let's go, the bike is safe here." Donning a pair of night vision goggles, the Juicer leaped out of the crucible, followed by the Crazy. After several acrobatic leaps, they had finally arrived at the floor of the foundry. The place had a few sub-levels which were probably massive furnaces. Below the furnaces would be a waste tunnel where ash and other unused products would be flushed. The sewers were probably connected down there or the Hammer Fists may have made their own entrance. Either way, the gang would be hiding out down below. Once on ground level, the pair stuck to the shadows and started to prowl amongst the machinery. The metal of the massive mechanisms was covered in dust, and some had long since turned a rusted brown color. Still, the smell of lubricants and other pungent chemicals hung in the air. To Rex it was all a jumble and the way to the lower levels could be anywhere. He turned to Shadow and shrugged. The Crazy put his hand on the Juicer's shoulder and stepped in front of him, taking in deep breaths through his nose. Rex remembered the Crazy's keen senses and followed Shadow's lead, who was now crawling along on all fours and sniffing the floor and the air like a bloodhound. Finally, after what felt like an eternity, the Crazy eagerly scampered toward an empty furnace located at the end of the foundry near where the Sky Cycle patrol had exited the building. Within the furnace was an open waste duct that had a makeshift rope ladder descending deeper into the facility. Rex followed Shadow down without pause. This led to a series of waste ducts that were easily ten feet in diameter. Judging by the amount of refuse inside, they were being used by someone. Fast food containers and junk food wrappers were everywhere, as well as empty bottles of booze.

The two determined intruders followed the tunnels until they ended at the top of a huge open area. The massive pit was several hundred feet long and easily 80 feet deep. Pipes twenty feet overhead covered the ceiling, while numerous smaller pipes ran along the walls. Shadow pointed to a metal ladder made of steel rungs embedded in the concrete and metal walls that led down into the cavernous basin. By the look of the area, this was where all the waste collected before it was drained away. That was, when the foundry was in operation. Having worked in a foundry before, Rex had imagined such a drainage holding bay would be filled with hardened sludge, but this area was clean as a whistle. In fact, it was so remarkably clean that it suggested to him that either the original clean up crew did a great job when the plant closed, or the CS might have plans to fire up this forge again.

Looking down on the open area, Rex and Shadow could see where the Hammer Fists made a temporary base. The area was divided by a variety of material, from old wooden pallets and chicken wire to blankets hanging on strung up ropes. Rex was ready to dive in and go looking for Doc Young's medical bag when Shadow grabbed him by the back of the armor. Quickly, the Crazy put his finger over his mouth and pointed to his right ear. Rex strained to listen. There was a faint whirring noise in the background followed by a thump, thump. Someone or something was down there. Rex nodded, agreeing with Shadow's observation, and studied the area a little more carefully.

Minutes passed with no one in sight, yet the noise continued, and finally both Rex and Shadow heard noises from behind them. By the sound of the commotion and laughter, a group of Cyber-Snatchers were returning and right behind them. Looking around there was nowhere immediate to hide. The nearest waste duct was too far away for both to jump. Their only option was to climb up on the protruding waste pipe they were in. It had a small lip above it and there were some pipes that could be balanced on.

Both modified men made a quick jump a distance no normal person could have done. Just as they cleared the waste duct, a group of a half dozen Cyber-Snatchers arrived, each taking a turn climbing down the ladder. Two had bionic legs and they just jumped, each carrying a sack, presumably full of stolen cybernetics and bionics. They were laughing and joking amongst themselves and by the sounds of it, had scored big. Two squabbled over who had finished off the Coalition officer and another called 'dibs' on the Cyber-Disguise. If they had really slain a CS officer, and the discussion about the Cyber-Disguise suggested they had, this gang was more vicious and dangerous than Rex had imagined. Any remaining doubt vanished when one of the thugs pulled the dead man's head out from a sack, his CS helmet and Dead Boy face plate tumbling to the floor in the process. To butcher a CS officer took guts and power.

With all the Cyber-Snatchers on the ground in the basin, Rex and Shadow quickly descended, with a series of acrobatic leaps placing them just where the others had come down seconds before. Rex planned to follow these chumps to see where they deposited their loot. However, it was never that easy, and this group had to stop at what passed for a bar within their makeshift lair.

Rex and Shadow could easily drop down and hide with all the commotion the group was making, however, as they were talking, Shadow could hear that sound again, and he made eye contact with Rex and pointed to his ear again. The noise was much louder this time, but unlike before, Rex and Shadow had a clear view of what was coming. Approaching the bar was a hulking brute of steel at least eight feet tall. Vulcan, I presume, Rex thought to himself. A full, freakin' conversion cyborg!

Cyborgs, more commonly called 'Borgs, were men or women who had given up their flesh and blood bodies for one that was fully mechanical. The only thing left that was remotely human was a brain and spinal column, and they were usually somewhere in the chest of the metal monstrosity. By the looks of it, this was a mining 'Borg. A full out Combat Cyborg bristled with weapons, had some of the heaviest armor in North America, and was strong enough to tear a man in half. This cyborg was apparently looking to upgrade, because he dumped the sacks that his Cyber-Snatcher minions brought in and began picking through various components. Or maybe he was estimating the value of their stolen cybernetic loot.

Mining 'Borgs could be just as tough as Combat Cyborgs, but typically had fewer weapons. This one still had a massive mining drill on his right hand. Around the drill were several protrusions, probably plasma torches to soften up rock or cut through stone or metal. They also made powerful short-range weapons. The left hand, however, appeared to have been recently upgraded with a mishmash of weapons. The forearm was sporting a pair of Vibro-Claws and the whole arm was a different color from the rest of the metallic body. It looked bulkier and probably had increased strength. The 'Borg's legs were also a different color, and by the looks of some of the weld marks, were also an upgrade from the original. There was no telling what kind of concealed weapons this cyborg might have.

Rex and Shadow watched as the cyborg picked through the newly acquired cyber gear while the others turned up some music and began to drink heavily. Good, Rex thought. The music should enable him and Shadow to move around unheard while these idiots party, and feeling safe in their lair made them loud and careless. There was no lookout, nor any security devices that he could see.

Rex nodded to Shadow in the opposite direction and they both dropped to the floor of the basin and began to make their way through the partitioned living area. Their first obstacle was a wall made of chicken wire and wooden pallets. Both modified men easily flipped over this wall, landing in what looked like a makeshift bedroom. After several more flips, the two made some headway towards the other end of the base, away from the party area. The place had disgusting living conditions, especially when Rex and Shadow flipped into what served as a makeshift latrine. It was nothing more than another pit in the ground where people did their business. Shadow was gagging over the smell when a single Cyber-Snatcher walked in. The Crazy was too busy pulling up his mask and vomiting to notice, but not Rex. He spotted the intruder the instant he walked in. The Cyber-Snatcher didn't have time to even look surprised as Rex grabbed him by the arm and flipped him into the large hole in the ground. The hole must have been much deeper than Rex thought, because it took a second before he heard a splash and crunch. Looking into the hole he could barely make the Cyber-Snatcher out as he was lying on the bottom, slowly sinking into the muck and water. That was the problem with bionics and cybernetics, they tended to weigh a man down. Rex clapped Shadow on the back and whispered to him.

"Don't worry, I took care of it."

The Crazy's face was flushed, but he nodded.

"C'mon, let's get going."

Shadow and Rex again leapt over the makeshift wall, however before the Crazy could land, there was an abrupt shaking of the ground, enough so that it kicked up the dust and knocked over a few baubles, causing the Crazy to grab on to Rex as he landed. They both realized the music had stopped and the cyborg was screaming at his henchmen.

"You idiots! You brought the Coalition with you!"

One of the Cyber-Snatchers protested and said, "No way, boss. There was no one around when we jacked these skin jobs, and we were not followed here!"

The cyborg was just beginning to speak when two more Cyber-Snatchers came climbing down from the same entrance as the other. Both landed with a mechanical thud. Holding up a C-14 Fire Breather laser rifle, one of them shouted, "Boss, Dead Boys are all over F4 and two Death's Head transports have landed outside. What do you want us to do?"

The cyborg began barking orders, telling his men to grab what they could and make a run for it. The cyborg wasn't bothering to hang around, either, and darted toward the exit on the opposite end of the basin, where a drainage pipe 15 feet in diameter led to the sewers below. He took six giant strides and lept into the air. A battery of little thrusters under his legs kicked in and propelled him the rest of the way.

"The Coalition," groaned Rex. That there was a complication he had not expected. Why did they have to raid the foundry tonight? Then he thought about the slain Coalition officer. The gang had pushed its luck. The CS might ignore a lot, but they never ignored the death of one of their own. These arrogant fools had brought the wrath of the Coalition Army down on their operation.

"C'mon, now we really have to get going!" said Rex, no longer trying to be subtle. He whipped out his Vibro-Sword and began to hack through the last wall that was in his way. The makeshift structure fell away to the deadly weapon, allowing Rex and Shadow to enter a room at the back of the lair. There they found crates of goods bearing the medical insignia Rex always saw at Doc Young's place. Jackpot! Now if only a company of Dead Boys weren't on their tails.

Looking around, Rex didn't see anything that looked like a medical bag. The next thing he knew, he was standing face to chest with the mining cyborg that had just burst into the room from the door. Both men stared at each other in surprise.

"YOU!!" shouted the cyborg. "You brought them here!" he bellowed, pointing his drill arm towards the Juicer and Crazy. Small bolts of plasma began to erupt from around the drill at the two interlopers. Shadow hit the ground, doing a split while drawing his NG Super-Laser pistol, while Rex flipped through the air, coming down next to the cyborg, and quickly brought his sword down, aiming for the 'Borg's elbow joint. The cyborg was faster than he looked and managed to move his arm enough to avoid having it sliced off. Instead, the Vibro-Sword went through the drill, cutting its length in half.

Rex was coming around for another cut when the cyborg spun his torso without moving his feet, catching the Juicer off guard and sending him flying towards the end of the room. The strength of the blow was strong enough to send Rex right into the wall, but he was fast enough to flip just in time, hitting with his legs, bouncing off and landing on the floor like a cat. Rex had no time to consider whether that blow had done any internal damage or not. He could already feel the flow of endorphins and the rush of adrenaline as he prepared to rush back in at the monstrosity.

However, before he could leap, Shadow had unleashed a burst of laser fire followed by a grenade launched from underneath the pistol. The explosion sent shrapnel flying everywhere and when the smoke cleared, the cyborg had a scorch mark on his thick armor and his drill arm was mangled. If a demonic mechanical face could look surprised and angry at the same time, it was conveyed by the hanging jaw of the cyborg. His response to the attack was to bring down the remainder of the wall that Rex and Shadow had come through. Both men could see it coming, but they had nowhere to go when it collapsed on them. Fortunately, it was just wood and chicken wire, and all it caused was an inconvenience. Rex was already chopping his way out with his Vibro-Sword and Shadow was using a Vibro-Knife. Rex could see the cyborg, who had the perfect opportunity to eliminate them while they were temporary subdued by the debris and wire, but instead he popped off his mangled drill arm while a compartment opened on his right leg. Reaching into the compartment, the 'Borg removed a bionic hand and wrist joint, which he promptly attached to where the drill had been a moment before.

Shouting could be heard up by the ladder, and the footfalls of standard Dead Boy armor were approaching. Apparently some of the Cyber-Snatchers thought they could stand up to the Coalition troopers descending on their base and decided to open fire. Idiots, Rex thought as he feverishly hacked his way out of the remaining chicken wire and debris. Shadow was struggling and appeared pinned by a crate that had shifted to pin his foot. Rex jumped to assist and watched as the cyborg scooped up a handful of small items, tossing them into a large rucksack. Among the items was a dull, black leather bag. It had a medical insignia on it along with the name Rex recognized as Doctor Young's from the diplomas he had seen hanging in his office.

Instead of heading to help Shadow, the Juicer leapt in the direction of the cyborg. All he had to do was grab that bag and they were out of there. Shadow would be okay for a few seconds, Rex reasoned. The cyborg had other ideas and was undeterred by Rex's assault. The monstrosity moved with mechanical speed, spinning around and grabbing a small cylindrical item from a chest compartment that seemed to open by itself. Before Rex could land, the item was tossed at Shadow.

No! Grenade!! Rex thought. Before he could alter his trajectory he connected with the cyborg, but instead of bringing down his Vibro-Sword on the cyborg's head as he had intended, he vaulted off of the mechanical body back towards Shadow. Rex could see that the grenade had landed just out of the reach of the Crazy, who still had his leg pinned. Rex landed on Shadow as smoke and sparks erupted from the grenade along with a loud bang. Rex had expected to feel the force of a high explosive grenade or shrapnel from a frag grenade, but instead it was a *flash bang*. The flash bang had served its purpose, by distracting the Juicer long enough for the cyborg to escape to a nearby set of rungs down to the sewers.

Rex couldn't see through the smoke and worked to unpin Shadow's foot. The Crazy was a little stunned from the flash and noise of the stun grenade, but was otherwise okay. The duo could hear the mechanical voices of the Coalition troops as they spoke through their armor. They were spreading out and conducting a thorough search of the area.

"Clear."

"Clear."

Then the sound of laser fire, the scream of a Cyber-Snatcher, and the word, "Clear."

Standard CS search and destroy operation. A mini-purge, you might say.

Obviously the Cyber-Snatchers had not been much of an obstacle or deterrent to the highly trained and well equipped storm troopers.

Rex and Shadow had to get going or they would be the next to fall before the might of the Coalition Army.

Rex lifted the crate off Shadow's legs, allowing him to pull free. Shadow's legs would no doubt be bruised, as he preferred to wear light padded armor, but at least he could walk – assuming they got out of there alive.

Rex was going to leap towards the rungs in the wall but hesitated, waiting for the Crazy. Shadow had a slight limp, and knowing that he would slow Rex down he pointed forcefully toward the drainpipes.

"I'm not leaving you behind, Bro." replied Rex, moving to grab the injured Crazy. Shadow put his hands up to motion for the Juicer to stop. He then gave Rex the thumbs up and pointed to himself and then to his mask. He winked at Rex and nodded for him to go.

"You better not get caught or your sister will kick my butt." said Rex. Shadow replied by slipping away from Rex and moving towards the shadowed areas of the lair.

Rex hated leaving him behind, but knew that Shadow was far more experienced than he was and had done this sort of thing in the past. Evasion and stealth were his specialties. Still, he was like blood and Rex was concerned for his welfare, even if he was a Crazy.

With his quarry getting away, Rex lept feet first into the shaft leading down.

Behind him he heard more gunfire and voices shouting. "There!" "Clear."

Rex hooked onto one of the ladder's rungs and made his way down fast, if a bit reckless. He knew Coalition troops were all over the place and the damn cyborg was making good with his escape. Thankfully, none of the soldiers had seemed to notice him . . . or Bruce/Shadow.

"Stay back!! I have a book and I'm not afraid to read it!" said a voice that Rex had recognized as Shadow's! It was a recording, of course, that was done years ago, but it still made for a nice distraction. The message repeated again and Rex could hear Coalition troopers rushing towards the location of the voice. With luck, that would leave a big gap for the Crazy to slip through.

"Damn tricky, you Crazy bastard!" Rex mumbled to himself.

With no time to waste, the Juicer poured on the speed and raced down the tunnel. The details of the subterranean corridor were a blur to him as he raced down it following the sounds of the cyborg's footsteps in the distance. Slipping on the passive night-vision goggles as he ran, Rex smiled. At least the cyborg's path would be obvious, as the giant machine left deep, enormous footprints in the muck that covered the floor of the tunnel. Furthermore, no normal sized manhole was big enough for the 'Borg to slip through, so his options for escape were limited.

The drainpipe ended at a large vertical shaft. Without even looking up, Rex knew his quarry was climbing up just ahead of him. He could hear the clang of heavy metal against the steel rungs the beast was climbing. The 'Borg was already at the top and climbing out, apparently having used the built-in in thrusters in his legs to leap half the distance up. The vertical pipe was smooth save for the rung ladder and various pipes that connected to it above Rex. Each pipe had just a small lip at a connection point, enough for the Juicer to catch his foot on. Making sure his sword and rifle were secured, he began leaping from lip to lip, going higher and higher until he was ground level with the foundry. Catching his breath for just a moment at the opening, Rex peeked out to see a large contingent of Coalition soldiers. Something big was going on. This wasn't just some raid on a Cyber-Snatcher gang. There had to be over 200 troops. There was a lot of commotion going on, but before Rex had time to figure out what all the ruckus was about, he heard what sounded like a jet engine.

Rex, along with dozens of CS troops, looked up to see the cyborg taking off in a large, souped-up hovercycle or rocket bike. It had the normal hover jets that kept the bike in the air, but instead of hover jets to propel the craft it clearly had some kind of dual engines that were big and powerful. The cyborg was forced to sit in between them with a rucksack clearly visible to Rex. Rex was running out of time and would never make it to Shadow's hovercycle, even if he could avoid all the Dead Boys, to give pursuit. Without any other recourse, Rex locked his sight on one of three Sky Cycles that had landed a short distance away. These vehicles where the Coalition's version of a hovercycle on steroids. Capable of reaching speeds in excess of 500 mph when the rockets kicked in, they also sported a decent weapon system. Rex had always admired the vehicle, now he was about to steal one.

The Juicer pulled out his Vibro-Sword and charged into a dozen or so Coalition troops still looking up at the escaping cyborg. It was all the distraction Rex needed as he flipped, rolled, and raced toward the vehicles. Along the way he grabbed a nearby length of chain and hacked it loose with his sword. Chain in one hand and sword in the other, he swung at several Dead Boys, who hit the dirt to avoid the whirlwind of metal aimed at their heads. That's what Rex wanted. He only needed to scatter and distract them long enough to get to one of the cycles. Still in the foundry compound, Rex realized that he was running through a maze of cranes and that several large pieces of machinery and cauldrons were suspended overhead. Each held in place by a chain anchored to the ground. With a few quick swings of his Vibro-Sword, the chains were cut and the items they held in place were let loose. It was as if the sky was falling, and Coalition troops scattered as not just a single piece of machinery fell, but dozens. Rex hadn't figured on the chain reaction, but it worked to his advantage.

At the end of his gauntlet run, the Juicer flipped in the air and landed on the nearest Sky Cycle. Rex hoped they operated the same as a hovercycle or else he would be in a world of hurt. Fortunately for him, most CS troops were also illiterate and the flight controls had a variety of symbols found on most hovercycles. The engine roared to life and the Sky Cycle shot into the air at a blinding speed.

Now this was a rush, Rex thought to himself. If he didn't live in the 'Burbs he would have loved to keep the Sky Cycle, but it would be too hot a commodity.

Leaving the Coalition soldiers behind, Rex focused on the contrails of the cyborg's souped-up hovercycle. He could see why the 'Borg who called himself Vulcan was the gang's leader, he was smart as well as physically strong. The damn cyborg had the perfect escape plan and vehicle to do it. If Rex wasn't so desperate to get that medical bag, he'd never have pulled the stunt he just did to give chase to Vulcan.

Rex quickly closed on Vulcan. While the cyborg's hovercycle was clearly built for speed, it didn't compare to the advanced Coalition Sky Cycle, and the cyborg's weight didn't help matters. Rex gained on the fugitive. The Sky Cycle even tracked the cyborg on a mini-display in the dashboard. Looking at the color coding, Rex could follow his target's every move while closing fast. The tiny circle that represented the 'Borg on the display was getting bigger and the color was changing from a blue to what Rex figured would be red. Now Rex understood why the illiterate CS troopers were so effective. Even though they couldn't read it was compensated for with their technology. Rex knew that Rachel would appreciate his observations. Watching both the display and the terrain ahead, Rex noticed that two smaller blips had appeared on the screen. The Juicer glanced behind him to see the two other Sky Cycles in hot pursuit. He shook his head, thinking how he couldn't just catch a break today, and kept focused on his quarry. Looking ahead, he noticed that the cyborg was descending into the streets of the 'Burbs. Good idea, Rex thought. They would be harder to track if they traveled at street level. The problem was, the sun was cresting the horizon and there would be people and vehicles hitting the streets. Rex had to risk it, and followed Vulcan with his Coalition pursuers hot on his tail. They were clearly experienced pilots and knew how to handle their vehicles, as they were quickly catching up faster than Rex had to the cyborg. The fact that they hadn't fired yet suggested to him that they were trying to recover the stolen Sky Cycle, and that might be something that could work to Rex's advantage.

Having lived in the 'Burbs all his life, the Juicer knew it pretty well, and there was a section coming up where he might be able to lose the CS troopers while still keeping the cyborg in sight.

Rex banked the Sky Cycle towards a parallel street and he slowed down, letting the CS troops get right up on him. Looking over his shoulder, he could tell by their gesturing that they were ordering him to stand down or else they would fire. Ahead of Rex the road divided and there were several large buildings at least five stories tall. He gunned his vehicle and shot it down a side street, heading back to his original course. As he swung across the street, between the buildings there were clotheslines full of clothes, just as he knew there would be. The lines of washed clothing were strung across at all levels from the second floor on up. With his knowledge of the place and his Juicer enhanced reflexes, Rex was able to avoid them, weaving the Sky Cycle up, down, left and right. The two CS pursuers didn't react as fast as Rex and the lead bike tried to burst through the obstacles sending bras, panties and linens flying everywhere. Worse yet, a blanket flopped over the pilot along with clotheslines that quickly tangled around him. His bike crashed into the fourth floor of a building. The pilot of that cycle hung suspended by the remaining clotheslines, like a bird in a snare.

The second pilot was fast enough to pull up on his Sky Cycle, gaining just enough altitude to avoid having himself tangled in the lines. He did, however, catch one of the lines that was covered in shirts and pants and it was like a kite's tail dangling behind the speeding vehicle. Before Rex could congratulate himself, the display on the Sky Cycle flashed red quickly and the dot that was the remaining Sky Cycle glowed an amber flashing red! Rex looked behind him to see a pair of mini-missiles screaming his way. He directed his Sky Cycle towards the nearest abandoned building and, at the last second, he veered to the left. The missiles exploded behind him, sending Rex and the cycle jarring forward. Even a near miss and Rex could feel the heat of the plasma from the missiles. This guy meant business and obviously didn't give a damn about the 'Burbs or any innocent bystanders who might get killed in his pursuit. To most CS citizens, the 'Burbs were an eyesore that would never go away, and most Coalition troopers didn't care about them or the people who lived there.

Another pair of missiles shot over Rex's head as the pilot had once again lined up a shot. Rex was able to avoid this blast and he started to zig and zag through the various streets, using buildings as cover. The remaining Sky Cycle pilot was good and kept pace with Rex. He hadn't fired again since Rex wasn't giving him the opportunity. Using what little breathing room the Juicer had, he carefully grabbed his shouldered JA-11 rifle. The weapon was supposedly based off of a pre-Rifts design and was three weapons in one. Rex opted for the ion setting that would allow him to fire the weapon in bursts. Piloting the Sky Cycle one handed wasn't easy for Rex, and a few times he thought he would lose control. He had to act, however, and act now. Clearing the next building, he whipped around, holding the rifle one-handed, and fired a burst. The first shot missed, the second hit the windshield of the trooper's Sky Cycle. It was the third shot that hit paydirt, blowing a clean hole in the Dead Boy's armored chest and causing him to spin out of control. Rex saw the Sky Cycle spiral to the ground, but there was no explosion. He figured the pilot had managed to land and only hoped he wouldn't renew his pursuit.

Rex quickly returned to the forward facing position, shouldering his rifle. His own Sky Cycle was veering out of control. Hugging the controls, Rex and Sky Cycle plowed through a nearby building. It was vacant and old, but it was only the vehicle's hard composite armor that kept the bike from being destroyed and the Juicer with it. Rex regained control as the vehicle burst through the other side of the building.

Dust and debris covered Rex's body and the Sky Cycle. Shaking it off, Rex searched the display screen for the cyborg, praying that it was still locked on to him as a target. It was, and he was close; a few streets over on a parallel path. Maybe his luck was changing, Rex dared to hope. Better yet, the cyborg's hovercycle gave off an oily smoke that allowed Rex to get a visual fix on its location, and he veered to get back on the trail.

No more playing around, Rex thought as he hit the Sky Cycle's overdrive. He wasn't belted in, and if not for his superhuman strength the Juicer would have been thrown from the bike. The buildings around him became a blur even to the Juicer. Normally, traveling at these speeds, pilots had the advantage of being strapped in to their seats and tried to travel in a straight line. Rex was still maneuvering the bike down streets kicking up large rooster tails of dust and grit behind him, and causing people to scream and curse the Coalition as he sped by.

The distance shrank down in seconds. Rex noticed that he was in the north part of the 'Burbs and his quarry was dead ahead. He could even see Vulcan's rucksack. Giving the Sky Cycle a little more juice, Rex was soon side by side with the cyborg, who looked over, shaking his head. With mechanical quickness, Vulcan pulled out a large bore energy pistol that looked alien to Rex and fired a massive plasma bolt at him. However, it only hit an empty Sky Cycle that seconds later, slammed into the ground, showering the area with debris. Rex had vaulted onto the back of Vulcan's hovercycle and was grabbing at the rucksack. The cyborg's arm pivoted and being mechanical, took a position that no human arm could take as the mechanical monster tried to aim at the Juicer for a second blast. Rex had had enough. He pulled his Vibro-Sword out with one swift move and swung at Vulcan's weapon. The sword connected, spraying a shower of sparks. Rex swung the sword again, before the gang leader could fire the weapon, and cut the straps of the rucksack. Meanwhile, the cyborg tried to shake the Juicer loose by jinking with the hovercycle. Rex was undeterred, sheathed his sword and grabbed the rucksack, pulling hard. Vulcan tried to grab at Rex as he flipped off the bike with his prize in hand. The cyborg wasn't about to give up his stash without a fight, however something caught his attention. It wasn't the fact that Rex had flipped onto the roof of a nearby building, it was the half dozen or so metal clinking sounds that caught his attention. Looking over his shoulder he saw that where the rucksack had been were several metal pins. The realization hit the cyborg as a small cylinder rolled into view. He didn't even have time to react as the grenades exploded, engulfing the bike in superheated plasma. A second later, the bike itself exploded.

Rex had cleared the bike and aimed for a small building that was quickly coming up. He hit hard and his momentum carried him off the building to land in a nearby alley. He was eating dirt when he heard the explosion. Vulcan had probably survived, he mused. Despite the explosion, mining cyborgs were heavily armored and tough as hell. Survive, yes, but he wouldn't want to pay for the repairs the 'Borg would need to get himself back in working order.

Rex sat up in the alley and grinned to himself. He had done it. Looking into the rucksack, the doctor's bag was safe and sound. There were even a handful of other cybernetic parts he was sure the Doc would give him credit for. Rex jumped to his feet and noticed he was bruised and bleeding in several places. He might even have a broken bone or two, but he felt fine. Great in fact, thanks to his drug harness and Bio-Comp. Rex knew that his Bio-Comp unit was automatically releasing thousands of microscopic robots into his bloodstream. They would begin to repair his body, stop the bleeding and patch him up as he made his way back home. Meanwhile, a drug cocktail kept the pain down to a bare minimum.

Rex looked around. He was on the northern outskirts of the 'Burbs, which meant he had a long walk. Rex moved on foot at an inhuman speed, dodging the occasional CS patrol. He was sure by now they found all the Sky Cycles and probably the wreckage of the cyborg's hovercycle. If he was lucky, no one would recognize him. Heck, if he were really lucky, the authorities would decide he must have died in one of the crashes. Rex made a mental note to keep a low profile for the next few months.

Chapter 6 - A not so pleasant homecoming

The sun was up and finally, after a two hour walk, Rex had arrived, first going to where Shadow stored his hovercycle. It was there. Good, Rex thought, Shadow had made it out, bike and all. But by the looks of it, not without a fight. Poor Countach looked barely flyable. Several laser blast marks and even some scorch marks that must have been from grenades or mini-missiles marred its surface. Rex put the rucksack down next to another bag that he had noticed. Glancing in the large sack, Rex discovered Shadow had made off with a few things himself, and by the looks of it, he scored some IRMSS (Internal Robot Medical Surgical System) and RMK (Robot Medical Kit) devices. They were very expensive and used in healing people who had broken bones or some kind of internal damage. They were more common in the mega-city, as they were typically manufactured by the Coalition States. Out in the 'Burbs they were worth their weight in gold. Leaping out of the hovercycle's hideaway, Rex headed home. The boys would probably still be asleep, but to be on the safe side he would enter in through his and Rachel's bedroom window.

As Rex expected the window to his bedroom was unlocked, allowing him to slip in without a sound. He tried to be as quiet as possible to not wake his wife, however before he fully opened the window, he noticed that the door was off the hinge and leaning against the bed. Panic welled up, giving him a jolt of adrenaline, and he slammed the window open, shattering it and sending shards of glass into the room. He was inside before the glass hit the floor. Flipping the door out of the way to make sure no one was under it, he grimaced at the sight of a bloodstain on the floor.

He ran to the boys' room – empty! The two beds were stripped clean with only a few scattered pillows. Rex fell to his knees, his wife, his children, what happened?

Who could have known he was married or where they lived?! Questions mixed with grief began to overwhelm him when he heard a thumping coming from the front of the apartment. Rex gripped his Vibro-Sword, flew to his feet and charged down the hall. The thumping grew louder and was accompanied by someone speaking.

"No, no, no, no . . ." Rex tried to calm himself, recognizing the voice. In his corner behind the couch Bruce was banging his head against the wall, uttering "no" over and over again. Rex couldn't remember the last time he heard Bruce speak in person. It had to be before Todd was born.

Rex knew asking the Crazy any questions right now would be useless, and whatever happened occurred some hours ago. Rex scanned the room, looking for any kind of clue, and sitting on the kitchen counter next to a picture of the whole family was a message disc. They were cheap, disposable handheld devices that just about everyone used in the 'Burbs, at least those who were illiterate. The Coalition produced them by the zillions and sold them very cheaply. The devices were very simple, one button to record a message the other to replay it. The green button was flashing, indicating that a message had been recorded. Rex scooped it up and played the message.

"Hello, Rex, it's your pal, Viper. I have a little proposition for you. I have three people you know very well. Oh, here's a little proof . . ." There was a momentary pause and the sounds of a person struggling before Viper spoke again. "Say something to your hubby, Dear."

Rex listened, having brought the memo disc up to his face, and even though he knew Rachel was the logical choice it still hit him hard when he heard her speak.

"Rex . . . there are two Juh . . ." She was suddenly silenced with what sounded like a slap or a punch. Then the voice of Viper returned.

"You've heard enough. Go to the **Rusty Cup** by noon for further instructions or I'll start with your youngest. You know, so your wife can watch!"

The message ended and the flashing green light turned a solid green. Rex crushed the device in his hand and threw it at the wall. Anger surged throughout his body and his Bio-Comp adjusted by sending a surge of endorphins. Normally the high was a welcome diversion, but Rex needed his anger and overrode the device with the handheld unit hanging from the right side of the drug harness. He needed his head clear. He looked over toward Bruce, who had stopped speaking and banging his head into the wall. He was standing in the corner looking towards Rex, his head held down in shame, and clutched in his hands was a stuffed toy tiger. Rex recalled it was the one that Jason had given Uncle Bruce, who was having nightmares at the time. The Crazy raised his tear filled face and looked at Rex.

"I failed them . . ." Rex was surprised to hear the Crazy speak twice in one day.

"No, you didn't, Bro, you were being a friend and helping me. Viper's my problem. I thought things would change once we were free agents. I don't know why, but he hates me. Jealous, maybe. Or just plain evil. Remember when I told you about my Bio-Comp malfunction? Yeah. Well, the Doc said it was sabotaged. Deliberately messed with. The only person I can think of doing that to me is Viper. He's the last person I remember seeing before I woke up in the clinic."

Rex suddenly realized he was still holding the Vibro-Sword and sheathed it. He walked over towards the Crazy, who was gently putting the stuffed animal on the couch.

"You with me on this one, Bro?"

Uncle Bruce wiped the tears from his face as it took on a hardened expression. Grabbing his ski mask, he slipped it on and nodded.

"Good, Here's what we're going to do . . ."

Chapter 7 – The Pain of Waiting

The wait until noon had been agonizing. Rex tried to distract himself by preparing for whatever might arise. He replaced the partially spent energy clip of his laser rifle and tried to repair some of the damage his armor had taken.

Uncle Bruce/Shadow had already left to make a few purchases. Rex had no idea what the Crazy needed to buy, but he promised he would be at the **Rusty Cup** by noon, and undercover.

Rex downed his third beer as he tapped the wooden table of the inn with his fingers. His eyes darted around the bar, looking for any sign of Viper or his partner. Rachel said "two." There were two men who were going to die this afternoon.

Time dragged on until noon when a young kid, probably around the age of 13 or 14, came into the bar. The kid had a wild eyed look to him with messy hair, disheveled clothes and track marks on his arms. He also acted super-hyper like a new Juicer just days after receiving a conversion. A *Wannabe Juicer*, Rex thought to himself. It had to be, and the kid was looking for his next high. Viper must have promised to hook him up. Wannabe Juicers were pathetic. They were usually kids who were too young or too mentally unstable to join any organization willing to do a Juicer conversion, so instead they opted to take whatever kind of street drugs they could get their hands on. Most were burnouts in a few years who lived from one high to the next. The Wannabe Juicer looked around the bar and seeing Rex, raced over to his table.

"AreyouRex?" the youngster blurted out, his words all strung together and his body visibly shaking as he waited for a reply.

"Yeah. You got something for me?" asked Rex, his anger fading to pity for Viper's messenger. The youngster pulled a memo disc out of his pocket and held it in his hand. He extended his other hand to Rex. "Fifty credits," he demanded.

The momentary feelings of pity faded to feelings of indignation. This punk actually thought he could pull some kind of scam on him. A variety of options raced through Rex's mind, most too violent to contemplate, considering the messenger was a kid.

"Listen, Kid, I only have one thing to ask you and I'll say it very slowly so you understand. How . . . much . . . is . . . your . . . life . . . worth?"

Rex looked deadpan and stared the smug kid down. To further punctuate his point, Rex grabbed the beer mug with his hand and with one quick motion, shattered the glass everywhere. The normally noisy bar quieted down and people started to stare in Rex's direction. Considering his options, the Wannabe Juicer set the memo disc on the table and ran out of the bar. Looking around, the bar's patrons resumed their conversations. Rex grabbed the memo disc and looked it over. This was a slightly more expensive memo disc, as it had a small screen for video messages. Rex pressed the green flashing button and the message started to play. The silver screen changed to a picture of Rachel, her mouth duct taped shut and next to her were the boys, wrapped up in their bed sheets, duct tape also keeping them secure as well. The image finally panned to Viper, who began to speak.

"Hey, BOSS! As you can see, your family is alive and well. How long they stay that way depends on you, Bro. Be at the base of the old Sear's Tower by 23:00 hours tonight. Come alone. Try anything and they're toast."

The message screen went blank. Rex looked around the room. He couldn't tell if Shadow had come in or not. It was lunchtime and the bar was full. Rex paid his tab and left. For some reason, Coalition patrols had picked up and not wanting to draw any attention, Rex ducked down the nearest alley. Shadow dropped down ahead of him.

"Damnit, I hate it when you do that!" said Rex, who had reached for his Vibro-Sword as a reflex action. Releasing it back into its sheath he pulled out the memo disc and played it for Shadow. The Crazy looked at Rex, waiting for a plan.

"Its probably going to take us all afternoon to get out to the Chicago ruins. The 'Burbs are crawling with Dead Boys today. There's no way we're going to be able to just jet out of here. Hell, after this morning, we're probably who they're looking for."

The Crazy nodded and started to head out of the alley, sticking to the shadows. Rex followed suit.

It took longer to get out of the 'Burbs than Rex had hoped. The Coalition troops had a perimeter and various checkpoints around the 'Burbs. While it was illegal to create Juicers and Crazies in CS territory, it wasn't illegal for the pair to be in the 'Burbs. Still, CS troopers liked to flex their muscle by detaining anyone they wanted to question, and Rex didn't have time to end up in a Coalition detention center. Since he and Shadow needed the hovercycle, it took extra effort to get out of the 'Burbs, but finally, having passed the last checkpoint, they were on their way to the ruins of old Chicago.

Getting out of the 'Burbs, while time consuming, was the easy part, getting into the ruins of Chicago would be another matter entirely. Several ley lines coursed through the ruins of the city, with a nexus at the heart of downtown. Practitioners of magic would often come to the ruins to make use of the untapped energy found there. Since the Coalition claimed the ruins as part of their territory, plus the fact that the practice of magic in any CS territory was forbidden, the CS created a large military perimeter around the ruins, and sent patrols inside them to exterminate anyone found there. Having a patrol on hand to stop trespassers was one thing, having a military presence was another. In addition to keeping people out, the CS troops stationed in the ruins were also charged with keeping anything that might crawl out of a Rift from leaving the ruins. Consequentially, they had a lot of heavy hardware on hand.

Outside the shattered ruins, Shadow had pulled the hovercycle into a small gully and handed Rex a pair of infrared distancing binoculars. From this distance, Rex could make out where the remains of the Sears Tower were. However, now was not the time for sightseeing. Rex focused on observing the Coalition forces in the area. He had never seen such a large concentration of Coalition hardware anywhere. Marching along the perimeter were massive robots with a large death's head for a body, large cannons on either side, and spider-like legs for mobility. Rex instantly recognized them as Coalition *Spider Skull Walkers*, one of the more deadly Coalition war machines. Watching them amble across the terrain always made Rex's skin crawl. Flying in the air were Sky Cycles and SAMAS power armors.

This wasn't going to be easy, Rex thought to himself. They would have to wait till night to approach. Using infrared and night vision, the two modified men could use the dark to their advantage. Now came the hard part: more waiting.

Most of the time, Rex reveled in being a Juicer. It was the times of inactivity that he hated the most. Juicers often had to take a heavy sedative to sleep. Rex knew the wait would be agonizing and would most likely cause him to try to foolishly sneak into the ruined city before it was dark. So he adjusted his Bio-Comp to put him into sleep mode for a few hours. Rex always tried counting backward from ten to see how long before he fell asleep. Until today he never made it past seven, four was a new record for the Juicer.

Rex was jolted awake by a sudden surge of adrenaline from his Bio-Comp. It took a few seconds for the cobwebs to clear and looking around, he saw Shadow was still meditating. Poking his head up from the gully, Rex took another peek through the infrared distancing binoculars. Coalition patrols were still tight, but there were a few spots where he and Shadow could slip in under the radar, so to speak. And Rex had a plan. He jumped on Shadow's hovercycle and fired it up. That was enough to wake the Crazy from his reverie. Lifting the ski mask, he gave Rex an indignant look.

"Let's go. I'm driving," said Rex as he donned a pair of nightvision goggles. Shadow knew that Rex wouldn't take no for an answer, and the Crazy reluctantly hopped on the back, securing a duffle bag to his side. Keeping the lights off, Rex headed towards the tower ruins at full speed.

The hovercycle was smaller than a Sky Cycle, but Rex hoped that on radar it would pass for one at a glance. Rex recalled from his jaunt through the 'Burbs on his "borrowed" Sky Cycle that its infrared sensors were forward facing and that the pilot had to rely on his own vision on the sides of the cycle. Rex hoped to use that to his advantage as he gunned the hovercycle on an intercept course towards the closest Sky Cycle patrol. As Rex predicted, one of the patrols was on an intercept course for the old city ruins, and it consisted of a pair of Sky Cycles. Hugging the ground and darting around piles of debris as the pair of cycles passed overhead, Rex hit the vertical thruster, sending the hovercycle up. Rex flew the hovercycle between the Sky Cycles and as Rex had hoped the pilots were concentrating on what was ahead of them, not what was just below and between them. It was only his enhanced reflexes that allowed Rex to maneuver so precisely between the pair of cycles as they entered the ruined city. Rex kept pace as the pilots darted in and around the shattered buildings and massive piles of debris.

He could see the ruins of the Sears Tower ahead. Part of it was glowing a pale blue from the ley line energy. The Sky Cycles were turning and Rex maneuvered the hovercycle beneath them to his left. As the building rapidly approached, Shadow leapt off the hovercycle, landing in a nearby shattered skyscraper. Rex was supposed to approach alone, and he would. The Crazy watched as Rex made a ruckus in front of the tower with the hovercycle at the base of the building. For several minutes he did donuts and figure eights, trying to look for a suitable place to land. He was kicking up dust and debris everywhere.

Not seeing any potential ambushers, Shadow set down a large duffle bag that he had been clinging to. He unzipped it and started to pull out its contents. It would take him a few minutes to assemble his gear and get into his heavy armor. Rex was buying Shadow plenty of time. Finally, Shadow fired his brand new grappling hook into the Sears Tower across the street and landed quietly several floors up.

Chapter 8 - End Game

Viper paced in the foyer of the Sears Tower. Its glass entrance was shattered long ago by the cataclysmic events that had transformed the Earth. Now the building was nothing more than an empty shell, the bottom filled with debris. The interior was lit up from the ley line that coursed through it, bathing everything inside with a soft blue light. The Juicer didn't wait alone.

Trussed up to one of the building's interior columns were Rachel and the boys. Her captors had finally taken the gags off. The boys were scared and confused and Rachel's only hope of keeping her own fears from surfacing was to talk to the boys. Throughout the day she had given them a history lesson on Chicago and even quizzed them on their spelling. The large Titan Juicer, for the hundredth time, came over to stare at Rachel and run his hands through her hair. He didn't say nice things, either. In fact, most were rather unpleasant comments about what he was going to do with her if Rex didn't show up.

There was also another person in the foyer. He had showed up unexpectedly early, much to Viper's annoyance. The man wore a long, black, hooded robe adorned with red silk and a variety of hanging bones, from animal to human. In his right hand was a bone staff with a skull on top of it. Blood ran from the eye sockets and flies circled around it. *Blood Reaper* was the powerful Necromancer who had financed Viper's Juicer conversion. The death mage had made the proper introductions and worked out a financial arrangement with the Black Market. Viper only had to serve a one year tour of duty, but once he finished, he had to pay off his debt to Blood Reaper. The death mage had told the Juicer of his plans to create an undead army, and the mage was looking forward to creating a *Murder Wraith*. Viper had learned that Murder Wraiths were undead Juicers who had to give themselves over willingly, and Viper wasn't ready to be an undead Juicer. Not when he had a chance to be immortal with a new process he had heard of called the *Prometheus Treatment*. That's why he had tried to disable Rex's Bio-Comp. Blood Reaper had a strange and twisted sense of honor, and had given Viper his word that if he could provide another candidate for the process, then he would be relieved of his debt. Rex was that candidate as far as Viper was concerned.

"This Juicer you promised me, Viper. He had better be a suitable specimen and not on Last Call. He needs to live for at least a year while undergoing the treatment."

Viper was annoyed. It was getting close to the time and now he had to answer to Blood Reaper.

"Two years, man. He's been a Juicer for two years. Ok?" Viper hadn't realized he had raised his voice as Goliath and their prisoners looked at him. The young boys looked especially surprised. Viper was about to leap over to them when he heard a sound from outside. It wasn't another CS patrol, it was a hovercycle coming to a landing and making a heck of a racket doing it.

"I trust you'll have this situation under control shortly. Place these manacles on him. I shall observe from the shadows." The death mage handed Viper a slimy creature that looked like a living pair of manacles. It had a pair of black, beady eyes and it squirmed in his grasp. Viper watched as the Necromancer walked away, uttering the phrase: "From light to dark, it is in the shadows that I must walk."

At the completion of the phrase, the death mage seemed to walk right into the shadow and disappeared completely.

"C'mon Goliath. I might need a hand getting these things on him," ordered Viper. Goliath leaned in close to Rachel, licking the side of her face.

"Don't go anywhere, beautiful. I'll be right back."

Shoving a gag in her mouth, Goliath felt something kick at his shin. It was one of the boys, Jason as he recalled.

"Leave my mother alone or else my Dad is going to kick your butt to kingdom come, Fatso!"

The large Juicer was surprised. This little one had guts. He grabbed the two boys by their necks with one hand, and duct taped them together with his free hand. After a few twirls with the tape he looked young Jason right in the eyes.

208

"Children should be seen and not heard, and if I hear you again I'm going to punt you like a football. Got it?"

Jason's eyes welled with tears. Goliath turned around and headed towards the entrance in the foyer. Had he looked up he would have seen Shadow clinging to a girder. The Crazy was clad in full Dead Boy body armor, modified to accommodate the metallic studs sticking out of his head. Instead of a death's head for a helmet it was a plain featureless mask with a tinted visor over the eyes. Shadow waited until Goliath was far enough away before descending to the ground. His approach was so silent that Rachel was momentarily startled when he touched her shoulder from behind. She whipped her head around expecting the evil mage, but was instead greeted by the sight of her brother, his finger over his mouth indicating silence. The boys reacted to their mother, but couldn't turn their heads because of the duct tape. The Vibro-Knife sliced through Rachel's bonds with ease. She quickly freed herself and made a move towards the boys when Shadow stopped her. He directed her to go up the knotted rope hanging behind the Crazy. Reluctantly, she complied while Shadow went to work freeing his nephews.

Rex gunned the hovercycle, purposely making a ruckus to get the attention of anyone in the building. He even did a few donuts, kicking up dust and debris. Finally, when he could see Viper and Goliath he parked the hovercycle and shut it down. The two Juicers approached and Rex tried to stall for more time by leaping out off of the seat of the cycle right towards Viper. Rex purposely didn't draw his Vibro-Sword, rather opting to plant a big juicy fist right in Viper's face. Instead, Goliath caught Rex in mid-air by the throat and hurled him towards a nearby wall. Rex slammed into the wall at Juicer speeds, breaking through the flimsy concrete. Well, at least he was inside, he thought to himself. He tried to glance around before jumping to his feet, but the two Juicers were on him in seconds.

"You were always in my way, man. Now you and your family are gonna pay!" sneered Viper.

Rex wasn't fast enough and before he could get to his feet, Viper planted a roundhouse kick that caught Rex across the jaw, sending his body spinning into the air. Not content with just watching, the Titan Juicer caught Rex before he could fall to the ground and kicked him square in the chest. The kick sent Rex flying further into the belly of the building.

When Juicers fought ordinary people they always had the edge, but when it was Juicer versus Juicer the action was often over before most people could blink. In that instant, as Rex was flying through the air, he noticed where Shadow was and that Rachel was with him as well. He just had to buy them a few more seconds to get out.

"What's wrong, old man? Bio-Comp not up to par? Hmm, wonder how that could be?" taunted Viper as he raced over to where Rex had landed.

Rex looked up as Viper approached him, Goliath two footsteps behind him. Rex just had to know . . .

"Why, Bro? I trained you. Taught you everything about fighting and surviving in the Black Market. Hell, I even got you a spot with me in Slasher's Mercs."

"You really don't want to know, man. I just took from you what I needed. Now I'll take the rest," said Viper as he grabbed at the battered Juicer's leg, caught his ankle and hurled him through the air toward a shattered escalator. Rex tried to roll with the coming impact, but the metallic stairs threw off his landing. Rex immediately felt a pop and crack in his left ankle.

Damnit, broken! Rex thought as he slammed his fist over his heart. This was an emergency stash of nanites that would flood the Juicer's system, repairing any damage. Fortunately for Rex, his Bio-Comp was already working to release natural endorphins and painkillers. All Rex felt was a slightly warm sensation in his ankle. Thanks to the drugs, he would still be able stand and fight.

Looking around, Rex noticed that Shadow was tossing Todd up to his mother, who was on a floor above them. His aim was true and the youngster landed right in his mother's arms, Jason was right beside them.

Rex was relieved. Now he could fight back. However, before he could draw his sword he heard maniacal laughter coming from a nearby shadow. Stepping out of the darkness was some kind of magic user. Oh Crap, was Rex's only thought as he quickly drew his Vibro-Sword.

"You're a fool, Viper. He's been playing you since he got here," said the mage as he stopped a few feet away from the battling Juicers.

"What are you talking about? We're just working him over a little," shouted Viper with a stupid grin on his face. He was clearly a man who enjoyed inflicting pain on others and was laughing in between blows. Goliath also had a taste for blood as he was laughing as well.

"Because you just lost all the leverage you had. Did you really think he would come alone?" replied the Necromancer, pointing his staff toward the empty restraints where the captives had been, then at the Crazy. For once Viper was caught off guard, but Goliath, on the other hand, was surprisingly quick on the draw. With Juicer speed he pulled his heavy rifle, pointed it at Shadow and unleashed a barrage of plasma. The Crazy was already somersaulting out of the way and behind a column as the Juicer was drawing his weapon. After landing on his feet, Shadow drew his own weapon, a heavy laser pistol with an under-mounted grenade launcher. He let fly a grenade that impacted on the Juicer's rifle. The weapon exploded, causing a shock wave that sent all three Juicers flying through the air. The mage was just far enough away to not feel the shock wave, but shrapnel from the grenade did impact on an invisible shield that covered the magic user's body. He laughed and retreated back into the shadows to watch the rest of the melee.

Rex was ready to fight back knowing that his family was safe. The concussion had put some distance between him and Viper, and Rex remedied that by leaping the distance with the intention of splitting his enemy's skull in half with his Vibro-Sword. Viper, however, recovered just as fast as Rex and had both his Vibro-Knives over his head to block the incoming sword strike, temporarily locking the blade between his two knives.

Taking advantage of Rex's momentary defenselessness, Viper kicked with his augmented strength, striking Rex right in the groin. Juicer or not, Rex felt the blow if only for a second as once again the Bio-Comp pumped painkillers into his system.

Yeah, gonna feel that one in the morning, Rex thought to himself. Doing a back flip and putting in some distance was the only way to free his Vibro-Sword. The two Juicers stared each other down in what felt like an eternity for two augmented men. Each waited for the other to flinch. It wasn't long before Vibro-Blade and Vibro-Sword rang out as cold, hard steel tried to find kinks in their opponent's defenses.

The explosion of a plasma cannon would normally have severely injured a man. Goliath, however, was no ordinary man, and even with his armor scorched and some burns on his face and body, like Rex and Viper, he would heal and at the moment his Bio-Comp was dulling the burning pain that he felt on various parts of his body.

Shadow had ducked to avoid the blast and when he finally got up, Goliath was charging his way. The explosion had sent a wave of pain and nausea through the Crazy as his enhanced senses felt overloaded by the explosive concussion. His armor did little to shield him due to its modifications and before he could react to the Titan Juicer, Shadow was kicked hard in the gut, sending him across the room to land in a large pile of rubble. Goliath, for all his bulk, was still a Juicer, and was on Shadow again, this time bringing down a piece of metal that he had picked up after kicking the Crazy. The strike landed across Shadow's face, sending part of his armored mask flying off and leaving a deep gash in his face. Goliath battered Shadow several more times. All the Crazy could do was keep his arms up, covering his face. Each blow could be felt through the hard armor.

Once Rachel had the boys in a safe location, she looked back as a battle of supermen was erupting down in the foyer of the shattered building. She had been so intent on watching Rex that it was only after the metallic clanging of Goliath hitting Shadow's armor that she noticed her half-brother was in trouble. She wasn't a combatant, but she looked around to see how she could help. Shadow had left most of his gear in a large duffle bag and Rachel rummaged through it, finding a Wilk's laser rifle. The weapons were small and sleek and easy to wield. She had used a rifle in her day, but that was before her sons were born. She took careful aim and squeezed the trigger with one gentle pull. Instantly, a trio of red bolts erupted from the rifle, racing up Goliath's large arms, causing him to drop his makeshift weapon. His arm was scorched and by the looks of it, his armor was pierced as well. She could smell burnt flesh and was shocked that she had actually hit her target.

Rachel had gotten the Titan Juicer's attention. He looked up at her, licking his lips. The Crazy wasn't moving anymore and blood poured out of his mouth. With one powerful leap through the air, the giant was standing next to Rachel before she could take her next breath. She tried to point the rifle at him, but Goliath was too quick and slapped it out of her hands. He then grabbed her by the neck, but not as roughly as she would have expected. With his free hand he began to paw at the bathrobe she was still wearing from the night before.

Suddenly an animalistic scream filled the air. Before the Titan Juicer could respond, Shadow had landed on his back. He looked like a feral animal, his teeth bared, a Vibro-Blade in his hand. The blade was driven into the Titan Juicer's right arm, causing him to release Rachel. Still growling and screeching, Shadow lunged at the side of Goliath's head, biting off his ear. Rachel was just able to roll away as both men fell to the ground, rolling around in an all-out brawl. Shadow unleashed a frenzy of blows, slashing with the Vibro-Blade and punching with his free hand. Even Goliath's great strength couldn't stop the enraged Crazy.

High density steel rang out as Rex and Viper clashed. Each had managed to get in a few shots with his blades, each only saved by his armor. Both were evenly matched and the battle would likely take hours but Viper was intent on ending it now. He did several back flips with Rex's blade inching closer and closer to his neck. After doing several more flips, Viper vaulted for some girders several feet above him. The girders were exposed, probably during the Great Cataclysm, and three hundred years caused the rest of the floor and wall to have collapsed decades ago. All that was left was a section of girders crisscrossing like a tic-tac-toe grid. Rex followed suit and just as he landed, Viper was sweeping at his feet. Rex had to flip again, this time to another girder. Both Juicers faced each other across the way.

"Getting tired, old man?"

Despite being a Juicer, Rex had at least ten years on Viper. He was breathing a little harder than the younger man.

"You're the one who's running his mouth. Looks to me like you're the one who's tired, or are you just scared?" taunted Rex.

He was counting on Viper to make a mistake. Taunting him, Rex hoped, would get his hotheaded opponent to get careless.

"I don't know what I saw in you," said Rex. "Hell, I can't even believe I vouched for you to Slasher. Don't think you're taking my spot in the merc company. Slasher thinks you're just a punk. And he's right. Without me, you'll always be nothing!" said Rex with a smile.

Viper could feel the rage building inside of him. Even with the calming drugs dispensed by the Bio-Comp he was still outraged. That's what he always hated about Rex. His smugness. He always knew Rex thought he was inferior. A punk.

Insulted and enraged, Viper leapt at Rex and hurled both of his Vibro-Blades ahead of him. Viper's shots were dead on and Rex was only able to deflect one of them, the other stabbing into his right leg down to the bone. Rex quickly dislodged it before it severed his whole leg. It left a large, gaping wound and Rex felt a small tinge of pain. Looking up, he saw Viper was next to him on the same girder, spinning around, trying to land a roundhouse. Rex caught it square in the chest sending the Juicer plummeting backwards. His only recourse was to flip backwards to right himself, and while still in the air he could see Viper had also leapt after him and was drawing another pair of Vibro-Blades. Rex used Viper's nanosecond of defenselessness to hurl his Vibro-Sword at the leaping Juicer.

Both Juicers landed nearly simultaneously, staring at each other face to face. Viper couldn't figure why Rex had a smug look on his face, but then it hit him. The pain. Oh, the pain. Looking down, he saw that the Vibro-Sword had pierced his armor and had gone through his chest. In one quick motion, Rex ripped the Vibro-Sword out and Viper fell to the ground clutching his chest, spraying blood and chemicals from his Bio-Comp. While Rex had pierced Viper's chest, the real damage was to the drug harness, which was spilling its liquid contents all over the place. Rex raised his Vibro-Sword, ready to sever the Juicer's head from his body when he was stopped by a voice.

"You need not kill him. I have plans for the Juicer that promise a fate worse than death."

The words came from the mage, Blood Reaper, who calmly walked toward Rex from out of the shadows. Rex pointed his Vibro-Sword in the direction of the mage.

"I have no quarrel with or your friends. If you'll allow me, I would be happy to assist your injured friend," he said, pointing to Bruce.

Rex looked unconvinced, so Blood Reaper pointed his staff at the Titan Juicer and uttered some words of magic.

"Your limbs grow heavy and your speed begins to fail, as your body moves at the speed of a snail!" A nimbus of energy flared at the conclusion of the spell, and Rex noticed Goliath had slowed down and that Shadow was once again in control.

Rachel had watched as Shadow and Goliath rolled around on the ground until the large Titan Juicer once again managed to get the upper hand and was kneeling on the Crazy's chest. Blow after blow had landed on Shadow's face, chest and arms. He could feel bones breaking from the barrage of punches and he knew he wouldn't last long. The frenzied outburst had left him fatigued. Shadow's only chance was to try and weather the blows and keep up a defensive posture while waiting for an opening. That's when he noticed that the blows were coming in shorter and shorter spurts. Opening his eyes, Shadow realized the Titan Juicer seemed to be moving in slow motion. Shadow returned the favor by landing a few punches square in Goliath's face. The large Juicer reeled back, allowing Shadow to escape.

Finally on his feet, Shadow prepared his next attack. He had noticed Goliath was teetering close to the edge of the upper level. The Crazy pointed his right arm up at a point behind Goliath and launched a built-in grappling cable. Hearing it strike a girder above him, Shadow jumped, heading right toward Goliath. The Titan Juicer could see the Crazy heading at him, but was too slow to respond. When Shadow's feet connected with the Juicer's chest, he sent Goliath plummeting backwards. The Titan Juicer entranced by the spell, couldn't react fast enough and landed on a pile of jagged debris that penetrated his armor and impaled the Juicer. He started to cough up blood.

"Even better!" exclaimed the Necromancer. "Two Juicers for the price of one." The mage walked over to the Titan Juicer, who was coughing up blood and was unable to move. "Fear not, you will live – for now."

Shadow landed opposite the mage and Rex was there as well.

"We're done here. Let's go, Shadow," ordered Rex, but before he and Shadow could leap up to the next level, the mage spoke.

"Perhaps, Rex, you will consider becoming immortal. Join me and the power you have now is nothing compared to what I could give you."

Rex looked up to the next level where Rachel and the boys looked down at him. He turned to look at the mage.

"No thanks," he said, and then added, "What do I look like, a Crazy?!"

Shadow looked a bit bewildered. He wasn't sure if he had been insulted or if Rex had made a joke. He looked over at the mage as if considering the offer, then shook his head no and followed Rex to join his family.

Blood Reaper had his answer and looked on as the family was reunited. He ordered his nearby Zombie minions to grab the two Juicers and carry them away. Both were incapacitated by their injuries, but were alive enough to be saved by his magic and used for his own sinister purpose. The mage chuckled as he disappeared into the shadows, followed by his undead minions.

Chapter 9 – A debt repaid and a decision to make

Sneaking out of the ruins and back to the Chi-Town 'Burbs was an adventure in its own right, and the young boys loved every minute of it. They had a million questions for their father, and Rex did his best to answer them while at the same time trying to emphasize the point that being a Juicer was *bad* and unhealthy. And how the boys would have to keep his being a Juicer a secret.

Rex was worried that there might be other enemies lurking out there, and that he had exposed his family to something he hadn't intended. Finally, after a few days of rest and healing, the family had settled in to a new apartment and Rex was off to repay his debt to Doc Young.

This time the doctor's office wasn't as crowded. Rex still hated waiting, and had to be content with plucking the flies out of the air and crushing them as they flew near him. By the eighth fly he was being called in to the Doc's office. This time it was cleaned up from before and even the doctor looked well, having replaced his eye with a new cybernetic one. This one looked almost real.

Rex plopped a large, dirty duffle bag full of cybernetics on the doctor's exam table.

"My word, did you clean out the Hammer Fists?" asked Doctor Young as he opened the bag. He carefully extracted his doctor's bag, examined it and its contents. The bag was dull, having lost its luster long ago, but the smell of leather was still present. Even the gadgets inside were still intact. The doctor looked pleased and smiled at Rex.

"Thank you, my friend. You've repaid your debt and kept your word as I knew you would. Do you mind if I look at the rest of the contents?"

"Go ahead, if you see anything you like let me know, otherwise I'm gonna pawn the rest." Doc Young opened the duffle bag, pulling out several more items. Some were familiar, like a Portable Laboratory and Compu-Drug Dispenser. He set those items aside and examined a small item the size of a deck of cards. He touched the screen and it came to life, with the following text scrolling across the screen.

No targets within range. Place scanner within 30 centimeters of target and press start scan to begin.

Curious, the doctor asked Rex.

"Do you mind if I examine you with this gizmo? Its looks like something I once saw on an old pre-Rifts science fiction show."

"Why not?" replied Rex as he shrugged his shoulders. The doctor brought the device near Rex and pressed the "Start Scan" button on the touch screen. Immediately an image of Rex displayed on the screen with all his vital statistics displayed. Passing the device over Rex, the screen followed suit by giving information about the man. It showed his Juicer implants, skeletal structure, circulatory system, and other numerous wounds, abrasions and fractured bones Rex had recently received. The doctor had a curious look.

"Did you injure your left leg recently?"

"Well yeah, as far as I could tell it was busted pretty good, but you know my Bio-Comp fixed me up good. How'd you know?"

"This device appears to be able to diagnose various symptoms. According to it, your left leg has several fractures and you have several broken ribs. However, all seem to be on the mend. You should really take it easy for a few more days. I'd recommend a week to let those nanites work. Your Bio-Comp is just masking the pain and swelling."

"You got all that from that tiny little device?"

"Yes, and I would like to buy it, as well as some of these other things."

Rex looked very pleased. He had planned on having to haggle with his Black Market contacts, but if Doc Young was willing to buy them, hell, all the better.

"Sure, Doc. I'm sure we can make a deal," replied Rex, smiling.

"Tell you what. In addition to any financial consideration, how about I include detox?"

"Whoa, Doc! I need to set my family up. I need to do a few more things as a Juicer before I go through that. Kids are expensive and I need to pay rent, heat and gotta feed those little monsters."

"Rex, I'm not going to lie to you. This little scanner is worth a fortune and I think I know the right people who would pay a lot of money for it. And I mean a lot. We could both be set for life and you won't have to do . . . whatever it is you have to do as a Juicer. You're better than that, Rex. You belong with your family."

Rex was taken aback. He had expected to be a Juicer for at least another year, probably two. He wasn't prepared for this kind of news and the thought of detox scared the hell out of him.

"I . . . I don't know, Doc. I mean, how valuable could that thing be?"

"Millions."

"Whoa. Are you sure?"

"Positive."

"Well, geez . . . detox, huh?"

"I know," said Doc Young. "It's a scary prospect, isn't it? Being an ordinary human again, I mean."

"Yeah . . . I mean no. I mean . . ."

"Tell you what, Rex. You think about it for a few days, get yourself all healed up and I'll talk to a few friends about this gizmo. Why don't you come back next week and, if you're ready, bring the family. If not, well then we'll work something out."

That's what Rex liked about Doctor Young, he was a decent, honest guy and that gave Rex hope.

"I'll let you know, Doc. Yeah, I have to talk this over with Rachel."

Rex left to be by himself for a while. He had to take in all the information he received. Having been a Juicer for two years, he had grown used to the power that coursed through his veins. And the last few days, as terrible as they had been, were also exhilarating. A normal man could never have survived any it. And now the thought of being a *normal man* again weighed on him. Rex headed home, taking a detour through one of the tougher neighborhoods in the 'Burbs. Maybe a little action would help him figure things out. Rex had a lot to consider, but at least for today he was a Juicer!

Epilogue

Deep in the heart of the Federation of Magic, hundreds of miles away from Chi-Town, two Juicers laid side by side. Blood Reaper looked on as his assistants replaced the normal Juicer chemicals with various magical concoctions. The mage had sufficiently healed their wounds to keep them from dying, and now they were fully conscious and manacled to iron slabs in a lab.

"What the hell are you doing, man?" screamed Viper as he fought against the magic chains that bound him. "You got him. Use him!"

Viper was nodding towards Goliath, who was writhing in agony. He complained numerous times about being hungry and that he was starving to death. Blood Reaper bent down so that his face and Viper's were only inches apart.

"Oh, I'll use him, don't worry. I'll be using you both," said the mage.

"Please, don't do this," begged Viper.

"You're weak. When I finish with you, you'll thank me for the strength I've given you."

"No! It's not my time you hear me? Not my time!"

"Oh, it's your time . . . my son," said the mage as he laughed, walking back toward another figure who was in the shadows. Blood Reaper bowed to the Deevil coming forward.

"Wahs Darb, I did not expect you today."

"Good," replied the Deevil, taking a long drink from a bottle in his hand. "I have a message from my master. He says, 'ensure that your army is ready, and the sooner the better.'"

"Why? If I may ask. The last time we spoke, his arrival was many years away."

"The situation has changed and we need to accelerate our plans. Have the minions ready." The Deevil disappeared in a puff of fire and smoke, having teleported back to his own realm. Blood Reaper smiled.

"Well, gentlemen. It seems you'll be seeing some action sooner than expected."

The mage laughed and both Juicers screamed in agony as their transformations began. In various cages and cells around them, Juicers by the dozen clawed at the bars. Some laughed and some wept, all appeared skeletal and emaciated. Blood Reaper's army was growing and he would be ready when the *Minion War* arrived on Rifts Earth, and no one would stand in his way!

Death, Friends & Life

By Braden Campbell
& Kevin Siembieda

Today marked the end of my ninth year on the Waiting List, and we celebrated with a funeral. Actually, it was a memorial service. One event has the actual dead body there, and the other does not. So, yes, we celebrated with a memorial service, since Rick Milne was lying somewhere inside the fortress city and we were all gathered here in my bar.

You'll have to excuse me. I've been into the rye pretty heavily since about noon. I know that those who serve the alcohol shouldn't be joining their patrons in the drinking of it, but today I don't care. It started with a little shot to calm my nerves before I gave my eulogy. Then, after the formalities were done, there were several toasts to our departed government overseer, in which I felt obliged to partake. My various sorrows began taking advantage of the situation, bubbling up to the surface, so I was drinking to drown them back down. Then, I had my epiphany. So I've cut myself off.

But I'm getting ahead of things.

I think I can safely say that Lieutenant Richard Milne was my friend. He came in every Tuesday and Thursday since I took over the tavern. When he drank, he ordered the exact same thing; a double whiskey sour, with ice. When he first started darkening my doorstep, he would come in and patrol the place, making a full circuit around the pool room, the bar area, and the tap room. He was every inch the neighborhood Coalition enforcer, resplendent in his grey Coalition uniform, boots shined to a mirror black, collar starched, hair perfectly trimmed. He would nod to me or perhaps say, "Good evening, Mr. Sussex," but otherwise he was stern and quiet. He made everyone nervous, which I guess was what he was going for. People are less likely to commit crimes against the State when they feel the unblinking eyes of the authorities on them.

The Lieutenant, back in those days, was under the impression that his tenure in the 'Burbs would be a short one. That this was just one unpleasant stepping stone in a much more glorious career. He didn't want to be here, and he felt no need to hide it. He took every opportunity he could find to put us non-citizens down, to make some snide comment about our homes, our habits, how we dressed, what we ate, how we behaved. He felt that because he was a Coalition Citizen, that he was somehow better than the rest of us. Funny thing is, we believed it.

Then the years began to go by, and for whatever reasons, Lieutenant Milne's promotion didn't come. He may have made calls, pestered those in positions above him, maybe even made some threats. Still he received no papers. His attitude began to change, and so did ours. I think somewhere along the line he came to the realization that he was more like us than he wanted to admit. He was waiting too. I sometimes wondered, but never found the courage to ask him, if he'd ever had a run-in with an attractive, dark skinned, blue-eyed woman who worked in some kind of administrative job. Did he demand of her where the hell his promotional certificates were, ask her just how much longer he would have to baby-sit the lot of us? And did she sigh, as she always did in my imagination, and tell him that it would just be a while longer?

He still showed up on his regular nights, but now he would sit at a small corner table and have a drink after he had finished having a look around. After a while, he started having two drinks. Later, he started sitting at the bar. Finally, he began making conversation, except that no one really felt comfortable talking with him. He was, after all, an officer in the Coalition Army, whether or not he was on duty. Still, I was the owner. I was his host for the evening, and so I had to listen and nod and sympathize. And after three years of pretending to be his friend because it was part of some ambiguous bartender's code, we became friends. I found I genuinely liked the man. Once he stopped trying to be so ram-rod straight and tough, he was actually a decent human being. In fact, I suspect it was that decency that held his promotion back.

He was our police constable for five and half years, and even though he made it clear that he did not want his current job, he never slacked in it. When the Brewsters' little girl went missing in the winter of 105, it was him who found her, forgoing sleep for three days straight until he finally tracked down the Boogie-Man who had taken her. When the hardware store across the street was broken into by vandals who stole the credit register and gave Mr. Lenn a pulverized arm for his troubles, the Lieutenant caught them. He maintained order as best he could with what few resources were sent his way from Chi-Town. And slowly, ever so slowly, those of us in the neighborhood who weren't here to push drugs, or snatch cybernetics, or sell illegal goods; the people who were just trying to live their lives until something better came along, started to like him too.

He was no saint. Not by a long shot. He arrested Tommy Lynch for trafficking "unau-thorized printed material" (that's books to folks like you and me), and turned his face into hamburger with a Neural Mace before dumping him in the back of a squad car. He hated D-Bees with a passion, called them all kinds of awful names. And he would try to trick you sometimes. For example, he sent us a lengthy, handwritten card for our wedding, which was nice of him, but later asked what we thought of it. That was a trap, because if you told him it was very thoughtful, or poetic, or sweet, or whatever, then it proved you could read. If you said anything else, you ran the risk of upsetting him. I just told him that I liked the picture on the front of it.

I don't know what killed him. Well, I know what physically killed him; he put a pistol to his head and pulled the trigger. I'm talking about what killed his ability to soldier on. That's real death, you see, when the spirit dies. Maybe it was the weather. Winters in this part of the country can be a fickle thing. One year, it might be reasonably cool and free of snow. Other times, there might be drifts up to your waist. The one just past was bleak, windy, freezing and too damn long. From the end of October until this, the middle of March, it just seemed to go on and on. Everyone started to get depressed by it.

Maybe he felt that his beloved Coalition was falling apart. The War against Tolkeen was still raging up north. Hundreds of thousands from our side had been lost or killed. And it wasn't just Coalition soldiers, either. Many young men and women from the 'Burbs had volunteered for service as a means of fast-tracking their citizenship. They had given goodbyes to their families that were often joyful, or tearful, or both, then boarded trains that whisked them away to basic training camps somewhere north of Bloomington. We haven't seen a single one of them come back yet. At last count, the CS had suffered over half a million casualties; and a war that we were told would be over in a few months just dragged on and on.

There was the Civil War as well, although we didn't hear much about it where we are. News and rumors trickled in from wandering adventurers and merchants that Quebec had seceded from the Union and that Coalition troops were now struggling to drag it back in. Fighting mages and monsters in Tolkeen was one thing, but this was man against man. It completely undermined the spirit for which the CS stood: a bastion of civilization where all humans are created equal and welcomed without reservation. So, it could have been the hypocrisy revealed that broke him inside. I know it's given me some pause on the nights when I can't sleep, when I sit by the window in my comfortable chair held together with duct tape and dream about going off to live in the fortress city. A citizen at last. That's what I want, right? That's what all this has been for, isn't it?

Hindsight has bionic vision, as they say. I should have noticed that something was wrong. That something was really eating at him. A few weeks ago, Milne came in on a Saturday night. The place was busy, and Lisa was out with a bad cold, so I was slammed. I was a bit shocked to see him on a day that wasn't one of his regular ones, but I was so busy that I couldn't stop to ask him about it. Every once in a while I would catch him out of the corner of my eye, talking to Kenny Philbrick. It was only after last call that I had a chance to say hello, and by that time he was getting ready to go. You could tell he was thoroughly drunk by the way he was struggling to pull his greatcoat over his armored chest plate. Now that I think about it, there were pockmarks across the front of it, like dents in a car's fender. Somehow, because I was tired and worried about Lisa, it just didn't register.

"Rick," I said, grabbing a stick match from the little bowl on the bar to light my pipe with. "How's it goin'?"

"Good," he muttered and finally forced his left arm into his sleeve. He shoved his hands into his deep pockets. "Good," he said again.

"Odd to see you here tonight."

"I was workin'," he slurred. "Big bust. They called a lot of us in."

I nodded politely, and drew on my pipe. The air filled with the sweet scent of imported Virginian tobacco. Cost me two cases of vodka in trade, but it was well worth it. The Lieutenant swayed slightly.

"You need a ride home tonight?" I asked. "I think Roger is still around here somewhere. He could give you a lift."

"No," he replied. There was a moment of quiet, which was just fine with me after so many hours of the jukebox blaring. Then he asked me how Lisa was.

"She's got a fever," I told him, "but we had Fixer Mortland come around, and he says it's just a bit of flu. She'll be alright. Kids are still worried, though."

"'Cause their dad died of influenza."

I'd forgotten that I must have told him that at some point in the past five years, and it took me back a bit. My initial thought was that Milne had been going over some confidential file folder containing all the sordid details of my life. Was there such a thing, buried somewhere in the computer vaults of Chi-Town, where our every move was carefully set down by hordes of unseen informants and spies?

"Uh, yeah. That's right," I said slowly.

He turned to go, almost knocking over the tables as he did. I watched him weave his way to the side door. "Have a good night, Rick," I called to him, and I turned away to start cleaning up the bar.

He stopped in the doorway, and I was about to yell at him for letting all the warm air out when he said to me, with heavy sobriety, "Allen, if I died, would anyone fight to resurrect me?"

Did a chill go through me, or was it just the heat escaping out into the parking lot? I can't remember. It was such a bizarre question that I immediately assumed it to be just one of those jabberwocky things that drunks say. I've heard them all in my time here. Though I had to admit, that was a new one.

"Go home, Richard," I said, and started dumping ashtrays into a large bucket. When I looked up again the side door was closed and he was gone. That was the last I ever saw of him.

The following Monday, I was in the office trying to go through some paperwork. Samantha was working alone downstairs since afternoons are always slow. All of a sudden, she appeared in the doorway. Her face was strained.

"Allen," she said quietly, "there's some Lieutenant downstairs asking to see you."

"Milne?" I asked.

"No. Someone else. Has a couple of Dog Boys with her."

That got my attention. The Coalition only breaks out their mutant canines around here when they are hunting for renegade psychics, demons, and magic users. Or sometimes, when they just want to put a good scare into someone. Who wouldn't be a little bit terrified standing nose to snout with a two hundred pound, talking German Shepherd? I ran a hand through my hair and quickly went downstairs.

Standing in the lobby was a young woman, twenty-five maybe, with caramel-colored skin, and dark eyes. Her blonde hair was pulled back into a tight bun. She cradled a helmet under one arm, but was otherwise dressed in a full suit of Dead Boy combat armor. With her were two Dog Boys. Sorry, *Psi-Hounds*, as we are supposed to call them. I didn't recognize their breeds, but they were both about five feet tall and broad across the chest. One of them narrowed his eyes at me and aggressively sniffed the air. I briefly wondered just how I might smell to someone who could accurately tell what I ate for breakfast three days ago.

Samantha was cowering behind me as if I could in any way protect her if things went bad.

"Can I help you?" I asked. Even though the day was cool, I felt sweaty under my arms.

The woman snapped her fingers, and the Dog Boy who wasn't staring me down handed her some kind of little electronic display tablet. "Allen Sussex," she read.

I nodded.

"You are the owner of this establishment, and have been since 103 P.A.?"

"Uh-huh."

"My name is Madlyn Reed. As of this morning, I am the new constable in charge of your Suburb's Sector." She waited for me to reply, but I just stood there. I honestly had no clue as to why she was introducing herself to me. She continued, saying, "My predecessor left instructions that whoever replaced him should make a point of coming here and meeting you."

Through the window behind her I could see several passers-by slow down and try to see what the trouble might be. It had been quite some time, I'm proud to say, since we'd had any incident in the bar that required the Coalition to investigate. For them to show up in the middle of a quiet afternoon was stranger still. Suddenly, I put things together.

"You're replacing Richard," I said.

She corrected me sharply. "I'm replacing Lieutenant Richard Milne, yes."

"Right. Lieutenant Milne. Sorry," I muttered. Trying to be upbeat I then asked, "Would you like a tour of the place?"

She looked around the lobby, her face scowling slightly. She looked like a woman who had just stepped into something unpleasant, like dog crap. Or our lives, perhaps.

"We have no weapon detectors," I said before she could. I smiled inwardly, assuming that next she would ask me if I owned a gun. Fresh out of the Chi-Town Officers' Academy she was, just like Rick had been when he first showed up, running through a standard list of questions and observations.

"I see," she said frowning. "I have to admit, Mister Sussex, that I have no idea why I was instructed to come here."

Her discomfort put me at ease a bit, and I shrugged. "We're a social focal point. The man you're replacing figured that it was important to have a good relationship with us. I guess he wanted to make sure that carried on after he got promoted out of here."

"Oh, Lieutenant Milne wasn't promoted," she said. "He's dead."

I couldn't have been more stunned had she hit me in the face with a brick. She snapped her fingers again, and with a jerk of her head the two Dog Boys went out into the street without so much as a word. I stammered for a second, and was about to ask her the details when she curtly said something about being in contact later in the week and left. Honestly, I can't really remember.

By collecting bits and pieces from different people in the neighborhood, and by grilling Kenny as to what he and Richard had been talking so intently about, I eventually found out what had happened. As I have said, the war against Tolkeen was dragging on and both sides in the conflict were getting desperate. Apparently, a group of mages had come down from the north and taken up residence somewhere in the 'Burbs. They were planning some kind of terrorist action like an assassination, or blowing up a marketplace, or something. One way or another, the guy in charge went and got himself killed. That should have been the end of things, but it wasn't. Instead of just quietly slipping back to Tolkeen, the remainder of the mages decided to bring their beloved leader back from the dead.

I think this is funny as hell, because we live in such a screwed-up world that some days I cannot fathom why anyone might want to live through it twice.

Anyway, resurrecting someone is no simple task. Between assembling the necessary components and then having a half a dozen sorcerers combine their power to make it work, the Coalition discovered where they were and what they were up to. A massive raid was launched against the shabby boathouse where the mages had holed up. By the time the fighting was over, nine CS soldiers and fifteen Dog Boys were dead, all the mages had been killed, and an entire block of river front property had been burned to the ground. This included the Stoble family stockyards, so maybe it was the sound of two hundred sheep being burned alive that finally broke Richard Milne. It would have screwed me up for life, I can tell you that.

After that, he walked to my bar and got wasted. He told Kenny a bit about the kind of night it had been, went back to his office in the Sector Security Compound, and sometime around dawn finally decided that he just couldn't take it anymore. His body was taken back into Chi-Town, where an autopsy would be performed before his final cremation and interment somewhere. Those who thought we knew him best wouldn't be allowed to go and pay our last respects, because as non-citizen riff-raff, we were forbidden from entering the fortress city. So, for the next week people laid wreaths or candles against the outer wall of the Compound, and I organized a memorial service here in the bar.

Lisa was a real trooper, I've got to tell you. Weak as she was from the flu, she still helped me set everything up. She cooked stews and casseroles to feed the guests, and baked several dozen fresh buns. Not once did she tell me that she thought this was a stupid idea, or a waste of time and money, even though that's certainly how she felt. Lisa never liked the Lieutenant. She didn't really have anything against the Coalition as a whole, she was waiting for her citizenship papers the same as many of us. There was just something about Richard Milne that put her off. Still, she saw that this was important to me, so she did all she could.

The flurry of extra activity caught the attention of her kids. Katheryn is seven years old and Ramona is nine. Two days following my visit from Lieutenant Madlyn Reed and her Dog Boy entourage, we were putting them to bed when Ramona asked us what was going on. She sounded worried.

"Is there going to be a party?" asked Katheryn, who probably expected a joyous repeat of Christmas, or the New Year's bash we had just recently had.

I was leaning in the doorway. Lisa looked over at me and raised her eyebrows, looking for help. I just stared blankly at the wall, preoccupied. I couldn't concern myself with whether or not we should now tell two children about the reality of death. I had my own issues to deal with. Without backup from me, Lisa sighed angrily, and then told her daughters that someone Allen knew had died a few days ago, and that yes, we were going to have a kind of party for him. One where all the people who had loved him would get together and share funny stories and other good memories.

"I thought you didn't like that man," Ramona said. "I thought no one liked him. So why are we having a party for him?"

The mouths of babes. As usual, Lisa came up with something much better.

"That's right," she said softly. "I didn't like him very much. But he was a part of our lives for a long time. Ever since you both were little he looked out for us in his own way, and he tried to protect everyone in the neighborhood."

"Like when he saved Allison?" Katheryn asked, referring to the Brewsters' daughter. Her big blue eyes were rimmed with tears. My heart was breaking.

"Just like that." Lisa ran her hand through Ramona's long, brown hair. "Would you want us to have a nice party for Roger if he died?"

Both the girls nodded enthusiastically. Roger had been good enough to watch the girls whenever Lisa and I were both working, and we paid him a little on the side for his efforts. They loved the crazy old man who they called "Mister Whiskers," and looked forward to their regular visits with him. He was quite fond of them as well, never having had a family of his own. He played with them, told them stories from his long-vanished youth, and took them down to the river to feed the ducks if the weather was nice. When I first showed up here, Roger Pittman was just another unemployed rummy who frequented my bar. Now, I realized, he was a surrogate grandfather.

As if she was picking up on my thoughts, Lisa then said, "That's because Roger's like a part of our family. And so was Lieutenant Milne. All the good people that you see around you, they're all part of your extended family, and you should never forget that."

The matter concluded to their satisfaction, the girls got under the covers. Lisa turned off the light, and shut the door behind her as we went out into the hall.

"Thanks for your help, Allen," she hissed.

I couldn't deal with a marital fight, not at the moment. I turned and started to walk away, but Lisa grabbed my arm. "What's the matter with you? You've been moody and detached all day."

I almost told her. I almost opened my mouth and let loose about what had come in the mail earlier that day. About the long, grey envelope and the heavy citizenship papers inside, emblazoned with the Skull and Lightning of the Coalition States. My citizenship papers had finally arrived. Mine. Not Lisa's. Not her children. How could I walk away from four years of marriage? Or for that matter, nearly a decade of friends? Of course, I didn't have to leave them. I could go ahead and start our life behind the fortress walls and wait for her and the girls until their papers came. I'd promise to be faithful, find work, get our apartment ready for their arrival. I'd visit whenever I could get a weekend pass to the 'Burbs. After all, wasn't this what we had been working for? Wasn't this the dream? Our dream? On the other hand, I could just pack a bag, and stroll into Chi-Town without so much as looking back. To hell with this life, the bar and everyone who calls it home. See you around, Honey. Thanks for four years of marriage. Tell your kids I'll miss them. You can keep the bar. Stuff like that happened all the time.

"I'm just really tired," I lied.

She squinted like she was trying to see through me, and for the millionth time I was thankful that Lisa had no psionic abilities. Then she nodded, said something about having to peel potatoes before she could go to bed, and went down the back stairs to the kitchen.

My tortured mind ran over every possible contingency, but none of them seemed right. The price of Citizenship came at too great a cost.

Then we had the memorial service. I wasn't even certain just how many people were going to show up, and I was surprised to find the bar packed by eleven o' clock. Simon Brewster broke down in tears three times as he praised Milne and said his farewell. His wife and daughter looked on with warm smiles as he thanked the Lieutenant for saving their little girl. All told, more than three hundred people came to celebrate Richard Milne's life. It struck me as bitterly ironic how a man who obviously felt lost and lonely enough to commit suicide had been surrounded by so much love the whole time.

I said my little piece about how I would miss him, and cracked a joke about his haircut, which got a much bigger response than I anticipated. I joined in the toasts. I listened to the others tell their stories not just about him, but about each other. About how we all got through with the help of our friends. At one point, I saw Kenny telling dirty limericks to a large crowd, and watched Roger pour juice for Katheryn and Ramona. I watched the room and felt lucky to have so many wonderful friends.

Since the day my brother was murdered in the streets, I had been a man with no blood relations. Even my girls weren't my blood, they were the children of Lisa's first husband, who died in the crossfire between two rival gangs. I had spent years convincing myself that if I could only get inside of Chi-Town, if I could just get those acceptance papers, that I would be adopted into another kind of family. Now, here I was, finally being offered just that chance, and it brought me no joy. How could I abandon these people here to go and live amongst a bunch of strangers? Family and love are more than blood line or security.

That's when I remembered something else Richard had said to me a few weeks ago.

"I envy you, Allen," Milne said out of nowhere.

"You do, huh?"

"I sure do. You have all this, my friend," and he gestured with his arms across the bar packed with people.

"Yeah? Great," I chuckled. "A home full of drunks."

"A home, Allen. A home filled with drunk friends."

We both smiled at that comment and Richard said, "What do you think you'll find in Chi-Town that you don't already have right here?" Then he got up, tipped his hat and left to go home. Home to Chi-Town.

As the party continued, I put the cork back into the bottle I had been drinking from. I climbed the stairs, weaving from one end to the other, entered my office and sat heavily in my creaky chair. I withdrew a metal box from a secret compartment underneath my desk, and reaching into a vest pocket, pulled out the envelope that held my papers. For a moment, I weighed it in my hand, listening inside my brain for any voice of dissension or reason. There was none. I dropped the envelope into the box and returned it safely to its hiding place.

I wasn't declining the Coalition States' generous offer. I was just delaying my acceptance until such time as Lisa and the girls received theirs too. Then the four of us would sit down and make the decision to walk into the city to start a new life or not, together, as a family. If their papers never came (women with children somehow often seemed to fail to make the cut for citizenship), so be it. If there was an expiration date for the acceptance of my citizenship (I didn't look), so be it.

I chuckled to myself. The decision felt good. It felt right. I felt happy. Truly happy. I would stay here with my beautiful Lisa, Katheryn and Ramona, among a family of friends. Hell, I would even probably get to like Lieutenant Madlyn Reed in time.

I said a prayer for my friend, Richard, grabbed my keys, locked the office door, and went back downstairs into the light and life.